Th Dragonmaster

A novel by

Nigel Conway Partis

Still Small Voice Publishing

The Dragonmaster

© 2009 - Nigel Conway Partis

The right of the author to be identified as the originator of this work has been asserted in accordance with the Copyright, Designs and Patents Act – 1988

First published 2009 by

Still Small Voice Publishing

23, Heol-y-Felin, Penparc, Cardigan
SA43 1RH United Kingdom

All rights reserved. No part of this book may be reprinted or reproduced or utilized in any form, or by any electronic, mechanical or other means, now known or hereafter invented, including photocopying and audio recording, or in any information storage or retrieval system, without written permission from the publishers.

ISBN No. 978-0-9561735-0-8

Printed and bound in England by IMPRINT DESIGNS – Exeter.

A catalogue record for this book is available from the British Library.

The stories, characters and situations portrayed in this book are entirely fictitious. Any similarities to persons or organisations, actual or not, living or dead, are purely coincidental and unintentional.

<~ Preface ~>

This book is a quasi-autobiographical, factual, action fiction! I have changed names, and whilst the storyline is purely fictional, many of the described events have been part of my personal experience. Others are a recounting of things that have happened to people I personally know. I will leave the reader to determine which is which.

My descriptions of certain heavenly realms are at best an educated guess, mostly formulated from my personal understanding of scripture plus accounts of the experiences of various visionaries. Whatever heaven may ultimately be like does not alter what it took to get us there. If this world with all its beauty and wonderment is merely a pale and 'fallen' reflection of what is to come, then truly 'We can't begin to imagine the wonders that God has prepared for those that love him'.

On the opposite extreme, many of the descriptions of the manifestations and tactics of the devil, our enemy, come directly from years of personal experience in ministry and spiritual warfare. From time to time, within the narrative, factual background with a biblical reference is given. Hopefully this will greatly assist in increasing the reader's understanding of the overall subject.

The 'meat' of the novel is set in the area in which I live. The foothills of the Preseli Mountains in West Wales, UK. This is the very place where the ancient circle of bluestone megaliths known as Stonehenge were quarried, back in antiquity. Also it's the very same area where the great Welsh revival of 1904 occurred. A spiritual battleground indeed!

It is the earnest hope of the author that through the pages of this book some will find salvation, as well as entertainment.

Nigel Conway Partis.

---------- O ----------

~ Dedication ~

This book is dedicated to my beautiful wife Erika. The kindest, most caring person I have ever known.

Without your constant love and encouragement, this novel would not have come into being. You have never complained or criticised when I worked hour after hour locked away in my studio. Instead you have given me your complete backing and support, every step of the way.

You are a precious jewel to me and my life is so much richer for knowing you. You are my best friend, my lover and helpmeet. Thank you for being my wife!

And also to . . . . .

My mother. ~ Thank you for giving me a love of words mum, and for passing on all those loquacious and poetical genes!

~ ~ ~ ~ ~ ~ ~ ~ ~ ~ ~ ~ ~ ~ ~ ~

The Dragonmaster

Chapters

1. The Palace of Accusation ………………… 1
2. Two Ancient Lands ……………………… 34
3. Dark Incantations ………………………… 61
4. Ask, Seek, Knock ………………………… 87
5. The Angharad Legacy ……………………146
6. Warrior ……………………………………188
7. As Above, So Below ……………………..231
8. Postscript …………………………………..284

~~~~~ O ~~~~~

The Dragonmaster

CHAPTER 1 **The Palace of Accusation.**

Hunching his shoulders against the driving sleet, Joshua Fishmen wearily tossed the last of three heavy canvas mailbags into the back of the small red van. It was 7.15a.m. on a cold December morning, four days before Christmas and the absolute busiest time of the year for postmen in the western world.

The previous evening had been the depot Christmas party, and in the time honoured fashion of young men at these sort of events he'd imbibed more alcohol than was sensible, in less time than was expedient. With eyes half closed against the icy wind, he very gently shut the van doors and shuffled zombie like to the front of the vehicle. The intense bright yellow of his foul weather coat seemed so loud he could almost hear it. Meanwhile the marching band inside his head played on in tumultuous repetition. Easing himself into the driver's seat he sat for a few minutes, almost dazed by the frenetic early morning bustle of the sorting office yard. The three paracetamol he'd taken some twenty minutes earlier began to take effect, and with a heavy sigh he gunned the engine of the eager little van. Last night one more drink had seemed like a good idea. Now however, it was merely another stone in an ever-growing wall of regret.

Leaving the yard he swung the van into the bustling flow of early morning traffic. The grey sleeting dawn seemed to mirror his consciousness. Last night his 6.a.m. start had felt an eternity away, now it was stark reality. The hollow monotone rumble of the van body was somehow amplified this morning by the dismal façade of the breaking day.

At twenty seven, Joshua Fishmen was ill at ease with his life. Being a postman hadn't quite matched up to his youthful ambitions and fantasies, in fact quite the opposite. He'd always felt he would do great things, that he would 'be someone' and be successful, (by the world's definition of the term). Like millions of other youngsters across the world, as a child he had been mesmerised by the dark box in the corner of the room. Programmed to believe lies, to be entertained by violence, and to worship the great gods, money and sex.

Though not at all what the world would term a criminal, Joshua was not adverse to the odd deal here and there. A new television of questionable origin, or a nice leather coat very cheap, would produce a smile and the appropriate wad of notes to complete the purchase. Like so many of his peers he smoked marijuana and did the occasional line of coke or speed at parties. His height was average with a muscular frame and, considering his social habits; he was generally a good deal fitter than most of his contemporaries having been a regular soldier for six years. He had seen action in Bosnia and the Gulf and was recognised by his associates as someone who could look after himself. Never the aggressor, he had nonetheless been in many fights. Most of these being the result of going to the aid of some unfortunate who was being bullied or picked on. On the odd occasion where he'd been attacked, his assailant usually had cause for deep regret. There was an air of chivalry about him, perhaps best described as 'a knight in rusty armour.' Albeit dented and battered by the world, with the faded emblem on his shield unreadable. One thing however was for sure. Joshua Fishmen was a warrior.

He had grown up on a large housing estate in Essex where he spent his first fourteen years under the guidance of an ex sergeant major father, (who ran the home like some sort of military unit) and a timid yet highly intelligent and artistic mother. In terms of material things he and his two brothers, one older one younger, had wanted for little. Their father had a well-paid job and they were clothed, fed and cared for excellently on a superficial level. Discipline was harsh and militarily enforced. The slightest seeming misdemeanour would result in weeks of punishment far outweighing the perceived crime. Often, over the top physical punishment would be meted out in anger on the spot. Josh's mother was generally preoccupied with keeping the home perfect, lest the wrath of the head of the household should descend on her.

Whenever Sergeant Major Fishmen was at home, orders were barked and immediate unquestioning compliance was expected. Failure to comply always resulted in a swift and harsh physical chastisement, usually followed by some form of stringent ongoing punishment. The human condition is such that we all need to feel loved to be able to function and develop fully. To attain anything like our true potential we need an environment of love and acceptance in our formative years. Sadly for Joshua, as for many millions world-wide like him, this was not the case.

After enduring over twenty years of control and mental abuse, when Joshua was thirteen, his mother finally left for a man with more heart than intellect, more compassion than strength. She had taken Josh's younger brother with her and Josh knew he would be the next to leave, especially after his father moved in a new 'step mother' within a few months. Just after his fourteenth birthday he had escaped into the Infantry Junior Leaders Battalion, and was posted to a barracks some three hundred miles away in Shropshire.

Some elements of army life suited him down to the ground. Weapon training – outdoor military manoeuvres – sport and the general camaraderie involved in a military lifestyle. However, he had real hard time with all the bull and polishing and the often twisted megalomaniac dispositions of some of his superiors, most of whom were way too much like his father for his liking. Still, by the time he was nineteen he was a full corporal and well on the way to becoming a sergeant. Career prospects: very good.

It was the gulf war that had put paid to it eventually. Out in the desert in a three-truck convoy they had somehow been identified as 'unfriendly' and an American heat-seeking missile had brought their war to a swift conclusion.

The shrapnel he'd caught in the right leg was enough to gain his discharge from H.M.Forces. The pittance he received in invalidity benefit was not enough to even half live on. Had he been an American serviceman he would now be on a good pension for life! The irony of this situation normally amused him, at least since he'd gotten used to it. Today however, it made him want to spit!

Four years now he'd been a postman and even in this short time he'd seen the job go downhill. He drove on towards the council estate where he would shortly be delivering his cargo of letters and parcels. Musing further he thought "No, it's not the job, that's basically okay if you overlook the early starts." He thought again "No" he said aloud to himself, "It's the people, the situations, the location!" His round began in the next street on the left, and more in deference to his pounding head than any concern for the possible fragility of his parcels, he eased the van gently into the sharp turn. The horn blast and simultaneous squeal of brakes from behind served, in no uncertain terms, to remind him that in his somewhat pre-occupied post inebriate state he had entirely forgotten to signal.

Bringing the van to a gentle halt just around the corner he swung the door open and pulled himself to his feet, fully intending to apologise to the unfortunate driver he had caused to brake rather sharply. At this moment a builder's van screeched to a halt level with him, its burly occupant looking decidedly aggressive. "Sorry mate!" said Josh raising his hand in an acknowledgement of guilt as the big builder exited his van. The reply was a tirade of expletives, casting aspersions on Josh's parentage and general sexual orientation, most of which made no grammatical sense but Josh got the picture. This was followed by a great lumbering ham sized fist hurtling its way towards Josh's nose. At this point instinct, plus several years of army training, took over. Josh neatly side-stepped the blow, ducked and drove the heel of his right hand into the assailant's Adam's apple, whilst the fist of his left hand delivered a crippling blow to the unfortunate mans midriff. In three seconds it was all over, at least for the time being. The attacker was on his knees in the road doubled over and choking. Joshua spoke calmly but firmly. "I didn't want trouble pal, I was about to apologise, but you decided to attack me . . . so you got it!" His opponent rose slowly from his knees, still coughing. He held up a hand in a gesture of submission and slunk back to his vehicle. Once inside of course his dented bravado returned. Through his half opened window he yelled "I know where you drink you scumbag – we'll 'ave you." Casting yet more aspersions on Josh's parentage and sexual habits, he roared away, his right arm out of the window mimicking someone shaking a bottle of milk.

Returning to his van Josh sank heavily into the driver's seat, his head pounding but his mind clear. This was about the limit. Four times now in the last 3 years he'd been attacked whilst at work. It seemed to him that since 9/11 the whole world was going mad. It seemed that people were losing the plot bigtime. Way more than even the dictates of a mad materialistic society should demand. There were wars everywhere, the weather was going crazy, new diseases were regularly appearing, and more and more control was manifesting from politicians who had promised freedom. Suddenly a strange wave of emotion engulfed him. It was at times like these that often the old childhood feeling of being different would surface. He would feel that somehow he didn't belong here, but it would only last momentarily, until some other thought would wrench his consciousness back into the world. The thought that did it this time was of Cathy. He would be seeing her this afternoon.

Cathy Hancock was the wife of Toby an old school pal. These days Toby was frequently away on Middle Eastern buying trips, and the lovely Cathy was warm and accommodating. And anyway it was common knowledge that Toby often took his secretary away with him 'on business'.

Josh shook his head to break his own distraction from his previous train of thought. "Yeah" he said to himself, "the whole world's going mad and I don't know why."

Three hundred miles away in a secluded cottage in West Wales sat a man who did know why. Quite precisely why. And how, and when, and through whom. He sat in a battered old fireside chair his feet up on the towel rail of the coal stove, puffing away contentedly on an old briar pipe. At sixty three Meredith Evans was still in pretty good physical shape. There was a slight rounding of the shoulders and a little thickening of the waistline, but he could still chop logs, get the coal in and push his battered old Morris Traveller when it occasionally needed assistance to start.

Polly the Jack Russell terrier curled up in the basket next to the stove, had been with Meredith some seven years. Ever since his dear wife Leah had 'gone to be with the Lord'. Expecting her usual early morning walk, the little dog cocked her head to one side and looked expectantly at her beloved master. "No, not now" he said, leaning forward and tapping the pipe ash into the coalscuttle. He sat back and closed his eyes. He was a short thickset man with swept back black hair, brown eyes and strong Celtic features. His temples were greying and the lines of age told the story of a life lived in moderation, truth and love.

He had accepted Christ as his Saviour in a chapel meeting some fifty-one years ago and had continued steadfastly to run his race. As the bible instructs, he had trusted the Lord with all his heart, not leaning on his own understanding and the Lord had dealt with him accordingly. In fact at this very moment he was being told of the disciple – a chosen one - who would soon be coming to him for instruction. He would come from far away. He would be a warrior, a seeker after truth and, a postman!.

------ O ------

At the same time, on the other side of the country, a thoroughly dejected and downcast Joshua reached a decision. As he sat there in his van a boyhood memory had begun to unfold. Years ago, when he was eleven, the family had gone on holiday to the mountains of North Wales.

Joshua had fallen asleep en route and still had vivid memories of awakening at a place called Horse Shoe Pass. It was very high up, and he remembered looking down in wonderment on the tiny little cars far below making their way up the twisting road that leads to the top. The splendour of the surrounding scenery had taken his breath away. So far his whole life had been lived in a relatively flat county on the other side of the country. This was spectacular! This was exciting! The whole of the two weeks had been an amazing exploration and he had fallen in love with Wales. This was where he would live when he grew up!

As the memories flooded his consciousness he made the decision. "Yes, that's where he would go. Where the people were friendly and the air was clean. Life in the hills. Maybe some chickens and a dog. Yes, get in touch with nature – freedom!" His head still in the daydream, his body drove the van and completed his round without further incident that day, save for his having to make a swift over the gate exit from a pursuing canine. By three thirty that afternoon he was clocked out and ringing the doorbell at Cathy's house. She answered the door clothed only in a bathrobe and ushered Joshua quickly inside, slipping the robe from her shoulders as she did. Drawing her to him Josh closed the door with his foot, shutting off the scene from the outside world, but not from the unseen observers. One guardian angel and two evil little demons – The Grey Ones.

----- O ------

On Christmas afternoon, sprawled across an armchair at the home of his best friend Ray Coughlin, Josh was deep in thought. Zara, Ray's wife was busy in the kitchen and squeals of delight were emanating from the playroom where Donna and Vernon aged six and seven were getting acquainted with a whole pile of new toys. The lights on the beautifully decorated tree twinkled and sparkled, diffusing the room with a gentle warmth. An excellent dinner, four brandies and some top quality South African grass had put the two friends in that 'special place'. The one most people only ever visit on Christmas afternoon. It's a state of total immobility in which people usually succumb to sleep. Yet if one can resist sensory shutdown it's also a potential Aladdin's Cave of ideas and inspirations. One such idea cart wheeled its way into Ray's consciousness. "China!" Ray suddenly exclaimed, "That's it, China!"

In truth, at that precise moment Josh's thoughts were centred more on the lusciousness of Cathy's body. However he was quite prepared to ditch that one for the time being and enter into his friends obvious excitement. "China?" said Josh, casting a quizzically expectant glance at Ray.

The two men had been friends for as long as they could remember. They had both grown up on the same large housing estate, Harold Hill in Essex. Together they had climbed trees, ridden their bikes, pinched apples, built model aeroplanes and pulled girls pigtails. Together they had fought Romans, Indians, Germans and Darth Vader. Together they had camped out in the forest, gone fishing, drunk beer and smoked grass. Together they had experienced their first real sexual encounters. Josh with Ray's sister Shirley and Ray with Shirley's friend Diane. And all this before they were fourteen. Ray had been devastated when Josh had told him he was "Off to join the army." Josh had tried his level best to persuade his pal to join up with him. Ray was actually up for it, but his father would not countenance the idea and Ray eventually went to college and on to business studies, gaining a degree. He now ran a small but very successful import/export company, dealing in hand made crafts.

Right now he was flushed with excitement and enthusiasm. "Yeah, it's got to be bursting at the seams with ethnic stuff." he said, rubbing his chin thoughtfully. "Zar! where's my atlas babe?" He rose like an animated statue from his easy chair and disappeared into the kitchen. Josh was pleased for his friend and knew also that this would be no idle pipe dream. He'd seen him do similar things in the past. Like the time aunt Davina had bought back an intriguing little carving from Sri-Lanka and Ray had tracked down the source and made a handsome profit from his subsequent importation. "Yeah" thought Josh "go for it mate!"

Zara came into the room exhaling a long plume of blue grey smoke and passed the joint to Joshua. She smiled a lovely warm and genuine smile, her green eyes shining and her long red hair catching the glow of the Christmas tree lights. "Ray is on one!" she said in the tone of a knowing wife, "Ray is definitely on one!" They both laughed and she studied Josh's face as he gazed at the tree lights, lost in thought. He was no Adonis but had strong features and deep blue eyes with a mop of curly mousy brown hair. Physically he was strong, about five feet ten inches tall and quite fit, the damage to his leg having long since repaired itself. She always enjoyed his lively and inventive conversation. Actually, if the truth be known, she fancied him like crazy!

------ O ------

Four years ago it had very nearly happened. Ray was away in France and Josh was 'keeping an eye out' for Zara and the kids. He'd come for dinner one evening and they'd drunk a bottle of wine between them and smoked a couple of joints. Somehow, though neither of them were really sure quite how, they had ended up in a passionate embrace in the kitchen. Kissing and fondling each other and fast approaching the point of no return. It had been Joshua who had called a halt, suddenly pulling himself away. "No Zar, this is wrong. We both love Ray. He's your husband and my best friend and we mustn't do this." Zara was relieved. In her heart she agreed totally, but with the wine and the dope her body was revved up and ready to go, and she knew she would have easily betrayed the man she loved, save for Joshua's strength of character. "Let's pretend it never happened" she said, buttoning her blouse and kissing him on the cheek. "Never again, eh?" Josh had agreed and left.

The watching Grey Ones had been furious, they had spent so much time engineering this event only to see it fail before their eyes. They had charged the atmosphere with lust and abandonment and fully expected to witness an act of adulterous betrayal. Instead this puny human over whom they exerted ever-increasing influence, had acted with a nauseating chivalry! A short distance away an angel smiled. The bargain had been kept, and from that time to this Josh made a point of never again being in a situation where he was alone with Zara. Scowling and muttering the Grey Ones plotted. They would try again.

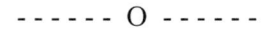

------ O ------

Still gazing at the shimmering Christmas baubles Josh inhaled deeply, sucking on the joint. Unbeknown to him something black vile and shapeless landed on the back of his neck. He looked up from the tree at Zara who was swaying to and fro to the sound of Bob Marley on the hi-fi. Lust exploded in his being. Her shape, her form, the fullness of her breasts and the tightness of her jeans. Her beautiful sensual femininity somehow screamed at him and he had to fight the urge to just grab her. The feeling was so strong that his rational mind kicked in and he gripped the arms of the chair, utilising every ounce of his remaining self-control. She turned away totally unaware of his turmoil and headed for the kitchen. Josh sat there, stunned by the intensity of his own feeling. Or at least what he surmised was his own feeling. The urge to ravish Zara had been so unbelievably intense. Josh found himself wondering whether quite possibly, that was how it was for some rapists. Uncontrollable, powerful, overriding feelings. The more he rationalised the smaller the disgusting black thing on the back of his neck became. When eventually he said to himself "For God's sake man, Zara is Ray's wife!" the thing withered and died and he returned to his own thoughts. And all the while the Grey Ones hissed and plotted.

------ O ------

At the same time far across the country, his feet crunching on the light fall of crisp snow, Meredith Evans was taking his customary Christmas afternoon walk. He was well wrapped against the elements and the two glasses of after dinner brandy he'd had, served to heighten his enjoyment of the occasion. He walked along the trickling bed of an ancient stream, his green rubber boots coping admirably with the water. It began to get rather steeper as he ascended the side of a hill and after a hundred yards or so he left the stream and joined an old track to his left. The gently ascending path took him beneath tall pines, across the bed of another stream and on and up towards the rocky crags of the hills surrounding the estuary town of Aberdigan.

As he reached the high point the conifers gave way to leafless deciduous trees and lifeless brown bracken, all dusted with a sprinkling of snow. Eventually he reached his special place. Special only to him, it was merely a spot where a tree had fallen, its branches forming a convenient armchair that gave him a magnificent view over the whole estuary. All around were rocky outcrops, gorse and spiky grass. A stranger would have passed by never noticing, but to Meredith it was an important place. He had spent many hours here in prayer. He looked out over the rolling hills at the sun that was shimmering on a silver sea to the west. The sky was blue and cloudless. Slowly turning his gaze eastward, inland he saw all the hills had a dusting of white and the approaching heavy looking snow clouds proclaimed a deeper garment to come. Polly ran back and forth, criss-crossing the track and occasionally disappearing for two or three minutes as she investigated all and sundry. Overhead a Buzzard circled unhurriedly, every now and then diving sharply for thirty or so feet before soaring again to maximum predatory height.

Looking back down the valley he had just ascended, Meredith could see the roof of his cottage with its surrounding wall of ash and laburnum trees, his corrugated

Dutch barn, and two of his three remaining fields. He used to have sixty-eight acres, now it was just seven, the rest having been sold off since Leah died. A thin plume of silver grey smoke drifted lazily from his chimney and his eye caught the barely discernible outline of the small summer house he had built for Leah, so she could paint in peace. She had only managed to use it that one summer. The cancer had come on quickly and God had chosen to let it be. He still missed her terribly, but the tear that trickled down his cheek went unnoticed by Polly, who had caught the scent of something small and furry and was barking and scratching at the snow covered undergrowth.

Collecting his thoughts and bidding Polly to cease, Meredith stilled himself. He sat with his eyes closed for a full minute. Then, lifting his hands skyward he prayed out loud. "Lord God, in the name of Your most precious son Jesus, I pray for protection for the one you are sending to me. Guard him Lord. May Your angels protect and keep him from the wicked schemes and plans of the enemy. Open his mind and his heart to the truth and reveal Yourself to him by your Holy Spirit. Amen."

------ O ------

At this precise moment Zara was turning to walk into her kitchen and Josh was being assailed by dark spirits of lust. The phone in the kitchen rang. Ray answered and after a short conversation called out "Josh, it's your mum." She knew he was staying with his friends for Christmas and so had phoned with season's greetings. Josh had long since repaired his relationship with his mother, and loved her dearly. The Fishmen family was actually quite large and as a result Josh had all sorts of uncles, aunts and cousins he had never met. This being mainly due to their reticence to visit a grumpy and overbearing ex-sergeant major who never visited them! So it was a pleasant surprise for Josh to learn, in the course of conversation regarding his plans to move to Wales, that his uncle, Hector Fishmen, was something of a bigwig in the postal hierarchy of that principality. His mother had said she'd "see what she could do."

------ O ------

The Grey Ones hadn't always been grey, far from it. At one time aeons ago they had reflected the glory of a pure and holy creator. They had been endowed with wisdom and beauty and had been given access to deeper knowledge than that of any subsequently created human. They had existed in the very presence of the Lord God Almighty and had carried out His bidding in places and situations man cannot begin to imagine.

However, one of their number had seen himself as equal to his creator. He was perfect in all his ways. That is, all his created ways, but he took pride in his beautiful appearance and his perceived ability to do things of his own volition. He was the anointed Cherubim, The holy angel who led the praise and worship of The Lord God in heaven, but pride got the better of him and he decided he would "Be like the most high God." He led a rebellion in Heaven, and astonishingly, managed to get around a third of the other angels to join him. This anointed angel's name was Lucifer, which means The Light Bringer.

The angels of heaven are said to be innumerable – so many we could never count them. Lucifer's rebellious army is one third of innumerable! All the angels who rebelled were cast out of heaven and into the atmosphere of the Earth. All the angels who rebelled were changed in nature from light to darkness. From angels to demons. They were given new names to compliment their new natures. Lucifer became Satan – the accuser and deceiver. His new nature is one of pure unbridled evil and hatred, with a desire to smash and destroy everything that is good and true. Likewise with all the other disobedient angels, they became demons of varying degrees of power and evil, totally subservient to their master Satan. They hate and loathe the things of God. Especially mankind who is made in the image of God – that

is, with the ability to love, think laterally, reason, show compassion and all the other attributes that differentiate us from animals. The sole purpose of demons and evil spirits is to get mankind to worship Satan instead of God. They do this via every possible means of deception, distraction, lust, pride and addiction. All of those things to which fallen man is eminently susceptible.
'Grey Ones' are assigned to everyone who is 'chosen' and they manifest in all manner of guises.

"For those who belong to The Lord were chosen before the foundation of the World" [Ephesians Ch.1v. 4]

------ O ------

Goomelt and Pusto were they Grey Ones assigned to Joshua Fishmen. They had been around since his conception. Their sole purpose was to prevent him from coming to a knowledge of the Lord God through the redemptive blood of Jesus Christ, the saviour of the world. They would do this by presenting their target with a vast array of distractions designed to appeal to man's senses. Sight, touch, taste, hearing and smell. Either pursued individually, or in devilish combinations, this strategy had worked well for Satan's armies since the fall of man, and hordes of demons just like these two were at work all over the earth. However, the very mention of the blood of Jesus filled their dark hearts with terror, for they already knew that at sometime in the future they would be placed in a lake of fire because of that blood, shed so long ago. They were also in constant fear of their superiors and the extreme pain they would be subjected to each time their charge did anything vaguely approaching good. This was enough to keep their twisted minds on the present, plus the constant need of the updating of dark plans and schemes designed to keep Joshua away from the light.

Although invisible on this plane, in appearance they were about two feet tall, quasi humanoid in shape and a sort of see through grey in colour. Inter dimensional in being, and thoroughly evil in intent, they sat on nothing apparent, just behind and level with the shoulder of their assignee. Had they worked together and formed cohesive strategies, their task would probably have been a whole lot easier. For the fallen heart of man is wicked and sinful and easily persuaded into wrongdoing. Instead they would argue and fight and being demons hated each other almost as much as they did the human they were attacking. Outside of their mandate to keep Joshua away from the light, their two main aims were gratification of self and their evil natures, and placation of their savagely cruel overlords. In the scale of things, Goomelt and Pusto were only a couple of rungs up the ladder from basic elementals. They had the ability to throw 'Spasmoides' onto the back of the neck of their assignee. Spasmoides were condensed forms of elemental spirit like anger, lust, envy and greed etc. The Grey Ones had the authority to launch a Spasmoide attack each time their human entered a situation which was contrary to God's law. If the situation persisted the Spasmoide would grow, gaining more and more influence in the area of its nature. Eventually it would be able to enter the body of the victim and exert high influence.

The idea of 'possession' by demons is generally far too strong a word, and the world's understanding of this matter has been coloured by such movies as The Exorcist and many others like it. A spirit has a nature and if it gains entry, a spirit of lust can only make that person lustful; a spirit of anger can only make that person angry, like wise with all the other elemental spirits. They are basically single natured one-track entities.

Goomelt and Pusto revelled in their limited power, savouring every moment in which they could attempt to exert any form of evil control. Yet in the overall scheme of their master's plan they were little more than expendable pawns in a strict hierarchy. In Satan's domain there lays a chain of command stretching down from dark and powerful spirit rulers of whole countries, to the likes of Goomelt and Pusto, and then the elementals, who scurry around scratching at the lives of individuals. There is a hate filled strategy, very real and precise, which goes on day after day, year after year. It is directed relentlessly at humans in general and believers in particular.

"For we are not fighting against people made of flesh and blood, but against the evil rulers and authorities of the unseen world, against those mighty powers of darkness who rule this world, and against wicked spirits in the heavenly realms." [Ephesians Ch.6v 12.]

------ O ------

The area commander of the Grey Ones assigned to Joshua was Scaybaz. A malevolent and particularly sadistic entity, he had managed to hold on to command of his area for the last six centuries of man time. On many occasions the two small demons had felt the full force of his wrath, especially when things hadn't gone to plan concerning their charges. Retribution would be swift and merciless from the razor sharp claws of this leathery winged, skull faced commander. The minions of Satan were not however, the only contenders in the ongoing struggle for lordship of Joshua's soul. Each chosen one had a Guardian Angel as well, and both the angel and the demons could hold one of two positions. There was 'The Position of Influence' which was right at the shoulder of the human, or there was 'The Position of Observation' a discreet distance behind. Strict spiritual laws governed the conflict and a chosen one automatically had a Guardian Angel at their shoulder from birth up to the age of accountability. Some say that age is 13.{*Bar-Mitzvah - which means in Hebrew 'Son of the commandment'- would tend to indicate that a person comes under the power of God's law around that age.*)

Nonetheless, there *is* an age where we leave childhood and become responsible before God for the choices we make. Once an individual has reached that age, the holders of 'The Position of Influence' would be directly related to their human charge's observance of God's law. Prior to each chosen one subsequently accepting God's offer of salvation, the holders of each position could change, depending upon the behaviour and lifestyle of their charge. The system was totally just.

'The Position of Observation' had suited the two demons better. True, they couldn't directly attack Joshua, but they were allowed to influence and manipulate people and situations around him. Also the painful visits of Scaybaz had been far less frequent. However, since gaining 'The Position of Influence' they had to work much harder, remaining alert and trying to steer Joshua into situations of increasing negativity and sin. They had tasted a fair deal of success up to now and were perplexed by Joshua's sickening morality towards Zara at this awful time called Christmas. They had been especially pleased when news of their master's plans to gradually dissipate the despised season by making it 'offensive to other religions' had filtered down to them. Soon there would be no more sickening carols or disgusting little children acting out the birth of the one they hated. The plan was underway, and it appeared to be working.

Shortly after Josh's refusal to pursue his lust towards his friend's wife, Scaybaz had arrived, his face contorted with rage. He slashed their backs with his razor sharp claws whilst screaming at them "Hit him with more lust you fools!" - "Yes Lord Scaybaz" they quivered through the agony "it will be done as you command."

------ O ------

The Grey Ones and the whole demonic hierarchy did not exist on the earth plane as we know it. Nor did the Angels. Joshua, his fellow human beings, and the birds, animals and insects of creation existed in time on a three dimensional plane amidst fixed parameters. This they chose to call reality. The rest of God's unseen creation existed in an interim, layered, overlapping dimension that had nearly been discovered by a certain Mr. Einstein at a point in earth time some while back.

The dark forces commanded the atmosphere around the earth and influenced the lives of the vast majority of its inhabitants, to varying degrees. That vast majority being totally unaware of the situation and abjectly disdainful of any attempts to educate them to it.

The tactics utilised by the darkness were always the same, mainly because man could be relied upon to commit the same folly over and over again. Man's fallen nature being such that his appetites would more often than not win out over his conscience. The ability of mankind to invent had paid Satan handsome dividends. Guns, bombs, rockets, and chemical and biological warfare. The tide of filth pouring into the average home via TV and the internet. The discovery of LSD which had led to the 'opening' of peoples minds to the point where society now felt marriage unimportant, drugs ok and illicit sex a thing to be coveted. Then there was the food situation. Ever increasing governmental controls and legislation. This line of attack managing to poison people's nourishment with chemicals and preservatives. The ongoing effect: a huge rise in cancer, diabetes and heart problems. An epidemic of obesity. The list was endless. At the same time of course there were also wonderful advances in medical technology and many other benefits cunningly disguised to make people think they're happy.

Satan always mixes a modicum of truth with his lies.

------ O ------

Joshua Fishmen knew nothing of the Grey Ones at his shoulder, even though they had been there since he was thirteen years old. Nor was he aware of the presence of Chakine the magnificent warrior Angel who stood shining and alert a discreet distance away.   He now occupied 'The Position of Observation' formerly held by Goomelt and Pusto.

Chakine had been assigned guardianship of Joshua from his conception. He had faithfully kept the Grey Ones and their associates at bay with divine right and authority. He had maintained 'The Position of Influence' and carefully watched over the growing boy. He stood nearly twelve feet tall, a muscular, shining, winged warrior Angel. One of the heavenly host of guardians assigned to 'chosen ones'. On his left arm he bore a circular shield capable of deflecting any of the weapons of the armies of darkness. At his side hung a scabbard housing a sword that cut great swathes of light, colour and perfect justice, whenever it was drawn. He was awesome and totally righteous with the bestowed power of God. His golden hair hung in ringlets on his neck and shoulders, and his robe and beautiful feathered wings were as white as snow. Around his waist sat a belt of plaited scarlet fastened by a clasp set with Beryl, Onyx and Jasper. Upon his head a band of gold edged with red, the insignia of a warrior Angel.

On Josh's thirteenth birthday Chakine had been particularly alert. He knew the Grey Ones would soon make some sort of move to try and gain 'The Position of Influence', and he was ready. Josh's protection was now no longer automatic. He had reached the age of accountability. Now he was responsible for his own actions, and should he transgress God's laws and choose to live to his own rules, then the influence of the Grey Ones would take over and become stronger and stronger.

------ O ------

Ray Coughlin was not a 'chosen one' and as such didn't have any Grey Ones assigned to him. They didn't need to be, he was, in spiritual terms, wide open. His grandmother had been a medium practising Tarot cards and automatic writing. His mother had committed suicide when he was seven, after years of hearing voices. He grew up influenced by his drunken father and a succession of assorted 'mums'. By the time he was eleven Ray had an unhealthy interest in horror stories, devils, demons and the like. However, not being a chosen one did not mean that he would never hear the call of God or be unable to respond to it. In fact, had he called upon The Lord or been shown the love of Jesus as a small child, then he would have had equal access to salvation through God's wonderful grace.

"God is not willing that anyone should perish, but that all men should come to salvation." [2 Peter Ch3 v9.]

Ray was three months older than Josh and had entered accountability the sooner. Just because a person does not acknowledge God's rules, does not negate their validity. Very soon Ray was wallowing in a mire of his own construction, heavily influenced by the darkness and spiritual condition of his family line, plus the choices he was now making.

A month or so before Josh's thirteenth birthday Ray had arrived at the Fishmen house looking rather furtive with something concealed under his jacket. "Is your dad in?" he whispered. Josh replied that his dad was at the pub and Ray had flopped into an armchair and tossed a magazine into Josh's lap. "Feast your eyes on that!" he said in a quivering adolescent tone. The magazine opened to reveal full colour pictures of several couples engaged in sexual activity. Hardcore pornography.

Chakine grimaced. Goomelt and Pusto, further back, squealed with delight edging slightly forward. Chakine shot them a glance over his shoulder, his hand moving to rest on the handle of his sword. They froze and shuffled back to the assigned place. Ray pulled a pack of cigarettes from his pocket and offered one to Josh. Then he produced several packets of sweets and tossed them on the coffee table. "I nicked 'em from Patel's" he had boasted. He did an early morning paper round for the newsagent at the end of the street.

And so the plan was hatched. Two nights later to the utter delight of the watching demons, Ray and Josh broke into Patel's, stealing sweets, cigarettes and more porno mags from under the counter. Soon, Chakine was finding being at Joshua's shoulder progressively more difficult. He could protect him, but he could not infringe the youngster's free will. Over the course of the month leading up to Josh's birthday the two young men became ever bolder in their criminal enterprises, eventually going into town and stealing CDs and electrical goods.

Angels hate to look upon the sins of men, knowing that it offends the Lord their God.

------ O ------

Goomelt and Pusto felt a tinge of fear when they heard the leathery beat of wings heralding Scaybaz's approach, but this time he was relatively affable merely scowling at them with obvious disdain. "It is the anniversary of the vile human's birth tomorrow, and then he is accountable. One more transgression of the law" his raspy voice barked "and we may petition at the 'Palace of Accusation'!" The two underlings quivered in anticipation. Scaybaz continued "One more move by this puny human towards rejection of" he almost gagged on the words "the Most High, and you two will assume 'The Position of Influence' at last!"

Chakine was facing the Grey Ones and their commander, his back to Joshua, his hand on his sword. He wanted to separate Scaybaz's skull head from his leathery body and could easily have done so in one deft move, but a warrior Angel must obey the rules and he stood motionless his eyes fixed on the large demon. Scaybaz was careful to avoid his gaze and kept his eyes fixed on the two Grey Ones. "One more transgression!" he screeched as his leathery wings carried him off into dimensional darkness.

Two days later Ray phoned Josh, "Wanna come over?" he said excitedly "my dad's gone out and Diane and Shirley are here". In two minutes Josh was en-route to Ray's house. Shirley was Ray's sister and she and Diane were both fifteen and innocent. Ray had gotten some marijuana from somewhere and stolen a six pack from the off licence. The girls had been reticent at first, but as the beer and grass took effect they became less and less inhibited. When the porno mags were produced they fell headfirst into the trap, surrendering that which they could never regain in a haze of booze and drugs. Chakine had long since turned away, refusing to look upon that which so offended his master. Nor did he look in the direction of the pathetic little demons who were now jumping up and down with delight. He merely gazed in the direction of the courts of heaven and praised The Lord in angelic tongues.

- - - - - - O - - - - - -

Goomelt lost no time in setting off for The Palace of Accusation. He knew the way even through the darkness of his master's kingdom. Following the trail that led from the Level of Elementals to the Plane of Control, he passed group after huge group of demons undergoing training. These were the ones especially reserved for attacking believers. The elementals had become relatively easy for spirit filled believers to detect, and they weren't multi functional, merely mirroring their nature in the actions of their victim. Whereas these special troops were far more sophisticated. Banner after banner he passed. Pride, False Doctrine, Tradition, False Humility, False Love and Religious spirits. By far the biggest group was Pride, a massive army being made ready to attack believers.

Several demons along the way snapped or hissed at him, but he just scowled back, far too intent on his delightful mission to pay them any heed or lose any time stopping to fight. Along The path he passed several other Grey Ones returning from his intended destination, each one sporting a satisfied triumphal expression.

In the distance, a huge cliff face rose up and up towards the heavens. As he neared it he became aware of a disgusting blue white light emanating from the very top. He quickly looked away, it made him almost vomit, but then it always did. He began to feel a sucking slime around his feet and lower legs. Cackling and shrieking, dark shapes swooped and dove out of the inky blackness, and a foetid stench struck his nostrils. He breathed in deeply; "Ah" he sighed "The Place of Witchcraft." For a few seconds he stood savouring the foul and heavily evil atmosphere, before continuing his journey to the wall of rock ahead. As the shrieks and incantations of the Place of Witchcraft gradually faded into the distance, Goomelt approached the cliff face. He was now acutely aware of the hated blue white light high above him and kept his eyes firmly on the ground in front.

The lower reaches of the cliff face were dark and comforting, the rocks covered in a slimy liquid putrescence. Up ahead an eerie red glow signalled the entrance to a small tunnel, which sloped gently upwards. Goomelt entered, ascending the slope and was comforted by the strong smell of decay. The tunnel eventually opened out into a small cavern and there sitting behind a desk hewn out of the rock sat a figure with the head and neck of a vulture, the body of a man, and the tail of a lizard which it flicked to and fro impatiently. On the opposite side of the cavern small bays were cut into the rock, each with a chimney like aperture above. In the eerie red light it was just possible to see each one was numbered.

Goomelt identified himself and stated his business. The creature, with a wave of his hand, directed him to bay number four. "Put the helmet on and don't forget the stone." croaked lizard tail. Goomelt had no intention of forgetting the stone, without it he was dead!

The 'Stone of Temporary Sanctification' allowed Grey Ones on behalf of their master the Great Accuser, to access The Palace of Accusation and lay their charges against their Chosen Ones. The palace was situated in the absolute lowest point of heaven, where God's glory was only twice as bright as the sun and temporarily sanctified demons could survive for just long enough to present their case and leave. This was the part Goomelt hated. He'd done it before in times past with other humans he'd been assigned to. He knew he'd be okay as long as he stuck to the rules. He knew that God's entire creation and each spiritual dimension were governed by strict rules, and a strong legal framework. Nonetheless, the thought of going up into that awful place made him shiver inside. From a pouch hanging on the wall in bay four he took a dark green pebble like crystal and swallowed it. From a shelf on the opposite wall he took a helmet resembling a welders mask and placed it over his worried head. Then he stood under the chimney. Lizard tail nodded a curt approval and pulled on a rope hanging down from the roof of the cavern.

High above on the cliff top, a formless being of blue white light twenty feet high, began to spin like a whirlwind above the chimney and a terrified demon began to rise into the lower reaches of heaven itself. His eyes tightly shut against the wonderful realms of colour and light he was passing through, he soon came to a halt in a huge shining room The destination of all the chimneys. The floor was like liquid marble and the walls danced and shimmered like mother of pearl. Arches and levels and doorways went off in all directions and the ceiling was a vibrant collage of semi precious stones. All around the room stood warrior Angels, swords drawn and alert. The darkness is never to be trusted.

Various other Grey Ones were arriving and leaving and the whole place had the air of a celestial airport. Without actually speaking the blue white light told him to report to the Admin Angel at arch seven. He was thankful that he'd' swallowed the stone of temporary sanctification, otherwise this disgusting blue white light would have killed him, never mind the warrior Angels! He'd finally made it to The Palace of Accusation and he knew his case was strong. Reaching the admin desk he was motioned forward. He stated his name, his commander's name, his area code and the name of Joshua Fishmen. He was about to launch into his accusations when the Angel held up a hand to silence him. He shifted from foot to foot. Temporarily sanctified or not he still didn't like this place. The awful gut churning smell of perfumed incense and the horrendous sound of distant choirs of Angels praising God made him want to run from there.

The admin Angel was checking lists. "Ah" he said, "yes, Joshua Fishmen, chosen one, right." Goomelt was again about to fire off his railing accusation, but another raised hand stopped him in his tracks. The Angel had opened a large book. Wonderfully decorated and encrusted with jewels, it was visibly vibrating. It was The Lamb's Book of Life. The little demon shuddered and shuffled backwards. The Angel perused it for a minute or more; then, slowly closing it he looked up, his radiant face tinged with sadness. "You may proceed." he informed Goomelt. The little demon gleefully laid out his case. God's law had been broken. Stealing, lying, fornication, also the breaking of human civil law with drugs and under age sex. He knew he was on a winner, Angels had to obey the rules. The admin Angel made some notes; then, reaching under his desk he produced a single white Angel feather, the tip of which was red. He studied it for a moment and then resignedly handed it to the excited little minion of darkness, who by now was almost shaking with fiendish glee. "You may return and assume The Position of Influence." said the Angel, dismissing Goomelt with a wave of his hand. The small grey being lost no time in exiting The Palace of Accusation with all its stomach churning goodness. He was eager to get back and increase the advantage he and Pusto would now hold.

Chakine had known what was coming and when Goomelt returned holding up the blood tipped feather he knew he had to relinquish his position. His face revealed none of the intense sadness he felt at leaving the shoulder of his young charge. He wasn't about to give these enemy agents that satisfaction. Instead he looked straight at them with a righteous and holy indignation, which in turn released waves of the hated blue white light rendering the demons extremely uncomfortable. They both looked away as Chakine retreated to a 'discreet distance' and then they shuffled warily past him to take up their newly gained 'Position of Influence'. The Grey Ones were gleeful, they'd done their job and won through. Now they would really begin to capitalise on the situation. Up until now from the

Place of Observation they had only been able to exert influence over situations from a distance. Now they had a free hand totally. Now they could mount a direct attack. From this point on Chakine could only intervene if Josh was in mortal danger.

------ O ------

That had been fourteen years ago now. Fourteen years in which Chakine had seen his young charge move steadily towards total capture by the darkness, and fourteen years in which that darkness had tightened its grip on an increasingly violent and dangerous world. Suicide bombers wreaked havoc across the world whilst the purveyors of pornography, alcohol and drugs reaped ever increasing profits. There was a vile and perilous assault on humanity. Nation rose against Nation and Kingdom against Kingdom. There were famines and earthquakes everywhere.
[Mathew Ch24 v 7].

Grey Ones the world over were now equipped with 'Spasmoides' and their master had succeeded in flooding the world with occult material. Children were encouraged to cast spells and enter into divination Harry Potter style. Each day millions of people eagerly looked to see what the future held in their star signs, and covens and spiritualists were reporting record growth. At the same time hundreds of millions of babies were being murdered. Ripped from their mother's wombs in abortion clinics across the world. The kingdom of darkness was growing ever stronger. The demons felt sure they were winning.

Although the last fourteen years had been strewn with apparent victory for the Grey Ones at Joshua's shoulder, there was something of which they were completely unaware. Something which Chakine knew would one day prove to be the ace hand that would put him back in The Position of Influence. He knew it would also stand Joshua back on his spiritual feet, as a true chosen one.

------ O ------

Many years ago, when Joshua was a little lad of seven, Chakine's area commander Captain Cherno had suddenly arrived unannounced at five a.m. on a Sunday morning. Goomelt and Pusto, at that time holding The Position of Observation, were a discreet distance away and fast asleep! Chakine was seated at the foot of the sleeping lad's bed. As Captain Cherno appeared, he motioned towards the slumbering demons, and held a finger to his lips. Usually protocol would demand that Chakine leapt to his feet and gave the customary salute "Hail to The Lord God Almighty – Holy – Holy – Holy." However on this occasion, as instructed, he remained silent and the two demons slept on, oblivious to developments. Chakine listened attentively. Cherno, his face shining, said "I bring exciting news from the Throne Room of The Most High." Chakine smiled appreciating the honour. "This day the child in your charge is to receive a verse of scripture, quickened by The Lord's Spirit, and this verse will be his future key." Chakine recognised the significance and grace bestowed upon his small charge and silently praised God for His wonderful love. Cherno continued, "We have special dispensation to suspend time around those two." indicating the comatose duo with a nod of his head. "I will see to that. You make sure the child attends St Mary's church this evening." With that, Cherno covered the distance between him and the sleeping demons in a flash. He drew his sword and whirled it around and around them with lightning speed until they were encased in a strange ball of purple light. They slumbered on, completely unaware. Cherno returned to Chakine's side. "I have also organised a company of Angels to attack a rather troublesome group of demons who inhabit a coven on the far side of Scaybaz's territory, so he'll be tied up there for the foreseeable future." They stood and looked at the small child asleep in his bed, and wondered and marvelled at the ultimate plans of their Holy Master.

At seven a.m. the young Josh yawned and rubbed his eyes. Chakine arose from the end of the bed flicking his wingtips. Cherno, from his position by the ball of purple light, which still contained the tranquilised slumbering demons, smiled and nodded to Chakine. Little Joshua swung his legs out of bed sitting upright as he did so. He stretched and yawned again. Outside a staggeringly beautiful sunrise had painted the morning sky myriad hues of pink and red. Joshua got up and went over to his window totally enraptured by this morning sky, the like of which he'd never seen before. Suddenly he began to sing. It was a strange and wonderful song in a language he'd never learnt. His little heart poured out in pure praise to the as yet unknown creator of this visual splendour. Both the Angels wings were fully open as The Glory of God filled the young lad's bedroom on that summer Sunday morning, and a tiny flame of knowing flickered in his young heart.

His Earthly father had always dismissed any notion of God as rubbish, and there had never been any form of spiritual guidance whatsoever. At one time Dean, Josh's older brother had kept a bible under his pillow, but he had been so berated and humiliated by his father because of it, that he never again sought solace in the truth nor considered the wisdom of the light therein.

That evening, under the pretence of going to visit Ray, Josh walked the mile or so to St Mary's Church. He knew nothing of churches, services or any sort of organised religious activity. Yet he knew he wanted to come here, he felt almost compelled. The church was an archetypal neo gothic building surrounded by the usual collection of dead people. He went through an ancient wrought iron gate, which opened onto a pathway leading between the gravestones and on to the church entrance.

Moss covered headstones, some very old and unattended, leaned at peculiar angles on either side of the old cobbled path. Some of the ancient stone caskets were cracked and split. He found himself frightened to look too closely lest a skeletal hand should emerge, or a pair of red eyes stare out at him from the darkness within.

As he approached the building, he looked up at the huge grey spire towering above him and he wanted to run away from this place. It seemed to bear no resemblance to the lovely feelings he'd felt this morning as he sung to the sunrise. Yet somehow he still felt he should continue. A huge oak studded door sat dark and brooding in an archway between two small spires. These were intricately decorated with all manner of frightening gargoyles and bizarre carvings. The whole building was grey stone and rather foreboding. Just behind Joshua, Chakine was extremely alert. He'd been in these places before.

The sound of people's voices behind him was a comfort to Josh. Twenty or so assorted people were following along the little path. A mighty creaking sound heralded the opening of the big arched door, and there stood a grey haired old man in a black and white dress! He had huge bushy eyebrows and hair growing out of his nose. Josh froze, rooted to the spot. The sudden ringing of the bells served to somewhat quench young Joshua's trepidation. Some of the adults had overtaken him and were filing through the door past 'dress man.' Josh followed suit.

Entering the main body of the church he gazed around wide eyed at its huge cavernous interior, high timbered ceiling and profusion of enormous stone arches. It was cold and not at all what he had expected, but he dutifully took his place in a row of pews on the right hand side. The low slung sun was streaming through the beautiful stained glass window above the altar, making a contrast of illuminated colour against the stark and unwelcoming dark shadows that seemed to lurk behind the huge stone arches. There was room for maybe two hundred and fifty people, so the little band of twenty-three worshippers looked sparse indeed, dotted around this strange, cavernous, echoey building. Josh sat patiently on the hard wooden pew. A white haired old lady began torturing a monotonous dirge from an old pump organ, and the oft repeated farce of religious ceremony began yet again in this place where once, long ago, God had truly been worshipped. Now however, Religion ruled and the release of Truth was sparse. Sparse, yet still there when the word of God was spoken or read, or the heart of a 'Sunday Christian' was moved upon by the Spirit. But the spectre of 'Tradition' loomed large.

The thirty or so elementals had shrieked in terror as the warrior angel entered the church with Joshua. They were black one-dimensional shadowy beings from antiquity. They had been here a long, long time. Now however they were scurrying about in all directions in a blind panic. Chakine knew the rules and acted instantaneously. This was his master's house. It had been dedicated to Him two hundred and thirty years ago. In the scope of things, earthbound elementals were considered fair game and had no legal rights outside of a living body.

Almost as he crossed the threshold he drew his sword with lightning speed and swung it in a wide arc curling upwards. This sliced in two the unsuspecting entity perched on the pew behind 'dress man'. Launching himself skyward, he hurtled towards the belfry dispatching two more on the way with a deft flick of his gleaming weapon. As his feet came to rest on the wooden beams of the tower, six screeching, slashing elementals flung themselves, in futile desperation at his back. Chakine swung hard with his shield, catching them in mid attack and sending them cascading from the ledge into space. He quickly followed, his sword flashing as he rolled and twisted through the air delivering the 'coup de grace' to each shadowy form before his feet touched the flagstone floor.

From the corner of his eye to the right, he just caught a glimpse of several dark forms scuttling towards the small door behind the choir stalls, in a desperate bid for freedom. In a flash he was out of the main door and round the outside of the building just in time to cut each one in two as they dashed from the doorway looking behind them. The remaining entities were dispatched in the cellars just as the drone of the organ ceased and the minister mounted the steps, which would raise him above the pews and thus psychologically elevate him above the people. He stood at the lectern and cleared his throat. Joshua still thought it curious that this man ascending the steps was wearing a dress, but nobody else seemed to mind so he guessed it must be acceptable.

His immediate task complete, and having secured the building, Chakine resumed his place at the boy's shoulder. The people stood up, sat down, stood up, and then sat down again as 'dress man' spoke unfamiliar words in a weird theatrical sounding voice. They didn't seem to speak the same English as Josh, and the man in the dress seemed to be almost chanting. Noticing that those around him were holding a white card, he picked one up from the pew in front and realised that this was a question and answer routine. Dress man would give the question and the answer was read out by the audience. Words like 'in-ik-wit-ee' and 'pur-dish-on' were totally alien to the young lad. He understood none of it, and was beginning to wonder why he had so wanted to come here. The white haired old lady began torturing the organ again, and the little congregation wailed and mumbled their way through several really boring songs he'd never heard. Next they bowed their heads and said a poem. It didn't rhyme. It was something about 'Our Father'.

Dress man cleared his throat again, and in a nasal whining tone continued, "Our text for today is from the Gospel of St. Mathew, chapter seven, verse seven." Chakine touched the ears of his charge, unfolding his wings as he did. Raising his arms heavenward he began to pray in Angelic Tongues. The minister continued "Ask and it shall be given you, Seek and you shall find, Knock and it shall be opened unto you."
No one but Chakine saw the Glorious Light that enveloped the little boy, and no one but Chakine knew that these words had entered Josh's heart. He had been given a 'key'. This verse would have special meaning for him. - And now, twenty years later, Chakine could only observe, watching and waiting for the Wisdom of God to unfold the plan.

------ O ------

The New Year came and went and Goomelt and Pusto were quite pleased with themselves. Their stock of 'Spasmoides' was growing in diversity and so was their hold over Joshua as he went deeper and deeper into the exploration of sensory gratification. Since just before Christmas they had managed to add adultery (with Cathy Hancock) and false witness (Josh had lied when taxing his car, saying it had been off the road when it hadn't). They had also managed to resuscitate and amplify the old desire for pornography, from teenage years. And with the advent of the Internet it had just been so easy. Scaybaz had even mumbled a curt "good" when informed of the advances!

On the surface, by worldly standards, Josh and Ray were ok guys – they were doing all right! Ray especially. They both had gainful employment and had never been in any real trouble with the law (mainly due to never having been caught). Nonetheless, everything looked promising. Ray was forging ahead with his plans to visit China, and Josh's uncle Hector was looking at the possibilities of wangling his nephew a transfer to West Wales.

Like most people, outwardly they appeared to be normal healthy human beings, but the reality was they were totally unable to recognise the condition of their hearts. They would be up in arms about anyone practising paedophilia, yet would quite happily sit and watch all sorts of gross perversion in pornographic films. They would be incensed if someone stole from them, yet they regularly stole from the taxman and the authorities, considering them 'fair game'. Any nice cheap goods would be purchased – no questions asked. Like so many, many others, theirs was a veneer of respectability. A mutually accepted 'front' through which society manages to retain the façade of civilised behaviour, whilst secretly indulging in all its lusts and perverted fantasies. Man looks on the outward appearance. God looks into the heart.

In reality they weren't any different from ninety eight percent of the rest of the population in respect of their lifestyles, beliefs and standards. Ray believed that making a pile of money was the answer. A big house, nice car, holidays in the sun. Whereas Josh felt that overpopulation of the planet was the root of man's problem, with too many people crowded together in enormous cities. He felt that each person should have their own piece of land on which they could grow food and be free, although he wasn't at all sure how to go about it. He cared passionately about the destruction of the rainforests and the ecology of the planet in general, yet still used all the carbon producing trappings of the society he found himself in. Had he to have categorised himself he would probably have said atheist-humanist, but in reality he was like everybody else. Searching.

Searching in all the wrong places Those that the wiles of the darkness had presented him with. Searching within the corridors of his own sensory gratification. Looking, but doing so without realising his own inward desperation. For God has placed in the heart of mankind the desire to seek their creator.

And all the while the 'Grey Ones' schemed and muttered.

<<<<--- END OF CHAPTER ONE --->>>>

The Dragonmaster

CHAPTER 2 **Two Ancient Lands**

Polly was by the kitchen door and barking long before Meredith Evans could discern the sound of the battered old Land Rover that was wending its way up the track to his cottage. He'd just finished a meal and it really was a breakfast. Food had not been on the menu for the last three days, as he'd sought God's will in prayer and fasting.

Easter had come and gone, and the fullness of spring was fast approaching summer. The hedgerows were a profusion of wild flowers and rampant vegetation. Bees hummed in search of pollen, and fledglings stretched their new-found wings, continuing to hassle for food from their increasingly disinterested parents.

Meredith had been asking God what, if anything, he should do with regard to the 'Chosen One' he'd been told to expect. In the three days of prayer one word had frequently returned to his mind. *'Accommodation'*. So he figured he'd wait and let things develop. He hadn't expected the speed at which they would.

The sound of the approaching vehicle grew louder, and a well used Land Rover came to a halt by the back door. Meredith rose from his place by the Rayburn to greet his old friend Emir Phillips. They spoke together in Welsh. "Well bach, 'ow are you then." Meredith enquired of the older man. "Not so good really Meredith," came the reply, "not so good." Turning to the sink to fill the kettle he motioned to Emir to sit in the fireside chair. He'd known him for twenty years now and had seen him lose his wife to cancer too. Emir had spent his whole married life in a cottage similar to Meredith's three quarters of a mile away on the same ancient drovers track. They were nearest neighbours, Emir being closer to the main road.

Although they were quite different, there was empathy between them. Meredith was educated, loquacious and generous, whereas Emir was a man of few words, little schooling and with a reputation for being something of a tightwad. "Anything I can help with?" Meredith asked warmly. Emir sighed, "Well" he said slowly "you know as 'ow my daughter Sian lives in England, and 'ow I've been finding it 'ard to cope since Rhian died, well, Sian's asked me to go and stay with 'er, see." His tone was almost apologetic and Meredith waited to see if anything else was forthcoming – but it wasn't.

After a short silence, in which he made Emir his mug of tea, he said "And?" looking quizzically at him. "Well, er . . . I was wondering like... if you would er... like... keep an eye on the place for me?" - "Certainly, but what about your animals?" quizzed Meredith, knowing he would be singularly unqualified to look after two horses, a jersey cow, and a ragged assortment of goats. "Oh, no problem man, Lynn Williams is 'aving the 'orses, that new English couple in the village want the Jersey and the goats can go to the mart!" He sat back in his chair and sipped his tea. "So you're going for good then?"- "Hell, yes boy! Nothing to stay 'ere for then is there?" Meredith thought for a moment. "So, are you renting your place out then Emir?" Emir cleared his throat. "Well, er,... that is... er... part of what I meant about keeping an eye on it like." He cleared his throat again. "Would you know anyone, you know, er ...looking for a place like?"

Meredith wanted to leap into the air and shout "Praise the Lord!" But in deference to his old friend, an unrelenting atheist, he merely whispered it. God works in mysterious ways indeed. Within a week all the legal stuff was sorted, and two weeks later Meredith was on the platform of Carmarthen station waving goodbye to Emir.

He smiled as the train pulled out of the station. and watched it disappear into the distance, taking his old friend off to the remainder of his life with his daughter in England. He would miss him, but he was certain that the property would not remain vacant for long. The cottage, with its two acres of fields and paddocks, was completely un-modernised, and almost as secluded as Meredith's further down the track. Reaching into the pocket of his waterproof coat, he jingled the keys and wondered how soon he would meet this 'Chosen One'.

------ O ------

Hector Fishmen had been surprised to hear from his brother's widow after such a long time, but being a far more affable fellow than his deceased sibling he had greeted her warmly on the phone. Having attained the position of Area Postal Director after nearly thirty years in the Post Office, he was pleased to discover that the nephew he had never met had chosen a similar path. Not only was he amenable to the idea of his kin transferring into his area, he actually had an office where one of the postmen was about to emigrate to Australia! That office was situated in the coastal town of Aberdigan. Blood being thicker than water, Joshua's application somehow went to the top of the list. It was approved, rubber-stamped, and signed and sealed, the very day that Meredith pocketed the keys to Emir's cottage.

------ O ------

As soon as he had declared his intention to import goods from their country, the Chinese Embassy became extremely helpful to Ray Coughlin. They furnished him with all the necessary visas, passes and documentation he would need as a foreigner travelling deep into the Chinese interior. They had even promised to provide an interpreting guide.

With the relevant inoculations administered and the airline tickets booked for the middle of next week, the Coughlin household was a hive of activity. On previous trips Ray had taken Zara and the kids, but this time, China being an entirely unknown quantity, he had decided he should go alone. Zara had never liked camping or the outdoor life, preferring the luxury of hotels, swimming pools and the close proximity of boutiques. That was how they'd conducted previous expeditions. Hunting down the artefacts Ray was after by taxi, and usually no more than about forty miles from whichever hotel they were staying at.

This time however the target area was a little further a field.

The village of Yantook in the mid China province of Sheng-Too-Lai, lay some four hundred and fifty miles from the nearest airport, with the last eighty or so miles being rough mountain tracks. Ray had decided on this particular area after being shown some photographs and two or three examples of Jade and soapstone carvings of exquisite quality. They were small enough to be able to pack a thousand or more into a small six by four crate. He knew they'd 'fly away' once he got them home. He was good at his job and he'd done his homework. Two crates after expenses should net him around thirty thousand pounds. He was slightly concerned about the language problem, realising that he would have to put his trust in an interpreter, who would be a total stranger, and a Chinese stranger at that! However, apart from this small worry, he was filled with the excitement of a potentially lucrative and stimulating adventure. He'd toyed with the idea of asking Josh to accompany him, but that would have meant Josh giving up his job, and Ray couldn't afford to take him on at present on a permanent basis. And anyway, Josh's heart seemed to be set on the Wales thing, so Ray had kept silent.

The farewell drink at the Coopers Arms on the Monday night was well underway. Ray and Josh had 'downed a few' and were relaxed and happy, totally unaware that they were being watched with malicious intent by a group of drunken skinheads from the building trade. Goomelt and Pusto, just behind Josh, were enjoying the predominantly demonic atmosphere of the place, whilst Chakine, sensing danger had tuned in to the conversation of the shaven headed group. There were elementals everywhere, revelling in the sleazy licentiousness that abounded in every corner of the establishment. Chakine, listening intently, could hear the plotting of the group of hostile inebriates seated directly opposite the two friends. They were just out of sight in one of the mock Tudor booths, and they were all very, very drunk. "That's 'im " slurred the biggest of the group, "that's the scumbag who jumped me from behind just before Christmas." The rest of the motley band murmured their drunken displeasure. Chakine noticed the dark shapes materialising in and around the group of men, and he recognised the large one as the man who had attempted to punch Joshua one morning just before Christmas.

The gang egged the big man on. "Do 'im Spud" – "Yeah, go on, slice him up!" The dark shapes were growing in intensity and one of the group produced a butcher's meat cleaver from under his coat and passed it to Spud. Chakine discerned the spirit of murder in the big drunken man, who was now rising to his feet, the weapon hanging in his hand. In the power and knowledge of his authority, drawing his sword he, leapt forward sweeping Goomelt and Pusto aside with his shield, and placing himself firmly between Joshua and his advancing protagonist. The spirit of murder, when suddenly confronted with this warrior Angel, sword drawn, shrieked and backed away, causing the object of its influence to crumple in mid swing of the cleaver. The first Ray and Joshua knew of it was when the edge of their table exploded in splinters and their drinks launched into space, cascading over the now prostrate figure of a sixteen stone skinhead who was 'kissing the floor' at their feet. Unseen, in the same instant, the warrior guardian, his sword flashing, dispatched the whole group of shrieking terrified demons with swift and righteous anger.

The pub bouncers moved in on the rest of the gang and in the ensuing mayhem Josh and Ray made it to the relative safety of the car park. Goomelt and Pusto had started to complain, but Chakine shot them a warning glance as he sheathed his sword, silencing them with two words. "Mortal Danger!" As the friends climbed into a taxi, Ray said to Josh "Nothing like a nice quiet drink is there!" – they laughed in humoured irony all the way home.

The following day, whilst out shopping for all the bits that would ensure her man had a comfortable trip, Zara decided she would buy Ray a special little present. Something that would bring him luck. She needed to get some more king size rolling papers for making joints and so went into 'The Wizard's Den', an alternative type shop that sold hash pipes and all sorts of smoking related materials.

During conversation with the Gothic looking girl behind the counter, she happened to mention her desire to buy her husband something that would bring him luck on his travels. The sales assistant, dressed all in black with a whitened face and thick black eye liner, smiled broadly exclaiming, "I've got just the thing!" Zara was impressed by the tale of an ancient Babylonian symbol of luck and prosperity, and soon left the shop with a gift-wrapped silver pentagram and chain. The five pointed star, symbol of the Horned Hunter of the Night. Satan himself.

Gothic girl giggled with glee, yet another amusing story she would be able to share with the rest of the coven. Later that day Zara presented Ray with his gift. He was genuinely pleased and kissed her with great affection. "Thanks sweetie, I'll wear it for good luck then." he said, as she fastened the dark symbol around his unsuspecting neck.

The assortment of spirits already involved with Ray's life almost purred with contentment when their host was willingly adorned with the symbol of their master, knowing that the assurance of their tenancy grew ever stronger.

The sound of the doorbell heralded Josh's arrival, and soon all three friends were sitting around the coffee table cups in hand. That morning news of his official transfer to Wales had come through and he would be leaving next week. Uncle Hector had very kindly sent him all sorts of peripheral details concerning his forthcoming move. There were various tourist guides and brochures, each one depicting a different place of interest worth visiting. All of them had one thing in common. Somewhere on each publication would be a depiction of a small Red Dragon. The national symbol of Wales. There was also an imitation parchment poster, showing a three-dimensional map of Wales. It advertised The Mabinogion, which is a Welsh book of 'The ancient Celtic legends of spirits, heroes and dreams'. Made to look like an antique scroll, the map showed the location of all the castles and places of historic significance, plus it had little drawings dotted here and there illustrating various episodes from the legends. Curved around the coastline, was an enormous Dragon. Its tail coiled around Mt. Snowdon to the North and its body following the contours of Cardigan Bay. The fire breathing head coming to rest in the Preseli Mountains further to the South. At the bottom of the poster it proudly proclaimed 'Wales, The Land of the Dragon'. Josh passed the map to his two friends who studied it for a while and then passed it back. Neither of them had ever been to Wales. "It looks amazing," said Zara, "All those castles and waterfalls and things." Ray looked at his old friend warmly, "You know, after that business in The Coopers Arms the other evening I understand now why you're going. If I didn't have this lot" he said jokingly, gesturing to Zara and the house in general, "I'd probably be coming with you!" Josh stayed for dinner, and after a few joints and some beers the men were 'chilled' in the easy chairs whilst Zara dutifully saw to the task of finishing Ray's packing. On the table, the now folded map of Wales and its accompanying brochures, had somehow slid beneath the pile of Ray's notes and schedules for his trip, whilst the rest of Uncle Hector's communication was returned to Josh in its buff envelope.

Having some annual leave still owing to him, Joshua took the following day off to drive the family to the airport so they could all wish Ray 'Bon Voyage'. With plenty of time to spare, Ray checked his baggage in and they all went for a vastly overpriced coffee. Eventually the flight call came over the tannoy, and Zara and the children said their tearful good-byes to Ray. Finally the two friends embraced. "Take care in the Land of The Dragon," Josh said sincerely. "You take care in the Land of the Dragon too, boyo!" quipped Ray, in a phoney Welsh accent. Then waving and blowing kisses to his family he disappeared from sight through the doors marked 'departures'.

On the drive home Ray's parting words seemed to go round and round in Josh's head. Until now he'd never really thought of Wales as 'The Land of the Dragon'. Then he remembered Uncle Hector's poster and resolved to find out more.

- - - - - - O - - - - - -

The pretty young girl behind the desk of The Aberdigan Chronicle smiled cheerfully. "How can I help you sir?" Meredith smiled back. "I'd like to put an ad in your accommodation to let section please." He handed her a piece of paper. "Oh yes, for two weeks please." The assistant filled in the relevant forms and requested the appropriate price. His business concluded Meredith stepped out into the narrow cobbled side street. "Well Lord, the ad's in and now it's up to You." he said, walking past the castle towards his parked car. The late spring sunshine was warm on his face and his heart was filled with anticipation.

Aberdigan was an ancient estuary town. In the past tall masted sailing ships had voyaged the oceans of the globe from what was once a bustling seaport of some importance. The Castle, with its commanding view over the estuary, had previously stood like a sentinel. A symbol of security over the affluence of the town. Now however, its crumbling walls were shored up with huge ugly steel girders painted bright yellow. Trees grew out of the masonry and many years of neglect had taken their toll. The complete mis-management of this ancient monument by successive local authorities had been a disgrace, and now huge quantities of public money were being eaten up in an effort to restore it.

Down at the tidal river, the once grand shipping lanes were silted up and bore only minimal traffic, the occasional shrimp or lobster boat, small private motor craft, and sundry canoeists. The huge old granary on the wharf was now a museum of local history, with flats above, and the ancient narrow bridge over the river, which was the main South road access into the town, completed the picture of a settlement that had seen better days.

The town itself was still alive and bustling in terms of commerce and tourism, but it wore a shabby old coat, and its shoes needed polishing. All in all it reflected the general economic state of the area, and everywhere, just everywhere, on walls, flags and buildings sat the symbol of the Dragon.

Polly turned round and round in circles on the front seat of her master's car, excited at his approach. Meredith smiled, he could always expect a large greeting from the little creature, and he loved her dearly. He loved his old Morris Traveller too. One hundred and ninety five thousand miles and still going strong! True, occasionally he did have to push it in an effort to coax it to start, but it had been more than reliable overall and he wouldn't swap it for a Rolls Royce. Year after year it had taken him to and from his job at Bangor University where he'd lectured in History and Art until his retirement three years ago. "Thank You Lord." he said, remembering, how all those years ago he'd prayed for a reliable car!

Driving through the town, Meredith prayed for the people he passed, and he prayed especially for the churches and chapels dotted along the way. "Wake them up Lord; please open their ears, eyes and hearts to Your word."

Many years ago in 1904 the area had witnessed a wonderful revival and The Holy Spirit had poured out His love, bringing many into knowledge of God's grace and truth. However, God has no grandchildren and each generation must have their own experience of personal salvation. A plethora of churches and chapels in the area bore witness to this previous move of God, but now sadly many of them had closed down and most of the others were sparsely attended by ageing believers. A small group of younger Christians regularly met at Meredith's house, and at the homes of one or two others. There were fourteen souls in all, and they loved to worship God and pray together.

One of their number was a stunningly attractive twenty four year old student, Cheryll Jameson. She was studying art and design at Aberdigan College. A lively quick and intelligent young woman, she came from 'alternative' stock. Her parents were hippies and she had spent much of her early life travelling with them in India. She now had a flat in town, whilst her parents lived in the Cych valley, some ten miles away. Her Doc Marten boots, ankle socks, bright leggings and baggy knee length multicoloured jumpers did nothing to lessen the impact she always had on males of all ages. Beautiful waist length blonde hair, powder blue eyes, strong high cheekbones and gorgeous cupid bow lips were matched with a generous and caring personality. This was well balanced by a great sense of humour, and rounded off by the ability to listen as well.

When she smiled, which was often, she would reveal a gleaming set of straight white teeth any Mormon missionary would have died for! Her body was the kind of shape that had made Hugh Heffner rich. In short she was what the world would term gorgeous!

In February five years ago, Meredith had picked her up hitch hiking. They'd talked about art and had 'hit it off'. A genuine friendship had developed. She then began to visit him regularly and they would often meet in town for coffee. Whilst his knowledge of art enthralled her, his knowledge of spiritual things enlightened her even more, and she became hungry to know the truth. After a few months, he gave her all of Leah's old paintbrushes and equipment and free use of the summer house studio.

Cheryll had been impressed by the fact that unlike every other man, (young or old) that she'd ever met, Meredith had never once 'tried anything'. He had always treated her with the utmost respect and been completely above board. By the end of that summer he'd led her to salvation in Jesus.

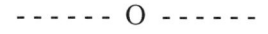

------ O ------

Thirty six thousand feet up, Ray Coughlin looked out of the window of the airbus down onto the carpet of thick white cloud below, wondering what his Chinese adventure held in store. Reaching up to the overhead luggage bay he pulled out his briefcase. He wanted to re-check his itinerary again to make sure there were no loose ends. As he went through his papers he came upon Josh's map and brochures and wondered how they had got there. As he perused the map he noticed the town of Aberdigan on the coast and just to the right of it a bit inland, was a place called 'The Cych Valley'. It had drawings of demons and goblins and the like, and bore the legend 'The Entrance to the Underworld'.

Ray smiled, thinking it curiously coincidental that both he and his good friend were independently on their way to two ancient lands, and that each of these was reputedly inhabited by dragons!

------ O ------

Goomelt and Pusto were puzzled. On several occasions now Joshua Fishmen had failed to respond to their Spasmoide attacks with any enthusiasm. Just last week Cathy Hancock had arrived at his digs one evening and he'd refused her obvious invitation to have sex, despite Pusto scoring two direct hits with lust Spasmoides. His excuse had been that he wasn't feeling too well, and she'd left shortly after. And then there'd been the incident at the fast food shop, where a drunk had pushed him in the back and invited him to fight. Despite a perfectly placed violence Spasmoide from Goomelt, there had been no response. Nothing.

Now, this evening, as Zara was pressing her warm soft body against his, in a slightly over enthusiastic 'thank you for taking us to the airport' cuddle, the two demons launched an all out attack. They threw Lust, Adultery and Betrayal. Yet nothing happened ...... Nothing at all! The watching demons were frantic, incensed, and totally terrified of what Scaybaz would do when he discovered the recent lack of dark responses from their human.

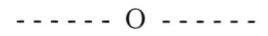

------ O ------

Far away, on The Plane of Control, Scaybaz was speaking to a larger and more malevolent looking entity, with horns, a wolf like face and a double set of wings. The eyes of this creature glowed with an eerie green light as he listened impatiently to the smaller demon. Globules of stringy brown slime dripped from his large yellow fangs and his foetid breath smelt like rotting flesh. At this point in time, little did Goomelt and Pusto imagine that soon they would long for the days when Scaybaz was their commander. For this horned wolf head was Kaisis, the commander of the area to which Joshua Fishmen was about to move. Feared even amongst the ranks of demonic leaders, Kaisis was the embodiment of evil. Cruel and full of hatred, he was the Ruler of the Western Province – Wales.

------ O ------

The twelve-hour flight now over, Ray was jet lagged, yet buoyed up by the excitement of his forthcoming adventure. Had he known at this time just how exciting it was going to get, he would probably have turned around and taken the first flight home, but ignorance being bliss, he continued through Beijing customs and out into the arrival lounge. The extreme presence of armed military unnerved him somewhat, but since 9/11 it had become pretty much standard practice at airports the world over. The global threat of terrorism had been a tonic to those individuals and governments who seek to overly control the citizens of their respective countries. A population in fear for its safety will tolerate ever increasing levels of security measures, to the great benefit of those with a hidden agenda. Behind each and every insane and evil action, lie varying degrees of dark spirits.

Scanning the bustling building for any sign of the interpreter who was due to meet him, Ray eventually caught sight of his own name held aloft on a white card. Signalling his recognition with a wave of his hand, he approached the small dark haired Chinese man. He was greeted with a polite bow. "Good afternoon Sir," said the diminutive oriental, "I am Simon Cheng, and I will be your interpreter and guide for the duration of your stay." He was smiling broadly, and, as far as Ray could ascertain, seemed sincere. "On behalf of my government may I most cordially welcome you to The Peoples Republic of China." He held out his hand, which Ray took, shaking it warmly as he secretly thought, "Well, at least the guy seems to be able to speak English ok!" As it happened Simon Cheng could speak English, and Arabic, and also Spanish and German, plus seven dialects of Chinese. A graduate of Beijing University, his father was

American and his mother Chinese. He worked for the Department of Trade, interpreting and assisting foreign buyers to locate sources. Taking Ray's holdall, Simon led the way. As they exited the building into bright sunlight, Ray was very pleased to be politely ushered into a large black limousine, which then proceeded to chauffeur him to his temporary destination. The Beijing Hilton.

On the short journey he was amazed to see just how many people seemed to throng the streets. It reminded him of an ants nest with people scurrying everywhere, busy, busy, busy.

His accommodation was excellent, the service impeccable and the food thoroughly delicious. "I could get used to this." he thought, as he slipped tired but happy into the world of air-conditioned dreams.

As arranged Simon Cheng was there on the dot of 8am. Ray, his business suit swapped for slacks, a pullover, a waterproof, and sturdy walking boots, settled comfortably in to the passenger seat of the luxury Jeep. The interpreter gunned the engine and the expedition began. They sped out of the city on the first leg of the long journey that would take them to the province of Sheng-Too-Lai in the Sichuan Mountains.

------ O ------

Four hundred and fifty miles away high in the craggy peaks of that distance province, the occupants of the village of Yantook went about their daily tasks. Accessible only via four footed transport, the small village nestled against a sheer rock face that rose grim and desolate some three hundred feet above the cluster of ramshackle buildings. All around and far into the distance the ancient mountains rose stark and foreboding, framed against a powder blue sky. Somewhere deeper in the rocky starkness lay the sources of the mighty Yangtze and Mekong rivers. Rows of tiered and terraced buildings perched lazily on great slabs of rock at the foot of the cliff. Their ancient red tiled roofs in stark contrast to the bleakness of the weathered rock. At the top end of the village stood a magnificent walled pagoda, its beautiful symmetry perfectly reflected in the crystal clear water of the small Mountain Lake beside it.

Stretching down the valley for a mile or more, an intricate patchwork of small terraced fields added a splash of colour that served only to highlight the harshness of the surroundings. The remote location had allowed Yantook to remain virtually unchanged for centuries. Even Chairman Mao's Cultural Revolution had made relatively little impact. True, a team of government officials did visit once a year, assessing the production of carvings and arranging the sort of buying trips that Ray was now on, but generally, life was as it had always been since antiquity.

Painted on the door of every building, and carved into walls and rock faces all over the village, the same symbol was visible everywhere. A triangle, depicting three intricately intertwined red dragons.

In a windowless room at the rear of the pagoda, amidst the eerie flicker of candles, a hunched figure sat cross-legged on a large black silk cushion. He wore a black silk robe, and he swayed to and fro as he chanted from an ancient leather-bound book that lay open on the floor in front of him. Every now and then, he would pick up a pinch of powder from one of three copper crucibles, which were mounted on a carved wooden dragon sitting on its haunches. The powder would be sprinkled over a glowing charcoal brazier. Each time he did so the area would fill with a cloud of heavily narcotic smoke, which would billow and curl, serpent like, around the room. This was followed by a strange luminous green glow, which would intensify and then gradually dissipate until the process was repeated. On the wall opposite, a large mural depicting the triangle of three intertwined dragons, seemed to be vibrating, and almost animated. The eyes of the three creatures glowed yellow and green and the room hummed with a low guttural growl.

Outside in the sunshine, skilled artisans were carving all manner of beings and creatures from Jade and soapstone. Traditional designs which captured the human world around them, as well as various mythological entities from times long past. Their workmanship was exquisite; utilising secrets handed down through the generations, and techniques known only to real masters of their trade.

------ O ------

Ray was thankful that the Jeep was comfortable. The drive was long and the going, slow. Once they'd left the main road they had needed to adjust their speed to suit the uneven and potholed surfaces. The first evening had been spent at a fairly modern and comfortable hotel and the second day's journey was much the same as the first, except that Ray felt as if each mile was somehow taking them further back in time. As dusk approached he could see, silhouetted against the red pink sky, the Sichuan Mountains rising like stalagmites from the plain ahead.

Simon swung the Jeep onto a small side road that led to what looked like some sort of military establishment. "We'll stay here tonight Mr. Coughlin." said Simon, exiting the Jeep. The small outpost was manned by at least twenty soldiers. The officer appeared to know Simon, greeting him with a salute followed by a polite bow. The accommodation was sparse but warm, Spartan but practical.

The officers and honoured guest ate separately from the enlisted men. At dinner Ray was relieved when Simon produced a spoon, after observing his pathetic attempts to utilise chopsticks, declaring "Empty chopsticks and an empty stomach lead a hungry man to despair!"

With Simon's skilful interpreting the three men passed a pleasant evening discussing all manner of things. Families, the problems involved in feeding hundreds of millions of people, and the merits of Manchester United football club, a favourite subject of Ray's. When Simon's officer friend had first been introduced to him, Ray had nearly choked trying to suppress his laughter at hearing, "Mr.Coughlin, this is lieutenant Mee-Too-Long." He had managed to feign a coughing fit and got away with it.

Later, when whilst discussing football, Lieutenant Too-Long, in heavy Chinese accent, had referred in all seriousness to the famous Manchester United striker Wayne Rooney, as "Wayne Looney." Ray had to turn away, biting his cheeks to avoid exploding in hysterical laughter. He had no wish to offend his hosts, but it was one of those times when your brain seems to lock on to that which strikes you as funny, and replay it over and over at the expense of your decorum.

Rolling around on the floor in hysterics is fine in the right setting. It soothes the soul. Right now however, Ray was not sure it would be received in a positive fashion.
Feigning yet more coughing, whilst desperately suppressing his laughter, he made his excuses and headed for the sanctuary of his bunk. On the washroom wall, taped between the two mirrors were a series of Playboy centrefolds. He smiled to himself, realising that despite language, culture or customs, men are basically the same the world over!

As he drifted into sleep his mind was awash with the sights of the last two days. On the long journey from Beijing he'd seen such an incredible mixture of the old and the new. Enormous tower blocks and state of the art glass and steel buildings with all manner of geometric design. Village after village and mile after mile of rice paddies, tended by simple folk tilling the earth with oxen. Old wooden carts piled high with reeds. Majestic Pagodas, huge advertising billboards and endless swathes of plain concrete houses that seemed to go on forever. It truly was a strange and intriguing amalgam of the ancient and the modern.

At breakfast next morning Ray was surprised to see Simon Cheng in military uniform, a revolver in the holster at his side. Sensing his disquiet Simon explained "Mr. Coughlin, by midday we shall have entered the province of Sheng-Too-Lai, where we will pick up horses and an escort for the two-day trek to Yantook. There are, unfortunately, brigands in these mountains to whom a fine cargo of Jade is a tempting proposition. Our uniformed presence may serve to deter them." - "Oh, ok, right… er …yes." Ray replied in the most nonchalant tone he could muster, desperately trying to give the impression that the prospect of armed brigands ahead was an accustomed inconvenience and a mere trifle.

The equipment loaded they began the next part of the journey that would take them deep into the Sichuan Mountains. As the four-wheel drive vehicle propelled them ever nearer to this lawless sounding area, Ray Coughlin found himself seriously wondering if this trip had been such a good idea after all.

------ O ------

In a different time zone halfway across the world, Joshua Fishmen his estate car crammed full of his belongings, approached the Severn Bridge that spans the Bristol Channel. Across the water lay the land he had fallen in love with at age eleven. He felt a sense of excitement as he queued for the tollbooth. A strange feeling. Almost as if he was coming home.

The fee paid, he continued his journey over the enormous bridge suspended hundreds of feet above the turbulent waters of the tidal estuary. The divide that separated England from Wales seemed to mark the end of a chapter of Joshua's life, and at the same time, the beginning of a bright new future. This really was it!

He could feel the strong wind buffeting his vehicle as he passed the halfway point of the huge steel-cabled suspension bridge. In the distance he could see the outline of the mountains silhouetted against the clear blue sky. He savoured the moment as his car made landfall in the Principality. The sign that proclaimed 'Welcome to Wales' in both Welsh and English, seemed to be there especially for him. Also, depicted in the centre of this sign was a large Red Dragon.

"Then, there was war in heaven. Michael and the Angels under his command fought the Dragon and his angels. And the Dragon lost the battle and was forced out of heaven. This great Dragon – the ancient serpent called the Devil or Satan, the one deceiving the whole world – was thrown down to earth with all his angels." [Revelation Ch.12 v 7-9]

The little band of believers close to Josh's destination had continued to pray for the protection of the one they knew was coming. Meredith having shared with them what The Lord had revealed to him.

Ever since Joshua had left that morning, Goomelt and Pusto had been hurling Spasmoide after Spasmoide at the back of Josh's neck. They'd tried all they could to cause an accident. They tried getting him angry with other drivers; they tried filling his mind with lust and depravity. Together they tried anything and everything. Eventually, in desperation even attempting to get him to make a wrong turn and thus delay the inevitable. Nothing had worked! Not one Spasmoide had adhered, and now here they were in The Land of the Dragon, directly accountable to area commander Kaisis.

Chakine, cruising directly above the vehicle, was extra alert. He'd done battle with this wolf headed demon before.

------ O ------

At the foothills of the Sichuan Mountains the road forked into two separate highways. One veering off to the North and one to the South, both skirting the mountain range. They took the South fork and after about two miles turned off the road on to a rough track that went Westward and upward for as far as the eye could see. An hour later they arrived at Mountain Station 27, which sat at the head of the gentle valley they'd been ascending since leaving the highway. The scenery was barren yet breathtaking, with craggy mountain peaks ever rising into the distance. Several horses and mules were corralled next to the main building, and six uniformed soldiers appeared. Quickly forming themselves into a line they saluted, as Ray and Simon climbed out of the Jeep. Returning the salute, Simon spoke to the men who quickly hurried off in compliance leaving the two of them to enter the building and partake of coffee. Inside the rest room the walls were similarly decorated by Playboy centrefolds, and

Ray smiled, his observation of the previous evening being confirmed yet again. Men are the same the world over!

As they sat by a window with their coffees, Ray took in the incredible vista. He had only ever seen views like this on the Discovery Channel! To the left a narrow trail led up and up, winding away from the station until it disappeared in the distance over a rocky ridge. "Wow," exclaimed Ray still taking in the panorama, "it's beautiful." The other man nodded. "Yes Mr. Coughlin, beautiful but very dangerous!"

Within the hour the small expedition was ready to leave. Ray, Simon, four soldiers, six horses and eight pack mules. Aware as he was that one day's pony trekking in Derbyshire, didn't exactly qualify as experience, nonetheless Ray had assured Simon the previous evening that his equestrian skills were up to it. No one likes to lose face. Two hours later and two thousand feet higher, Simon Cheng was well aware that this fair-haired foreigner's horse riding skills were somewhat less than those of a second rate Cossack! Still, he admired the man's determination as the line of riders and animals snaked its way up a steep and slippery rock strewn trail.

Ray, completely out of sync with the animal beneath him, was swaying erratically from side to side, looking for all the world like a rat being shaken by a terrier. Pulling alongside him Simon chided the unfortunate animal in Chinese before turning to Ray. "A thousand apologies Mr. Coughlin, this foolish animal is completely failing to respond to your horsemanship." Ray's face saved, Simon slipped a halter over the animal's head and proceeded to skilfully lead the grateful Englishman's horse. Onwards and upwards they went, along an increasingly dangerous and difficult trail. Here and there red legged ravens hopped amongst the rocks and the occasional bird of prey eyed them warily from the safety of a rising thermal. For several hours they made steady progress. Sometimes in the shadow of steep rocky gorges, sometimes high on windswept ridges. Mile after mile they edged along this trail that snaked and twisted over the beautiful yet inhospitable terrain.

Just before dusk, as they traversed the ridge of the latest rocky obstacle, they encountered two men with a large herd of goats. Ray noticed Simon unclip his holster and turn in his saddle, scanning to the right and to the left. The two goatherds seemed friendly enough, their leathery faces wreathed in smiles as the line of men and animals passed them. Simon exchanged a few words with the two, and Ray was again aware of an acute alertness about him. A mile or so on they stopped to camp for the night. Two of the mules were loaded with firewood, and soon, tents erected, they settled down around a comforting blaze.

"I was surprised to see those two guys way out here." said Ray, sipping on his tea by the fire. "That was unfortunate." replied Simon. "How do you mean?" queried Ray shifting his position. He was aware that he was rapidly seizing up from the unaccustomed pounding his posterior had taken, not to mention his thighs and lower back! Simon, his face animated by the flickering orange glow looked up from the fire at Ray. "This trail we are on leads only to Yantook. The people of Yantook sell Jade and Soapstone carvings, nothing else. You are, if you'll pardon me for saying it, an obvious foreigner. And the presence of the empty mules merely confirms the fact that we are on our way there to buy." Ray sighed heavily with the realisation. "And the goatherds will tell the bandits, right?" - "That is correct Mr. Coughlin."

------ O ------

Meredith Evans felt bad in one respect about withholding Emir's cottage from the twenty or so callers who had phoned since the ad appeared in the Aberdigan Chronicle. He'd asked the same set of questions to each inquirer, taken their numbers and in due course would politely let them know they'd been unsuccessful. None of them had been the tenant he was looking for.

Four miles away on the opposite side of town, Joshua Fishmen, perusing the local paper, relaxed in the stream of sunlight pouring into the little café just opposite the castle. The sausage, egg and chips had been most welcome after the long journey. His hunger satisfied, priority two was to find some 'digs'. Initially as he'd told Ray, he was expecting to stay in bed and breakfast until he could find something more permanent. The little ad in the 'Accommodation for Rent' section virtually leapt of the page and hit him between the eyes. - 'Two bed. Cottage in 2 acres. Long let - No unemployed.' - Paying his bill, he enquired of the café proprietor and was directed to the nearest public phone box.

The phone rang yet again, the tenth time that day. Meredith was outside checking the progress of the Jasmine and Clematis that would soon cloak the front of his cottage with a blaze of softening colour. Josh was about to put the receiver down after a dozen or so rings, when a slightly breathless Meredith answered, some scissors and a ball of green twine still in his hand. "Hello, Meredith Evans here."
"Good afternoon, I'm enquiring about the cottage you have advertised for rent." - "Oh yes, right, can you tell me please, are you currently employed?" - "Yes," Josh replied " I've literally just moved here from Essex and I'm looking for something reasonably permanent."

Meredith was suddenly aware of his own heartbeat, and the now familiar feeling of the manifest presence of the Holy Spirit in a special way. "And may I ask, what is the work you do?" Josh wished he could have said poet, writer or architect or something glamorous or highly remunerative. Instead he told the simple truth. A truth which to the ears of Meredith Evans, was the only reply he needed. Confirmation of what he'd been told to expect. Here at last from far away was the one he'd been expecting. A Postman and A 'Warrior'. A Chosen One.

"When would you like to view the property?" Meredith asked in a matter of fact tone, although his spirit was swirling and bubbling inside of him. "Would this afternoon be alright?" Josh retorted, his voice tinged with amazement. Meredith gave him directions and half an hour later was waiting at Emir's cottage for the new tenant to arrive.

Goomelt and Pusto, worried as they were about Kaisis, and Josh's apparent immunity to Spasmoide attacks, nonetheless like Aberdigan immensely! An air of decay emanated from the crumbling castle that dominated the town, and they'd noticed several leathery winged forms perched on the battlements like a row of preening pterodactyls. Whilst Joshua was eating they'd clearly seen a whole bunch of spirits of addiction go into the pub just down the road. When Josh had taken a stroll around prior to going to view the cottage, they had noted with glee the tattooist and body piercing shop, and several shops brim full of occult paraphernalia and images of false gods. Eastern religion and philosophy abounded and spirits of sex and drug abuse were everywhere. The nasty little pair were very optimistic, in a demonic sort of way.

Emir's cottage had been the home of godless people for many years, and as such all manner of spirits had taken up residence there, nor would they leave. Rather they would wait for the next inhabitant to be installed and cast the influence of their elemental natures on whoever it was. They were all there because they had been invited. Not consciously in some dark ritual, but by the failure of the previous occupier to observe God's laws. God's law is like an umbrella. Stay underneath it and you're ok. Step out from that covering and you are unprotected and at the mercy of the dark angels. The ancient stories of hobgoblins have their basis in truth. A whole host of unseen demonic beings lie in wait for the sons of disobedience, those who reject God and the teachings of His word. However, there is one name to which all demons must bow. That of The Lord Jesus Christ. He is the name above all names, and, all power in heaven and on earth has been given to him by God. In turn He has made His power available to those who truly follow Him, and He has given them the authority over the darkness in the power of His name.

With the total assurance of that authority, Meredith entered the empty cottage of his old friend. Behind him, his guardian Angel, Salzar. He entered each room, commanding every dark entity to vacate. In the name of Jesus he served notice to quit, effective immediately. This was rigorously enforced by Salzar. Those that left when commanded disappeared to the waterless places. Any who hesitated or tried to argue their rights, were swiftly dispatched by

Salzar's flashing sword. Soon the task was completed and Joshua's new home was swept clean, at least for the time being. Shortly, maybe the Postman would bring along his own demons, but for now Meredith was happy.

After briefly wandering around, Josh headed out of town to view the cottage. Driving north he made a mental note of where the Spar supermarket and one or two other important establishments were located. Ever alert, Chakine had noted all that Goomelt and Pusto had observed, and more. From his vantage point flying above Josh's car he had seen all the dark entities.

As they passed the college on their left, coming from a side street was Yolan, a fellow warrior Angel. He was at the shoulder of a beautiful blue eyed girl with long blonde hair. Chakine and Yolan had exchanged salutes and knew without speaking that their master's plans would soon cause them to interact. Josh had seen the girl too. It was a brief almost subliminal glimpse as his vehicle passed the narrow side street, but it was enough. "What a cracker," he thought as he continued towards his rendezvous with Meredith. "Hope I deliver to her door!"

With half his head thinking 'blonde' thoughts, Josh had missed the track the first time, but remembered being told that if he came to a bridge with a telephone box, he'd gone too far. Putting his brain into priority mode he turned around and soon was bumping along the little tree lined track that would lead him to his meeting, and hopefully his new home. "First cottage on the right." he thought as it came into view. Only cottage on the right as far as he could see!

Outside, an old Morris Traveller was parked askew. As Josh drew up, a dark haired man with leather patches on the elbows of his ancient tweed jacket appeared in the doorway, smiling broadly. Goomelt shrieked and fumbled in his pouch of Spasmoides, spilling them everywhere. Pusto froze in abject terror, thrown into total turmoil by the disgusting white light emanating from this nauseous human and the warrior Angel who stood at his shoulder. The older man approached, his hand outstretched. "How do you do, I'm Meredith Evans." he said, warmly taking Josh's proffered hand and shaking it vigorously. "Joshua Fishmen, nice to meet you!" Josh was aware of an incredible warmth and sincerity in they eyes of the older man, and liked him immediately. The two Grey Ones sat motionless, frozen in fear and almost unable to bear the proximity of the deadly white light. At the same time they knew they couldn't back off. To do so would mean voluntarily surrendering the position of influence, and thus, a certain and painful lingering torment at the hands of Kaisis.

Chakine and Salzar greeted one another with the customary salute. "Hail to the Lord God Almighty, Holy – Holy – Holy." The two humans entered the dwelling. The cottage was un-modernized, stone built with sash windows. The walls were nearly three feet thick and the downstairs floors were all large slate flagstones. At one end was a huge oak beamed inglenook fireplace, housing an ancient Rayburn. At the other end a set of very steep and narrow stairs clung precariously to the wall, accessing the two bedrooms above. The exposed beams of the ceiling joists completed the feeling of antiquity. To the rear was a single storey kitchen and bathroom, a recent addition some forty years ago. From the upstairs windows there were superb views over the rolling hills of the surrounding area, and to the rear there was a garden that opened out to the paddocks and two acres. Meredith could sense Josh's elation. He could also sense the presence of darkness around the young man, but knowing God had plans for him he brushed that aside. "Time enough for that." he thought.

The two men discussed monetary arrangements, settling on a rent of sixty-five pounds a week furnished, in consideration of the basic condition of the property. Meredith would see the solicitors in the morning, and no, he didn't require any deposit! In fact Joshua could move in now if it suited him!

Half an hour later, Meredith gone, Josh sat on the sofa opposite the Rayburn soaking in the atmosphere of his new home. He almost couldn't believe his luck. The very first place he'd tried, and not only that, the rent, at sixty-five pounds a week was almost unbelievably cheap! And for as long as he wanted it! Turning around on the sofa he surveyed the room. "Excellent," he said out loud. "Absolutely excellent." He still had a week before he started at Aberdigan Post Office, so tomorrow he would explore the area.

The Grey Ones were agitated, extremely agitated. Their Chosen One seemed to have developed something of an immunity to Spasmoide attacks recently, and now they had to cope with him having an awful follower of Jesus as his landlord. They knew too that soon they would receive a visit from their new area commander, the dreaded Kaisis All in all things didn't look particularly good, but they squabbled to the conclusion that if they could keep Josh and the nasty believer apart, all would be well.

At home, three-quarters of a mile away, Meredith was praying. "I thank you Father for this young man you have sent to me. Please keep him safe from the plans of the enemy, and prepare his heart to receive the truth. I pray too that by Your sovereign power his home may remain clean and free from the influence of dark spirits, Amen."

From a distance, Chakine looked at the two Grey Ones by Joshua's shoulder, and fingered the handle of his sword. He knew it wouldn't be too long now, and that sometime soon he would regain The Position of Influence. He would of course keep to his master's rules on the matter, but he also knew that the very second the young man received salvation, then he would be free to send these demon's to await their ultimate punishment. In patient obedience he relished the thought.

The birds were singing and the morning sun was streaming through the windows as Josh awoke. It took a few seconds for him to orientate himself . Yes, he really was here, living in a cottage in Wales! He jumped out of bed, stretched, spun round a couple of times and said out loud "Excellent!"

The rear of the cottage was south facing, the two acres of land sloping gently downwards. In the distance the town of Aberdigan was still swathed in early morning mist, which hung ghost like over the estuary.

Breakfast outside seemed to be the obvious choice, and the front of the cottage bathed as it was in morning sunshine, seemed to be the obvious place. He took a shower, threw on his bathrobe, and making some tea and toast, headed outside. "This couldn't get any better." Josh said to himself, sitting on a slate bench in the warm sun sipping tea and listening to the gorgeous song of a Robin.

A faint 'ting-a-ling-ting' in the distance caught his attention. It was the sound of a bicycle bell bumping over the rough track, and he wondered who this might be. As the cyclist came into view, Josh reviewed his previous statement realising, things could indeed get better! Approaching him on a mountain bike was a vision of loveliness, her long blonde hair billowing and shining in the warm rays. It was the girl he had glimpsed yesterday! As she drew almost level with him she smiled and waved, bringing the bike to a halt. "Hiya, I'm Cheryll a friend of Meredith's." she volunteered, remaining seated on the bike. Frozen in terror at yet another sickening 'white liter' the two demons remained motionless. Yolan and Chakine nodded acknowledgement of each other whilst maintaining a high state of alert. At the same time, Josh still in his bathrobe, cup and saucer in hand, stood up to introduce himself. Unfortunately for him, the belt of the bathrobe had caught behind the slate bench, so that as he stood, the robe was drawn like a curtain to one side, revealing his ample manhood. In his frantic reaction to cover himself the cup tipped in the saucer, cascading hot tea down his naked front and causing him to leap like a dervish clutching his groin and yelling ""Arghh!"

Cheryll, sucking in her cheeks, turned her head away desperately trying to fight off the rising tide of laughter. She lost the battle. Exploding into uncontrollable mirth she lost her balance, falling sideways the bike landing on top of her. She just lay there laughing and laughing. Eventually, far more embarrassed than hurt, Josh regained his composure. He lifted the bike from the still giggling young woman and helped her to her feet. Her hand still in his, their eyes met and they stood motionless, 'locked on' for several seconds. Finally, Josh, his heart racing and speech impeded, mumbled

"Er, I'm er... Josh," his eyes still lost in hers, " I've... er" he nodded over his shoulder towards the cottage, "moved in." Gently removing her hand from his she smiled "Are you um ...ok?" She motioned to his midriff. Thankfully the tea had been well below boiling point and Josh replied "Er....yes...yes, no lasting harm done." Cheryll was aware of an incredible electricity in the air. When Josh had taken her hand to help her up she had tingled all over. It was just the nicest feeling. "Whew," she had thought "whatever was that?"

Climbing back aboard the mountain bike she turned to Josh, "Well, nice to meet you Josh, see you again." She waited until she was a few yards up the track before calling back over her shoulder, "Oh, and thanks for the cabaret!"

Josh stood and watched her cycle off in the direction of Meredith's place until she disappeared round a bend in the track. "Great." he said to himself, "So much for Mr.Smoothie." He'd just acted like a brainless zombie, made a complete fool of himself and spoken in monosyllables. This had never happened before. He was always really cool with the ladies, always had the right chat up lines and knew just what to say. Usually aimed at persuading them into bed, and it had worked many times. He stood there in the morning sun confused, bemused and totally smitten!

<<<<---END OF CHAPTER TWO--->>>>

The Dragonmaster

CHAPTER 3   **Dark Incantations**

Ray Coughlin was finally getting the hang of the horse thing. Up when the horse goes up, down when the horse goes down, simple really. Mile after mile they followed the rugged trail. He was warm now after this arduous feat, and the exertion of merely trying to stay in the saddle had caused him to break out in a sweat. He unzipped his coat and unbuttoned his shirt. The afternoon sun felt good on his face. However, the rest of his body, his shoulders, lower back, posterior and thighs were an aching mass of knotted muscle, strained by the sudden and prolonged use they'd had after years of relative inactivity. Two days hard riding as a complete novice was taking its toll. He was just wondering how much longer he would be able to hold out, when Simon Cheng on the mount in front of him leaned back saying "Just over that next ridge Mr.Coughlin, and we shall be in Yantook." A sense of relief flooded over Ray. He had long since realised that he was well out of his depth in this environment, and generally uncomfortable in the harsh rocky terrain. He thought about Zara and the kids' way over the other side of the world, in their cosy, carpeted, centrally heated home, and for a long moment wished he was there with them. It was the thought of the potentially lucrative deal he would soon be striking that brought him back to reality as his horse surmounted the crest of the ridge.

There in the valley before them, nestled at the foot of an enormous sheer rock face sat the village he had traversed half the world to come to. The tiered fields softened the grey starkness of the ceaseless crags and outcrops, and it was refreshing to see some real greenery after nearly two days of mostly barren rock. The track descended from the ridge to the floor of the valley below, and they passed between rows of small terraced fields, vibrant and productive. In the distance a gong was being beaten, heralding the approach of the little caravan of horsemen. By the time they reached the village square beside the walled pagoda, quite a crowd had assembled to greet them.

Most of the inhabitants were dressed in hardy looking two piece garments, resembling grey sackcloth. Each person had a brightly coloured woven belt around their waist, and some wore curious little pointed patchwork hats that reminded Ray of the Dutch dolls he'd seen on his travels. Dragon symbols were everywhere, and he made a mental note to enquire about them from Simon. In the meantime, despite his aching limbs, he was enjoying being a celebrity, being acutely aware of how closely he was being scrutinised by all and sundry. Amidst the lively chatter Simon was conversing with a group of men and indicating Ray as he did. The Englishman understood not a word of their dialogue, yet knew from their awe filled expressions that Simon must be outlining the scale of the proposed purchase.

With the creak of wood on metal hinges, the gates of the pagoda swung open. Immediately all discourse ceased. Silence descended upon the square and the villagers in their entirety assumed submissive postures. Hands clasped together, heads bowed. "Mr.Coughlin, please come." motioned Simon, dismounting. Ray, his aching body temporarily forgotten, followed suit and the two men approached the pagoda gates. As they walked Simon said "Mr. Coughlin, you must please bow when you meet Yan-Ti the village Overlord." Suddenly ten feet in front of them as if from nowhere, stood a figure robed entirely in black. On his head he wore a small pillbox hat, replete with the symbol of three intertwined dragons. His silk garments shimmered in the afternoon sun and his long drooping beard and moustache reached his chest. Ray suppressed a chuckle as he thought "Any minute now Christopher Lee is going to appear!"

Simon bowed and spoke to the man, introducing Ray. On hearing his name, Ray clasped his hands together and politely bowed his body forward. As he did so, the silver Pentagram, Zara's parting gift, swung out from his partially open shirt, hanging in full view from the chain around his neck. Yan-Ti's eyes widened when he saw the symbol, and the gasps from the watching villagers were clearly audible when he slowly and deliberately bowed towards Ray. He then spoke again to Simon, before turning and walking back inside the building, leaving a servant to attend to the needs of his houseguests. The amazement on the interpreter's face was self-evident as he said, "You and I Mr. Coughlin are to stay tonight in the pagoda, as special guests of Yan-Ti."

Simon Cheng was puzzled, extremely puzzled. On five previous occasions he'd visited Yantook, always interpreting and assisting foreign buyers. On each previous occasion they had been accommodated in one of the tiered buildings opposite, interacting with Yan-Ti only upon arrival, and then just prior to departure, when payment for goods was due. He had always felt that their presence was merely tolerated by the Overlord for the sake of the money to come. Now however, they, or rather Mr. Coughlin, seemed to be highly honoured. He concluded he would just enjoy the perk, and get on with his job.

As Simon attended to the needs of his men, Ray was left alone in the cobbled courtyard, whilst the rooms he and Simon would occupy were made ready. He sat on a wooden bench surveying the almost surreal scene. The whole place looked like some kind of film set, and he chuckled to himself again as the possibility of Christopher Lee suddenly appearing re-entered his mind. The pagoda had five tiers to the main roof with a succession of smaller tiered annexes and archways leading off in all directions, each roof was supported by gold painted pillars, with much gold leaf work on the many ornate carved timbers. The painted stone walls were predominantly red and green, and everywhere he looked was the symbol of three intertwined dragons.

In a windowless room at the rear of the pagoda, Yan-Ti sat cross-legged on his black cushion, swaying back and forth. The room was again filled with heavily narcotic incense, and the luminous green smoke swirled and spun about him. On the floor in front of him lay open a large ancient 'Book of Magik', and on the left hand page was a large illustration. It was a drawing of a pentagram.

Yan-Ti was very surprised that a foreigner would posses The Ancient wisdom. All the ones he'd met previously had merely been rich fools, but he knew his eyes had not deceived him and he determined to find out more that evening. From far back in time, since the years of the early Chinese dynasties, his ancestors had walked in the ways of The Ancient Wisdom. For the last seven hundred years the first born male of his line had been schooled in these arts from childhood. Instructed, prepared and initiated into ways that would eventually qualify them to be a Dragonmaster.

He had spent all his life in these mountains. Most of it here in Yantook, except for five years spent learning the deeper secrets in a monastery far into the mountains. A remote and deeply dark place, known only to a select few. Being without technology he knew little of the outside world. Nor did he care for it. Here as Overlord he was number one, feared and respected. As Dragonmaster he held the power of life or death over his subjects.

His men and animals catered for, Simon returned to the pagoda and soon he and Ray were relaxing in a luxuriously draped and well-cushioned room. Ray's aching limbs had returned to pole position in his consciousness, and he decided he would like to lie down for the two remaining hours before supper was due to be served. Before he did however, he asked Simon about all the dragon symbols he had seen. "This is a relatively primitive society Mr. Coughlin, lost in ancient ways. Things here have remained unchanged for aeons. I think the symbols you have seen are much the same to these people as are the crosses you have on religious places in your country, symbols of worship I believe." - "Oh I see," Ray answered, "It's a religious thing, Thank you Simon." He arose slowly, his throbbing body almost creaking, and made his way to his room.

Twenty minutes later, lying on a comfortable bed of silk cushions with his mind drifting, he had a brilliant idea. He sat up with a groan, his taught back and shoulders nowhere near as impressed with the idea as his brain was! Tipping out the contents of his travelling bag he found what he was looking for. It was a small circular mirror, about seven inches in diameter, set into a carved wooden frame. The carvings depicted three lizards, running nose to tail around the perimeter of the inset mirror.

It was one from a series of excellent Balinese carvings he'd imported the previous year, and the quality was so good he'd decided to keep one for his travelling needs. Next, rummaging through the pile of his stuff now strewn on the bed, he found a small tube of super glue. Zara always packed some for him 'just in case'. He'd always laughed at her before, but now he blew her a long distance kiss. Taking the nail scissors from his travelling manicure set, he rooted around and found all of Josh's brochures and began to meticulously cut out all the little Red Dragons he could find. This done, he very carefully stuck them, evenly spaced, like the numbers on a clock face, all around the rim of the mirror. Finally he placed a larger one directly in the middle. The result was rather good Ray thought, quite professional. A small gift for his host who was obviously into Dragons! A little 'sweetener' to better his chances of an advantageous deal on the morrow. He lay back on the bed and drifted into dreams.

A knock on his door fetched him out of his brief slumber, and a servant using sign language intimated it was time for food. Summoning Simon, he led the two men into a superbly decorated room. The walls were powder blue and hung with wonderfully embroidered silks, the ceiling a timbered pattern of geometric gold leafed carvings. The floor was luxuriant in white animal skins and large silk covered scatter cushions. In the centre of the room a long low table spread with all manner of delicacies, beckoned their taste buds. Seated at one end of the table, Yan-Ti bade them sit, and with few words the meal commenced.

The Chinese takeaways Ray and Josh would frequently get on a Friday night bore absolutely no resemblance to this fantastic cuisine whatsoever. Simon spoke a few words to Yan-Ti, and then handed Ray a spoon and fork, for which he was most grateful.

Eating then commenced and Ray, to the obvious enjoyment of his host, sampled everything. The meal done, Ray produced 'The Dragon Mirror' and through Simon addressed himself to the village Overlord. "As a small token of my appreciation for your wonderful hospitality, would you please accept this Mirror of Meditation?"

Ray was a fast learner, and pretty skilled in the art of negotiation. He thought the term sounded suitably 'spiritual' for something he'd made up three seconds earlier, but he wanted the best deal he could possibly get on the jade carvings, so he'd pander to this weird old guy's beliefs.

When he saw the mirror, Yan-Ti let out a little gasp of pleasure, a broad smile creasing his leathered face as he nodded enthusiastically. "I thank you for such a wonderful gift, where did you come by such a mirror?" translated Simon. Ray, the salesman in him now firing on all cylinders, replied "I too come from a land of Dragons, a distant land far across the oceans. Like yours it is a land of mountains." As Simon translated, Ray produced from his pocket the 'antique' map of Wales and handed it to Yan-Ti. The Overlord was captivated by it, and motioned the two men to come and sit beside him as he spread it on the now cleared table. He says, "This is wonderful," Simon said, "especially the large Dragon all down the side of your country." Ray was really getting in to this. He pointed out the illustration of the 'Entrance to the Underworld' situated in the Cych Valley. Simon translated and Yan-Ti let out a long sigh his head nodding. "When do you sacrifice to your dragons?" the old man asked. Ray's mind was racing. "Oh we don't need to sacrifice at present, they're all sleeping." Ray waffled, remembering the schoolboy stories of St. George, he continued, "Many, many years ago a great warrior named St.George did battle with the dragons and he cast a powerful spell on them. Since then they've all been sleeping and no one can wake them." Ray was well pleased with himself. He felt sure the old headman had believed it; by the way he was now studying the map and murmuring to himself.
In reality Ray Coughlin had no idea just who this old man was, nor had he a clue just what he was getting himself into.

Their host spoke again to Simon. Eventually the interpreter turned to Ray and with a slightly perplexed expression said "Mr.Coughlin, Yan-Ti asks if you would like to take the smoke with him?" Ray was chuffed, "I've cracked it" he thought, "well in!" - "Certainly," he replied "I'd be honoured." Simon relayed the information and turning again to Ray said "I am not invited to accompany you; therefore I shall be retiring for the night." He looked at Ray with genuine concern "Mr.Coughlin, please be careful." Simon thanked his host for the meal, bid them both good night, bowed and left.

Yan-Ti motioned Ray to follow as he rose and crossed the room. Hidden behind the silk hangings was a small doorway that opened onto a small corridor. This led the two men into a windowless candlelit room. Ray knew they grew hash in these mountains, and was eagerly anticipating a good smoke to ease his horse battered frame and help him to sleep. The last time he'd gotten high had been with Josh back around Christmas and he found this invitation extremely appealing. Simon's obvious concern was quite amusing. Ray felt "He probably thinks I've never smoked dope before!" but at the same time it was sort of comforting to know his protector was on the ball.

With the lack of interpreter, Ray decided it was probably best just to try and emulate his host so as not to inadvertently offend him. Yan-Ti sat on a large black cushion and indicated to Ray to sit on one opposite. As he did so, he noticed a large mural painted on the wall they were both facing. It was the same triangle of three dragons he'd seen everywhere in the village. Ray concluded that this must be some kind of chapel or prayer room and did his best to affect an air of reverence. The Overlord sprinkled something onto the glowing charcoal brazier to his right, and instantly thick plumes of luminous green smoke curled and danced about the two men. The smell was unfamiliar to Ray, but within seconds he was aware of all sorts of peculiar sensations flooding his body and twisting his senses. This was a powerful narcotic, and way stronger than any of the recreational drugs he'd been used to. As he'd been expecting the much gentler effect of hashish, he was momentarily thrown, and felt himself sliding into unconsciousness. Dark spirits were everywhere, and during the few seconds in which Ray lost control of his senses, several of them gained access to his being, joining those already in residence from a Godless lifestyle. He was only out a short time, but it was long enough for him to unknowingly acquire three more uninvited, shadowy guests.

He regained consciousness with a jerk, still sitting cross-legged on the cushion. Next to him Yan-Ti was rocking backwards and forwards chanting a strange incantation. Spread out on the floor in front of him was the map of Wales. Ray, feeling very, very stoned, yet remembering his decision to do whatever his host did, followed suit, voicing the only chant he knew. The one that was usually heard on the terraces of Manchester United Football Club! - "C'mon you reds.... c'mon you reds.... c'mon you reds." As he was still repeating the phrase and rocking backwards and forwards, the Dragonmaster threw another handful of narcotics onto the brazier. The mural on the wall opposite seemed to come to life pulsating and vibrating, and Ray felt himself being sucked into and through the triangle in a swirl of green smoke. Then he was spinning in a dark tunnel, going down and down, still chanting, unable to stop. In the background he could hear Yan-Ti's strange repetitive chanting, but it seemed a long way off.

Suddenly he was in a huge cavern. Torches burned and flickered at intervals along one side of the cavern wall, causing the opposite side to shimmer and gleam with eerie green phosphorescence. He thought at first it was plastic, then he realised – he was looking at a solid wall of Jade. At the back of the cavern, deep in the shadows, something moved. Ray heard a sort of scraping sound followed by a long low guttural growl. It was bestial and terrifying, causing the hairs on the back of his neck to stand up. From within the darkness two malevolent yellow green eyes seemed to pierce his soul, and he was very, very afraid.

The distant chanting ceased and he opened his eyes, relieved to find himself still seated on a cushion next to Yan-Ti in the windowless room. The Headman was nodding and grinning at him, so he nodded and grinned back, hoping the fact that he was thoroughly shaken was not too obvious. By sign language his host indicated it was time for sleep and two minutes later a servant guided him back to his room. Ray stumbled into bed. He was still pretty 'out of it' as he lay awake longing to sleep. Each time he tried he would see those yellow green eyes staring out of the darkness at him. "That certainly wasn't grass I just smoked," he thought, recalling the relatively innocuous experiences he'd had with marijuana in the past. "That was anything but relaxing!" Eventually after another half an hour the effect wore off, and he drifted into a deep sleep. Totally unaware of the presence of the new entities that now bore legal rights to his life.

------ O ------

Meredith had just finished his morning prayers when his favourite girl in all the world arrived, and collapsed in his fireside chair in fits of laughter. For a full two minutes he could get no sense from her as she tried in vain to tell him of her recent encounter with his new neighbour. Each time she tried to recount the episode she'd merely get as far as saying "I pulled up on my bike." and then the imagery of the ensuing scenario would replay in her brain, causing her to dissolve into fits of uncontrollable mirth. Meredith waited patiently until she regained enough composure to finally describe the entire interlude. This resulted in him also sinking into a chair amidst great guffaws, and the two of them laughed till the tears ran down their cheeks. "Oh, my sides are hurting." chuckled Cheryll, finally returning to a semblance of normality. "Mine too!" declared Meredith as he wiped away the tears of laughter with the back of his hand. Composure finally regained, the two of them began to pray for the salvation of Joshua Fishmen.

------ O ------

Fortunately for Goomelt and Pusto, Josh was sitting by a stream on the boundary of the bottom field smoking a joint, when Kaisis arrived. He'd swooped down on them from above snatching them up in his razor sharp claws. And now he held them around their necks, their black eyes bulging as he squeezed them both. With his foetid breath and yellow fangs only inches from their terrified faces he growled, "You two will keep your charge away from the believers," he tightened his grip "Understood?" Pusto felt that at any moment his eyes would exit his head like corks from a bottle. After shaking the pair almost senseless, Kaisis hurled them to the ground and threw a pouch after them. "These are new Spasmoides, stronger, stickier. Antichrist. Use them well!" As he turned to go, he recognised Chakine standing a discreet distance away. He knew of course there was a warrior Angel assigned to this filthy Chosen One, but he hadn't realised it was one of his old adversaries. "Har, Angel" he called mockingly "So you're here to protect him eh?" Chakine remained motionless, aware of the hundred or more demonic fighters lurking in the darkness behind Kaisis. "And you're going to keep him safe, just like.... Now what was her name?" he drew his sword and swung it mimicking a decapitation "Oh yes, I remember, it was Angharad!" he sneered as he spoke the name. "The Lord rebuke you!" countered Chakine, as the big demon rose shrieking with laughter into the darkness.

Painful memories surfaced for the Angel. Memories of a time long, long ago. It was an age well before this current time of God's grace. An age well before this present time in which men can be saved through salvation in Jesus. These were memories Chakine would rather forget, but the foul demon's taunting with the name of Angharad had caused them to temporarily resurface.

------ O ------

Tossing the joint end into the stream Josh watched it bobble and spin away into the distance, as he endeavoured to puzzle out the earlier events of the morning. Try as he may, he could not understand why his usual silver-tongued eloquence with the opposite sex had deserted him. After all she was only a girl this "Cheryll." he said her name out loud, and then he said it again, "Cheryll." The warm sunshine on his face reminded him of her; the busy water flowing over shiny pebbles reminded him of her. In fact, he'd pretty much thought of nothing else but her since their encounter this morning! Where did she live? What did she do? Did she have a boyfriend? He resolved to enquire of his landlord.

- - - - - - O - - - - - -

The carving workshops were a hive of activity on this clear sunlit morning. The artisans of Yantook were proudly displaying their wares in readiness for the foreign buyer. Earlier that morning Yan-Ti had sent word from the pagoda that Ray was to be treated with the utmost respect. The workers had already been more than surprised when their Overlord had bowed to the stranger, and then to see him invited to stay in the pagoda, well that was unheard of. In all the years they'd been doing business with foreign buyers, never once had Yan-Ti socialised or interacted with any other customers. So now, as is wont with simple men, rumour was fast elevating Ray Coughlin to an almost 'divine' status.

Simon Cheng noticed how much more affable Yan-Ti was this morning, as the three men breakfasted together. He was also very surprised to learn of the Overlord's intention to accompany them to the workshops to view the carvings. Yet another first!

Breakfast over, the three men made their way from the pagoda across the square and through the village to where the workshops hugged the sheer rock face. Laid out on ancient wooden trestles were several thousand handmade pieces. The craftsmanship was exquisite, just as Ray had expected from the samples he'd seen previously. Nearly all the carvings were of single dragons between three and eight inches high. Each one carved from a beautiful deep green piece of Jade. Ray's calculator brain was working overtime, as he pictured the hundreds of little gift shops in Wales that would snap them up. He was also immensely enjoying being treated like a king. It caressed his ego and fed his carnality, and the spirits within revelled in the admiration he was receiving. The degree of surprise on the faces of the workers was evident, as Yan-Ti smiled and acted in a generally amicable fashion to all and sundry. Simon was utterly astonished when the time came for 'hard bargaining' and the handing over of cash. Yan-Ti was offering Ray all of these carvings at nearly half the price he usually charged!

Within the hour the deal was struck, and the workers began placing the figurines into small sacks padded with straw, to load on to the pack animals for the long trek back through the mountains. Refreshments appeared and as the three men sipped their tea Yan-Ti enquired as to whether or not Ray would care to see the Jade mine, whilst he attended to some other business. The reply was affirmative. After ensuring the loads on the pack mules would be evenly distributed and safely fastened, Ray and Simon were led to the entrance of the mine. Two villagers held burning torches aloft and the little group set off down a dark twisting tunnel reaching into the heart of the mountain behind the cliff face. Ray felt somewhat apprehensive after his experience of the previous evening, but, when after three hundred yards or so the tunnel opened out into a small illuminated cavern with four men diligently hacking away at the walls, his fears were dispelled. An obvious bright seam of Jade ran right through the rock and the two men watched with interest the ancient mining techniques unchanged for centuries.

Back in the pagoda Yan-Ti was sprinkling his narcotic powder on the charcoal brazier in a small windowless cell behind his smoking room. On the floor huddled in the corner sat a young Chinese girl of fifteen. She was terrified and shaking, not daring to look at the man she knew was the Dragonmaster. As the green smoke began to fill the room, he left closing the door behind him and locking it. Crossing the corridor he entered another room full of artefacts and antiquities. From an old chest in the corner he removed a large carving. A triangle of three intertwined dragons, carved from one piece of top quality Jade. The chosen piece in hand he made his way back to his smoking room and was soon seated, rocking back and forth whilst he chanted amidst the green swirling smoke. The Jade carving sat on the floor in front of the dragon mural, and as the chant increased the mural began to vibrate and sparkle with energy, rippling from top to bottom and back again. For a full ten minutes it grew ever faster, ever stronger. Yan-Ti's chant increased to almost a scream, manic in its intensity.

A low guttural growl filled the room, rising like orchestral timpani to a thunderous roar, and a rushing wind spiralled round and round, causing the brazier to glow red hot. The mural, now alive with evil power, leapt from the wall and dived, hissing into the Jade carving. Then all was silent. The wall totally bare.

The Dragonmaster summoned his servant, and together they unlocked the little cell, leading out the now stupefied young girl. In his hand Yan-Ti carried the carving; his servant carried a burning torch. Going through an archway into a tunnel, they began descending stone steps, fifty or so, which terminated in a small cavern hewn from the rock beneath the mountain. Set in the centre of the cavern floor, a large flat circular stone covered the mouth of a deep dank shaft. A heavy chain was attached to enable its removal by means of a pulley on the cavern roof. On the wall opposite a timber spoked winding wheel held the other end of the chain.The girl stood dazed and motionless as the servant placed the flaming torch in an iron wall holder. Taking hold of the wheel with both hands he began to slowly wind in the chain. As the circular stone dislodged and began to rise, there was a sucking hiss and a rush of putrid air filled the room causing the torch to flicker wildly. At the same time Yan-Ti ripped the flimsy gown from the poor girl who barely seemed to notice in her drug induced state. A faint snorting growl was emanating from deep within the blackness of the gaping shaft, as the Dragonmaster pushed the shuffling young female ever nearer the precipitous drop. She moved in slow motion, thankfully not really aware of what was happening, until, just by the edge she voiced a half conscious "No!" The black robed demoniac swung the heavy statue upwards; It caught her full on the back of the skull, pitching her headlong into the stinking abyss. Her echoing scream fading with the depth.

Lowering the stone back into place, the two men climbed the stairs up into the pagoda. "It was a good sacrifice, the statue is now empowered." Yan-Ti said, more to himself than to the servant.

Deep below ground several minutes before, Ray had heard what sounded like a muffled scream, far away. "Did you hear that Simon?" he enquired, but Simon had been preoccupied watching the miners at work, so he replied in the negative. Ray shrugged his shoulders and thought no more of it.

Twenty minutes later the two men were back in the sunlight, double checking the animals and equipment, and making sure the precious cargo was well secured. Ray was still enjoying being bowed to by all and sundry when the gates of the pagoda swung open and the Dragonmaster appeared with his servant. Silence once again descended on the villagers. With solemnity in his gait the dark master approached the little column of men and animals. Stopping before Ray, once again he bowed. Simon translated as he said, "Mr.Coughlin, the people of Yantook," he gestured towards the gathered crowd of villagers, "would like very much to thank you for coming from a land far away to trade with us." he paused, "We recognise that you too come from a land that honours the Dragon," there were murmurs of approval from those gathered, "but because of the evil man 'San Jodge', and the spell he cast long ago, your Dragons are all asleep." He motioned to his servant who approached Ray, the Jade carving of the three dragons on a black silk cushion in his outstretched hands. "Please accept this gift which will undoubtedly wake them all up again."

The villagers voiced their assent, and the Overlord smiled handing Simon a letter as he did. "This contains specific instructions as to how this matter should be accomplished, please translate it carefully and give it to

Mr.Coughlin." As he was thanking them all, through Simon, Ray was admiring the statue and thinking "Wow! This'll fetch a couple of grand in town!"

They mounted their horses and were about to set off when Yan-Ti called out "Misah Hofflin!" Ray turned to look over his shoulder. The black robed Dragonmaster, his hands clasped together, chanted "Khum Oyu Rez - Khum Oyu Rez - Khum Oyu Rez!" He bowed, turned around and walked back into the pagoda. The Englishman raised his arm and waved, and with a jerk the train of men and animals began the arduous journey back to Mountain Station twenty-seven. It wasn't until they'd cleared the ridge that led them into the next valley that Ray realised just exactly what Yan-Ti's parting words had been. The rallying cry of countless Manchester United football supporters! 'C'mon you reds!'. The very chant he'd used when he'd 'taken the smoke' with the Dragonmaster.

For several hours they made steady progress in the watery sunshine, their pace somewhat slower with the weight of the cargo. Ray, now sitting much easier in the saddle, noticed that the soldiers held their weapons crooked in their arms instead of slung across their shoulders as they had been on the outward journey. Simon too was far more active. Sometimes riding at the head of the column, sometimes at the rear. He seemed extremely alert, constantly scanning the ridges on either side of their route.

Each of the four soldiers had two heavily laden mules in tow. Two soldiers at the front, then Ray, then two more soldiers, all in single file. Ray was a little tense, sensing a degree of vigilance amongst the military men, which he found slightly disconcerting. The temperature was falling, and Simon drew alongside Ray as the shadows were beginning to lengthen. "Just over that next ridge there is a cave in which we can pass the night." These were the words Ray had wanted to hear for the last couple of hours. "Fine." he replied, by now very much looking forward to dismounting. "Unfortunately it would be unwise to kindle a fire tonight Mr.Coughlin, it could easily draw unwelcome attention to our presence here."

They located the cave and, with the animals tended and a guard rota organised by Simon, they passed a cold but otherwise uneventful night. Ray slept fitfully, his dreams frequently invaded by the sound of a low guttural growl, and those piercing yellow green eyes glowing in the darkness.

Just after dawn the little column was underway again. They were heading due east and the morning sun was directly in their eyes, making it difficult at times to see anything in the distance. Simon was quite animated, frequently communicating with his men whilst also maintaining a state of high alert. After an hour of travelling, the trail began descending towards a steep sided, narrow gorge, obviously part of the path of a long gone glacier which had cut its way through the rock, leaving a cleft sixty feet wide through sheer rock faces rising hundreds of feet upward. Ray remembered passing through this gorge on the way to the village.

They were still several hundred yards from the entrance to the gorge when Simon, at the front, wheeled his horse around barking orders to his men as he did so. He drew alongside Ray. "MrCoughlin, I have no wish to alarm you, but I sense danger ahead. This gorge is the perfect place for an ambush, and therefore we need to pass through it as quickly as possible." Simon rode back to the front and spoke again to the leading man, before returning to Ray's side. The Englishman's pulse rate had already leapt up two gears, and his mouth had gone rather dry. "Ambush?" he thought, "what the hell have I got myself into?" Trying to disguise the fear in his voice he said "Okay Simon, what do you want me to do?" Simon looked at him hard. "Just stay in the saddle Mr.Coughlin." He took out his pistol and checked it, then slipped it back in its holster.
"I will take your reins a short distance from the entrance to the gorge, and we shall gallop." Ray found the confident authority in Simon's voice comforting. He wanted to say, "But I don't know how to gallop." yet simultaneously realised the futility of such a statement when the reality was possibly, you gallop or die! He pushed Yan-Ti's parting gift further into his saddlebag and quickly tightened the buckle

another notch. Simon, taking Ray's reigns, eased his mount in front. "Lean into it Mr.Coughlin, and keep hold of the horn of your saddle!"

Momentarily, Ray felt as if he were on a film set again, but the fear stabbing at his insides and pounding in his temples, quickly yanked him back to reality. They were now about one hundred yards from the gorge. With a final reassuring glance over his shoulder, Simon said, "Hold on!" as he dug his heels into the side of his mount, urging it forward, at the same time signalling his men to "Go!"

The line of men and animals surged forward, picking up speed. Ray decided the best thing he could do was to mimic the jockeys he'd seen racing at Newmarket, and so he transferred his weight to his legs, knees bent, almost standing up in the stirrups. He found it got him by.

As they entered the gorge, at what was really no more than a fast canter due to the loads on the mules, rocks began to rain down on them from above. Ray felt the wind as one whistled past his forehead missing him by a whisker. Another ripped a gash in his thigh, curiously as he thought, without any pain. He saw another one strike the rump of Simon's horse, just as a burst of automatic fire threw the leading soldier from his mount, almost cutting him in two. The shots were coming from a rocky ledge to the right; two bandits were firing an old belt fed machine gun. Drawing his pistol, Simon loosed off four shots in quick succession. The first took out one of the men, hitting him square in the chest and sending him toppling backwards. Two and three ricocheted screaming into space, whilst the fourth caught the other man in the calf, delaying him just long enough for a fusillade of shots from one of the soldiers at the rear to take him out of the picture. Up ahead three more bandits opened fire from ground level rocks to the left. The remaining soldier in front of Simon managed to get one of them, the other two going to ground as the men and animals thundered by.

In the confines of the gorge the noise was incredible, amplified as it was by great rushes of adrenaline amidst the screeching of ricocheting bullets and the pounding of hooves. The now rider-less leading horse took the full force of a burst of fire from up ahead, causing it to crash to the ground, its flailing legs entangling with those of the mule behind it. As a result the unfortunate soldier behind them careered into the tumbling mass of equine mayhem and was catapulted from his mount into the rock face, breaking his neck. With lightning reactions Simon swung his mount around the stricken animals, still leading Ray. The two soldiers behind followed suit.

Up ahead two more bandits opened fire on the advancing troupe, one either side of the now narrowing gorge. The thunder of hooves and gunfire roared in Ray's head as he hung on to the terrified animal beneath him. He knew that to fall was to die, and the thought of never seeing Zara and the kids again spurred on his resolve to remain mounted. Simon remained cool as a burst of rounds from an old Thompson sub machine gun whistled past his head from the guy on right. The gap between adversaries was closing fast as he levelled his pistol squeezing off three rounds with measured precision. The first one missed, the second and third didn't. The Thompson sent a hail of bullets bouncing off the ravine wall as the target toppled backwards, his finger still on the trigger. The little interpreter winced in pain as a bullet ripped into his thigh from the gunman on the left, half a second before the soldier behind Ray put two well placed rounds into the bandit's midriff. The way ahead was now seemingly clear and they rode on towards the end of the gorge.

Ray remembered hearing the first few rounds of the long burst of machine gun fire from behind, as it kicked up the dust and ricocheted of the canyon walls. And then the brief searing pain which melted into inky blackness.

------ O ------

The staff at the Chinese Embassy in London had been marvellous. Ever since the news of Ray's injuries had been broken to Zara they had provided non-stop assistance. First a chauffeur driven car, to take the kids to Zara's mother. Then, a visa processed within the hour. And finally the female interpreter who now sat beside her on the long flight to Beijing. Zara however was in no mood for conversation. Frantic with worry she stared out of the window, lost in thoughts of her seriously wounded husband, and fearful of facing the future, possibly without him. The Ambassador had been kind but honest, supportive but realistic.

Ray it seemed had been caught in an ambush in the Sichuan Mountains. Two of his party had been killed, and he and another man had been wounded by gunfire. His wounds were apparently quite serious. Five in all. One to his right shoulder, one to his lower middle back, another to his left buttock and a further two to his left thigh. He was at present in intensive care. However, he was in the most modern and well-equipped hospital in China, under the care of specialist staff. All she could do was wait, as hour after interminable hour; the aircraft bore her on towards her destination and the uncertainty of whether or not her husband would live or die.

Meanwhile in Beijing Hospital, in a sterile room full of high tech medical gadgetry, Ray lay pale and still, his body festooned with wires and pipes. His life a slow weak green blip on a life support monitor screen.

------ O ------

Zara had no way of contacting Josh before she left for China, as he'd not yet been in touch with his new address. So instead she'd phoned Josh's mum and left the details with her, knowing he called her regularly. That evening Josh had received the devastating news about Ray. The Grey Ones, seizing their opportunity had managed to score a direct hit with two Spasmoides. Anti Christ, and Anger, and they'd stuck fast. Right now God was not Josh's favourite person. As is often the case, people who fail to acknowledge Him and His wonderful creation, are often the first to blame Him when things go wrong in their lives! However, God doesn't believe in atheists.

The knock at the door plucked Josh from his depressive contemplation of recent events. Wearily he rose from the sofa, crossed the room and opened it. There stood Meredith. "Good evening Josh, just called to see if you are settling in alright and if there's anything you need or I can help you with." he smiled. Goomelt and Pusto recoiled, hissing. Josh, relieved to have someone to talk to about Ray's situation, invited him in, motioning him to sit in the armchair by the Rayburn. Over tea, Josh related as much as he knew about his best friend's current situation, plus several reminiscences from the past. Meredith could see that Josh was deeply disturbed by the news, and so volunteered what was for him, a second nature option. "I'll get all my fellowship praying for him." he ventured. Josh's reaction momentarily took him by surprise. "Pray for him?" he exclaimed, the anger Spasmoide working its poison, "Who to, the so called God who let it happen in the first place?"

Uncomfortable as they were in such close proximity to the nauseating white light around Meredith, the two demons were enjoying this. The man of God, discerning that now was not the time to elaborate further, merely said "Well, if there's anything else that I can do to help, don't hesitate to ask." and with that he thanked his host and was on his way.

After he'd closed the door behind his landlord, Josh realised that he'd actually been a bit rude and resolved to put the matter to rights and apologise next time he saw him. "So," he thought, "old Meredith's a bit of a bible basher then. Oh well, everybody needs their emotional crutches." He locked the doors, switched off the lights and, inhaling deeply from the freshly ignited joint in his mouth, mounted the stairs singing a line from an old John Lennon song. "Whatever gets you through the night, it's alright – alright."

Back at home, in his kitchen, Meredith stoked the Rayburn and made himself a pot of coffee. It was going to be a long night. Settling in his fireside chair with Polly curled up in her basket; he was silent for a few minutes. Still, before God. Then he commenced in prayer. "Father God in heaven, all praise and honour and glory be to you. Lord, build Your kingdom here on earth and cause it to be perfect in formation and obedience, just like it is in the heavenly realms. Father provide for our needs, and forgive us our sins in the same way that we forgive other people, for we have all come far short of Your great glory. I pray also Father for Your protection from the evil one and his minions, for You alone are mighty, majestic and worthy of all our praise. I thank You for sending Your only Son to die for me, and in His precious name I ask the following – I ask Lord that You spare the life of Ray Coughlin, that You keep him alive. Heal and restore him Father, snatch him from the very jaws of death, at least until such time as he can hear the Gospel of Life and make his choice. Please Lord don't let him die, heal him because You love him, heal him because of the great price You paid for him – the life of Your only Son."

Hour after hour, deep into the night, Meredith fervently prayed on behalf of Ray Coughlin. At three a.m. he suddenly stopped. He had the confirmation. In his heart he knew His prayers had been answered. He yawned and stretched as he rose and made his way to bed. "Thank You - thank You Father God."

'The effective, heartfelt, believing prayer of a redeemed spirit filled man will do great things'.
[James Chapter 5 v 16] *Amplified.*

------ O ------

High in the Heavenlies in an enormous silver and sapphire room, just above and behind The Palace of Accusation, two warrior Angels were receiving urgent orders from their Captain. "You are to proceed to Beijing immediately; at the hospital is an Englishman, Raymond Coughlin. The enemy are about to take him to the fiery places, but we have had special orders from the office of The Lamb – Praise His holy name – One of the Sons of God has pleaded successfully with The Most High and you are to keep him on the earth plane for the time being – go in the authority of The Lord God!"

------ O ------

Ray opened his eyes. Everything was hazy. He was in a room. He tried to move but couldn't. To His left he could see a monitor screen, which came in and out of focus, although he could clearly hear its monotonous bleeping. There appeared to be 'ropes' all around him, but he didn't know why. He tried feebly to call out, but his mouth wouldn't respond. Then he remembered. The horses, the frantic galloping, the terror, the awful noise followed by the sudden searing pain across his back.

Relieved that he felt no discomfort at present, he realised that he was in a hospital. The constant bleeping suddenly stopped and was replaced by a monotone hum. He tried again to sit up and was relieved when he felt himself moving. However, the momentum of his movement caused him to float from his bed and up towards the ceiling! Somehow it seemed perfectly natural and he felt good, but puzzled. Looking down he was shocked to see himself still lying on the bed, festooned with pipes and wires.

Suddenly the door burst open and a whole host of medical people began feverishly working on his body. He couldn't understand anything they were saying, he half laughed as he said to himself, "It's all Chinese to me!" but he began to have increasing misgivings, people don't float on ceilings observing themselves below. Then he realised he was moving. Up he went, passing through the ceiling, and then through all sorts of colour and sounds. Soon he found himself in a long tunnel, going faster and faster. He had the sensation that it was going gradually downwards, and as the seconds ticked away he became ever more fearful.

Without warning, something grabbed his wrist dragging him along, and he could hear terrible moans and shrieks off in the distance. He was powerless and utterly terrified as yet more bony hands fastened on him out of the darkness. All at once he was in a dimly lit cavern that flickered with an evil reddish glow. The moment he saw his tormentors he began to scream hysterically, much to their amusement as they slashed and tore at him with their claw like hands. The pain was intense and unrelenting and the whole place was unbearably hot, seething with dark entities that were mercilessly torturing their unfortunate captors. Through the haze of awful pain, Ray felt he was in the worst nightmare ever possible. He realised that he and the other prisoners were being herded ever nearer to a foul and gaping abyss on the far side of the cavern, the apparent source of the dreadful heat. Several warrior demons waited by the edge of the stinking precipice and began to pitch the hapless screaming souls over the edge into the volcanic void. A large demon had grabbed Ray's head and was about to toss him into the molten morass, when a shaft of white light suddenly enveloped the terror-stricken man. The roof of the cavern above Ray collapsed with a thunderous crash as two warrior Angels, swords drawn entered the scenario. Tormentor demons scuttled into the shadows like cockroaches, shrieking in terror and temporarily leaving their captives free. Ray, still entirely bathed in white light and frozen between relief and total disbelief, noticed that all the other people were Chinese, yet didn't know why. Many of them were now on their knees, pleading with the Angels to help them, but their cries were to no avail. One of the warrior demons spoke out "You cannot come in here!" he pointed to the pleading humans "these belong to my master, legally!" "Not so demon," the Angels said in unison "this one has been claimed by a believer – you know the rules!"

The warrior demons snarled and spat but remained where they were, and all the while the desperately frightened people continued to beg for help. One of the Angels addressed the entities already residing within Ray. "You have your legal rights - until the curse is broken!" The other Angel reached out and touched the middle of Ray's chest with a glowing red crystal, saying "Return and remember nothing." The white light carried Ray away as the Angels spun upwards in a time reversing spiral, sending the rocks back into the cavern roof and leaving the unfortunate souls of the humans to their eventual eternal judgement.

  The limp body in intensive care convulsed as the charge from the resuscitation paddles surged through, kick starting the heart and reanimating the continuous green line on the monitor screen. The heartbeat grew stronger and stabilised, the breathing deepened. The extremely efficient Chinese medical team went about their business, completely unaware of the two warrior Angels who now stood at either side of the bed.

By the time Zara arrived later that evening, Ray's condition was much improved. Although he was still unconscious, his monitored breathing and heartbeat were remarkably good and his overall condition was stable.

She was not allowed into the intensive care room as a precaution against infection, but she could look in from the adjoining room. She stood tears streaming down her face as she gazed at Ray's motionless form, festooned with pipes and wires. As she studied the monitor screen with its now steadily recurring 'blip', she closed her eyes and said "Please God, don't let him die."

In another part of the hospital two floors down, Simon Cheng sat propped up in bed writing. The bullet had passed right through his thigh, narrowly missing the bone. He'd lost quite a lot of blood, but the wound was clean and he was in no danger, only some discomfort from the pain. Right now he was in the process of compiling his report to his superiors. His written account was precise, military and factual. Completely underplaying his acts of selfless heroism. Totally failing to mention that were it not for him, then they would probably all have died . . . .

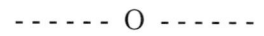

------ O ------

They had been nearly at the end of the gorge and the relative safety of the wide valley beyond, when Simon had felt the scorching pain in his thigh. Holding tight to Ray's reigns he'd urged his mount forward. A long burst of automatic fire from behind kicked up the dust, and sent screaming ricochets spiralling into the sky as the remaining bandits sought to bring down the Jade laden mules. The tail end of this fusillade had raked across the back of Ray Coughlin and the rump of the mule at the rear.

Ray had pitched forwards barely conscious, yet still gripping his horses mane. The mule at the rear had crumpled to the floor, its heavily laden weight snapping its tether to the one in front. They had cleared the end of the gorge, and swung hard left into the relative safety of some rocks at the base of a sheer cliff. They were safe from above, and stretching before them was the wide valley that fed the trail fifteen miles down to Mountain Station 27.

Simon had leapt from his mount, just in time to catch the now unconscious Englishman as he slid sideways out of his saddle. He laid Ray against some rocks and, barking orders to the two remaining soldiers, he'd taken an automatic weapon and some clips and headed back towards the ravine. One of the two remaining soldiers was instructed to stay with Ray, whilst the other unhitched his mules and galloped off down the valley to summon help.

Ignoring the pain from his heavily bleeding leg, Simon had edged along the rocks towards the opening into the gorge. He could clearly hear the voices of the bandits as they attempted to loot the cargo from the stricken mules. He'd figured they were no more than fifty yards round the rocky corner. His heart was pounding but he knew what he'd got to do. Cocking his weapon and taking a deep breath, he'd spun himself out into the gorge squeezing the trigger as he did so. The three bandits had been taken completely by surprise, the hail of bullets cutting down two of them. At this point, Simon's injured leg had given way, and he'd crumpled to the ground just as a burst of fire had filled the space he'd occupied an instant before. Thinking he'd hit him, his adversary had run forward as Simon rolled sideways and fired a quick burst. The hijacker had seemed to freeze, the weapon had dropped from his hand, and he'd pitched forwards face first into the dust, as death came to greet him.

Further into the ravine several of the gang members were retreating dragging the heavy Jade filled saddlebags as they went. Simon, realising he was in no condition to expedite a pursuit, had emptied three of his remaining five clips in long bursts after the fleeing robbers, thus encouraging their hasty departure. He'd waited for five minutes, alert to any possibilities of their return, before dragging himself to his feet. Using rocks for support, he'd hopped and hobbled to where Ray lay, guarded by the remaining soldier. Still ignoring his own needs he'd dressed and bandaged Ray's wounds and sent the soldier to retrieve the saddlebags that were near at hand. His estimate of the time it would probably take the other soldier to reach help had been spot on, and it was only when he'd heard the distant 'chudder' of the helicopter rotors that he'd finally slipped into unconsciousness.

< < < < - - - END OF CHAPTER THREE - - - > > > >

The Dragonmaster

CHAPTER 4   **Ask, Seek, Knock.**

As Josh awoke, his head pounding from the previous evening's alcoholic excess, Goomelt and Pusto were the demonic equivalent of happy. The antichrist Spasmoide was firmly attached and growing. Anger was all around, now well established, and last night Pusto had scored a direct hit with a lust, causing Josh to fantasise about defiling the nasty blonde believer. For three days now, by working on his concern for Ray Coughlin, they had managed to keep him away from the awful 'white liters', and with an optimism born of ignorance, they felt sure they were winning. When Kaisis had made a sudden whistle-stop appearance, he had only kicked them backwards, scowling "Make sure he continues to sin!" as he took off to oversee the murder of some children. All in all the dismal pair felt rather smug.

Chakine however knew different. He knew that the prayers of the believers for Josh's salvation were being gathered together in a great golden bowl in The Arc of Prayer, one of the highest reaches of heaven, a glorious realm. Unimaginable to the mind of man and unreachable by anything earthly that was not washed in the Blood of Christ.

It was Saturday morning and yet again Josh was regretting a Friday night spent wasted in alcohol. He'd lost count of the times he'd said "Never again." Not That he was an alcoholic in the literal sense of the word, far from it. But it just seemed to be the place to run to when things got a bit much. He was aware of the pernicious nature of too much alcohol, but at the same time he was weak. He was also aware of its toxic qualities and ability to damage his body, but usually more so the morning after than during the event. At times like these, Josh felt as if he had a degree in The Wisdom of Hindsight. He sighed heavily. There was a feeling of helplessness over Ray's situation. He wanted to do something, to make a difference, to be able to comfort Zara, anything except do nothing. Yet there was nothing he could do but wait for more news.

The current worrying situation aside, he absolutely loved his new home, and during the last few days had been exploring the area in and around Aberdigan with the aid of an Ordinance Survey Map. Following the road alongside the dilapidated castle and over the bridge, a pleasant drive adjacent to the river bought him to the coast. Where the river met the sea he'd found a magnificent golden sanded beach almost a mile wide, bordered by dunes sprouting spiky grass and wildflowers. The whole mouth of the estuary was ringed by rolling hills, and the white tipped turquoise surf danced and dived in the shallows of a safe, blue flagged bay.

He'd travelled deeper inland and discovered an impressive series of small waterfalls several miles further back up the same river. Locals told him of the salmon that would leap here in due season when the relatively gentle falls would be a raging torrent of furious white water. The same river cut its way through steep sided heavily wooded valleys, on its unrestrained descent to the sea. A few miles from Aberdigan another old castle stood sentinel, high above its fast flowing banks. From there it began to slow and meander across wide gentle plains strewn with sheep. It played host to canoeists and fishermen, and delighted walkers on riverside paths. It slowed increasingly as it neared the estuary, lazily passing below the castle and the town of Aberdigan, its determined progress finally mixing it with its saline brother in a dancing swirl of currents and swift eddies.

Everywhere the transition to summer was exploding with verdant plenitude, and the whole area was vibrant with life, growth and energy. Outside the cottage, tea in hand and paracetamol in system, Josh surveyed his immediate surroundings. His garden and the banks of the lane were ablaze with colour, as all manner of wild flowers vied for the kiss of the sun. Beneath tall foxgloves, with tiers of purple flowers, pink Campions and yellow and white Daisies jostled one another for space. Bright blue Forget-me-nots squeezed between the Vetch and wild garlic dotted along the banks, and nettles and grasses of all kinds completed the picture.

House Martins were putting the finishing touches to this year's accommodation on the gable end of the stone built woodshed. Chattering excitedly they flew back and forth about their business.

Josh exhaled a deep and troubled sigh. Here he was living in the midst of all this beauty in a wonderful location, yet something was missing. And he knew it was more than the trouble his best friend was in, but he couldn't put his finger on it. The bark of a terrier broke in on his contemplation, and looking up the lane he saw Polly investigating the hedgerows a hundred or so yards ahead of her master. Chakine smiled. At the same time The Grey Ones shifted uneasily at the approach of the nauseous white light. They could clearly see Salzar, Meredith's guardian, close at his shoulder. They hoped that Josh would ignore the man and that he would just walk right on past. Their hopes were dashed on both counts.

"Morning." called Meredith with a wave and a smile, striding ever closer, "Hi" Josh replied. He was glad to see him, as he'd wanted to apologise for his outburst the other day, but had actually been too embarrassed to go to his house. It certainly seemed though from the older man's general demeanour that he had not been offended.

As Meredith arrived, Josh said sheepishly "Oh, um, about the other day . . I was a bit rude and", Meredith held up his hand to silence him saying, " It's okay Joshua, no problem nor any offence taken. In fact I've actually come to invite you to dinner this evening, that is of course if you're not doing anything?" Firmly under the influence of the antichrist Spasmoide, Josh was about to make his excuses when Meredith added, "Oh and Cheryll's coming as well. I think you met her the other day. Young lady, long blonde hair?"

Goomelt and Pusto were screaming "No! No!" but the lust Spasmoide from the previous evening was still firmly attached to Josh's neck, and drew him heavily in the direction of acceptance. Also the mere mention of her name had crushed his unconscious spiritual resolve like a hammer would crush a grape. Despite everything the demons had done, he found himself saying "Thank you, I look forward to it." - "About eight then?" smiled Meredith as he lit his pipe; clouds of aromatic smoke billowing about him. Salzar smiled and nodded to Chakine who smiled back and then looked directly at the cowering demons, once again nonchalantly fingering the handle of his sword. "Eight will be fine." retorted Josh, already buzzing on the idea of another encounter with the beautiful blonde. Meredith turned and with a wave strode off up the track "See you later then". The little Jack Russell ran to Josh her stumpy tail wagging furiously. A quick lick of his outstretched hand, a quick sniff of his shoes, and she was off again and at the heels of her master.

The idea of having a little dog of his own was very appealing. He'd thought of it several times in the last week. As a child he'd always longed for a dog, but had always been denied the opportunity. Now though, there was nothing to stop him from fulfilling the desire. More to the point, there was no one to say "No." As he sat in the sunshine the idea matured into a decision, and entering the cottage he found his local paper and looked up the address of the nearest dog's home. A phone call confirmed the availability of dogs of various shapes and sizes, and half an hour later he was on his way to the Rhyd-y-Meirch Animal Sanctuary.

During the course of the fifteen-mile journey, he imagined all sorts of possible dogs, not at all sure of which type to get. In the end though he had the overwhelming feeling that the right dog would choose him, and as he swung his car into a parking space at the sanctuary he felt completely at ease with that feeling.

Rhyd-y-Meirch was a privately owned affair, typical of a thousand other such charitable organisations across the country. It was efficiently run, albeit on a shoestring budget, by two somewhat eccentric sisters, Dulcie and Wilhemina Frogett-Smythe.

Their appearance completely belied their aristocratic origins. The family fortune long since depleted; they had both devoted their lives to the care and protection of homeless animals, almost to the point of neglecting themselves. Their house was in desperate need of repair. Tiles were missing off the roof, grass and weeds grew from the gutters, and several of the windows, bereft of glass, were taped over with blue plastic fertiliser bags. Row after row of dog pens and sheds festooned the immediate area from the edge of the car park right up to the house, some one hundred and fifty yards away.

As he exited the car, an aromatically pungent cocktail assaulted Josh's nostrils. It appeared to be an amalgam of strong disinfectant and wet dog. Everywhere he looked there were animals. In the sea of pens, dogs barked or howled, relative to their disposition of the moment. Chickens, Ducks, Peahens and even an ancient limping Turkey, scurried about scratching and pecking hither and thither. In, on, and under the various buildings, cats of all shapes and sizes, prowled, played or slept in the sunshine. To his left in a small field, two horses, five donkeys, several goats and a Vietnamese pot bellied pig, sojourned in relative harmony. From the edge of the car park, a very old looking one eyed sheep, watched him warily.

In various locations, several young girls were engaged in the processes of cleaning, feeding and grooming. It was one of these who approached Joshua. "May I help you sir?"

Having explained who he was, and the nature of his business he was led along a pathway between two rows of pens, towards the house. The noise was cacophonous as all manner of canines voiced their opinion of the passing stranger. Some of them were throwing themselves at the mesh fencing of their enclosures, scrabbling with their paws, almost seeming to say "Me, Me, notice me!" One or two were leaping high in the air barking frantically and spinning round, whilst others, perhaps inmates of a longer duration, sat silently, heads down, seemingly resigned to their incarceration.

Eventually they reached the gate to the overgrown front garden of the house, and the young girl instructing Josh to wait, went inside. Atop a dry laid stone wall to the right of the gate was a large cracked and fading white painted sign, proclaiming:- *'Rhyd–y–Meirch' Animal Sanctuary* – Proprietors: *W&D Frogett-Smythe.* Beneath this was written: 'What is man that you are mindful of him? – The son of man that you care for him? You made him a little lower than the heavenly beings and crowned him with honour and glory. - You made him ruler over the works of Your hands – You put everything under his feet. All flocks and herds and beasts of the field – The birds of the air and the fish that swim in the sea.- O Lord our God how majestic is Your name in all the earth'.

Psalm 8. V.4-9

Chakine studied Josh carefully, as he read, re-read and then read for a third time, King David's words from the book of Psalms. It made total sense, and struck Josh as singularly true. All the animals we categorise as domesticated, we control. And the ones we can't control we are rapidly exterminating, directly or indirectly. In that sense, rightly or wrongly, all the other species with whom we share the planet, are 'under our feet'.

Goomelt and Pusto scowled at the script with rebellious disdain, but the Angel smiled to himself. Spasmoides or not, he knew something was happening deep in the heart of the man he had seen born. The one whom his Master had chosen.

Wilhemina Frogett-Smythe strode down the garden path. It was just after midday "Good morning Mr Fish Man!" she exclaimed in a loud upper class accent. She had a slight nasal whine and spoke in an almost aggressive staccato fashion. Her appearance was extraordinary. Green rubber boots, a bright blue floral print dress, custard yellow cardigan and a red knitted bobble hat. "Lovely day, what!" Josh tried in vain to squeeze in a reply "So you want to give a dog a home eh?" She strode towards some sheds beckoning him to follow. "Come along! Come along!" she ordered as if Josh were one of her charges. They stopped outside a large shed. "Right then, what do you do?" Josh felt as if he were being interrogated . "I'm a postman" Josh replied almost sheepishly, "Wife?" barked Wilhelmina, "Er, no" came the reply. Josh was feeling more and more like a naughty schoolboy. "No good, no good, can't leave a poor animal at home all day long, most certainly not!" she scolded. "Oh no, you misunderstand" Josh managed to interject. "I can take it with me on my rounds each day." She looked straight into his eyes for several seconds. He was extremely surprised by the warmth and sincerity he felt from her. "Small then!" she said, as if she had already made up his mind for him. "This way!" Striding briskly off again she led him to another shed further along the path. Inside were twelve individual pens, each housing its temporarily vagrant canine occupant. "Terriers, all sorts, look around, choose one!" she said in staccato fashion. "Only open one pen at a time if you want a closer look. Keep the main door shut at all times. I'll be back in fifteen minutes."

Off she went closing the large shed door behind her. Josh wondered if she was on speed, but the time he'd spent looking into the eyes of this eccentric old lady had assured him that she was basically okay. Several of the dogs were yapping furiously and leaping excitedly against their wire mesh prisons, as Josh sauntered down the gangway perusing the occupants. There were a couple of Corgis, and five obviously quite old animals, none of which caught Josh's interest. One little Jack Russell however was superb. Short haired and well muscled with distinctive black and white markings; he stood wagging his tail looking alert and keen. Josh opened his pen, and like a viper striking, the dog was out, hurling himself in a snarling frenzy against the mesh gate of the cage opposite, as its occupant snapped and snarled back. He took no notice of Josh whatsoever, merely intent on killing the object of his wrath. Spotting a pair of heavy-duty motorcycle gauntlets hanging on a nail, Josh put them on and grabbed the small animal from behind as it continued to assail its quarry. The dog twisted round repeatedly sinking its teeth into the thick leather as Josh tossed it unceremoniously back into its pen. None of the next three cages proved to house suitable applicants for the recently created position of 'best friend' for Josh.

The dog in the last cage was curled up in its basket; its head tucked into its haunches, and as such was of indeterminable appearance, except for being brown. Standing by the gate Josh made little kissing noises. "C'mon boy," he coaxed, unaware that 'he' was a she. "C'mon boy." There was no response and he was about to give up on the idea, when the little brown ball of fur lifted its head and opened one eye. Squatting down he tried coaxing again, patting his own shoulder as he did. "C'mon boy, c'mon, come see me."

The little dog began to slowly uncoil, and, tipping its head back, yawned lazily. Next it flopped two large paws forwards out of its basket, and rose slowly on its haunches stretching, with its backside up in the air. It yawned again; simultaneously 'shimmying' its whole body as it did so. Josh gently opened the gate and moved inside squatting down again, the little dog was still standing half in and half out of its basket a few feet away. Very slowly it began to wag its tail, almost as if this was too good to be true. As Josh encouraged it again it cocked its head to one side as if listening intently to something far away, and then it looked directly at him.

Without further ado the little creature stood up, walked straight to him, and in a gesture Joshua Fishmen would never forget, placed its little head on his knee, looking up into his face. He had been chosen!

The ticket on the animal's pen ascribed to it the name 'Boots' and stated it was a year old bitch. She was beige brown with black legs from the knee down, wiry hair, lop ears and four huge paws. An accidental cross between a Bedlington Terrier and an 'Allsorts'.

Just then the door swung open and in strode Wilhelmina Frogett-Smythe "Oh yes, knew you'd choose Boots, absolute right dog for you." she said, almost matter-of-factly. "Tragic, tragic, owner killed in a car crash you know, last month it was. Still, life goes on, what, eh?" - "That's really sad" was as far as Josh managed to get before she carried on "We can only do what we can until the Good Lord whips us orf, can't do more than that eh?" Josh dived in quickly "Has she been inoculated and such?" - "Yes, yes, got all the bumpf, come along and we'll sort it out" she replied, clipping a lead to Boots's collar and striding for the door. Josh followed along behind, realising that although he hadn't even said he would have the dog yet, the decision appeared to have been made by Boots and by Wilhemina. So he figured he'd go along with it.

At the office, which was merely another shed, full of paper, Josh met Dulcie. She was of the same mould as her sister and the two of them together were almost a cabaret act. An 'adoption' form was duly signed and Josh made a donation of twenty-five pounds.

Wilhemina walked with the man and his dog down to the car park. As soon as Josh opened the door, Boots jumped straight in and curled up on the passenger seat as if she'd always been there. Josh, his face beaming, extended his hand to the eccentric old lady. As she took it she said, "Good food and plenty of exercise now, young man." Once again she fixed him with her gaze, and yet again he felt real warmth as she looked intently at him. "Thank you so much." he said. He climbed into the driver's seat and she walked back up the track a way, but then stopped and called out "Mr Fish Man!" Josh looked up attentively. As he wound down his window she said " Dominus Vobiscum!" and turned and walked back to her tasks. Although he knew it was Latin, Josh hadn't the faintest idea what it meant, so he resolved to ask Meredith that evening at supper.

On the drive back, Boots acted as if she'd always been in the passenger seat and Josh, his concerns for Ray temporarily allayed, stroked her every so often. He arrived home that afternoon a much happier man.

Within a couple of hours Boots was acting as if she'd always been with Josh. She would follow him everywhere and if he sat down she'd flop at his feet. Obviously having had some training, she responded to all the basic commands. Sit, stay, lie down etc., and seemed to be a highly intelligent little animal. A trip to planet Tesco in Aberdigan furnished dog food and a large cardboard box for her to sleep in, and the local charity shop had just the right old woollen blanket.

Josh drove around town and located the sorting office depot, where he would be starting work on Monday. It looked fairly new and he hoped it would be an okay place to work from. Sitting in his car he glanced at the row of familiar looking red vehicles parked in the compound and wondered which one would be his, and how easily, or perhaps not, he would adjust to his new round.

Over the last few days, in preparation he had been studying the local Ordinance Survey map and a town plan of Aberdigan, with all the street names. But with the majority of these being in Welsh, he found most of them totally unpronounceable.

As he pulled away from the sorting office and headed out of town towards home, Josh thought again about Ray, and again he felt frustrated at his total inability to assist his friend or be of any real use in the situation. However he shrugged it off this time, consoling himself with thoughts of the beautiful young woman he would be dining with tonight.

Back at home he spent the next two hours showering, shaving and generally preening himself in preparation for his evening sojourn. Goomelt and Pusto were frantic. Short of relinquishing the Position of Influence, and the ensuing deadly repercussions that would incur from Kaisis, they had no choice but to endure the imminent close proximity of two white liters. Their attempts to increase lust in the life of their charge had backfired spectacularly, merely serving to make Josh more and more interested in the awful girl, albeit for less than chivalrous reasons. Nonetheless he now <u>wanted</u> to be where she was.

This was disastrous. They knew also that soon the wrath of Kaisis would fall upon their heads for not keeping Josh away from the believers. Chakine, ever present behind them was unnerving enough, and now they were going to have to endure Yolan and Salzar too!

The antichrist Spasmoide was however still firmly adhered, although it had stopped growing. "It's that thing." Goomelt said to Pusto, pointing at Boots who was lying on her back on the sofa, as her new master gently stroked her tummy. "That's what's making him nicer, yuuk" The pair of them ruefully bemoaned the fact that Spasmoides didn't work on animals.

Josh was sitting relaxing after his shower and bonding well with his new companion. The little creature had already provided a degree of peacefulness for the man and hence the demons were plotting. Unaware, Josh smiled and stretching out full length on the sofa, he rolled himself a joint. Soon he was in 'Marijuana Land', allowing his imagination to take him straight into Cheryll's boudoir. In this particular fantasy, he was not behaving like a gentleman. The Grey Ones seemed satisfied. At least, for the moment.

Chakine sensed the agitation of the two demons and smiled to himself. He knew that Meredith, Cheryll and the whole fellowship were praying for Josh's salvation, and he always had in his mind the memory of the small boy in the grey stone church all those years ago.

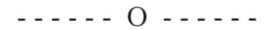

------ O ------

Cheryll Jameson had spent the afternoon at her parent's smallholding in the Cych Valley and now she too was preening and preparing for the dinner at Meredith's with the handsome young man she'd recently met. She realised she was extremely attracted to Josh and she knew too of his calling, and wondered if there might ever be the possibility of a proper relationship. She stepped into her shower and as the warm water cascaded over her body, she began to feel quite sensual, letting her mind drift into unguarded areas. For a brief time she allowed her self to go with it, imagining a somewhat different outcome to her previous meeting with Josh, until she suddenly said, out loud, and with real spiritual authority, "No! - Lust, in the name of Jesus. Get out of here!" Reaching up she turned the dial of the shower to cold, and gasped, gripping the handrail. The icy water sent shockwaves coursing through her system, bringing the zeal of her passionate imaginings, to a swift conclusion. Stepping from the cubicle she began to laugh as she dried herself. "Wow!" she thought, "First time I've ever had to take a cold shower!" She continued giggling as she said "Praise You Lord for delivering me from my own nature."

It had often struck her as funny that guys at college called her 'iron pants' or 'the female eunuch', amongst other things, just because she wouldn't do what virtually all the other girls did. They intimated that something was wrong with her because she exercised self-control. They seemed to assume that she had no sexual feelings because she wasn't a slave to them.

On the contrary, she was an extremely sexual being, passionate and demonstrative, but first and foremost in her life was the fact that she had freely chosen to follow Jesus, and as such did her best to live the life the Master had prescribed for those who would follow him. Not that she never stumbled, nor did or said anything she shouldn't, but she had a firm grasp of what is right and what is wrong and was trying her best to live it. She understood clearly that when a thought just 'pops' into your mind then it's not necessarily wrong. Or sinful. What you might call the arrow thought can come from all sorts of stimuli. Some good - some bad , and some totally neutral. She knew the problem lies with what you do with a thought once you recognise it to be negative or plain wrong.

Yolan had been at her shoulder for some five years now, from the very night she had accepted Jesus as her saviour. Her two Grey Ones had stood no chance. The moment she made her decision Yolan's flashing sword had sent them, bound in chains, to a dark place. A grim prison, where they would have plenty of time to contemplate their fate. Time to dread their eternal torment in a burning lake of fire prepared for the devil and his angels.
[Matthew Ch.25 v 41]

Like Chakine with Josh, Yolan had also seen Cheryll come into this world. He had protected her until her own decisions had ultimately ousted him from the Position of Influence. With great sadness he had observed her becoming wild and promiscuous, smoking dope and doing Tarot Cards. Getting drunk and wasting her God given talent and beauty on sensual self centred pursuits. Now though, she shone with the light of his Master. The Holy Spirit of God and the saving power of The Blood of Christ had entered the equation, and another life had been changed for eternity.

None of the Angels could understand however, why, on occasion, these servants of their Master would do and say very ungodly things, just like every other believer the world over. Their wicked human thoughts and deeds were completely beyond the Angels comprehension, for they originated in the free will that God had decreed for the human race. Since Lucifer's transgression, Angels no longer have free will in that way. They do only that which their Master instructs. Therefore, actions outside of God's will, resulting in sins being committed by beings who also have the Holy Spirit living inside of them, leave the Angels totally flummoxed. Completely unable to understand. Nonetheless they continue to perform their allotted tasks with integrity and precision.

------ O ------

Meredith's battered old Morris Traveller pulled up outside Cheryll's place at the pre-arranged time, and he sounded his horn. A few minutes later, a vision of loveliness emerged. She had woven her golden hair into dozens of beaded plaits that hung nearly to her waist. Even in a huge red baggy jumper, multi coloured leggings and Doc Marten's, she looked stunning and very, very feminine. Meredith smiled a knowing smile and said in a teasingly complimentary tone, "We're supposed to be getting this lad saved, not tempting him!" Cheryll laughed and turning her head away from him said in a phoney Southern drawl "Well sir, I'm sure I don't know what you mean." Within ten minutes they were putting the finishing touches to the dining room layout at Meredith's place.

Josh meanwhile, having already showered and shaved, was trying on the seventh of his many shirts. He stood in front of the full-length mirror in his bedroom and turned this way and that, scrutinising every detail of his appearance. With a sigh he unbuttoned the rejected garment, tossing it on the bed amidst a heap of previously discarded shirts and trousers. The mid blue Levi's that now adorned his lower half, had taken twenty minutes and several changes of mind and trouser to arrive at. And now he was in consternation as to the correct choice of apparel with which to ornament his upper torso. Catching sight of himself complete with worried expression, he stopped, shook his head and began to laugh, flopping forwards into the pile of clothes on the bed. "What the hell am I doing?" he said to himself "She's just another pretty girl, and I've had loads of them." He stood up again looking at the pile of clothes. "C'mon Fishmen, get yourself together." he said as he snatched up a green check shirt and put it on.

The whole time, Boots had sat in the corner observing the ritual. Then, titling her head to one side, she stood up and jumped onto the bed. Josh stroked her behind the ears affectionately and, not even bothering to look in the mirror, left the room and descended the stairs. Boots followed right behind him, negotiating the descent of the stairs with a curiously animated side to side movement. Josh stood at the bottom watching her cautious progress, his heart growing in affection towards the small creature. Grabbing his torch and his keys he headed out the front door and up the track towards Meredith's, happily accompanied by his new canine companion.

The Grey Ones were hurling Spasmoides like there was no tomorrow, realising that if they didn't do something very quickly, there might well not be a tomorrow for them! They knew Josh was heading for an appointment at the home of the old white liter and that the disgusting young female one would be there too.

Fear, Anxiety, Panic, all were forcefully thrown, yet not one stuck fast, all of them falling to the ground and disappearing in a little puff of smoke. The antichrist Spasmoide was still in place and the two demons were cursing that it would work.

Josh stopped dead. He had gone about a hundred yards from his place when he suddenly wheeled around and ran back down the track towards his cottage. Goomelt and Pusto squealed with hate filled excitement. The antichrist Spasmoide was working! They wouldn't have to account to Kaisis after all!

Arriving at his door, Josh fumbled in his pocket for the keys, and, opening up strode across the room to his sideboard. Reaching out, his hand closed around the neck of a bottle of Chardonnay. Boots was running excitedly around him. "Nearly forgot the booze Boots!"

--- --- O ------

High in the courts of Heaven, way beyond The Palace of Accusation, in a place of softly undulating synergy, The Arc of Prayer gently expanded and contracted, as if it were breathing. Compared to the splendour there, an earthly rainbow, (God's sign of His promise never again to flood the whole earth), was merely a small reflection. Millions of miles long, high and wide it housed the seven primary colours of earthly creation, plus many more either side of our recognised spectrum. Limitless layers of colour, sound and light, danced together. And wove swirling, visual, sonic harmonies that gently flowed and billowed like the finest multi-coloured silks in a serene breeze. Oscillating tones of pure sound colour pulsated, cavorting in every direction in wondrous random symmetry. Each colour, each tone and each shade vibrated on a specific frequency producing a musical note in harmony with all the others. The result, being a glorious organic symphony that rose filling the heavens with living praise to The Almighty God.

Up into this wondrous plethora rose the prayers of the believers world-wide, mystically transformed into sound, light and colour, yet still retaining every nuance and aspect of their human request. Countless golden bowls were being gradually filled as millions of Prayer Angels criss- crossed the Arc incessantly collecting and transmitting the petitions and communications into the throne room of God. Merged within this vibrant symphony of colour and sound, were the prayers of Meredith, Cheryll and the other Aberdigan believers. Prayers for the salvation of Joshua Fishmen!

In the heavenly realms, God's perfect will is totally balanced harmonious vibration. God is Spirit and He spoke all things into being. He took pure vibrations (which we deem to be sub-atomic) and by His awesome power fused them into matter, to become, in all its myriad complexity, what we perceive to be the third dimension. The realm in which, for the present, we have our existence.

'By faith we understand that the entire universe was formed at God's command. So that the things which are seen were not made of things which are visible'.[Hebrews Ch.11v3]

When God answers prayer, the interacting of light and sound, woven with the glorious colours of His holiness, manifest themselves like luminescent rays into the soul and spirit of man. They bring light into darkness; they break chains of bondage, and bring healing. And they bring a hunger for knowledge of their origin to men of ignorance. For the believer they will also bring leading, guidance, instruction and wisdom, as well as a whole host of practical provision.

'Every good and perfect gift comes down from above, from the Father of Lights in whom there is no variation or inconsistency' [James Ch.1v17]

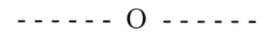

------ O ------

It was these humanly invisible rays that were now gently shining down on Josh, making new Spasmoides ineffective and preventing further growth of any already in place. They filled the Grey Ones with terror - Joshua with relative calm- and Chakine with praise and anticipation.

Torch in one hand and bottle of wine in the other, Josh set off again down the lane again for Meredith's as the clock struck eight. Boots ran excitedly to and fro sniffing all in her path, and exploring the hedgerows in the fading light. As he neared his host's home, Joshua felt calm and excited, peaceful and agitated, confident and fearful. He put it down to his ridiculous reaction to Cheryll. He was totally unaware of the terrified desperation of the two little demons at his shoulder, and the influence of the still firmly attached antichrist Spasmoide.

As he reached for the knocker, Meredith, who'd spotted him arriving, opened the door, greeting him warmly. Polly dashed out to investigate Boots who eagerly participated in the canine sniffing ritual. Handing Meredith the wine, Josh was explaining the acquisition of his new companion, when Cheryll emerged from the kitchen. "Hiya Joshua." she sweetly called, her smile lighting up the whole room. Boots and Polly ran in, still engrossed in their doggy introductions. When Cheryll caught sight of Boots she immediately went dog silly, fussing and cooing over the little creature. "Oh! Isn't she gorgeous," said Cheryll, continuing to pet her, "Where did you get her Josh?" Once again, Joshua Fishmen, ladies man par excellence, suddenly and inexplicably became Mr. Brainless, king of the monosyllabic response. Except right at this moment he couldn't even manage monosyllables. He stood there his tongue in knots, staring vacantly at her. She looked at him quizzically, trying not to laugh, whilst enjoying the effect the innocent beauty of her femininity was having upon him. "Oh, er, the, um, dog place." he finally replied, trying desperately to remember the relevant information, and acutely aware of coming across like a complete moron. Eventually he mumbled "Two sisters, er...." Meredith, coming to his rescue interjected. "Dulcie and Wilhelmina Frogett-Smythe?" - "Yes" said Josh, finally managing to speak coherently. "Strange pair I thought."

A couple of glasses of wine with the meal seemed to return the rest of Josh's vocal and intellectual faculties, and soon all three were seated around a log fire sharing bits of personal history. Meredith felt it right to wait until Josh aired the subject of things spiritual so as not to give him the impression of being outnumbered and preached at. He knew God was calling Josh and therefore recognised that the timing must be His. Not that he disbelieved in preaching the gospel, but in this particular instance, the timing must be The Lord's.

The conversation turned again to Josh's acquisition of Boots, and he was explaining how he felt the dog had chosen him, when he remembered Wilhelmina speaking to him in Latin. "Do you understand Latin?" he enquired of Meredith. "Well, some, why do you ask?" Josh explained and quoted as best as he could remember.

"Dominoes Vibscum?" Meredith thought for a moment and then, his face creasing in a broad smile said "Dominus Vobiscum – The Lord be with you!" - "Oh, they're bible bashers as well then?" blurted Josh, instantly regretting what he'd just voiced. "I'm sorry, I didn't mean to be rude" he apologised. "Oh that's all right, we don't mind do we Cheryll?" Meredith retorted. Josh looked stunned. Cheryll looked at him, and smiled a forgiving smile that melted his insides. Looking directly at her he sat forward in his armchair. "So you believe all this bible stuff then?" Still smiling she replied, "Yes Joshua, but only because it's true!"

Josh sat back in the armchair, stunned. He knew Meredith was religious, after all he was getting on and his wife was dead, so perhaps he needed the crutch of religion. But this beautiful creature?

Goomelt and Pusto's agitation was increasing by the second, and Yolan and Salzar close by their charges were enjoying every moment. "So that's the connection between you two then?" Josh enquired. "Yeah, Meredith led me to Jesus about five years ago." The antichrist Spasmoide was pulsating and Joshua felt a sudden sense of derision toward the two believers. Lust was also trying to re-assert itself as the highly agitated demons pulled out all the stops to try and hold their ground. Josh found himself thinking, "Huh, led her to Jesus, I'd have led her straight to my bed!"

She continued, "So what do you believe then Josh, about how we got here, who we are etc?" Josh looked again at Cheryll who was looking at him with an interested expression. He fixed his eyes on the ceiling as he gathered his thoughts, and then drew a deep breath. "Well, first off, I have to say, and no disrespect intended, that I don't believe all the bible stuff. Science has proved that evolution is how we got here, and anyway it's all been translated so many times now that it's nothing like the original. And all that stuff about a virgin having a baby, well that's obviously some primitive myth, and then there's those stories about people living for nine hundred years and well, it's all pretty ludicrous as far as I'm concerned." Josh felt himself becoming irritated with these people, plus a strong desire to have sex with Cheryll was welling up inside of him.

Within The terror of their situation, Goomelt and Pusto could still sense the workings of the two Spasmoides that had stuck. They were happy that Josh had spoken his mind about the horrid book, and they knew that his intentions towards the nasty believing female were ideally opposed to God's law. Meredith, sensing the presence of spirits holding sway over Joshua's will, went into the kitchen to make coffee, and as he did so he prayed. "In the name of The Lord Jesus Christ, I bind every spirit in the life of Joshua Fishmen that seeks to blind him to the truth of the gospel. I command you to back off and be silent"

A few minutes later with three coffees on a tray, Meredith returned to his lounge to find Cheryll and Josh in deep conversation. The two demons behind Josh were rigid, bound by the prayer of this righteous man, and unable for the time being to exert any more influence over him. Taking a coffee from Meredith, Cheryll said "Josh was telling me how he believes that each person should have some land and be able to grow his own food. And that he feels strongly that humanity is destroying the planet. – So I explained that man's original purpose, in work terms, was gardening, horticulture."

"Precisely." her mentor agreed "Not only that, but the bible also has a great deal to say about rulers and societies who oppress people and won't allow them to make a living. Furthermore, it states quite plainly that eventually the planet will be so polluted both physically and spiritually that it won't function properly anymore." - "Really?" said Josh, looking at the older man with renewed interest. "Let me ask you a question." Meredith ventured, aware that he was now talking to the 'real' Joshua Fishmen, who for the time being was unfettered and virtually free from demonic influence. "This bible that you don't believe in, have you actually read it?" Josh looked a little sheepish. "Well, in honesty, aside from the odd thing in 'Comparative Religion' at school, no, I've read hardly any of it. But lots of people say the same thing about it." - "Lots of people believed the earth was flat." Cheryll added. "Point taken." Josh agreed. "Actually," continued Meredith, "the word we call bible is really a plural, it comes from the Greek word biblios – meaning books. There are sixty six of them bound into the unit we call a bible, and that is divided into the Old and New Testaments." Josh was genuinely surprised. "Well I certainly didn't know that before tonight." Meredith resumed his explanation. "The bible is multi-faceted, inasmuch as there are many levels to explore. On one level it is a record of God's creation of the world and His dealings with mankind, mostly in the Old Testament, on another it's prophetic of the coming of Jesus and the redemption of man, so that . . ." Josh cut in. "I'm not sure I understand what redemption means in terms of man, and all this stuff about Jesus, well a lot of people don't even believe he was ever here." The anti (Jesus) Christ Spasmoide, although very subdued, was still there under the surface. Meredith thought for a moment. "If you redeem something you get it back, like if you had placed something in a pawn shop. When you go to get it back, you are said to 'redeem' it, yes?" Josh nodded. "Well, what Jesus came to do was to get man back from the darkness into the light. To rescue us from the clutches of Satan and bring us back to God our creator." –

"I can't go along with all this 'Satan' stuff, that belongs to the Dark Ages." Josh countered. "Okay, let's put that to one side for a minute, as I'd like to try and answer the other part of the statement you made regarding whether Jesus existed or not." again Josh nodded his assent. Meredith took a coin from his pocket and handed it to him, "Is there a date on it?" he asked. Josh studied it and replied "Yes, nineteen ninety one." - "One thousand nine hundred and ninety one years since what, Joshua?" Josh looked a little puzzled so

Meredith explained. "From the birth of Jesus, Josh. He's the man around whom our time is calculated." Cheryll looked at the young postman, sensing the beginnings of an inner turmoil. He looked from Meredith to her and said "Yeah, that's pretty convincing, as far as to whether he was here or not, I suppose." Meredith spoke again. "Not only that, but the historicity of Jesus is proven in many writings outside of the bible. The Koran acknowledges him as a prophet, and various historians wrote about him. Whomever you may consider him to be, it's a dead certainty that he was here on earth two thousand plus years ago."

Josh thought for a moment. "Well okay, so he was here, but I think that he was just a clever philosopher, a great mind, a man ahead of his time like Plato, Albert Einstein or perhaps Steven Hawking these days." Cheryll unleashed another disarming smile. "I used to think pretty much the same way, until Meredith pointed out some of the things Jesus said, like 'I am the way, the truth and the life, and no man comes to the Father except through me'."

This was the 'key' verse that had opened Cheryll's heart and mind to the reality of Jesus. Just as it had done for countless thousands of others, century after century. She continued. "When you really look at it, this statement is immense. Jesus is saying He's perfection, the all-sustaining power, and the absolute only way to get to God. Now, to my mind Josh, this statement is one of two things. It is either the most egotistical, megalomaniac ranting of a deluded madman, or it's true! To say you are the 'only way to God' leaves no room for any middle ground. An all-encompassing statement like that leaves absolutely no room for any grey areas. No 'clever philosopher' or any of that stuff. It's a cut and dried statement. He is either who he says he is, or he was a raving madman suffering from delusions of grandeur." Cheryll looked deep into Josh's eyes and then continued, "And then of course there's the fact that He backed up what He said by healing all sorts of people, feeding thousands from a tiny amount of food and raising people from the dead!"

Goomelt and Pusto bound as they were, could still hear the conversation. They were reeling under the power of God's word, held only in their place by their abject terror of what Kaisis would do if they voluntarily surrendered The Position of Influence.

Josh was feeling his own inner turmoil as the battle for his soul began in earnest. The words Cheryll had spoken to him felt like the truth to part of him, yet a voice within was saying, "Nonsense, rubbish, religious fanatics, make some excuse and go home, you've got some nice marijuana there." He was surprised therefore to hear himself say. "Show me where it says about being the only way to God, Meredith." Picking up his bible the older man opened it to John's gospel, chapter fourteen, and pointed Josh to verse six.

The onslaught came like a battering ram. Seemingly out of nowhere a horde of screeching demons descended upon the little dwelling. Yolan and Salzar reacted like lightning, leaping upwards to meet the incursion, their swords flashing with righteous brilliance as they dispatched one after another of their fiendish assailants. Half a second later they were joined by Chakine, and the three Angels formed a back to back circle above the heads of the three humans. Goomelt and Pusto continued to hurl Spasmoides at Josh.

The heavenly trio were hugely outnumbered but stood their ground, valiantly defending their charges as time and again the enemy furiously hurled themselves against the little band. In the room below them, on the earth plane, Meredith had suddenly become aware of an extremely malevolent presence. A highly oppressive atmosphere had filled the little room and he began to pray in tongues under his breath. Cheryll too was silently praying, commanding the forces of darkness to leave. The two Spasmoides on Josh's neck had started to grow again and as he looked at Meredith he thought, "Whatever am I doing here, listening to this bible basher?" He looked back down at the open bible in his lap and it made him feel angry. Polly and Boots were both growling at something unseen. As Meredith turned to calm them Josh looked at Cheryll, lust again burning in his heart. Goomelt and Pusto were now leaping up and down screaming obscene encouragement to Josh, when the edge of a golden shield sent them sprawling.

Summoned through the prayers of the believers, a dozen more warrior Angels led by Captain Cherno had burst into the fray, driving back the demons with righteous authority, their swords exacting a swift and heavy toll. The forces of darkness, reeling under the power of the counter attack, retreated into the black void. Cherno and his warriors greeted the three guardians. "Hail to the Lord God Almighty – Holy – Holy – Holy." The Grey Ones nervously re-assumed their legal position without a word, knowing the Angels would play by the rules. On the earth plane the whole incident had taken no more than thirty seconds. Suddenly Josh felt relatively calm again.

Cheryll and Meredith were both aware that something very dark had attacked, but also that the power of the light had intervened to repel it, so Cheryll continued. "So what do you think of that statement then Josh?" The influence of the Spasmoides had again diminished, leaving Josh to think reasonably clearly again. "I don't know about that at the moment, but I was just thinking about what I read today at the animal sanctuary. Psalm eight it was, something about 'why do you pay attention to man?' and that we've been given authority over the animals'. So why does God pay any attention to man then?" - "Because He loves us" the two believers said in unintentional unison. Josh looked hard at his landlord. "How do you know that for sure?" he queried, "and please don't say it's because the book, or should I say books, say so, because that proves nothing." Meredith smiled the smile of a man walking a familiar and much loved route. "No Josh, not just because the bible says it, although it certainly does have a lot to say about God's love for us, but I know He loves me through fifty years of personally experiencing His love. I could seriously talk for hours about the things God has done in my life. Time and time again He's proven His great love for me." There was a brief silence. Meredith thought for a while then quoted John Chapter 3 verse sixteen. "For God so loved the world that He gave His only begotten Son, that whosoever believes in

Him should not perish but have everlasting life." Josh felt the power in these words, even though he didn't fully understand their meaning. Something pushed a button inside of him that said 'Truth'.

------ O ------

In the Beijing hospital Ray was still comatose, though no longer in intensive care. His condition had stabilised and his vital signs were much improved. Zara now spent a good deal of her days sitting holding his hand and talking to him about anything and everything, trying to stimulate a response. At this moment in time the doctors couldn't say when he was likely to come round, but they had reassured her that there was no paralysis or serious long-term damage. At least she now knew he would eventually be ok. Simon Cheng was up and around, his leg wound healing nicely.

He had met Zara, but she was as yet, unaware of the part he had played in the saving of her husband's life. With conscientious efficiency, from his hospital bed Simon had also arranged the transportation and secure storage of Ray's remaining cargo. Right now it was all packed and crated up awaiting collection at an army base just outside the city.

In the initial rush and her concern to get to her husband's side, Zara had completely forgotten to bring her telephone, and so consequently, all her contact numbers. But after racking her brains, she did finally remember the email address of Josh's mother, and with the help of her interpreter found an Internet café and sent the following message. – 'Dear Mrs. Fishmen – would you please tell Josh that Ray is going to be alright. The doctors tell me there is unlikely to be any serious long-term damage and they expect him to come out of the coma anytime now. Send him our love, and tell him not to worry – Regards, Zara'.

------ O ------

Back in Meredith's cottage, just as Josh felt the power in the words of John Chapter 3 verse sixteen, just as he felt he was hearing truth . . . . . his mobile phone rang, cutting like a knife and severing the moment.

We live in Satan's system. God never designed us to live this way. All day, every day, we are bombarded with radio waves, satellite beams and electromagnetic pulses. The signals from mobile phones, television, radio, taxis, CB sets, and a whole host of other 'technological advances' saturate our bodies with cancer causing electronic frequencies. Even while we sleep all this stuff is passing right through us causing untold damage, and resulting in the ultimate slow and painful deaths of hundreds of thousands of people world-wide. These incredible innovations are hailed as progress and technological advancement, and whilst that may be true perhaps on one level, the whole system is driven by the love of money. This in turn causes manufacturers to produce ever better-faster-bigger units of their particular consumer drug. It's all designed to push our 'must have' buttons that have been cleverly put in place by a relentless campaign of 24hr. worldwide advertising. We were not meant to live this way.

The systematic poisoning of our food is now de rigueur. Unscrupulous manufacturers whilst telling us how healthy it all is, routinely place additives, preservatives and colouring, known to be carcinogenic, in our food. Why? The answer is <u>the love of money!</u>

We are living in a world -wide system that Satan designed, because even though he was defeated at Calvary, until Jesus returns, he is The Prince of This World. Adam and Eve handed the title deeds over to him way back in the Garden of Eden. In the wilderness Jesus was offered the whole world if He would worship Satan. [Luke Ch. 4 v 6-7] Satan could only make that offer if the world were (temporarily) his to command. Jesus acknowledged Satan as Prince of This World. [John Ch 14 v 30]

The whole world is filled with violence, greed and murder. Predominantly it's <u>for the love of money</u>. For personal or national gain. Satan is evil and 'The love of money is the root of all evil'. [1 Timothy Ch. 6 v 10]

The two go hand in glove. Wherever you find the love of money you will find Satan at the root. God's Kingdom is about giving and receiving whilst Satan's is about buying and selling. A mobile phone itself isn't evil, it's the power and system behind it all which is.

------ O ------

The message from Josh's mum about Ray's condition filled him with jubilation. But the timing of that message, just as Josh was about to apprehend a real truth, closed the door on further discussion of the subject that evening.

When Josh relayed the gist of the message concerning Ray's condition to his hosts, Meredith said, "Praise The Lord!" and Cheryll added, "Thank you Jesus!" They then explained how they'd been praying for Ray ever since Josh first told them about his friend's desperate situation. "Wow," Josh thought to himself half in derision and half in admiration. "These guys really believe this Jesus stuff!"

All three chatted for a while longer, but Meredith, discerning that now was not the time, did not broach the subject of God again. Once more Josh found himself 'looking' at Cheryll with his loins, and Goomelt and Pusto breathed a temporary sigh of relief. The antichrist and lust Spasmoides were still working!

As the evening wound down to its natural conclusion, Josh thanked his host, shaking his hand warmly. As he turned to say a warm goodnight to Cheryll, his confidence bolstered by several glasses of wine, he was stunned as she leant forward and gave him a brief yet sincere kiss on the cheek. "Goodnight Josh, see you again." The demons recoiled in horror, Chakine and Yolan smiled at one another, and Josh 'floated' off down the track with a big stupid grin on his face and a small dog at his heels.

For Meredith and Cheryll, the next hour was spent in sincere prayer, petitioning that the enemy would not steal away the seed that had been sown. That it would fall on fertile ground.

------ O ------

Meanwhile, way up in the heavenlies at the realm of the 'Arc of Prayer', the petitions and supplications of the little band of believers continued to accrue. The golden bowl was filling with beautiful vibrating colours. Yet more prayers for the salvation of Joshua Fishmen.

------ O ------

It was about eleven when Josh finally awoke. It had taken him ages to get to sleep. Partly because he couldn't get Cheryll out of his head, especially after that kiss, and partly because some of the things they'd discussed the previous evening kept coming back. As he lay drifting, Boots bounded onto the bed from her box in the corner and gave him an early morning face licking. He gently pushed her away saying firmly "No Boots, no face licking!" The little animal looked scolded and curled up by his feet. It was Saturday morning and outside the sun was shining on a vibrant bustling world. Deciding a nice relaxing joint would set him up for the day, he reached for his 'stash' box only to discover he'd been a bit over enthusiastic of late. There was barely enough for one small joint. As he smoked it he resolved to seek out a new line of supply.

It had always seemed totally crazy to Josh that it was illegal, when alcohol was freely available. He'd never met or heard of anyone who liked to get stoned and then go out and beat people up. Most folk seemed to get very talkative, creative, passionate or inwardly contemplative. Music took on new dimensions, and frequently transported you to a world of colour, imagination and poignancy. Of course, the actual act of sucking smoke into your lungs wasn't particularly cool, but hey, it's everybody else who gets cancer! The part he didn't like about it all, was having to go to dodgy places to obtain it.

Often in the past he'd been offered Heroin, Cocaine, Speed, and Acid amongst other things. Trouble was, occasionally he'd partaken, being a weak and foolish man. Of course aided and abetted by the two entities at his shoulder, perpetually encouraging him to take the wrong path. 'Occasionally' wasn't strictly the truth. A few years back he and Ray had come by some Amphetamine Sulphate, a rather large quantity actually, and they had indulged themselves for a couple of months. Josh remembered how he had started out feeling like superman, able to party all night then go straight to work the next day. Smoke endless joints and get very, very stoned, yet not feel tired. And the ladies loved it too, particularly its ability to make viagra seem like aspirin. Yet bit by bit it was taking a subtle hold. Little by little it lost its efficacy, requiring ever-larger quantities to achieve the desired effect.

Though he always tried to suppress the memory, Josh clearly recalled the afternoon he'd woken up to discover there was none left! He remembered suddenly feeling a tremendous anxiety, almost desperation. "Oh no, where can I get some?" He had literally just awoken and was pacing around his bedroom. Chakine was becoming increasingly concerned about his 'Chosen One'. Goomelt and Pusto had recently succeeded in leading him into dangerous drugs and had plans to introduce him to heroin if they could engineer the right circumstances. Although the Angel was not allowed to intervene in matters of Josh's free will, he could in an emergency, petition his superiors to gain permission to give Josh a spiritual experience. This he did, and Captain Cherno had duly visited, assessed the situation and granted that permission.

As Josh paced around his bedroom 'wired' and anxious about obtaining more drugs Chakine had swooped in and spun in a blur of speed just above Josh's head. The demons were paralysed and Josh's spirit was sucked out of his body to the other side of the room. Standing there aghast, he could clearly see himself distraught and agitated on the other side of the room. It was a pathetic sight and impacted him immensely. He actually heard himself say "Oh no, where can I get some?" The experience only lasted a few seconds. That was all it needed. With a jolt, Josh was back in his body with full cognisance of what he'd just seen of himself.

He remembered sitting back down on his bed, a hard realisation dawning. "Oh my goodness" he'd said to himself, "I'm one step away from being a junkie!" The next two weeks had been hard, but he and Ray had got their act together and stayed completely off the stuff and away from places where it was available. Several years had passed since and neither friend had succumbed.

------ O ------

Josh decided he'd go into Aberdigan and look for some 'alternative' types. They were usually a good bet. And even if they didn't have any smoke for sale you could pretty much guarantee they'd know someone who did.

Half an hour later he was parking his car in the riverside car park. He wound the windows down a little, to give Boots airflow, and walked up the hill towards the café by the castle. The little creature sat carefully watching him until he disappeared out of sight, then contentedly curled up on the front seat, confident of his eventual return.

At the café, tables and chairs were placed outside on the pavement in the sunshine, and Josh seated himself at one, next to a bearded, multi- ear ringed guy with a guitar case by his side and a dog on a lead at his feet. The guy looked happily stoned to him. It transpired his name was Andy.

After a few minutes of ice breaking conversation over coffee, mainly about bands, where local gigs happened and the like, and the fact that he was new to the area, Josh posed the question, "You wouldn't happen to know where I could get a decent smoke, would you?" Andy fixed him with a penetrating gaze and replied "Excuse me man, but I have reason to believe you can turn me on!" Josh exploded in laughter at this direct and very famous quote from an old Bonzo Dog Doodah Band track, where a very obvious 'undercover' cop is trying to ensnare dealers at a gig.

"Well," he replied, "I'm afraid I haven't got brown plastic sandals, blue serge trousers or an imitation plastic rose behind my ear!" Josh's reply was a paraphrase of the next line of the monologue.

Now satisfied that Josh wasn't some undercover policeman, Andy relaxed and smiled back. "Yeah, actually there's a guy where I live who's got some very good home grown, but you'd have to come with me. I'm waiting for the bus now." - "My car's just down the hill." Josh gesticulated in that direction.

Twenty minutes later they were on a winding back lane heading up into the Preseli Mountains. To the right was a long peak crested with rugged bluestone. Andy informed Josh that it was known as 'The Dragon's Back' and he could immediately see why. The arc of the top of the mountain looked just as if a scaly backed dragon was laying down sleeping along the crest. "Did you know man, this is where they mined the stone for Stonehenge?" Andy enquired. Josh was impressed, no he didn't know. "Yeah, there's some really cool places around here man, really cool vibes, specially if you do a handful of mushrooms as well."

Goomelt and Pusto were loving it, whilst Chakine flying along just above and behind the car, kept a careful watch for danger. He knew this place, and a tinge of sadness momentarily passed across his consciousness. It wasn't far from here that Angharad had died.

They turned left off the narrow road, into an even smaller lane and after a few hundred yards Andy directed Josh to turn into a gateway. A painted sign read 'Maen-Du' and Josh was duly informed that it meant 'Black Rock'. They continued for several hundred yards down a rather steep and rough track. At the bottom several old vehicles, some long dead, were parked in an area in front of an ancient stone built farmhouse. Various seemingly random outbuildings dotted the immediate area in an ill-conceived jumble. A large old Dutch style barn was to the left of the yard, and to the right two Tepees stood in a field, amongst some smaller tents. A little further across the field a domed sweat lodge reflected the sunlight from its polythene walls.

All around festooning the trees, bushes and buildings, were 'Dreamcatchers' and various mobiles. Several youngish children ran past playing and laughing. Josh found the place intriguingly inviting, and the two demons hoped that Kaisis would choose now as a time to pay a visit.

Chakine noticed a handful of terrified elementals quickly scurry into a barn on seeing him, and he made a mental note of their whereabouts. Atop the house two large leathery winged demons eyed him with malice and he drew his sword inviting them with a 'come hither' motion of his hand. They wisely declined.

Boots stayed in the car as Josh followed Andy into the house, and Chakine moved in as close as the rules of his current position allowed. There were spirits everywhere. Spirits of divination and witchcraft, Druidic spirits, spirits of eastern religion, native American spirits, a whole host of them.

There were several people in the house; all of them stoned, yet very friendly and welcoming to Josh. Inside the house there appeared to be a kind of organised chaos. He instantly liked the place and was soon rolling himself a joint from the proffered bag of grass and chatting amiably with the residents who were sitting around a large old pine table in the huge kitchen. The old house was completely unmodernised and had the feel of belonging to yesteryear.

------ O ------

Society labelled these folk 'hippies' or at best 'alternative types'. The reality was that they were spiritual searchers. Each one of them had individually looked at the society around them and concluded it was not the way they wished to live their lives. Some of them had been presented with a weak, dogmatic, powerless and traditional dead church as youngsters, and had perhaps, been made to attend. Others had been raised in atheistic surroundings, yet had been aware that there is a spiritual dimension out there. The Father of Lies – Satan, had successfully drawn them and many thousands like them, into a web of seemingly benign yet deeply occult activities. The inadvertent worship of demon deities, masquerading as 'gods'.

Many of these movements are really colourful on many levels, they have an immense and immediate attraction for artistically and musically inclined persons. Much of the music associated with these organisations is vibrant and interesting, unlike the downright boring sound of a church organ played by an old lady with no musical 'soul' and even less rhythm. Satan for the most part, had pretty much succeeded in doing a hatchet job on the so called Christian Church in this part of the world. Not that there weren't vibrant and lively spirit filled churches anywhere, just that these young folk and many more like them had been carefully kept away and fed lies, so that Christianity was considered as some old people's religion that was completely irrelevant to them. A lot of them would talk about Christ consciousness and how Jesus was an Avatar or some sort of guru.

In truth, though they may have heard the name, they had never really been introduced to anything other than 'Churchianity'. They had never been shown the person of The Lord Jesus. The Christ. The Saviour of the World.

------ O ------

Andy introduced Josh to Tarquin, the owner of the property. Apparently his parents were 'in oil' and he lived here on his generous monthly allowance, growing organic vegetables and marijuana. He was dressed in a long flowing eastern robe and wore a colourful beaded pork pie hat on his head. He was well spoken and privately educated. He was also deeply into Native American rituals.

The other residents of the house and assorted tents, all helped out in the vegetable gardens, or worked at producing various craft items for the local tourist trade. All in all Josh found them to be a colourful, likeable bunch of people.

Over coffee and a second joint, Tarquin suddenly said, "Okay Josh, so how much do you want then? – ask and it shall be given – seek and you shall find – knock and it will be opened unto you – for the right amount of money of course!" Many of those present laughed, but Josh found himself rather disquieted. He knew he'd heard that somewhere before. It seemed to mean something deeper to him but he didn't know what. "Where's that from, that saying about ask, seek etc? Josh requested, "I've heard it before somewhere." - "It's from the bible," Tarquin replied, "Mathew chapter seven, verse seven. My father has it on a wooden plaque above the mantelpiece, but don't worry my friend, I'm not religious or anything!" Everybody laughed again.

Josh concluded his business, and the visit was at an end. He was warmly invited to drop by anytime. Saying his goodbyes, he made his way back out towards where his car was parked and Boots was patiently waiting.

Ever watchful, Chakine followed on, sword in hand. He knew the two large demons were still on the roof, although because of the angle, they couldn't see him yet. Like greased lightning he launched himself into the air, coming at them from the gable end. Their two heads barely had time to turn before they were separated from the leathery bodies. The Angel used his momentum to continue the dive, straight down and into the open-ended outbuilding where he knew elementals were seeking refuge. His sword flashed as he twisted and turned dispatching swift and righteous justice. Without breaking his flight he exited the other end of the building, having sent them all to join the legions of demons already bound in chains. Those dark spirits awaiting their eternal torture in the lake of fire.

On the drive home the young postman felt a strange mixture of emotion. He was glad to have found somewhere he could get some decent smoke, and pleased to have made some new acquaintances, but this bible verse troubled him. It just wouldn't go away. "Ask and it will be given. What will be given?" he thought, "and what are you supposed to look for, and what's this door thing all about?"

Much as The Grey Ones had enjoyed the atmosphere at Maen-Du, and the soothing proximity of so many other demonic influences, they were rather perturbed at the way their target kept repeating this filthy bible verse to himself. They could clearly see the two Spasmoides still firmly in place and were at an agitated loss to understand. They hadn't witnessed the Angel's foray, but Josh's preoccupation with this awful scripture was enough to cause considerable consternation. They were even further alarmed when on arrival at the cottage Josh discovered a note pinned to his door. - 'Hi Josh, if you get back in time and fancy a walk this afternoon, I'm at Meredith's – Cheryll'.

Once again, the lust Spasmoide was backfiring on the hapless pair. Josh thought about it for all of two seconds before rushing indoors for a quick 'preen' and splash of breath freshener. Five minutes later he was striding down the track towards Meredith's cottage, with Boots running up and down behind him. The demons dreaded the encounter, but at least for the moment he wasn't reciting this horrible verse from the hated book.

Cheryll opened the door, a vision of loveliness and feminine beauty. Her wide smile was warm and welcoming. "Hi Josh, I'm really glad you could make it, it's a lovely afternoon for a walk." The two demons almost retched as she lent forward and gave him an innocent kiss of greeting on the cheek "Come in, Meredith's out back, but he's going off to town soon so it'll just be you and I for the walk." Josh wanted to somersault! A chance to get her alone and weave the old 'Fishmen magic'. "Oooh!" he thought, " I can almost taste those lips already." as his imagination took him even further down the road of unbridled lust. "Why don't you pop out and see Meredith while I get my boots on?" Cheryll suggested. The demons were relieved to be quickly exiting the cottage, as they loathed the atmosphere of a white liter's home. Chakine had greeted Yolan, and now did likewise with Salzar as Josh approached Meredith who was busy chopping logs. The older man was perspiring a little but enjoying his task. He greeted Josh enthusiastically.
Once again the young man was aware of how much he liked this old guy, and wondered why sometimes he was so irritated by him.

Meredith looked him straight in the eye. "Josh, you behave yourself now, with my beautiful little sister." - "Sister?" He thought for a moment, and then realised it must be meant in some religious context. "Oh yes ...er.... of course Meredith, ...you er... don't have to worry on that score, I wouldn't dream of ..." - just then Cheryll appeared in the doorway. "Ready?"

Meredith suggested they took Polly along to keep Boots company and soon the two humans, with their two dogs, two demons and two Angels were disappearing up the track that led to Meredith's favourite place.

Cheryll was well aware of Josh's various uninvited guests. In truth they weren't exactly uninvited, as they'd all gained access through disobedience of God's law. But she had no fear of this young man walking alongside her either, and on top of that she knew that Meredith and the rest of the fellowship would be praying for her protection. She'd made the phone calls to the others earlier. She also knew that right now Meredith was engaged in prayer for her and Josh.

As the little group of seen and unseen beings ascended the hill track, the two humans chatted about all sorts of things. With every step Josh found himself becoming more and more captivated by this beautiful young woman. Everything about her was just right. The way she looked, the sound of her voice and her amazingly warm, friendly and bubbling personality. It was a shame though about the religion thing.

She too was starting to perceive a depth of strength in him, despite the obvious spiritual shortcomings and the fact that he wasn't saved ... yet! She knew she liked him immensely, but she also knew God's will must come first.

It didn't take long until they'd reached Meredith's special place. He'd taken Cheryll there when she first got saved. Since then they would frequently come to this high place to pray over Aberdigan and the surrounding area. Goomelt and Pusto loathed the place and especially the close proximity of Yolan at Cheryll's shoulder. But they had no option in the matter. The two Angels remained alert but comfortably content with the present situation, Yolan close by and Chakine at his customary discreet distance. He looked at the two dark tormentors with Josh and felt it would be very soon now. Very soon indeed.

Sat on Meredith's fallen tree, overlooking the shining blue sea in the bay, the young man and young woman continued to talk, getting to know one another. The effect of the lust Spasmoide seemed to wax and wane in conflict with the prayers of the other believers. Josh felt like he was on some sort of pendulum. At times he just wanted to take her in his arms and kiss her passionately until she succumbed to his base desire. Then, just as quickly he would feel that what he really wanted to do was to hold her tenderly and stroke her beautiful hair. The Grey Ones were ceaseless in their nefarious attempts to incite a greater lust in their subject, but the power of prayer held firm.

Meredith had driven to the home of Dave and Lucy in Aberdigan and had been joined by several other members of the fellowship. Lucy began to get a 'word of knowledge' from The Spirit that the enemy was about to launch a heavy attack on Cheryll. Their collective prayers became even more fervent.

High up in the hills, seated on the fallen tree, Cheryll became aware of an exceedingly evil presence at exactly the same time as Chakine and Yolan were drawing their swords. Swooping out of nowhere the furious form of Kaisis crashed into the backs of the two Grey Ones. His powerful claws locking on to their scrawny necks, he lifted them up shaking them violently, their anguished cries drowned out by the roar of his wrath. Just behind him stood two hundred hate filled warrior demons. Chakine was at Yolan's side in an instant, sensing possible 'Mortal Danger' for his charge. The two Angels stood directly above the heads of the humans, their shields raised and swords at the ready, vastly outnumbered.

Kaisis hurled the two demons to the ground. " Resume your legal position!" he snarled. Chakine raised his sword threateningly. "We are not here to harm your precious Chosen One, Angel," he growled, spitting slime in all directions "This is merely an internal disciplinary matter." With that his claws sliced the backs of the terrified two who were scrambling back to The Position of Influence. They howled in pain. "You know the rules Angel, let them back!" Chakine shot a glance to Yolan who gave a slight nod of his head. The warrior Angel then took a pace backwards and stood his ground. Goomelt and Pusto scrambled into place whilst the horde of demons began an Antichrist chant. The point of Chakine's sword was two inches from Pusto's terror stricken throat. Kaisis rasped "You are in violation angel, that is not a discreet distance." Chakine calmly replied " The law of Mortal Danger, demon," he looked directly into the evil eyes "Do you wish to challenge it?"

The Antichrist chant was getting louder and more frenzied as Kaisis bent down, his huge ugly head between the two demons. His claw-like hands dropped something into their laps. "Use these, and make them work you useless scum!" He took several steps backwards joining the still chanting horde. Goomelt and Pusto lost no time in hurling these powerful new Spasmoides at the back of Joshua's neck. Three of them stuck immediately. Two 'Rapes' and one 'Murder'. Chakine knew he was 'stretching it' remaining where he was. He would obey his Master's law. However, he absolutely knew he could not interfere with Joshua Fishmen's free will.

As she felt the evil presence, Cheryll had begun to pray in tongues under her breath. Josh, thinking she was crying had reached out and put his arm around her just as the first 'Rape' Spasmoide had made contact. Lust exploded in his being and the desire to have her began to eliminate reason. She was saying "No Josh, not now!" because she knew she needed to pray against the evil presence, not realising what was happening to him. The demon chant was building to a fierce and furious crescendo, and Josh was on the very point of committing a serious sexual assault, when, borne on the prayers of the believers, sixty warrior Angels crashed into the chanting demon throng. Their swords cutting righteous swathes of light through evil leathery skin and scales. Captain Cherno and his brothers wreaked a swift and devastating judgement fuelled by the prayers of Meredith and the fellowship. The Demons broke ranks, fleeing in all directions, on into the darker voids of their dimension.

At that instant Josh awoke as if from a spell, the new Spasmoides falling from his neck and disappearing in a puff of brown smoke as they hit the ground. Although she knew there had been an enemy attack, and something acutely evil had been around, thankfully Cheryll had no idea regarding what Josh had been about to do to her. Suddenly she was aware again of the warm sunlight on her face, and the restoration of peace to the situation.

Josh however was horrified. He knew exactly what he had been about to do, although he also knew that it wasn't him. It was some sort of extraneous influence, almost as if something had taken over. Then he remembered the time back at Christmas in Ray's house. Similar feelings had nearly caused him to assault Zara. He remembered he'd had to grip the arms of the chair because of an intense unbridled sexual urge. Aware that something strange had occurred he turned to Cheryll and said "What the heck was that?" She looked at him with quite the most serious expression he'd so far seen on her lovely face. "Well, I know it sounds weird Josh, but something very evil just attacked us. Its okay, it's gone now, the blood of Jesus has protected us." Part of him wanted to laugh at this statement, but another increasingly aware part of him somehow knew that what she was saying was correct. Sensing some sort of inner turmoil in the young man, Cheryll continued "May I ask you some questions Josh, like a sort of little quiz? – But you <u>must</u> answer truthfully, okay?" - "Okay." he replied, expecting something like 'truth or dare'. "Before I do though I just want to fill you in on what you might call some background information relevant to the quiz, alright?" Josh was intrigued, "Go ahead."

"Way, way back" she began, "God gave a set of rules to mankind, basically about how we should live. Ten relatively simple rules. You may have heard them referred to as 'The Ten Commandments'?" Josh gave a nod of acknowledgement, "Yeah, I heard of them." - "Well," she continued, "If everyone followed these rules we'd have a pretty much perfect society. Trouble is; no one can. Not one human person, not ever, not back then and certainly not now. . . . Strange isn't it, no one can manage to keep just ten simple rules." Josh sat silently listening. "Only problem is Josh, at the end of your life God will judge you on whether or not you kept His ten simple rules." The young man looked vaguely uncomfortable. "I'll tell you what the rules are, and then we'll do the quiz, yeah?" - "Okay" replied Josh, looking somewhat apprehensive. Cheryll looked warmly into his eyes for a second, and said, "Okay, here we go. This is my easy to understand version.

One, God should <u>always</u> be first in your life.
Two, Never worship or bow down to anything but God.
Three, Don't use your lips to dishonour God.
Four, Don't neglect the things of God, especially a day each week dedicated to Him.
Five, Honour your father and mother.
Six, Do not murder.
Seven, Do not commit adultery.
Eight, Do not steal.
Nine, Do not lie.
Ten, Don't desire what belongs to someone else.

There they are Josh, ten fairly straightforward simple little rules." - "Yeah, I've heard some of them before, I think." he answered falteringly. Cheryll, full of compassion, continued, "Right then, lets try the little quiz, and remember you must answer truthfully or it's a waste of time." - "I'll be truthful" he replied. Wondering what was coming next.
"Okay, Josh, have you <u>always</u> put God first in your life?" He answered straight away "No" - "Have you ever worshipped anything other than God?" again he said "No, but I don't believe in God anyway." - "You realise that you can be 'worshipping' a band when you have your arms raised in adoration at a gig. Or worshipping on the terraces singing to your favourite football team. If you're masturbating whilst looking at pictures or movies, that is a form of worship of the object of your lust. Not to mention the love affairs some people have with their cars, houses, and material things etc."

He was quite shocked to hear her speak about masturbation so forthrightly, knowing she was a Christian, but at the same time he understood the truth of her statement. "I guess the answer's 'yes' then!" - "Okay, have you ever used the name of God or Jesus as a swear word?" Josh thought for a moment and suddenly realised the amount of times he'd said "Oh for Christ's sake" or "Jesus flipping Christ" or even worse. "Well yes, but I never really meant anything by it." said Josh, trying to get off the hook. "That's a yes as well then." Cheryll continued, "Have you always put aside a day a week to pursue the things of God?" - "No" he said resignedly. "What about your mum and dad, have you always honoured them?" Josh had a sudden vivid rush of long forgotten memories, the times he had 'slagged off' his father to his friends after he'd been beaten or severely punished for some inconsequential misdemeanour. "No, I haven't always honoured them, but . . " Cheryll stopped him with a raised hand. "It's not about the why's." she said. Josh's head dropped for a moment, then she said "Well I feel pretty sure you haven't murdered or killed anyone." she was smiling broadly. Josh wasn't. There was a long silence as another vivid episode was pile driving its way into his memory.

  It was the gulf war, they were on an offensive push when they came under heavy small arms fire and were pinned down in a single storey flat roofed building. The bombardment was incessant from one particular three-storey house two hundred yards away. Josh was section lance corporal and had sanctioned the unclipping of phosphorus tipped tracer rounds, which were every fifth one in the belt of machine gun ammo. They would literally glow in the dark so that you could see where your bullets were going at night. In essence they were little missiles of fire.

  They had made up a belt entirely of tracer and raked the house with a prolonged burst, till smoke began pouring out of the windows. Eventually the door had burst open and burning people spilled out onto the street. The soldiers had all been so hyped up that they loosed several bursts of automatic fire before realising it was women and children.

Burning women and children. The memory still haunted him, but so far he'd suppressed it and justified it by saying to himself "Hey, war's a dirty business."

    Cheryll had picked up on the heaviness during Josh's silence, and felt a little sad, but at the same time happy because she was aware things were getting through to the young man. She decided to move on without waiting for his answer. "Adultery?" he was about to say "No," but then he remembered Cathy Hancock, so instead he tried to justify it with "Yeah, but only once!" - "Ever stolen anything, even if it was only a pencil from work, or an apple from somebody's tree?" He remembered his raids on Patel's corner shop with Ray, along with many other less than honest episodes. "Yes." - "Have you ever told a lie?" - "No." he said, mimicking Pinocchio's nose growing rapidly, then sighing, "Yes, Cheryll, I have." - "And lastly," she said, her face absolutely deadpan, "have you ever looked at someone else's partner with lust, or desired to have something that belonged to another person?" Josh took a deep breath and exhaled loudly, then honestly said, "Yes, often." She held up both hands. "You scored ten out of ten Josh, unfortunately the only pass mark in this test is zero out of ten!" Josh looked perplexed. Cheryll continued,

"When you die, and that's the one certainty for all of us, and God judges you against His ten simple rules, will He find you innocent or guilty?" - "Well," said Josh pathetically, "I hope He'll find me innocent, that is if He exists!" - "How could He find you innocent Josh?" she said forcefully, "you've broken all of His commandments." - "Yeah, but I'm not really a bad person, I didn't mean to break them to piss God off or anything."

Cheryll looked at him with the love of Jesus overflowing in her heart. "Josh, if you were done for say, housebreaking or robbery, or even just speeding, and you found yourself in court, do you think it would be any sort of defence to say to the judge, 'But I didn't mean it your honour, and actually I'm a nice person!" She folded her arms and looked at him, she could almost see the conviction flowing over him and knew the Holy Spirit was moving. Unfolding her arms she leaned forward and gently but firmly said, "You broke the law! The judge would sentence you accordingly!" Josh was staring at the ground.

She continued. "God is a pure, holy and righteous God, and He works to a finite set of rules. In one sense Josh it doesn't matter that you broke all ten laws, because the bible says if you break just one you are guilty of them all!" He looked up at her. Now he was a forlorn and troubled man, aware of his condition, and under conviction before a God he wasn't sure he even believed in. "So," said Cheryll repeating her earlier question, "If you were to die tonight, and God ultimately judged you, would he find you innocent or guilty?" Joshua Fishmen struggling with it, but now aware of his sinful state, looked her in the eye and said "Guilty."

Goomelt and Pusto shrieked, cursed, blasphemed and ranted, whilst the two Angels smiled at each other. Suddenly, seemingly out of nowhere, a very low flying jet fighter screamed across the sky from behind, right over the little group's heads. The noise was deafening and the two humans almost jumped out of their skins. It seemed to bring the situation to a natural conclusion and Cheryll discerned it was time to 'shut up'.

"Wow, that thing came in so fast, literally out of the blue, and the noise! My ears are still ringing". Josh was slightly shaken, and so was his female companion. It was a horrendously loud and truly soul shaking, frightening, experience.

"Josh, that's just what it will be like when God's judgement comes, swift, terrifying and totally unexpected." She wanted to say more but felt constrained by The Spirit and so held her peace.

Changing the subject she continued "It's the only trouble with living here, as soon as the weather is nice the fighter jets use these hills as a training ground!" Josh was still musing over the implications of his transgression of these laws, even though he didn't really believe in their supposed author. It was a dilemma countless thousands had faced before him.

Summoning the dogs from their exploration of the undergrowth, they began their descent back to Meredith's cottage in the valley far below. Cheryll was quietly praying, and rays of invisible multi coloured light were bathing Josh with gentle revelation. The God who loved him so was beginning to remove the scales from his eyes. Goomelt and Pusto winced, again desiring to 'get the hell outa there'. Nonetheless they remained at their post, for fear of Kaisis far outweighed their immediate discomfort.

As the young couple walked back down the track, side by side in comfortable silence, Josh found himself looking around with new eyes at the flowers, bushes and trees. The two little dogs, oblivious of human complexity, jostled and played scampering in never ending circles. Floating high above, a Buzzard cried, and Josh stopped for a moment and looked up at this creature suspended in the air as it glided in lazy circles on the rising thermals. He looked down the valley, across a carpet of myriad shades of green. He looked out to sea at the shining white crested waves, then he turned his head slowly looking from left to right and was overwhelmed by the wonder and beauty of it all. Cheryll had stopped a few feet further down the track and was looking up at him quizzically.

The sudden realisation that none of this awesome beauty could have just come into being by itself, cascaded into his senses. In that moment he clearly saw the whole evolution thing for the unequivocal farce it really is. This was all designed and had been created, he could see it so clearly now. He plucked up a blade of grass and studied it, concluding that he could spend the rest of his entire life trying, and he would never be able to make one blade of grass and make it grow. For the first time he was truly perceiving the beauty of creation, God's creation. And that beauty included the stunning young woman not ten feet from him. He studied her for a few moments as her quizzical expression melted into a broad smile, and he said quite loudly "There is a God Cheryll, there is a God, and He made all this!"

She wanted to cartwheel down the hill, and if she had done so Joshua would have probably followed suit. Instead she just walked, praising God all the way to the bottom, as Josh walked alongside her still lost in the realisation of his new discovery.

By the time the two reached Meredith's cottage, he had returned from the prayer session at David and Lucy's. Cheryll was so excited that the older man knew something had transpired, but he waited until Josh went home to hear all about it from his favourite girl.

From that time on Goomelt and Pusto had relatively little influence on Josh. Even when he smoked marijuana, his thoughts were predominantly with regard to things appertaining to God. Although on a couple of occasions under its insidious influence, lustful thoughts towards Cheryll had managed to get the better of him.

Though still firmly attached, the two Spasmoides were slowly shrinking and the little demons were sorely afraid. Nothing they threw adhered anymore, and they were feeling quite unwell from the continued proximity of the foul white liters. In truth the only thing holding them there was their abject terror of Kaisis. That was only marginally beaten by their dread of their ultimate destination, the terrible, eternal, Lake of Fire. The one track elementals living inside of Josh were becoming extremely agitated too, but their tack was to lie low. Meredith had deemed it prudent to allow The Holy Spirit to do His work on Joshua, and so he and Cheryll gave the young man some space for a few days.

------ O ------

Josh started his new job in the Aberdigan Postal Depot and was enjoying it immensely. The guys working there had made him feel welcome and one of the team, and his new delivery round took him to farms, down long tracks and to all sorts of picturesque locations. For the first two days he was accompanied by another postman, whilst learning his new route, but he had soon picked it up, even though his pathetic miss-pronunciation of certain place names caused great mirth amongst his new Welsh colleagues.

There was however one small problem. Boots. On his second day his supervisor had made it quite clear that it was against regulations for Josh to have the little animal in his van, and that in future Boots must remain at home. Later that morning, having finished his round he had bumped into Meredith in the Castle Café, and over coffee, upon hearing of Josh's dilemma, his landlord had offered to have Boots whilst he was at work. "Oh, she'll be great company for Polly, especially as they get on so well." the older man said. Josh had gratefully accepted the offer.

Since his experience with Cheryll, he was still deeply musing over his realisation that there must be a God. He spent long hours deep in conversation with himself regarding various issues he still had about the whole thing. He still didn't understand what 'Ask and it will be given, seek and you will find, knock and it will be opened' <u>really</u> meant, though he said it to himself frequently. But all in all he was much happier. He loved his new job. The fact that his round mostly took him along tree lined lanes festooned with flowers, and then down private tracks to so many beautifully located homes, was a constant joy. Especially when he'd think about the hectic, soulless rat race he'd left behind in Essex.

One place though made him feel distinctly uneasy. 'Y Ddraig Goch'. It was down a long winding track bordered on either side by very thickly planted conifers. These kept the light out and rendered the ground beneath them lifeless and eerie. To the left, rising high above the firs, a craggy rock strewn hill ascended to the 'Dragon's Back' and Josh had realised that Tarquin and the others lived somewhere on the other side of the mountain.

The track concluded at a large dismal looking old house, where the faded curtains seemed to be perpetually closed. Even on a sunny summer's morning, this place remained in heavy shade, due to its location. It seemed to Josh to be an old quarry that had been hewn out of the mountainside. The stark grey stone rose up a hundred feet or so, dwarfing the dark, bleak, building, and almost encasing it in a semi circle of gloomy, lifeless granite. So far, he had never seen anyone here, although there was often a fairly new 4x4 parked at the side of the house. He often had a sense of being watched and felt a disquieting 'something' that always made him want to deliver the letters and get out of there as quickly as possible. The letters were always addressed to a Mr. De'Ath at: 'The Headquarters of The Temple of The Golden Dawn'. He knew the name was somehow familiar, but just couldn't place it. When he enquired of the guys back at the depot, he discovered he wasn't the only one who didn't like delivering to 'Y Ddraig Goch' – The Red Dragon.

Unseen, inside the dilapidated old house in a large and darkened room devoid of furniture, a huge Pentagram, the symbol of the Horned Hunter of the Night – Satan Himself – The Old Dragon, was marked out on the floor, with black candles at each of the five points.

------ O ------

Since Josh's perception that things had been created, (which had in fact been a divine enlightenment) the small group of believers had prayed fervently for the young man. They were well aware that like so many others, his mind, ethics, values and conscience had been blunted by years of subtle (and sometimes not so subtle) enemy attack. His philosophies were as full of holes as a Swiss cheese, and he was decidedly double minded. Like so many other people who wouldn't dream of stealing from their friends or neighbours, he would, without a second thought, steal from companies. False insurance claims or stuff so cheap as to be obviously stolen, these things he pursued with impunity. The philosophy was "Oh well, they can afford it, look at how much profit they make." or "They steal from us, why shouldn't we do the same to them?" The world of Joshua Fishmen operated on a set of values very far removed from those of its creator.

------ O ------

One evening Josh had found himself in the peculiar situation of praying this prayer. "Look God, I'm not even really sure if You're there or not, or if You can hear me – but if You are there then I think it's important. I realise that all this stuff didn't make itself and I'm pretty sure that I didn't just 'happen' – so, please tell me what to do."

His two demons were shrieking blasphemies and curses in desperation, as they realised the prayers of the believers were out gunning the power of their Spasmoides.

At that moment, Joshua started to understand what 'Ask and it shall be given, seek and you shall find, knock and it will be opened to you', actually meant. At least, he understood that he had asked, and that must mean that he was somehow seeking for something, though right now he wasn't sure exactly what it was, although he couldn't shake off this feeling of being guilty and somehow tarnished. The 'knock and it shall be opened to you' bit remained a mystery.

Over the course of the next ten days he'd visited with Meredith several times. Their arrangement was that Josh dropped Boots off in the morning, leaving her in a cosy little basket in the woodshed, until Meredith, arising an hour or so later, at around 7.00a.m, would let her out to frolic with Polly.

She had howled for the first couple of days, but soon got used to the arrangement once she was sure her master would be returning. Knowing she had hours of play with Polly to come, she would curl up contentedly as Josh left for his early morning shifts. When he returned around midday, he would invariably have some sort of theological question for his mentor, and that frequently resulted in an invite for coffee and a discussion. Meredith was still holding back somewhat under the very real conviction that God had purposed a definite time for this young man's salvation. He was aware that the bible says <u>now</u> is the time for salvation, but that 'now' would be when The Holy Spirit moved on Joshua's spirit.

So far they had discussed all sorts of things that were 'sticking points' for Josh, with his as yet limited understanding, but the wisdom of the older man could clearly see him being gently led towards the ultimate freedom of the knowledge of the truth.

Josh posed today's question. "If God is supposed to love everybody, then why are there millions of people starving to death in lots of places?" It was a genuine and heartfelt question, and one that Meredith had heard many times before. He puffed thoughtfully on the ever present briar pipe. "When God created mankind he gave us a free will, we've already discussed how Satan conned the first two people into using their free will to disobey God, yes?" Josh nodded his affirmation. "Well," Meredith continued "Your free will is allowing you to sit cross legged in that chair, and pick up your coffee when you want to. Think for a moment, how would it be if you didn't have this amazing thing called free will, what would you be like?" Josh mused, rubbing his chin for a few seconds and then answered, " I suppose I'd be like a robot or something." the older man smiled. "That's exactly it Josh," he moved his arms in a jerky staccato fashion and mimicked the sound of a robot voice " like-a-robot." The young postman smiled at his pathetic attempt at robotic emulation but nonetheless got the picture. Meredith continued, "So this free will which we take for granted is quite an amazing thing, it gives us the ability to make choices." He paused and took a sip of coffee. "Now, there's enough food in the world to feed everybody, in fact God has provided enough resources for every person to have food and a roof over their head. There is no doubt as to this. The trouble is, that some greedy people are fabulously wealthy and own vast holdings and have huge reserves of cash, hoarded at the great expense of others. They have ostensibly done this via their free will." Josh interjected "So why then did God create us with this free will, surely it would have been better to just have us obey Him, like you said the Angels do?" - "Well that's a reasonable point Josh, but had He done that we wouldn't have been able to love Him, or anyone, for that matter." The young man looked puzzled. "Okay, let's put it this way. Hypothetically speaking, I could put a gun against your head and make you do virtually anything. Except. . . love me! Because love is something we each have to choose to do. You can't be made to love someone, but you <u>can</u> choose to love them, by an act of will. Your <u>free</u> will. So if we didn't have free will, there could be no love. Free will validates love. If God had, by an act of creation, forced us to 'love' Him, then it wouldn't be love! He gave us the ability to choose to accept Him or reject Him, to love Him or not to love Him. That's the only way it's valid!" Josh understood, "Yes, I can see that, it makes sense." - "Unfortunately," Meredith added, "because of the fall, where man became separated from the close relationship with God that He had originally intended, a side effect if you like, was that mankind, now out on his own so to speak, used his free will to go the wrong way. So the answer to your original question about 'why are all these poor folk starving' etc, is man's free will, <u>not</u> God's neglect or lack of provision!"

Goomelt and Pusto just hated, loathed and despised hearing God's truth expounded by this nauseous human, whilst Chakine and Salzar grew ever more confident that soon this young man would be firmly in their master's Kingdom.

------ O ------

In Beijing, Zara continued her bedside vigil. The doctors were confident and had assured her that one day soon Ray would regain consciousness. She already knew that his physical condition was going to be all right, but she found the waiting very difficult. She missed her children terribly, and despite the wonderful treatment she had received from all concerned, she was desperately lonely. However through it all there was a quiet, unruffled sense of calm, with which she was unfamiliar. Back in Wales the believers continued to pray.

------ O ------

Josh had so many questions, but now he was allowing Meredith to answer them. Previously, like many others in his position, he would ask something and then halfway through the proffered explanation would ask something else, showing that he wasn't really interested in the answer, only in scoring points and thus deflecting having to acknowledge his sinful state in the light of God's law. Now however, since his afternoon with Cheryll, he knew he was in need, and as such was listening intently. Not only that, he'd bought himself an old bible from the second hand shop, and was avidly reading it, much to the chagrin of his Grey minders.

"You know Meredith, I find it really hard to accept that people lived to the incredible ages the book says, you know, Adam lived for 930 years etc, surely then that's a misprint, or rather a mistranslation?" Meredith puffed on his pipe, sending sweet smelling clouds of smoke swirling round the room, Josh really rather liked the aroma, even though it was one of Meredith's less endearing habits. "Okay, I'll have to explain a few things first, to paint the picture so to speak, but stick with it and hopefully by the time I've finished it will make sense." Josh stretched his arms out, clapped his hands and sat back in the chair, all ears. Meredith began. "When God created the Earth, He created it perfectly, with everything in balance from the smallest microbe up to man, the final pinnacle of His creation. The whole set up was in absolute harmony. Everything vibrating in sympathy with everything else, a perfectly tiered and ordered symbiotic creation designed to be self-sustaining in perpetuity." he puffed on the pipe, again filling the room with blue aromatic clouds.

"Scientists are now saying that they think there may have been a skin of water around the Earth. Not surprising, when the bible clearly states it to have been so! Yes, the Earth was originally encased in a skin of water"

'And God said "Let there be space between the waters, to separate water from water" And so it was, God made this space to separate the waters above from the waters below. And God called the space 'sky'. This happened on the second day'. [Genesis Ch1 v 6-8.]

Josh was looking really interested and listening intently. "This water was not on the surface, although there were also seas. This water was up above the atmosphere, in the sky! Now, we know that Saturn for instance has rings of gas around it, and other planets have their own peculiarities, so why should a skin of water having been around the Earth seem so strange? As I'm sure you're aware Josh, water refracts or bends sunlight, so it's reasonable to assume that when the suns rays shone upon the skin of water encasing the globe, they would have 'bent' around, thus warming those parts of the planet not directly in the sun. The warm air would also have been contained by the 'ceiling' of water, and the heat kept in." Josh's body language indicated his mental assent.

"Also with this skin of water, which is reckoned to have been about three miles thick, the atmosphere between the spinning Earth and the water above would have been very stable. Nowadays because the Earth is denser than its atmosphere, we have what we have termed 'weather'. As the Earth spins we have all these varying pressures and wind patterns which in turn cause conditions to vary from day to day. Back then, in God's original plan, the whole Earth would have been a wonderful balanced place of temperature equilibrium. Constant favourable conditions. In other words, just the way the bible describes the paradise that was Eden. This skin of water accounts for the fact that fossilised tropical plants have been found at the poles, and many other anomalies science is at a loss to explain."

Josh interjected. "So basically what you're saying is: the Earth that we live on now is not how it was originally designed to be?" - "Yes that's right," continued Meredith "but it's not only the Earth that isn't how it was originally designed to be, it's the whole of creation, man, the animal kingdom, all of nature."

'All creation anticipates the day when it will join God's children in glorious freedom from death and decay' [Romans Ch.8 v21]

So how does this relate to people living to fantastic ages?" Josh genuinely enquired. Meredith picked up the thread.

"We were originally created to live forever, if man hadn't sinned. Right in the beginning – Genesis Chapter three verse twenty-two - after Adam and Eve have sinned, God says, 'Let's get them out of the garden in case they eat from the Tree of Life and live forever'. There were these two special trees. The Tree of the Knowledge of Good and Evil and The Tree of Life. He had only told them not to eat from the Tree of the Knowledge of Good and Evil, so they would have been free to eat from The Tree of Life. I'm certain God's intention, until man's free will messed things up, was for us to live forever. Otherwise He certainly would have forbidden them to eat from that also. So consequently the early people lived to great ages. It's also interesting to note that scientists have discovered that air bubbles trapped in Amber from thousands of years ago, are far richer in oxygen than our atmosphere here now. The air was cleaner and way less toxic. And they also know people breathing oxygen rich air heal more quickly and generally have more energy, so that living in that sort of clean environment would have been infinitely superior health wise." - "I still find living 900 plus years at bit hard to swallow." said Josh honestly.

Re-lighting his pipe, Meredith revived his explanation. "Medical science says it doesn't know why we grow old and die. We have within ourselves the propensity to be self re-generating. They know of course what it is that takes place, but they are at a complete loss as to why. Yet the bible says quite clearly in Romans Chapter six, 'The wages of sin is death' – In other words it is this thing called 'sin' that brings about death. Now the early people, it seems got affected in a progressive sort of way and finally died at what to us seems an incredibly old age. But, if man was supposed to live in God's perfect creation forever, then they died at no age at all really."

"So how did just two people populate the entire world? I can't see that Meredith."

"Okay, just for a minute let's take the bible at its word, inasmuch as Adam lived for nine hundred plus years etc, yes?" Josh agreed. "There was no contraception in those days, so Eve would have produced one child per year, let's say she continued producing children for 750 years, (remembering the oxygen and skin of water around the Earth, plus the fact that we were originally designed to live forever). Once you get into about fifty years, those children are all breeding, then at one hundred years the grandchildren are all breeding and when you get to five hundred years you already have hundreds of thousands of people. All from just two beings. You see Josh, the bible is a true account of all things, despite the unlearned opinions those who speak to the contrary."

Josh was sure he had spotted a big hole in Meredith's argument, and the Antichrist Spasmoide was still attached; though losing power. "So what you're in effect saying is that the whole human race comes from incest, which God says is wrong!" he said almost triumphantly. Meredith smiled, again he'd heard this many times before, and knew that the enemy uses the same tired old methods on unbelievers, about the bible being full of contradictions etc. Basically because the lies work. That is until the light of the truth blows them out of the water.

"Actually Josh, at that time as far as God was concerned, there was no such thing as incest, inasmuch as intercourse with your brother or sister or any other close relative only became wrong when God gave the law to Moses, saying it was wrong, much later. It's the law that gives sin its power. Until a thing is declared wrong, to do it is acceptable and not sinful. In fact, I suspect God made that part of the Law because the sin that had entered the human race, was actually beginning to degrade our DNA. Though that is only my personal opinion. I said earlier that Romans tells us 'The wages of sin is death'. In other words it is this thing called sin that brings death, disease, decay and every other manifest attack on what was originally a perfect creation."

"Okay," said Josh, "but what about babies and young children, they haven't done anything, so how can they be sinners?" As Josh spoke these words, Meredith felt an almost overwhelming love for the young man sitting opposite him, and again he could sense the turmoil raging within him.

"It's because you misunderstand what sin is Josh, in the first instance it isn't what you do, rather it's a condition. Think of it like a 'spiritual Aids'. Every single baby born to human parents since Adam and Eve, was, and is, contaminated by this disease. The whole human race has it, and it has separated us from a pure and holy God who hates sin."

Just then there was a knock on the door, it was Cheryll who had felt led by the Spirit to cycle over to Meredith's. She entered the cottage and soon all three were deep in conversation about the things of God.

------ O ------

Goomelt and Pusto were extremely worried. The horrendous white light in the room seemed to be increasing with every minute, and now some of the hidden colours were manifesting as well! They knew they had to make a decision, and soon. It seemed to them that these filthy 'white liters' were drawing their charge closer and closer to believing the 'Lie of the Book'. And they knew that when that situation threatened, it was their duty to summon Kaisis. They also knew however, that their fearsome overlord would see this as failure, and that they would pay a heavy and unmerciful penalty.

The alternative though was instant despatch from the flashing sword of Chakine, should their human accept 'The Lie of the Book'. In reality, they knew that it was now only the immense demonic power of Kaisis who could rescue the situation, and so, with great reticence and trepidation they blew on 'The Horn of Impending Disaster', sending the message out into the blackness.

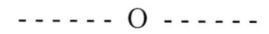

------ O ------

Meredith was aware of a strong presence of The Holy Spirit. Yes, this was it; The Lord's perfect timing in the life of Joshua Fishmen. Tapping his pipe out into the bin next to the Rayburn, he turned to the young man.

"Josh, God didn't leave man in this dilemma, floundering around in a cesspool of sin, separated from Him and without hope. God loves His creation and He loves each one of us despite the things we do. He hates the sin, but loves the sinner, and the bible tells us that God is not willing that anyone should perish, but that all men should come to salvation. So He made a plan, an awesome almost unbelievable plan to put us right with Him again." Josh was motionless listening with every fibre of his being. "He sent His only Son to the Earth to tell us about God's Kingdom, and how He is going to put all things back to rights and do away with sin. But because His laws have been broken, there was a price to pay. A great legally imposed punishment. The penalty for sin, or the 'wages' of sin, or what you get for doing sin, is to die! And remember, everyone is contaminated. Yet God loved us so much He came up with this incredible solution. He sent his own Son to die in our place. To undergo an agonising shameful death as a criminal. And that blood He poured out on the cross, did it! It actually paid the price! For your sin, for my sin, for Cheryll's sin, for the sins of the whole world! This means that for those who accept what Jesus did in their stead, they can now live forever, just like God originally intended, but in the new Kingdom God is going to bring about soon." Josh sat there staring at the floor, his mind whirling with all he'd just heard.

'For God so loved the world, that He gave His only begotten Son, that whosoever believes in Him should not perish but have everlasting life'. [John Ch.3 v 16]

Josh felt very strange as Meredith said, "Would it help if we prayed Josh?" Praying was an alien concept, yet something inside of the young postman desperately wanted to but didn't really know how. At that point The Holy Spirit gave Cheryll a verse, and she quickly looked it up in her bible. Finding it, she read it out loud.

"Behold, I stand at the door and knock. If you hear me calling and open the door I will come in and we will share a meal as friends" [Revelation Ch3 v20]

The power of the white light and its associated colours was intensifying, and the two demons were leaning backwards, as far away as they could get from Josh, without actually relinquishing their position.

The scripture he had just heard was echoing around in his head, and a realisation was dawning. 'Ask, seek, knock, - yes its true - no it's not - yes it is – no its not' It was all happening in Josh's head. He wanted so much to pray, but didn't believe in praying. He wanted to get up and run out of there, but felt he needed to stay. He wanted to tell these 'bible bashers' to get lost and at the same time he wanted them to help him to knock, or open the door or whatever the heck it was that he needed!

Meredith said again, "Josh, do you want to pray?" This time his reply was instant.

"I don't really know how to pray Meredith, please, will you pray?" Josh shut his eyes as the old warrior began, "Lord, I pray that You'll show Josh that You're there, that You love him, and that he needs You in his life."

------ O ------

Way above in the heavenly realm, at The Arc of Prayer, a swirling mass of colour and vibration began, like a boiling pot, to spill and bubble over the edges of a golden bowl. Instantaneously, from out of The Throne Room of God, came a pure shaft of golden light flashing earthward, its destination the mind and heart of Joshua Fishmen.

At the same time Kaisis materialised right behind Joshua in the room on the earth plane, sandwiching the two demons between him and the human. Above the house a thousand demons formed a 'dome of darkness' as Kaisis utilised every ounce of his evil power to bind the heart and mind of this 'Chosen One'. Chakine, Yolan and Salzar, swords drawn and shields raised, were ready to defend their respective charges, but they also knew the rules. At a time like this when the darkness officially held 'The Position of Influence' the Area Commander had the right to try and influence the outcome by working on the mind and emotions of the 'subject'. Chakine, under the 'Mortal Danger' rule had come to Joshua's side, and looking directly at the large foul demon said calmly, "Physically harm him demon, and I will despatch you."

------ O ------

On the earth plane, the room was in total silence, both Cheryll and Meredith praying under their breath. Shortly after Meredith had prayed that God would show Josh His love, the young man had started to feel all sorts of things he couldn't account for. His breathing started to go haywire, as if he'd been running, and he was aware that he was shaking too, although he had no idea why. Then he began to perspire, feeling hot and cold. The room was in silence and he felt completely, totally, and utterly, alone.

Suddenly he was aware that the corners of the room were getting very, very dark and an oppressive feeling came upon him. He felt some sort of battle was taking place in his mind as this dome of darkness descended upon him. It was as if there were a pendulum inside of him taking him from light to dark, yes to no, and all the while the oppressive darkness pushed down. He was not afraid, but it certainly was weird. But then it suddenly got freaky. What felt like two steel arms wrapped around him and pulled him back into the chair and he could barely breathe as Kaisis exerted every ounce of evil power he possessed. The dome of darkness was almost touching him and he felt as if he was about to pass out.

In the sky outside, Captain Cherno and his warriors, were in formation around the glorious shaft of light that was boring like a drill down through the tightly knit dome of demons. The warrior Angels were cutting, slashing and thrusting their swords into the evil formation. Their steadfast resolve won through, and the dome collapsed with demons swooping and diving off in all directions pursued by sword wielding fighters full of righteous indignation. In that instant, the shaft of light entered the mind of Joshua Fishmen, and he knew he needed Jesus in his life. The two 'steel arms' were still about him, and it was difficult to breathe. He had to fight to get the words out, he had to fight very hard! Chakine's sword was pointed directly at the throat of Kaisis, as he monitored Josh's well being. It was a full ten seconds before Josh almost shouted the words.

"Jesus, please come into my life and forgive my sins, take over and sort me out - please!"

Instantly, a great rushing spiral of light, fire and wind enveloped him from above, spinning all around. He could also hear the sound of Angelic voices, as the spiral sensation rushed up and down his body from the top of his head to his toes and back again. He could see flames swirling around him. Kaisis's iron grip was instantly blasted away and he cunningly wheeled off to the left and sped into the darkness.

In one lightning manoeuvre, Chakine's sword removed Goomelt and Pusto's heads, consigning them in chains to the underworld, before they even had a chance to move at all. A single red tipped Angel feather fluttered, spiralling gently downward in the space where the two demons had been half a second before. Chakine caught it in the palm of his hand and tucked it into his belt. The Angel was deeply satisfied.

For Josh, right at that moment, it was as if a turtle shell he'd had around him for all his life had exploded into ten thousand pieces. It just fragmented giving him an instant, tangible, freedom. As he stood up with flames of fire dancing all around him, he was laughing and crying at the same time, and he felt as if he was floating several inches above the floor. Cheryll jumped up and came to put her arms around him, but when she touched him she got a 'jolt'. Meredith too, putting his hand on Josh's shoulder, felt like he'd received a mild electric shock.

The three Angels were praising God and adding their voices to those of their brothers in the heavenly courts who were rejoicing over another sinner saved. Another newly redeemed life purchased by the precious blood of Jesus.

Chakine was very happy in an Angel sort of way. He'd never doubted that eventually his young charge would make the right choice, he just didn't like having to allow demons to manipulate humans. However, when the human in question transcended God's law, rules were rules, and Angels always obeyed. As he looked again at the young man, shining in the glorious light of new birth, his memories of a small boy in a large, cold, and grey stone church, came flooding back.

He rejoiced in the faithfulness and wisdom of his Master who had implanted part of His word deep in the child's innermost being.

A 'key' phrase that had indeed eventually caused him to Ask, Seek and Knock, and had brought him, washed, cleansed and forgiven, into The Kingdom of God.

< < < < - - - END OF CHAPTER FOUR - - - > > > >

The Dragonmaster

CHAPTER 5   **The Angharad Legacy**

Two months had passed from the day of Joshua's salvation. Two months in which he'd undergone an amazing and radical transformation. He was truly Born Again, or, more clearly, Born from Above as the translation should really read.

Solely on the strength of his acceptance of what Jesus had done for him at the cross, he had been forgiven all sin, accepted, washed clean, regenerated, rejuvenated and now had The Holy Spirit living within him. He had begun to learn how to pray and was realising that prayer is a powerful weapon when used in line with the will of God.

Meredith and Cheryll had helped him enormously and he was keen to learn and devour all he could with regard to God's word and the things of God. He had also met with Dave and Lucy and the other members of the little independent band of believers, and had felt welcome and totally accepted.

For a few weeks he had continued to smoke joints to relax after work, or to get a good night's sleep. But after God had spoken very clearly to him one Saturday morning, that particular 'hang on' from the old life was curtailed too. It had transpired like this.

It was the weekend and Josh had the day off, so he'd lain in until 9.00am, drifting in a cosy world of thoughts and dreams. Outside, the sun was caressing the earth with a warm hug, This promised to make the proposed afternoons jaunt to the beach a memorable one. He and Cheryll, plus a few of the younger ones from the fellowship had arranged it earlier in the week at the prayer meeting. They would hook up at 1.30pm.

Josh lay there thinking of Cheryll, and smiled. He realised he was falling in love with her and felt good about it. He had already resolved to treat her with the utmost respect, and had read what the bible teaches with regard to how men should conduct themselves around young women. Then something said to him 'A joint would be nice' and he found himself agreeing, and very soon he was reclining on a sun lounger in the morning sunshine, a cup of tea in his hand and a joint between his lips. He still retained some of his uninvited guests, and, as the consciousness enhancing marijuana took its insidious effect, they began to exert their one dimensional influence.

Quite suddenly he found himself imagining what Cheryll would look like in a bikini. But instead of dismissing the rogue thought he began to dwell on it. Consequently, the spirit of lust he was still carrying wove its dark spell with whisperings and lewd imagery, until Josh was thoroughly aroused and following a line of thought and actions displeasing to the Holy Spirit.

He realised what was happening and stopped, exerting his will over the other influences. "Lord I'm sorry, please forgive me." he said, horrified at how very easily the voice of lust had managed to sway him from the path of righteousness. He was stunned to hear God immediately reply. "My son, you can't expect to hear only from Me whilst you continue to smoke this stuff." The inner voice he heard so clearly was loving, yet authoritative, factual yet not condemning. He was thoroughly convicted and that night burnt the remaining dope in the fireplace. He went on to learn from Meredith about the way dark spirits work, and spent long hours reading his new bible and digesting the food therein. Any questions he had, [and there were many], were usually adequately and skilfully explained to him by the older man.

On two occasions, as the Holy Spirit had revealed things, Meredith had cast out an array of elemental spirits. Lust, pride, violence and dishonesty, to name but a few. His mentor had also explained that although many Christians didn't believe a Born Again person could have indwelling spirits, this was a false and dangerous assumption and not at all based on reality. Some believers maintained it was impossible for the Holy Spirit to share the same space as evil spirits. Whilst in one sense this is true, what they were failing to apprehend was the fact that in a regenerated person, the Holy Spirit dwells in the spirit area. That is the part that is connected to heaven and allows the believer to 'Come boldly to the throne of grace' – [Hebrews Ch.4v16] - and to interact and have fellowship with God once again. Just as God had originally intended in the Garden of Eden.

"Obviously," Meredith had said, "demons and dark entities can't be connected to heaven in the same sense, or share the same lines of communication as the Holy Spirit - Evil spirits dwell in the flesh and operate through our five senses. The Holy Spirit dwells in our spirit. Two completely different realms."

Josh felt it made sense that a person who has been wandering around in Satan's kingdom for say 27 years, and then gets saved, is highly likely to have picked up spiritual infection during his or her time in the wilderness disobeying God's laws. Also, Meredith pointed out that the bible says the 'Gifts of the Spirit' are given for the edification of the body of Christ, and that the body of Christ is comprised of those who believe. So if Christians can't have evil spirits why then did God give 'the discerning of spirits' as one of the gifts to help believers be free of bondage to Satan? Everything the older man taught him, Josh weighed up, and looked at for himself in God's word. And all of it seemed sound to him.

Some six weeks after his salvation, he was sitting at home reading from the book of Acts, Chapter two, which describes how on the day of Pentecost the apostles were gathered together for breakfast in the room above an inn. His mouth fell open as he read, "Suddenly there was a mighty rushing wind, and tongues of fire descended on each of them" He read, re-read and then read it again. This was unbelievable! He said out loud to no one in particular, "That's what happened to me!" Then he read on a little further to discover that everyone was 'filled with the Holy

Spirit and began speaking in tongues!' So he enquired of the Lord "Father, I know that this describes what happened to me, but why did I not 'speak in tongues'?"

Two days later he was sitting in the bath scrubbing his back, when suddenly a cascade of words seemed to bubble up from his innermost being and he began to speak out in a strange language he had never learnt. He sat there just praising God in this wonderful new prayer language 'till the bath water went cold!

Joshua Fishmen learned many new things, with much more to understand. His earthly mentor recognised that God was putting the young man through some sort of 'crash course', and that daily he was increasing in spirituality and knowledge of the word.

It seemed that the Holy Spirit was distributing to Josh almost the whole range of gifts, and Meredith was at pains to point out that a gift is exactly just that. It is freely given by God, unmerited, gratis, and totally unearned. He verbally underlined this statement, lest as the recipient, Josh should become full of pride. He also carefully pointed out that God's word, in referring to true believers says, "By their <u>fruits</u> you shall know them." <u>Not</u> by their gifts. And that fruit has to develop and grow before it is palatable. Also, that the fruit of the Holy Spirit is available to every believer by an act of will and obedience.

Josh soon learned that love, joy, peace, patience, kindness, goodness, gentleness, faithfulness and self-control are the essence of Christian living. They are the very building blocks of a stable and caring society and the potential fulfilment of God's law.

Chakine never left Josh's shoulder nowadays. He was glad to be back in the Position of Influence, and he, Yolan and Salzar, along with the other guardians protecting the rest of the small fellowship, remained particularly alert. They knew that since the young warrior's salvation, and the demise of Goomelt and Pusto, Kaisis had vowed revenge. They knew that he would be scheming and planning and looking for a weakness to exploit. Looking for a 'chink' in their armour, any way to capitalise on man's natural propensity to sin.

Josh had told the other believers all about his hippie friends at 'Maen Du', and the whole fellowship had been praying for them. It was now the weekend, and a fine day, so Josh and Cheryll decided they'd pay the hippies a visit and maybe talk to some of them about Jesus.

Just as they'd turned into the track leading to 'Maen Du' a vehicle was coming up from the yard, and they'd had to back up onto the narrow lane to allow it out. It was Fran; one of the community members Josh had met before. Stopping at the top of the track, she jumped out of her van and came round to Josh's open window. "Hi Josh," she said smiling, "can't stop, I'm really late for my circle dancing group, and the rest of the guys are away at Glastonbury for a couple of weeks." She smiled and acknowledged Cheryll, "See you guys another time." With a quick wave, she hurried back to her battered old van, which was ticking over and belching out huge clouds of stinking diesel fumes.

As she drove off, leaving a heavy trail of toxic grey smoke hanging in the air, Josh couldn't help but muse over the irony of an 'Eco warrior' driving a poison gas machine! Cheryll looked at Josh and said wryly "I guess she's off to save the planet, eh?" They laughed, and then prayed for Fran's salvation.

Josh swung the car back onto the road. In front of them in the distance rose the 'Dragon's Back', the very mountain from where the stones for Stonehenge had originally been quarried. "Fancy a little walk then?" Cheryll asked, "there's a pathway right to the top and the views are amazing!" - "Sounds good" replied Josh, responding to her indication to drive further along the road. A few hundred yards later they turned right onto a rutted and ancient cart track, lined on either side by high banks topped with gorse. There was still the remnant of large muddy puddles, situated around the indentations made from centuries of wheeled traffic. An indication of how much water fell here in the winter months. After about two hundred yards, the track split into a 'Y', the right hand fork leading off to a little cottage, the left hand track terminating in a rough turning area by a five bar gate. Beyond the gate, a vast area of heather and gorse, crisscrossed by small streams and well worn sheep trails, rose gently to the foot of the rock strewn mountain.

The 'Dragon's Back' rose steeply upwards, revealing ever more massive slabs of granite. This is known as Preseli Bluestone, a rock unique to this place and found nowhere else on earth. Way up at the top, all along the ridge, pointed mounds of stone rose high in the air, giving the illusion of a slumbering dragon stretched out atop the mountain.

Parking the car, the young couple climbed over the gate, whilst Boots managed to squeeze under it. They stood for a moment surveying the splendour of God's creation, and then hand in hand began walking along the ancient path that would eventually lead them to the summit.

Chakine and Yolan were ultra alert They both knew this place. They'd been here before, a long, long time ago. . . . . . .
. . . .

------ O ------

It was three hundred years before 'The Wondrous Event'. Satan ruled the earth unchallenged and darkness prevailed in the everyday lives of human beings. Fear, superstition and demonic practice co-existed alongside agriculture, the arts and the work of highly skilled artisans.

With the salvation of men yet to be realised, no Angels had been permanently assigned to human charges, and no 'Chosen Ones' had as yet been born to women. There were however a few individuals worldwide, who, by the evidence of their eyes and senses had perceived creation. They had realised it transcended the possible efforts of any idol of wood or stone. They refused to accept the pre-eminence of any earthbound, horned, or part animal deity. There was a tiny unconnected band dotted all over the Earth. People who, when they looked at the heavens on a clear night, could sense the enormity of creation. People whom, when they beheld the beauty of a wild rose, or the graceful flight of a gliding bird, or heard the cry of a newborn child, ascribed it to a single and all-powerful creator. Angharad of Garth Eryr was one such person.

The daughter of a tribal chieftain, she was a much sought after prize amongst the young Celtic warriors. Her red golden hair hung almost to her waist, cascading over the marble white skin of her lovely shoulders. Her strong high cheekbones framed clear and sparkling eyes of emerald green. Her lips were red and full and her smile was radiant. She was full breasted and lithe and walked gracefully like a princess amongst her people.

She was virtuous, kind, honest and caring. An upright young woman born into a world of darkness and superstition. When she was alone at night, she would often gaze into the heavens and secretly speak to the Creator. They were simple, yet faith filled, prayers. And The Holy One had heard them.

Chakine remembered well the day he and Yolan had been summoned by Captain Cherno and instructed to go down to the earth on a special mission. It was a great honour to be sent to the earth to serve The Holy One and help outwork His purposes. At that time the angels had no idea that one day in the future, their Lord and Master would himself be incarnated into a human body on the earth, to bring about the redemption of mankind.

Captain Cherno addressed them. "It seems a human female has acknowledged the Master, and He has ordained that the two of you should descend to the earth and bring to her a message. Chakine, you will deliver this message. - 'I come from the Lord God Almighty, The Holy One. He has heard your prayers and seen the longings of your heart. Your acts of kindness have come before Him and so He has sent me to strengthen and comfort you'. - You will remain with her for three revolutions of the earth, and protect her from harm. You may use whatever force is necessary. She dwells in the land of Briton on the coast of the West, beneath the mountain of great magnetic stones. You will arrive there at dusk tomorrow."

Later, in the heavenly Courtyard of Warriors, the two Angels were the centre of an excited buzz. As they reclined on layers of gently undulating colour, their fellow angels questioned them about their forthcoming mission. There was no envy or jealous comment, as would probably be the case in human circles, only excitement that a fallen human had acknowledged their master. At that time very few warrior Angels had ever visited the earth, so when Salzar returned from his current duties of assisting Michael – [Mik-a-el] - the Archangel, the warriors eagerly questioned him as one who had previously been on a mission to earth.

They needed no instruction in combat nor tactics, for as warrior Angels they were created with awesome abilities in those departments, but they had benefited from Salzar's knowledge of humans and what they could expect from beings created in the image of their Master. Fallen beings.

It was the first evening of a new moon in the late spring. In less than two days the festival of Beltaine would be upon them. Angharad felt happy and glad to be free of the cumbersome heavy animal skins she'd had to wear throughout the winter. She decided to walk down to the lake about one third of a mile from the settlement. As the daughter of Hwyldalach the tribal chief, she was in effect royalty. The expertly crafted gold Celtic neck ring and the golden bangles that adorned her arms denoted her superior status. Atop her head sat a finely woven golden hair band. And golden embroidery embellished the hem and breast of her shimmering green silk gown. The fastenings were fashioned from gold wire, and a thick shawl of purple wool hung about her shoulders. Though a fierce and warlike race the Celts also produced artisans of commensurate skill, their gold and bronze artistry unequalled for its grace and complexity.

Usually, if she left the sanctuary of the village compound, her handmaiden Riach would accompany her. But this time she went alone, instructing Riach to prepare supper for her return. As she walked out from the relative splendour of her father's large thatched long house, those working in the compound bowed to her with genuine affection. She smiled and greeted each of them by name asking after them and about the health of their families. The whole camp was encircled with a defensive barrier of wooden stakes sunk into the ground, their tops pointed. Smaller circular thatched huts served as accommodation for the ordinary people and storehouses for the necessities of Celtic life. Pigs and chickens rooted around and asses and oxen were tethered beneath a thatched shelter. A group of little children ran towards her calling "Angharad! Angharad!" She knelt and stroked the hair of each one, before rising to continue her journey.

As she moved towards the gate in the wooden fence that surrounded the compound, a group of young warriors bowed and one called out "Greetings Angharad, most beautiful of all women." She blushed and turned her head away to disguise a happy giggle. This was Canach the young warrior whom she secretly hoped would one day win her hand. They had been childhood sweethearts and in their teenage years had shared some intimately tactile moments during various licentious tribal celebrations. "May we provide you with an escort my lady?" he enquired as she continued her walk towards the gate. She stopped and turned to face them, her regal smile softening the words. "Be about your business, and leave me to mine!" They laughed as she turned and continued on and out through the compound gate. Outside, the men tending cattle and those tethering and grooming the horses similarly greeted her. Her response was always warm, friendly and genuine.

The path that led through the cultivated fields went due west. In front of her the sky was turning pink and red, and to the left the Dragon's Back rose majestically, silhouetted against the evening sky. High above her a lone Skylark performed its last aerial opera of the day.

As the fields gave way to gorse, heather and rock, she turned hard left onto a path that gently inclined down to the lake. Her favourite place in all the world. The rapidly setting sun was still shimmering on the water, reflecting undulating shades of pink in the small ripples of a gentle breeze. Down by the waters edge a large lump of bluestone provided a natural seat, the one she always used. Deftly jumping from rock to rock she ascended the eight or so feet and in no time at all was sitting with her knees raised to her chest gazing on the beauty before her.

She looked up at the crest of The Dragon's Back remembering the stories she had heard of the great temple that was built with stone quarried from the mountaintop. A hugely sacred place – Stonehenge. Her grandfather had been there as a young man on guard duty to the Druids, but no one else from her tribe had experience of the place. It had been a huge and mighty feat of engineering, costing the lives of many slaves and warriors, and she wondered of its purpose.

The sky was clear and the sun just minutes from setting. She drew a deep breath as she gazed upon the staggering beauty of the sinking orb against the backdrop of hues of red and pink. She glanced quickly right and left making sure she was alone, and then she closed her eyes and raised her hands skyward. "Great first God," she said with a quivering voice "I see such beauty as no God of wood or stone could have made. I see that the sun comes up and goes down each day. I see that babies are born from the lying with a man, and I see a design in natural things like trees and flowers. Please show me how I can know You. I *so* want to understand and know more about You."

As she spoke she was shaking, for she knew she had entered the realms of the forbidden. Only the Druids could speak with the Gods, and that only after much placation and ritual. She was taking a great risk openly praying where she might possibly be seen, but she desperately wanted to know more of the Great First God. Her arms were raised and her eyes closed when she heard her name called. "Angharad." She quickly lowered her arms, not daring to look, fearing a villager had spotted her, or worse still one of the Druids. She hugged her knees tightly, her eyes still closed. Again the voice came.

"Angharad, daughter of Hwyldalach." She slowly lifted her head from her knees and opened her eyes, what she saw made her gasp! Standing before her at the water's edge were two radiant beings of light, who shone like the stars themselves. Burying her face into her knees again she hunched herself even tighter, terrified by what she had seen.

Chakine spoke again, "Angharad, do not be afraid, I come from the Lord God Almighty. The Holy One. He has heard your prayers and seen the longings of your heart Your acts of kindness have come before Him and He has sent me to strengthen and comfort you."

Still terrified, the young woman lifted her eyes and looked at the two beings that stood before her. Suddenly her fear just melted away and they moved closer. Chakine reached out and touched her on the forehead and she instantly felt peace and serenity. "What must I do, my Lord?" she asked. Chakine smiled at her and said, "Love the Lord God with all your heart and continue to live in truth and kindness, treating others with respect. Do not bow down to Gods of wood and stone."

"Where is the Great First God?" she asked, "where can I find Him?" the Angel replied, "You found Him already Angharad, that is why He sent us, to confirm to you what you have already understood – There is only one God! – The creator of everything!"

The two Angels disappeared from her conscious view, though remaining close to her.

By now there was just enough light left to illuminate her path, and climbing down from her vantage point she began to wend her way up the hill and back to the settlement. As she walked her mind raced and her heart still pounded, yet through it all she felt a deep sense of peace and resolved to know more about the Great First God. Chakine and Yolan accompanied her unseen and spent the night at either end of her bed, alert and watchful.

As the first rays of the sun chased the darkness from the mountaintops, the settlement at Garth Eryr sprung into its daily routine. Riach awoke her mistress and served her some warming porridge to ward off the early morning chill. Outside, with banter and bravado, the warriors were preparing for a cattle-stealing raid on a settlement some twenty miles to the west.

Angharad's quarters were a daub and wattle partitioned room at the end of the long house, next to the similar rooms of her father's three wives. The dividing walls were made from woven hazel and willow partitions plastered with mud. Her father's room was of the same construction, and the walls were hung with woven fabrics depicting hunting scenes and scenes of ritual to placate the gods. Ten thick upright wooden pillars supported the long house, which was about sixty feet in length. There were five on each side holding up the thatched roof. The space between each of these was filled with mud coated woven partitions. The exterior wall constructed of carefully fitted logs. At the end opposite the sleeping quarters there were several very low tables, merely inches off the dirt and straw floor. Around these were scattered thick woven mats for diners to sit upon. Hanging from the walls were various tools and implements. Hoes, rakes, scythes, axes and the general accoutrements of Celtic life. Just inside the entrance in the centre of the floor, a fire pit burned, warming the large cauldron that hung above it suspended from a roof beam. On each of the large upright poles supporting the roof, there was a severed head, nailed to the pole. These were the heads of lesser foes who had been easily conquered in battle. The heads of men of importance were kept in a huge oaken chest, preserved in cedar oil. This chest took pride of place in the long house and visitors would be proudly shown the collection. Hwyldalach would often get them out to be passed around his admiring guests at dinner.

Although she had grown up with this practice, Angharad had never felt quite right about it. This morning however, the shrivelled grimacing heads nailed to the poles positively repulsed her. She knew she had to do something about it, though she had no idea what. She was about to exit the long house when her father called to her from his sleeping room. "Yes father?" she enquired as he came out dressed ready for battle.

Despite his being a fierce and generally ruthless man, Hwyldalach genuinely loved his only daughter deeply. "Come my lovely, let your father give you a farewell squeeze," he said holding out his arms. She ran to him and he embraced her warmly. "We shall return later with fine cattle and many heads!"

Outside, enjoying the bright morning sunshine, the warriors were mounted and ready, and waiting for their chief. Their short hair and long moustaches were accentuated by woad, a slate blue paste that they had daubed upon their arms and faces, giving them a fierce and ghoulish appearance. They were dressed in brightly coloured, chequered sleeveless tunics and long pants, and the shoulders of each man were adorned with a thick woven poncho-like cloak that hung behind him, down to the ankles. They were armed with spears, swords and knives and carried an oblong wooden shield, decorated with a personal emblem.

The restless horses snorted and whinnied, eager to run, and the mounted men held them in rein as they jostled one another, impatient to be underway.

Angharad wanted to wish Canach and the others good luck, but could not exit the long house ahead of her father. So she followed him out and was only able to wave a goodbye to the backs of the raiding party as they galloped out of the compound.

The women of the village were busy cooking, making garlands, and checking on the mead, and strong beer, for the coming Beltaine celebrations. This year the village was to be highly honoured, as they were to receive a visit from Zandorch, the Chief Druid, who was to officiate at the ceremonies in the sacred grove. The cattle raid had been carefully timed so that their triumphal return would coincide with the approximate arrival of their honoured guest and his entourage.

------ O ------

In the realm of demons, Kaisis the great wolf headed Lord of the West was receiving reports of a disturbance in the sector of Briton. Some elementals had apparently witnessed a manifestation of disgusting 'white light' around a young human female. He had immediately dispatched a troop of demons to investigate.

--- --- O ------

It was around noontime and Angharad was sitting in the doorway of Riach's hut, watching her weave cloth on a handmade loom. The two Angels stood watchful and alert, one on either side of the open wooden doorway. Their discernment told them danger was imminent so they unsheathed their swords and held their shields ready. The attack was sudden and forceful. Cascading out of the inky blackness of the netherworld, twenty screaming demons launched themselves at the readied Angels. Despite being outnumbered ten to one the two warriors met the devilish onslaught with commensurate skill.

With flailing claws the first demon dived at Yolan, slashing at his face. Yolan swung his shield hard catching his assailant full on and catapulting him backward into his following companion. A swift upward sword thrust nailed the two in one. Chakine launched himself right into the oncoming melee, the arc of his sword humming as it flashed at lightning speed, separating heads from bodies in rapid fluid motion. As a demon leapt on Yolan's back another dived at his midriff. The Angel's sword jerked over his shoulder splitting the one demon's face in half whilst at the same time his shield came down on the neck of his frontal opponent. In a matter of seconds eight of the enemy were vanquished. And as Chakine and Yolan tore into the remaining group with righteous force, the dismayed demons turned and fled back into the darkness from whence they came. None the wiser as to why the two servants of The Most High were at this place.

Oblivious to the entire incident, Angharad had continued to sit in the doorway of the hut observing Rhiach's skilful weaving. Her eyes witnessed the scene, but her mind was far away, contemplating the events of the previous evening. She wondered if it had all been in her mind. Or perhaps some of the dried ritual mushrooms from last autumn had been mistakenly added to the stew, for the experience seemed quite similar to some of the 'journeys' she had been on whilst under their influence during past Druid festivals. Except, she had felt so incredibly peaceful when the being had touched her, whereas mushrooms always made her feel jittery. Also the beings she had seen in the past often seemed dark and furtive, whereas these two had been light and beautiful.

As she thought about them she again experienced the sense of peace. A great questioning was beginning to rise within her. The things she had always been uneasy about took on a new clarity, and she saw that many of the things her people did were wrong, and thus displeasing to the Great Creator God.

Chakine and Yolan remained alert, knowing that the enemy would doubtless return in greater strength sometime soon. Their orders were to remain with the human woman and protect her, and this they would do, come what may, until the end of three revolutions of the earth.

------ O ------

In the dark realms at that very moment, the hapless commander of the demon raiding party was being shaken like a rag doll in the powerful claws of the wolf headed Kaisis. "You will attack again tonight, and if you fail me this time, you will beg for the Lake of Fire to alleviate your pain!" He hurled the miscreant into the middle of the other surviving demons who were furtively lurking in the shadows. "This time take eighty soldiers, and finish the job!" he screamed, as his leathery wings lifted him into the darkness.

------ O ------

Twenty miles away to the north, the mounted attack by Hwyldalach and the warriors had taken the unfortunate little settlement completely by surprise. Coming out of the bright sunlight they had swept down the hillside and into the cattle pens before the villagers knew what was happening.

The defending warriors who had run out to meet the attack fought valiantly, but most of them were cut down before they could reach their horses. Their heads were quickly severed and tied through the mouth and neck to the raider's saddles. The cattle and horses were loosed, and the pillaging band quickly and efficiently herded off their spoil amidst the thunder of hooves.

An expertly hurled spear found its mark between the shoulder blades of one of the fleeing attackers, who with a scream of agony tumbled backward off his mount, but the rest escaped unscathed. Warriors from the raided village fell upon the unseated attacker quickly removing his head, which they held aloft in consolation as the rustlers disappeared over the brow of the hill.

------ O ------

The chief druid Zandorch and his entourage were in sight of Hwyldalach's tribal enclosure. It was just across the valley a half-hours walk in front of them, as they slowly descended from the jagged peak of the Dragon's Back. Behind them, on a stone altar atop the mountain, lay the corpse of a young man, his heart cut out in placation to the gods. A ritual which had further empowered the ancient dark entities inhabiting the high places. The dragon spirits of old.

All around the Druid in the unseen realm, dark spirits whispered and muttered. His authority was unquestioned and absolute. His word was law. He held the power of life and death over all ordinary people. Their great respect of the Druids was mostly born of fear, and that fear was not misplaced. For these dark masters knew many arcane secrets and wielded great power through the realms of the demonic. It was through such men as these that the Evil One outworked his rebellious plan against Almighty God. Satan ruled over the earth by the power of fear, superstition and dark magic. Adam and Eve having handed over their God given dominion by disobedience, way back in the Garden of Eden. The tree from which they had eaten – The Tree of the Knowledge of Good and Evil – had, through their sin, opened the doorway to the knowledge of all sorts of dark and dangerous practices. And The Prince of Darkness had encouraged and rewarded their use. The whole world was swathed in superstition and fear, and the need to placate and appease the many gods, who were not gods at all, but scheming demons masquerading as such. For this season of time, prior to the coming of the Holy One, it was man's free will, under Satan's influence, that held sway.

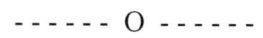

------ O ------

With Hwyldalach at the fore, the triumphant raiding party thundered across the open country herding their spoil of cattle and horses back toward the settlement. Dripping blood, the grisly toll of heads bounced and swung slung from the saddles of the horses, as the warriors skilfully kept the plundered beasts together.

Back at the settlement, warriors who had not gone raiding had been busy down by the Sacred Oak Grove opposite the lake. They had built two huge bonfires of oak and green yew topped with maypoles. These fires would be lit tonight, on the eve of the feast of Beltaine, May 1st. The cattle and all other livestock would be driven between the two conflagrations, herded through the thick smoke. This would ensure great fertility, health and a good harvest. Tomorrow would be a great day of celebration, feasting and games, but first this dangerous eve of Beltaine must pass without the anger of the gods descending.

Those whose job it was to look after the livestock, had spent the day extending the pens to accommodate the hoped for increase in cattle. And those whose job it was to steal them, were now no more than a mile away and approaching fast, replete with their ill gotten gains.

Zandorch and his band, still out of sight of the settlement, were ascending the gentle incline that led to the main gate of the compound five hundred yards ahead, when the druid suddenly stopped and inclined his head slightly to one side, as though listening to something. In truth, that was exactly what he was doing. And the demons whispered and muttered in his ear. They told him of a great evil that had been done at this place. How one who was not an initiate had dared to pray to the gods and that because the correct rituals had not been properly observed, rogue spirits were now in the vicinity. Dangerous spirits who would seek to usurp his authority.

He motioned to the others to sit down. From a small chest the servants were carrying; three polished human skulls were produced along with various other 'magical' artefacts, and they began to divine the omens.

The Druids held great sway over the people. They acted as judges, doctors, lawyers, military advisors, astrologers, soothsayers and priests. They were educated men, skilled in an ancient oral tradition. None of their learning was written down. It was merely passed on by word of mouth and, as such, meant that they alone were privy this secret knowledge. Knowledge is power, and this ancient sect wielded incredible power over the people. The instructions of the Druids had to be obeyed. And the word of the Chief Druid was sacrosanct.

Zandorch was a man of average height, but his head-dress decorated with the rays of the sun, made him look substantially taller. His flowing white robes of office were adorned with a circle of gold neck rings and a finely decorated golden belt. Across his shoulders sat a heavy woven purple cloak. A long flowing beard and moustache framed his stern features. All in all he cut a formidable figure, striding serenely at the head of his cortege. He had seven other men with him. Three Druids and four servants who dutifully carried all the accoutrements of his craft.

Back in the village, Chakine and Yolan were made suddenly aware of an approaching power of darkness that was very strong. Consequently they became super alert. Angharad had left Rhiach's dwelling and was sitting playing with some of the village children by the grain store. She was happy in this temporary distraction and the children obviously adored her.

The women of the settlement were still busying themselves with preparations for the morrow, and an air of excited expectation prevailed. From the distance the thunder of hooves grew ever louder, mingled with the shouts and whoops of the returning raiding party. Angharard and several of the other women rose to their feet and hurried to the gate of the stockade, anxious to determine the safety of their returning loved ones.

Once the cattle were safely corralled the warriors galloped up the track and in to the compound. Dismounting they held their trophy heads aloft and cried "Hail Hwyldalach, chief of chiefs, mighty warrior!"

Whilst the other women cheered and whooped, Angharad felt a deep pain in her soul. A great numbing sadness. She was about to cry out "This is wrong!" when the wife of the warrior who had not returned let out a great piercing wail and sunk to her knees. Angharad rushed to her side and knelt with her holding her tightly, whilst the other warriors, Hwyldalach included, came one by one and stood briefly before her, each bowing his head in acknowledgement of her loss.

The warriors did not fear death as the Druids had instructed them that it was no more than a passage to the realm of the gods. Celtic heaven was similar to earthly existence but infinitely better. There was neither sickness nor problems, no one grew old and the women were stunningly beautiful and readily accommodating. The sun shone always and the air was full of birdsong. No one ever wanted for food or drink.

------ O ------

It is curious to note how on a world-wide basis, differing cultures hold to very similar beliefs with regard to an afterlife. Militant Muslims willingly blow themselves up, convinced that they will be going to Paradise and the attentions of 70 'perpetual virgins'. Right across the globe various diverse cultures believe strikingly similar afterlife scenarios. Often predating Christianity. These apparent 'proofs' that Christianity is built upon preceding beliefs, fail however to apprehend one enormously salient point. And that is: The need for salvation. The requirement to be made right with God so as not to be totally consumed by His holiness upon entering His wondrous realm.

The fact is, that world wide, the fallen Lucifer – [originally The Light Bringer] – now Satan, has sowed erroneous beliefs laced with half-truths, into the folklore of cultures across the globe. His strategy has been to remove the need for salvation. And by releasing pre-emptive descriptions of aspects of heaven to early civilisations, he has to some degree succeeded in his purpose. He is well acquainted with the heavenly realms. He used to live there!

------ O ------

Finishing their deliberations, Zandorch and his band rose and continued up the hill. The omens had not been good. The Chief Druid knew well that on this eve of Beltaine they were particularly susceptible to the wrath of Belenos the god of fire and fertility. The god whom they would shortly entreat to purify the livestock in the smoke of the fires down at the sacred oak grove. He also knew that luck could easily change, unless he made offerings and placated the Gods. The lying spirits who constantly whispered in his ear convinced him that what was needed was the sacrifice of a young male warrior, whose strong heart would placate the gods. The issue of who had upset them by daring to pray, would wait till later.

An alert guard tending the cattle first spotted the Druid's approaching party and quickly relayed the message of their imminent arrival. A great buzz of excitement rippled through the camp and many people ran to the stockade entrance and began to walk down towards the visitors, forming a welcoming committee on either side of the track.

Angharad still sat cradling the now sobbing widow in her arms, a rising anger growing within her against the barbarity and senseless death that pervaded her world. Chakine and Yolan sensed the approach of yet another very dark enemy force, and moved nearer to their charge, swords drawn.

Hwyldalach and the warriors assembled in front of the longhouse, ready to receive their honoured guests, whilst women ferried bowls of food and jugs of mead and wine inside, to the prepared eating area.

Zandorch thrived on the praise and respect of men, especially when it was mingled with ill-concealed fear. In curt acknowledgement of the genuflections of the villagers lining the route, he nodded his head this way and that. The visitors entered the gates and approached the assembled warriors by the longhouse. "Greetings Zandorch, I trust you are well and have had a pleasant journey, please enter my home and partake of the food we have prepared." said Hwyldalach, motioning the Druids inside. Zandorch responded with a slow nod of his head and the three other Druids followed him into the building. The matter of the needed sacrifice and its reasons could wait until after they had eaten. "In fact," thought Zandorch, "it can wait until we begin the evening's divinations, just prior to the purification ceremony. The gods will be pleased. And the people's fear of upsetting them will increase their obedience to me."

The very low wooden tables were arranged in a circle radiating out from the centre. Each table was surrounded by animal skins laid on the earthen floor. Zandorch was seated in the middle with Hwyldalach next to him and the other Druids on either side. The remaining warriors were seated in order of diminishing importance, the least being furthest from the centre.

Canach's tribal standing caused him to be seated about halfway between the middle and the periphery. The Chief Druid gave the appropriate 'blessing' and the meal commenced.

Wild boar, mutton and fish from the lake were all consumed, along with oatcakes, cheese, butter, milk and honey. All washed down with wine, mead and beer.

As was the custom, the young warriors began boasting of the day's exploits and how they had vanquished the enemy. Each one in turn rose to his feet competing for the 'hero's portion' which would be awarded by the chieftain for the most convincing story.

It was Canach's turn. "As we carefully approached the enemy's camp I urged my horse ever faster, until it was galloping like the wind and as we came upon two of their sentries, I rode between them. With a slash to the right and a hack to the left I removed both of their heads, snatching them up at the same time and quickly threading them on my saddle rope as my swift horse continued to gallop towards their cattle stockade. With a single leap I cleared the stockade gate, slashing its fastening rope as I did so. I then rode around the inside of the stockade driving the cattle out to my waiting brothers who were all some distance behind me, none of them quite possessing my extraordinary equestrian skills. – Hwyldalach was a hundred yards away, directing the plunder of the horse corral. As I drove the cattle out to my waiting brothers, I spied an axe wielding assailant bearing down on him from behind, and so, hurled my spear whose straight and true flight went right through the attacker, saving my chief. This head also hung from my saddle by the time we returned."

The other warriors also boasted for all they were worth, but Canach won hands down. He was duly awarded the haunch of a fine boar. Zandorch had also listened carefully to the stories of derring-do, and had agreed thoroughly with Hwyldalach's assessment. The heart of a great warrior like this should indeed placate the gods on this Beltaine eve!

Whilst the revelling warriors and their guests slept, the ordinary folk of the village continued with their endless preparations for the morrow, and the needs of the coming evening's purification ceremony. Angharad stayed with the new widow, accompanying her back to her hut, and had continued to hold her and her two small children, all the while praying to The Great First God to comfort and provide for them. For the last hour, Rhiach had sat uncomfortably with her mistress; terrified the Druids would somehow hear the whispered prayers. She was torn between her loyalty to Angharad and her tribal understanding of how the gods would react. Chakine and Yolan were almost back to back on either side of Angharad. Swords drawn and shields up. They knew that there in the inky blackness of the netherworld, just out of sight, a vast number of demons had congregated, and that some sort of attack was inevitable and imminent. They were certainly not afraid, but nonetheless were aware of the potential danger to their charge.

------ O ------

The demons couldn't kill them – just as *they* could not actually kill the demons. Any they had vanquished were only temporarily disabled. Out of the immediate fight and bound in chains to await their ultimate fate in God's great judgement. If they decapitated a demon that entity was merely rendered into immobile captivity - it couldn't die. Demons, like Angels, are spirit beings and God will eventually destroy all demons in the Lake of Fire, along with their master – Satan. Demons *can* induce situations whereby humans are killed. Most often by other humans, or by suicide or madness caused by interacting with them. But it was not to be for several centuries yet, until after the coming of the saviour of all mankind, that mortal men, through the power of The Son of God, would be able to bind and banish demons themselves.

------ O ------

Eventually around 6pm, the warriors and their Druid overlords were awakened and began, with the rest of the settlement, to form a ritual procession to make their way down to the sacred Oak Grove. The cattle, horses and other livestock were already there, corralled in temporary pens erected for the ceremony. Angharad had no desire to attend, but she was the daughter of the Chief and she knew she had no option, as she would be immediately missed. So she took her place with the other females as the entire community slowly descended the valley to the Sacred Grove. Torches were lit and they all began to sing a song in praise of Belenos, everyone that is except Angharad, who had vowed to herself she would follow the instructions of the beautiful beings sent to her from The Great First God. She would not worship idols of wood and stone anymore.

In the general hubbub, no one noticed her failure to sing as the procession wound its way down past the lake and on to the Sacred Grove. Each of the warriors carried with them their most precious severed head, which they joyfully held aloft with both hands as they sang and chanted the ancient songs prescribed for the placation of Belenos, god of fire and fertility.

The Sacred Grove consisted of a rough circle of mature oak trees about one hundred and fifty feet in diameter. At one end underneath a yew tree, a great low slab of granite bluestone served as an altar. And in front of the altar stood a large wooden effigy of Belenos. Behind the altar was a semi circle of small standing stones. The branches of the yew were decorated with strips of coloured cloth, skulls, both human and animal, and various bones and carved sticks essential to the processes of divination. These branches formed a natural canopy over the standing stones, statue and altar.

The whole place was crawling with dark spirits. Death, murder and divination sat leering above the altar, whilst lesser elementals scurried around at the base of the oaks waiting to cast their one-dimensional influences over the approaching humans. Chakine and Yolan knew they were walking into an extremely difficult situation. They had already silenced several elementals whose recognition of their presence had threatened to expose them to the Druid.

Since the arrival at the camp of Zandorch's party the two Angels had transformed themselves into the likeness of two human servant girls, who, amongst the general busyness remained un-noticed. In this guise, the radiance of God's glory that they carried was temporarily masked and they were invisible to the soldiers of Kaisis. However, they equally knew that another attack would certainly come some time soon, in one form or another. They had earlier sensed the proximity of a large group of demons, out in the inky blackness of the netherworld, and they were also aware of the strong resolve of the young Angharad. They knew that sooner or later they would have to defend her.

Zandorch and his Druids took up position just in front of the altar, and the rest of the community stood some ten feet back, virtually filling the broad circle of oaks. With an air of solemnity the dark masters performed the various required rituals whilst the assembled onlookers excitedly sang, chanted and danced. Strips of brightly coloured cloth were laid in front of the altar in a semi-circle, thus completing the half circle of standing stones behind the altar. And upon these cloths the severed heads were laid.

In the westerly distance, the Dragon's Back stood starkly silhouetted by the dying rays of the sun setting on the sea behind it. The Druids rituals intensified, the chanting increased, and the presence of dark spirits grew ever stronger. A bolt of lightning struck the ridge of the mountain, briefly illuminating the entire area. At the same time Zandorch, his arms raised skyward, spun around to face the congregated people. Immediately there was total silence.

He stood like that for a few seconds, staring and motionless. Then lowering his arms he spoke. "People of Garth Eryr, the gods are displeased with you, there has been a great sin and atonement must be made. The gods require a life, which will ensure you have a fine and prosperous harvest and that your livestock will multiply." He took several steps forward, bringing him to the edge of the semi-circle of heads. Hwyldalach and his warriors comprised the first few rows of the assembled villagers, and the eyes of the Chief Druid slowly scanned their ranks. He stopped when his gaze fell on Canach. He slowly raised his arm his finger pointing directly at the young man. He called out "Canach, hero of the day. The gods have chosen you!"

At the same moment, a nano second before she let out a piercing "No!" Yolan had quickly touched Angharad's lips, rendering her unconscious. The two disguised Angels supported her and they remained unnoticed.

Canach strode out of the ranks of warriors, almost eager to meet his fate. He had no fear; such was the indoctrination of the Druid masters. He was confident his destination would be the land of the gods, the place he deserved as a faithful warrior. This tactic and the spirits behind it had served Satan well through several millennia, and would continue to do so, eventually manifesting itself in the suicide bombers that would plague the time of the end.

It was almost dark now, and the flickering torches held aloft accentuated the bizarre scene as Canach entered the circle. He went and knelt before Zandorch and the other Druids who handed him a drinking horn containing a narcotic sedative concoction.

Meanwhile the assembly resumed their chanting, singing and frenetic dancing as the young warrior drained the entire contents of the horn and stood up. The Druids stripped him naked and led him to the stone altar, which he climbed upon and then laid down. All around in the shadows more and more elementals were gathering, waiting for their chance to enter the assembled humans. Above, on the spiritual plane of darkness, Kaisis's warriors surveyed the scene, unable to see the Angels and eagerly anticipating witnessing the demise of yet another despised creation made in the image of The Holy One. The chanting and licentious dancing grew ever wilder as the Druids waited for the potion to take its full effect upon Canach. Many of the participants had taken psilocybin (magic) mushrooms and large quantities of ale, and the proceedings teetered on the brink of a full-blown orgy. Chakine and Yolan were not comfortable in the midst of all this sin, but realised any exit with Angharad would immediately expose them.

The intensity of darkness thickened and the Druids encircled the altar around the now motionless form of the young warrior. Zandorch lifted a knife high in the air, and plunging it down he quickly removed the heart, holding it aloft whilst the crowd of villagers squealed and screamed with demonic relish. At this moment hundreds of elementals launched themselves from the shadows right into the bodies of the watching humans. Their approval of the despicable deed being all the invitation that was needed.

------ O ------

It is a law that is universally applicable to humans. If one agrees to, or accepts, or condones anything that is contrary to God's law, then that person is deemed complicit. Guilt by association. And therefore that person becomes subject to the penalties prescribed for the offence. – Just as if they themselves had committed it.

To witness, and then fail to speak out against a ritual murder, makes the onlooker as guilty as the perpetrator. These spiritual laws are still active today and equally binding in God's sight. If you vote for any politician who approves of abortion or homosexuality or anything else displeasing to God, then you are effectively endorsing those positions. The list is endless. The outcome the same.

------ O ------

Complicity in dark magic rituals gives elementals the right to enter your body! And so now all of the assembled residents of Garth Eryr had indwelling spirits in varying degrees. For some of them this was the first time they had ever witnessed human sacrifice. For others it was merely another incident in a long line of many.

Canach's lifeless body satisfied Zandorch that the gods were now placated, and the purification and fertility ceremony could commence. The question of who had offended the gods would provide interesting entertainment during the feasting of tomorrow.

The ritual bonfires were ready to be lit and the livestock were all present in the temporary corrals, so the Chief Druid motioned the assembly to exit the grove. As they filed out in the torchlit darkness, the two disguised Angels were able to slip away with the still subdued chieftain's daughter, whilst everybody else gathered to witness the animals being driven through the purifying smoke between the two large bonfires.

------ O ------

At the same time in the spirit plane, the demon commanding Kaisis's raiding party was frantically questioning every elemental indwelling the humans, ever mindful of his master's threat should he fail in his mission. "Have you seen any disgusting white liters?" he would grab each one of them, his claws inflicting pain. "Tell me where they are!" he screamed, his red eyes burning with anger. The process was repeated again and again, until he came to the elementals indwelling the widow whose husband had died in the cattle raid. The terrified spirits quickly volunteered the information. "Yes master, today master, we heard the daughter of the chief praying to the Most High! There were two of them with her." The warrior demon grabbed the face of the elemental, screwing it up like paper. "Why didn't you report it fool?" he screamed, his face contorted with rage, "Where is she? Find her. Find her!" he barked at his following soldiers. Groups of them scattered in all directions.

------ O ------

The two Angels had taken the still slumbering Angharad to a cave high in the mountains, where they resumed their normal appearance. There they were safe; the enemy could not see them. Only their master was omniscient and omnipresent. The hordes of darkness would have to search for them. Yolan passed his hand across the girl's face, "Angharad, wake up!" She instantly opened her eyes and the great sense of peace once again flooded her being. The Angels explained what had happened and where she was and comforted her as she took in the news of Canach's fate. For a while she sat grasping her knees, rocking back and forth gently sobbing, tears rolling down her ivory cheeks. The Angels remained visible, a source of comfort and warmth.

Down in the valley the purification and fertility ceremony had concluded successfully, and the tribe and guests had retired happy in the knowledge that the gods were placated and a good harvest and fecundity was predicted. Copious amounts of strong ale, wine and hallucinogenic mushrooms had temporarily ensured that Angharad's absence had not been noticed by anyone, except her maidservant Rhiach. The young woman found herself on the horns of a dilemma and she spent hours tossing and turning on her bed. She was torn between her love for her mistress and her knowledge of the 'great evil' Angharad had done in daring to speak to the gods. She knew her mistress was the reason that Canach had been sacrificed and she was terrified that she would be somehow implicated. Her mind raced and, as she eventually fell into fitful sleep, she knew she had to make a decision.

Up in the cave, a warm shaft of morning sunlight caressing her face awakened Angharad. For a moment she was not sure where she was, then she remembered. The chill of her temporary boudoir caused her to wrap her cloak more tightly about her. The Angels were gone, at least in the sense that she could not see them, for they had promised her that they would remain until dusk of this new day. She trusted them implicitly.

She had awoken with a new and strong sense of resolve. She understood that The Great First God was the only God, and that the Druids and their barbaric practises were leading her people astray. She knew she must speak out. And she also knew how it would be received.

The settlement was visible in the distance, and as she picked her way down the mountainside, stepping from boulder to boulder she began to pray. "Great First God, I thank You for revealing Yourself to me, and for sending spirits to help me. I know my people are doing bad things because of the influence of the Druids and I intend to speak out against this. I ask You to give me courage and wisdom. I will not bow down again to idols of wood and stone, You are the only God."

She continued her descent with a fiery resolve in her heart and the light of the knowledge of The Creator God in her eyes.

Back at the settlement, children were running around excitedly in expectation of what this special day would bring. There would be a fair, and games and tests of skill, and the day would culminate with a special time of feasting to Belenos. Women were busily preparing food and lighting fires, whilst some of the men folk practised throwing axes and spears in preparation for the afternoon's games.

Bleary eyed, Zandorch and Hwyldalach were breakfasting together when the Druid mentioned the great evil that had necessitated the previous evenings sacrifice. "Today Hwyldalach, we shall root this out and discover who dares to insult the gods by approaching them in ignorance." The chieftain was hung over and in a foul mood. He looked up from his plate and snarled, "I swear Zandorch; I swear by all the gods, that when we discover the identity of the miscreant I myself shall remove his head!" Zandorch smiled and nodded as he visualised the entertainment to come.

As Angharad climbed the last slope that would bring her to the gate of the settlement her heart was pounding. Again a voice whispered in her ear "Fear not Angharad, The Lord of Hosts is with you." She stopped momentarily, drew a deep breath and walked on and up into the compound. Within seconds she was surrounded by squealing children, "Angharad, Angharad!" She picked one up and swung him round and they all wanted the same treat. Everywhere villagers greeted her; many of them secretly aware of how she had felt about Canach, having seen them grow up together. No one was surprised to see her return, understanding that she had needed to spend the night alone to mourn his loss. She made her way to Rhiach's hut seeking breakfast. Her maidservant bowed and acknowledged her, but she sensed that something was wrong from the mono-syllabic replies she received to her questions.

Having eaten she walked to her fathers longhouse, once again being joyously accosted by a gaggle of boisterous children. When she entered the eating area her father and Zandorch were still seated. Hwyldalach looked up and his demeanour instantly changed upon seeing his daughter. He rose to his feet his arms outstretched. "Come my lovely, give a hug to your father." his enormous arms encircled her. "Good morning Angharad" said Zandorch, "I trust you slept well?" Angharad bit her tongue. Now was not the time. She merely nodded. "Will you be competing in the spear throwing competition today?" he further enquired. Hywldalach interjected, "Of course she will, and she'll win! Don't let that beautiful face and slender body fool you my friend."

Like many Celtic women Angharad was skilled in the use of sword, spear and dagger. Although she had never used any of them in anger she would frequently do very well in competitions of skill, especially the throwing of the spear. This daughter of the chief was well loved and respected by all her tribal kin. But best of all in her mind, she was now loved and accepted by The Great First God. And she would not let Him down.

------ O ------

In the heavenly realm Captain Cherno had just received notification that he was to re-inforce Chakine and Yolan's mission with a troop of warriors. The deadline remained the same, dusk that evening. They were to protect the young human female until the sun went down. Cherno would lead a troop of forty Angels with Salzar as his deputy. His instructions were to remain 'cloaked' and observe. Only intervening if the situation looked like the young woman would lose her life before dusk. That was it. Beyond dusk they were not to intervene. Angels never question instructions from The Great I AM. They have no free will since Lucifer chose to disobey God and led many of their number astray. They merely obey – and obey to the letter.

------ O ------

Whilst Zandorch was busy satisfying his physical needs he was not listening to the mutterings of the spirits. He was well known for his predilection for buxom servant girls, so, as a good host, that morning Hwyldalach had sent him Edain, one of his own favourite mistresses. The games began at the hour before noon, so for the next three hours Zandorch could avail himself of her ample charms whilst the chieftain would oversee the remaining preparations for the celebration. Hwyldalach and his daughter exited the longhouse and made their way down to the field where all was being made ready for the coming festivities.

Angharad had earlier asked Rhiach if anything was troubling her but the maidservant lied, saying she had drunk too much mead last night and just felt a little queasy. The poor girl was really in a quandary. She loved her mistress dearly, but her fear of the gods and what the Druids might do to her was rapidly winning out. She decided she would tell what she had witnessed, but it would have to wait until the feast later that afternoon.

Various guests began to arrive from friendly outlying settlements and once again the two Angels assumed their guise of servant girls. The rather dulled senses of the hung-over people meant that they were able to blend in perfectly amidst the general hubbub, accompanying Angharad at a discreet distance as she followed her father who traversed the field, bellowing orders to all and sundry.

Even at this early hour, mead, beer and wine were being consumed like it was going out of fashion. This was one day when all people everywhere knew that they were safe from attack. For all the other tribes would also be celebrating Beltaine in similar fashion. It was an unwritten law that could be counted on.

Thousands of years earlier since before the Great Flood, men had practised lawlessness, murder and dark incantations in high places. They had worshipped dragons in this land, and their ritual sacrifice of hundreds of human beings had greatly empowered the demons that masqueraded in the form of dragons. In every high place where these entities had been worshipped they were now imprisoned as result of God's judgement through the Great Flood. Although imprisoned, literally locked into the ground, they were still empowered by sacrifice and ungodly ritual done at the site of their imprisonment. The worship of these ancient entities had long since been superseded by the druidic culture, and they lay dormant. Spirits cannot die. They lay like slumbering giants; patiently waiting for the day they would be released.
And there were hundreds of them.

------ O ------

The great festivities commenced the hour before noon. The wooden statue of Belenos had been brought up from the Sacred Grove and placed just in front of where the Chief Druid and all the dignitaries would sit. There were several maypoles decorated with bright strips of cloth, skulls and other artefacts. A fire pit was burning in preparation for the roasting of several wild boar and sheep, and a platform was sagging under the weight of jars of beer, mead and wine.

A long blast on a horn signified the start of Beltaine celebrations and the people were in the mood for revelry and enjoyment. Zandorch, being thoroughly distracted by the courtesan skills of Edain had thus far paid the spirits no attention this morning. With a satisfied smile he took his seat along with Hwyldalach and the other dignitaries.

The first event was axe throwing. A dozen or so warriors were assembled in front of the seated Chieftain, eager to begin. Some fifty yards away on a firmly secured pole, the eye of a bull hung threaded on a thin strip of leather. One by one the warriors took their turn, each hurling his razor sharp axe with all the precision he could muster. The pole was about eight inches in diameter and most of the axes whistled quite close by, one or two glancing crazily off the pole. Two embedded themselves into the upright timber but none actually hit the bull's eye.

"Stand aside!" roared Hwyldalach as he rose and strode over to the throwing point amidst the cheers and encouragement's of his people. Several horns of ale had improved his earlier demeanour and he waved and smiled broadly at his enthusiastic supporters who continued to cheer him. He held up a huge hand and immediate silence descended. Pulling his axe from his belt he weighed it in his right hand getting the balance. He took one large stride forward with his left foot, his eyes narrowing as he did so. He rocked slightly backward and forward for a moment, then with a blood-curdling yell hurled the weapon end over end towards the target. There was a great thud as it sunk into the timber splitting the pendulous eye in two. The assembled onlookers erupted into praise of their chief chanting "Hwyldalach! Hwyldalach!" The big man, his arms raised turned this way and that in happy acknowledgement of their adulation before turning to face the statue of Belenos. He bowed low. "Great God Belenos, I give you all honour and glory for my victory." Again the crowd cheered as Hwyldalach retook his seat amongst the honoured guests.

The day wore on with music and dancing, wrestling and all manner of events which tested the skills of the warriors, both men and women alike. The winner of each event, after bathing in his or her glory would present themselves to the statue of Belenos and repeat the prescribed mantra, bowing as they did.

The mouth-watering aroma of spit roasting boar and sheep was beginning to waft amongst the assembled revellers, as the final event before the great feast was announced. The spear throwing contest.

Two poles were set in the ground fifty yards from the throwing line. They were eight inches apart. Five feet behind them another pole was set, this one with the eye of a bull threaded on a thin strip of leather hanging on it. The contestants were required to throw their spears between the two front poles and pierce the bull's eye on the pole behind. For this event each competitor could only throw once. There were many entrants for this competition as it was considered to be the most prestigious. However, several of the young warriors had been less than prudent in their consumption of ale and could barely stand, much less place a spear with deadly accuracy.

The first contestant was wobbling from side to side as he held his spear aloft prior to his run up. He took several uncoordinated running steps before falling sideways in a tangled heap. The crowd roared with laughter and showered him with appropriate comments as he was dragged unceremoniously to one side. Similar scenarios were repeated by the first few men attempting to throw. The stewards had carefully assessed the condition of each entrant and placed him or her in the throwing order accordingly.

Eventually, after seven hugely entertaining inebriate misfortunes, a young warrior threw his spear between the two front poles and it stuck into the third pole quivering eight inches above the dangling eye. A roar of appreciation went up from the crowd.

Various other near misses were duly appreciated and several spears were embedded in the two front poles. Finally it was the turn of Angharad.

As the previous years champion she was throwing last, but she was definitely the favourite of the rowdy crowd. It was a tricky throw made even more difficult by the fact that the two spears stuck in the front two poles, were at a slight angles, greatly reducing the available gap. A rousing chant of "Angharad! Angharad! Angharad!" began to swell from the lips of the excited onlookers.

With great composure, determination and purpose she approached the throwing line, her weapon held upright. A flick of her wrist tossed the spear upwards causing it to turn in the air, and she deftly caught it at her shoulder, balanced and ready to throw. Her red hair hung in cascades over her shoulders and down her back, and it shone and sparkled in the late afternoon sun. She glanced over at her smiling father who nodded at her, as he bellowed "Silence! Let the girl throw."

Once again compliance was immediate, and in total silence Angharad took five slowly measured steps backwards. She stood spear at the ready, for what seemed like the longest twenty seconds, breathing deeply and centring her concentration on the job in hand. Then springing forward like a gazelle, with fluid co-ordination and unequalled symmetry, she hurled the perfectly balanced missile straight and true. Even as it left her hand she knew it was a winner. Her eyes followed it almost in slow motion, as it flew through the other spears, right between the first two poles and thudded into the rear pole, splitting its pendulous target asunder. She leapt in the air, twirling round as the watching crowd erupted into thunderous vociferous approval. Again the chants began "Angharad! Angharad! Angharad!" Chakine and Yolan still in human guise and fairly close to their charge, were intensely alert. There were dark entities everywhere, and as the people became more and more inebriated the indwelling elementals they carried gained more and more control.

Angharad basked for several minutes in her victor's glory enjoying the deserved praises of her tribal fellows. During this time the servants had begun slicing great succulent cuts of meat from the roasting animals, and the mouth-watering aroma permeated the whole area, signalling the time for feasting.

Amidst the revelry, inebriation and gastric stimulation most people failed to notice that Angharad had not given due reverence to Belenos as they tucked into their Beltaine feast. Everyone that is, except Zandorch.

It was at this time that the Druid began to tune his ears to the whisperings and mutterings of the dark spirits that directed his life. The sun was starting to grow low in the sky. Dusk was approaching and the influence of the darkness was increasing with the growing abandonment of the humans to their baser instincts. Hwyldalach was devouring a huge cut of roast boar when the Chief Druid leaned over to him. "Hwyldalach my friend, do you remember our conversation at breakfast?" The big man grunted, wiped his mouth with the back of his hand and peering at the Druid through half inebriated eyes said, "I do!" He took another enormous bite from the meat. "And do you also remember your oath to remove the head of the miscreant personally?" The Chieftain stopped eating and turned fully to face his questioner. "My sword is sharp Zandorch, find me the person responsible and you shall have their head!"

The Druid smiled and turned away and began rocking back and forth listening to the spirits. Just behind him the demon commander and his warriors waited on the edge of the inky blackness. Some of the more intoxicated villagers had begun to openly engage in various sex acts and an air of lascivious debauchery and evil grew, thinly disguised by the raucous music and laughter. The feasting continued for an hour or so before Zandorch slowly rose to his feet. The spirits had furnished him with what he needed to know and his twisted mind relished the task in front of him.

He raised his arms and bellowed "Silence!" Even amongst the drunken orgiastic crowd the response was immediate. All eyes were on him. "Angharad, daughter of Chief Hwyldalach, come here!" She was sitting eating with some of the warriors and maidens and rose at once approaching the table of dignitaries. "Angharad, I congratulate you on your victory, but I am disappointed that you failed to honour Belenos. I am sure you must have forgotten in all the excitement." They stood looking straight at each other. All else was absolute silence. "You may do so now, bow to our god," he said in an affected friendly manner. Angharad stood rooted to the spot an icy fear invading her senses.

Instantly the two Angels were at her side their guise discarded. All the demons and elementals recoiled in momentary surprise and fear. The two huge shining beings stood there, swords drawn and shields at the ready. On the physical plane no one could see anything different yet Angharad instantly had peace again, and she knew her Angels were with her. Again Zandorch addressed her, "Angharad, will you bow down to Belenos!" The young woman stood her ground, defiant.

Still seated, Hwyldalach was wildly gesticulating to his daughter in the direction of the statue.

It was at this moment that Rhiach cracked. She could sense what was coming and in fear of the savagery of the Druid should she be implicated, she cried out, "My Lord Zandorch, I am her maidservant and I have seen and heard this woman speaking out loud to the gods. She is the one who displeased them!" Then the woman recently widowed stood up, a victim of the selfsame fears. "I too have heard her praying out loud to the gods, just yesterday!" Hwyldalach sat stunned; his mouth hanging open. Angharad gathered her thoughts. At the same time the enemy commander launched his attack and a barrage of demons cascaded out of the blackness at Chakine and Yolan who fought valiantly to defend the young woman.

Still 'cloaked' and watching closely, Captain Cherno gave the order for Salzar and the rest of the angelic company to assist their brothers. They instantly entered the fray reinforcing the beleaguered duo. The shining Angels were outnumbered two to one, but held their ground in a tight circle around the young woman, keeping the demons at bay.

Zandorch addressed the Chief's daughter again. "Is this true? Have you offended the gods even before this offence to Belenos?" He theatrically looked around the assembled faces, avoiding Hwyldalach's. "Speak girl!" On the spiritual plane the battle continued to rage.

Angharad felt a wonderful peace as she looked directly at the evil man before her. She spoke calmly but in a voice loud enough for all those assembled to hear. I have not offended the gods you worship. You cannot offend that which does not exist. Do you really think that these gods of wood and stone made this beautiful land we dwell in. Your gods bring death and fear. The God I worship now brings life and health. He is The Great First God and there is no other. These gods you worship you have made yourself, from a tree or a rock."

A screaming rage contorted Zandorch's face, and likewise the faces of many others to whom the words of the young maiden were also blasphemy. Yet they were powerless. No one could move until Angharad had finished delivering the words that she felt bubbling up inside of her. Turning to the people she continued, pointing all the while at Zandorch. "You follow this man who takes the lives of young warriors and says it's the will of the gods. He tells you when to do everything! You keep the heads of your enemies because you think they hold power, but they hold nothing but death. Death and impending destruction! The Great First God is a God who loves us. He made us and He loves us. Your gods are no gods at all! Ask forgiveness and follow The Great First God. I will not bow down to false gods of wood and stone!"

Then she turned again to face Zandorch, her arms folded defiantly.

The sun had started to sink on the horizon and Captain Cherno knew that he and all the Angels must withdraw. He had heard the young female give the message from the Most

High and she had been protected for three revolutions of the earth, so their mission was accomplished. Angels obey their master. To the letter. He was quickly devising a strategy for retreat as the furious battle continued on the spiritual plane, when with a devilish screeching noise Kaisis and another great horde of demons suddenly joined the melee. Salzar and his brother Angels were swept back by sheer weight of numbers, leaving Cherno, Yolan and Chakine desperately trying to defend the girl.

As the Angels were pushed back, on the physical plane all hell broke loose and several screaming warriors and Druids came running at Angharad. Cherno and Yolan were knocked off their feet by the demon assault and slashed, clawed and stabbed repeatedly.

Chakine managed to keep his feet and remain right next to the girl, his sword flashing at the speed of light as he fought off demon after demon. The spiritual plane being outside of time, as we know it, this was all taking place in an instant before the running humans got to Angharad, the object of their wrath. Dusk was ending and Captain Cherno gave the order to withdraw, just as Kaisis and twenty other demons managed to knock Chakine over and pin him down, their claws cutting and slashing. He was overpowered and could not move. The rest of the Angels withdrew as per instructions.

Zandorch reached Angharad a fraction of a second before her father. He grabbed her roughly by the arm screaming "Blasphemy! Blasphemy!" Hwyldalach, tears streaming down his cheeks gently but firmly took hold of her other arm. She looked in her father's eyes and smiled. It was a smile of love and understanding. A smile that said 'I know what you have to do, and it's ok'. Kaisis had his foot on Chakine's throat, whilst other demons held him immobile. The helpless Angel could only watch as the dark scene unfolded.

Just as they would in a few hundred years time at the trial of Jesus, the demon horde now hovered over the assembled onlookers spewing out hatred and murder. The same crowd who an hour before had chanted her name in victory, now began to chant "Kill her! Kill her!"

Chakine, pinned down as he was, was pouring out every ounce of peace he could muster, into Angharad, who was now in the middle of a huge circle of screaming demonic villagers, all baying for her blood. Zandorch thrust her to her knees, then turning to her father he said "You made an oath to the gods, do it!" Peace outside of human understanding was all over the young woman and she looked up with loving eyes at her distraught father before bowing her head forward to receive the coming blow.

With foul brown slime dripping from his fangs, Kaisis stood over the struggling Angel, his cackling laughter splitting the air. "How now, servant of The Most High!" he shrieked, pressing his foot ever harder downward. Hwyldalach agonisingly drew his sword as Angharad shouted, "Great First God – You are the only God – there is no other!" A demonic cheer erupted as they witnessed the curving arch of Hwyldalach's sword separate Angharad's beautiful head from her shoulders. Kaisis savoured the moment, and many more elementals gained access to human bodies that night.

- - - - - - O - - - - - -

Angels and demons cannot die. But Angels don't get sent to await the Lake of Fire. So Kaisis had to let Chakine go, and he returned to the heavenly realms shortly thereafter. He had fulfilled his mission. For three revolutions of the Earth he had protected the girl.

The mystery of salvation was still in the future and unknown to him. On his return journey he thought about what Salzar had told him of his previous highly blessed journey to earth with The Most High.

It concerned a human named Abraham. This man had trusted The Most High and it had been accounted to him as righteousness. It occurred to Chakine that this was just what Angharad had done.

-------- O --------

As the two young believers continued the climb up the narrow winding path to the Dragons Back, Josh had a sudden urge to veer off to the left. He turned to Cheryll.
"Let's look around a bit." Hand in hand they picked their way across large bluestone boulders, and soon came across the entrance to a small cave that had not been visible from the ancient path. "Wow!" Cheryll said excitedly, as they explored the echoey cavern, "I wonder who has slept here in times past?"
The two Angels looked at each other but said nothing. Each clearly remembering a night spent here, a young human named Angharad, and the sad events of 2,300 years ago.

------ O ------

<<<< - - - END OF CHAPTER FIVE - - - >>>>

The Dragonmaster

CHAPTER 6 **Warrior**

It was now mid August and Josh and Cheryll were deeply in love. So far they'd managed to resist all the natural urges that would have seen them disappoint their guardian Angels and cause The Holy Spirit to distance himself. There had been a few 'close things' but their now combined sense of what is right, plus wanting to please God, had always won out. So they had resolved not to put themselves in situations where temptation could get the better of them.

------ O ------

In many respects the old fashioned way of having a chaperone present at all times prior to marriage, was a good thing. Teenage pregnancy was virtually unheard of in the days when it was not socially acceptable for young people over a certain age to spend time alone together.

In other cultures right across the world, unsupervised contact between young unmarried couples is frowned upon. In some places it's even illegal. Since the sixties and the time of so called free love, Western society has changed enormously. Women have become liberated. Liberated to murder their unborn babies, liberated to have illegitimate children, liberated to contract all sorts of sexually transmitted disease, liberated to swap and change from sexual partner to sexual partner. The list of 'freedoms' they have won goes on and on, and all the while standards in society sink further and further down.

The whole thing is part of a planned and carefully orchestrated manoeuvre from the 'Father of Lies'. Jesus bestowed that title upon Satan and it aptly describes his methods of operation.

He feeds lies to humanity. Lies that always target the sensual side of our fallen nature. His attacks are always through our physical senses and the ability we have to imagine all manner of events.

Our enemy is patient, he takes his ground little by little, almost imperceptibly at first, until suddenly – when it's too late - there is a realisation that the individual or society is wallowing in a morass of filth, perversion, lies and corruption. Whilst it is true that because of the fall of man there have always been those people and organisations that were drawn to follow diverse lusts and perversions, it was usually done in secret – always undercover of one pretence or another. Now however, in the 'enlightened' 21st. Century [And bear in mind that Lucifer was *originally* the Lightbringer ~ the one who enlightens] it seems that in the Western world nothing in the social sense, with the exception perhaps of paedophilia, is now considered taboo.

The concerted attack began in the sixties. Computers were in their infancy but the ground was being firmly prepared for what was to come. Two carefully planned and devastating world wars had happened in the recent past, priming the current crop of youth for rebellion against what they saw as the failed values of their parents.

Vast quantities of marijuana, LSD, and a plethora of 'uppers' and 'downers' flooded the whole youth market, and new and exciting sensual music emerged as the glue that gave cohesion to the whole cleverly marketed deception. The philosophies of Eastern cultures, fuelled by drug consumption and its subsequent libertine consequences, produced the whole Hippie movement. The ethos of free love cleverly sabotaged biblical moral codes, whilst demonic spirits of lust, rebellion and anti-Christ descended in vast and organised armies on the youth of the Western world. This time of Love and Peace and Flower Power was Satan's great counterfeit of the real love of Jesus.

There certainly was a great feeling of change and the expectation of the dawning of a coming New Age. It was easy to get caught up in the optimism of it all. But it was completely, totally and utterly false. For there is no salvation in it, and man's dilemma is his continued separation from God.

Around the same time other spirits of anarchy, death and destruction were being released. Some groups, like the Black Panthers and the Baader-Meinhof gang grew in the Western world, but mostly the activity of these spirits was centred in Middle Eastern countries. Here the predominant area of assault was via religious spirits. As television and the growing global media spread news of the ever-increasing decadence of the West, these religious spirits caused a fanatical lashback, and the re-emergence of an ancient philosophy – Jihad.

Now, in our wonderful computerised 21st Century, we have witnessed an incredible explosion of knowledge and information. Many people travel the world, routinely jetting from country to country. Many of our leaders and famous citizens are often found doing things that the Word of God says, are abominable. Yet they are idolised, given positions of authority, honour and celebrity. Millions of babies are routinely murdered for convenience. Filthy language and profanity abound on television and in film. Pornography is rampant and the fastest growing industry on the planet due to its easy accessibility via the internet. Sick men fly out to third world countries to have sex with children.

As our knowledge and technology has increased so has our depravity.

"But you Daniel, seal up the words of this book until **the time of the end**, when many shall run to and fro across the face of the earth and knowledge will be greatly increased." [Daniel Ch. 12 v 4] *Amplified.*

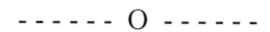

------ O ------

One late July evening, after the youth meeting, a rather troubled looking young girl came to speak to Cheryll. She was Jenny, the fourteen-year-old daughter of Dave and Lucy who attended the Aberdigan fellowship. Cheryll made some cocoa and they both sat down. "Is there something I can help you with Jen?" enquired Cheryll. The youngster looked right at her, tears welling up in her eyes. "It's school, the other girls won't leave me alone." she took out her handkerchief and wiped away the tears. "They know I'm a Christian and they keep taunting me." Cheryll smiled and reaching out, took her hand "Don't worry Jen, the bible says we are to count it all joy when people persecute us and say bad things about us because we follow Jesus." The younger girl looked at her seemingly unconvinced. Cheryll went on "I get it myself at college, all the time."

Jenny shifted in her seat and sighed, "Yeah, but they keep calling me a particular name and it really bugs me." - "They call me the same old names over and over," the older girl replied, "but I just ignore them." - "What do they call you then?" Jenny asked. Cheryll cleared her throat, "Well, sometimes it's 'iron pants' and other times it's the 'female eunuch'." The two girls looked at each other for a moment and then began to giggle. After a few seconds Jenny spoke again. "They call me. . . virgin girl." she said, her serious demeanour quickly returning. Cheryll studied the young girl with a mixture of emotion. "Virgin girl" she thought – "how I wish they could call me that!"

She sent up a silent prayer. "Lord, please give me wisdom for this young lady, I need to know how to best comfort and encourage her." The bible says if anyone lacks wisdom, then let him ask God, who will give it liberally, and, true to His word God did just that for Cheryll.

"Jenny, I understand that it's hard when people call you names. But look at it from God's perspective. What these girls are really saying to you is 'Obedient girl!' or 'Faithful girl!' - What a fantastic compliment!" Jenny's eyes lit up "I hadn't thought of it like that, yes, I am obeying God!" she smiled and sighed as if a big weight had been lifted from her shoulders. "And furthermore," continued Cheryll "here's what to say to them the very next time they 'accuse' you. Say, 'Listen, I can be like you any time I choose to – but you can <u>never</u> be like me again. What I have will be surrendered to my husband on my wedding night."

These imparted words passed on from the Spirit seemed to lift the young girl, and she went home resolved to meet her tormentors with that selfsame wisdom. Offering a prayer of thanks to God Cheryll wistfully wished she'd been more restrained at Jenny's age, instead of having given away such a precious thing in a haze of booze and drugs.

------ O ------

The next day, Josh was even happier than usual, that morning he'd received a call from Ray Coughlin, direct from Beijing. Ray's business mind had recalled Josh's mobile number, and the news was that he was healing well and would be heading for home soon.

Josh hadn't mentioned his new-found faith, feeling he'd rather wait until he and his old friend were face to face.

When he shared the news with Meredith and Cheryll they too were excited and happy. Although they had never actually met Ray, Josh had spoken of him often and since the incident in China, they had all been praying regularly for the man and his family.

------ O ------

On the other side of the world, in the other 'Land of the Dragon' Ray Coughlin and Simon Cheng sat opposite one another in easy chairs in a comfortable hospital lounge room. Simon was visiting, as he'd been discharged some six weeks previously, his wounded thigh having healed up quite quickly. Ray of course was still an inmate, though due to be discharged the day after tomorrow.

Simon had just finished, in a completely self-effacing fashion, filling in the details of all that had transpired after Ray had lapsed into unconsciousness, and the Englishman knew he owed the little Chinese guide a great debt of gratitude. Furthermore, Ray was pleased to be informed that approximately two thirds of the jade carvings had been rescued and that the parting gift of Yan–Ti was also safe. The whole cargo, under Simon's supervision, having been stored in two crates at a secure facility. All that was now needed was Ray's signature on the shipping dockets, which Simon had brought along. Ray signed them and duly passed them back to him. "Simon, thank you so much for all you have done," he said, pulling out his wallet.

In the time honoured fashion of English wide boys, he was about to offer Simon a 'drink', when the little man frowned, holding up his hand. He looked somewhat insulted. "Mr Coughlin, what I did I did because I am paid to do it. It is my job. My job was to get you safely back to Beijing. From your perspective, the fact of whether or not I accomplished this is open perhaps to one's interpretation of the word 'safely'. However, you are here and thankfully alive. Yet all I have done is my job, and for that I have already been remunerated." - "Well then," said an embarrassed Ray, putting away his wallet and getting slowly to his feet, "Let me shake you by the hand." Simon stood and the two men met in the middle of the room. Ray shook Simon's hand, then taking him by the shoulders he looked into the little man's eyes and said "Simon, I owe you my life – thank you, thank you so much." Simon bowed, "Mr Coughlin, it was my privilege." he said, as he reached into his inside jacket pocket and produced a letter. "Here is the translation of the document Yan –Ti gave to you. I hope you are able to make more sense of it than I." He Handed it to Ray. "And Mr. Coughlin, please be very careful, goodbye!" With that he turned and walked from the room, leaving Ray to muse over his good fortune at having had such a competent guide and interpreter.

The whole time Ray had been recovering, the Chinese authorities had accommodated Zara. First at the hospital whilst he was in intensive care, and then in a hotel close by so she could visit him each day. She was certainly not 'born again' nor really a believer in the conventional sense of the word, yet she had prayed and prayed for her man, unaware of course of all the prayer that had gone down on the opposite side of the world.

Unlike many people whom God bales out in an emergency, and then they go and forget Him, Zara was still thanking God each day. Not one of the bullets had struck a bone or vital organ, and although he would always bear the scars, her man was now 95% ok again. And they were scheduled to fly home in two days time! She thought to herself "Well, at least we'll never have to face another trauma like that in our lives!"

Little did she know what was waiting in the wings, and what dark doors had been opened by her 'harmless' little gift of a Pentagram as a good luck charm.

- - - - - - O - - - - - -

The hand of divine grace lay strongly on Joshua Fishmen. His relationship with his woman was right and pleasing to God and he was eager to devour all the teaching he could get. Evenings that weren't spent with the fellowship, praising God and sharing with the other believers, were spent in bible study with Meredith or Cheryll or a combination of the two. Recently he had felt led to enquire about spiritual warfare and the whole 'casting out demons' thing. His mentor instructed him well and Josh learnt quickly.

"So," he said to Meredith, "It's impossible for someone without the Holy Spirit, someone who isn't saved, to cast out a demon from another person?" - "That's correct, but with the possible exception of some Satanists who, through the powers of darkness, can exert some control over the lesser demons. However of course, their agenda is totally different and not at all concerned with the freedom of an individual." Joshua thought for a moment. "Should we cast out demons wherever we detect them?" - "Most certainly not!" came the reply. "For instance - If you are walking through town and pass someone on the street and discern that they have a 'non paying guest', what would be the point in casting it out? –

Unless the person concerned got saved or was saved and requested it be removed, or really intended to change their lifestyle, it would leave only to quickly return with seven more, in effect you'd be doing them more harm than good!" [Mathew Ch12 v.43 – 45]

Meredith sucked on the ever-present pipe, then continued "The whole spiritual area of what is termed 'deliverance' is one of the most misunderstood and mis-ministered areas of the Christian walk. Personally, when I hear someone proclaim they have a deliverance ministry I am always rather sceptical. Not that I don't believe in deliverance, it's totally biblical and I've been personally involved many times. But unfortunately there are quite a few believers who have set themselves up in this ministry without the leading of the Holy Spirit. And that spells eventual disaster!" Josh nodded his assent. "So how do you know if you have the gift?" "We all, as believers, have the authority to cast out demons. In fact we have the authority and mandate to do all the things that Jesus did!"
[John Ch14 v.12]
"Great," Josh exclaimed, "I'll start making my own wine!" They both laughed.

The warrior was growing fast in biblical knowledge, because his heart was open to the things of the spirit. He longed to serve his Heavenly Master and understood that he was saved solely by what Jesus had accomplished on the cross at Calvary. He understood that nothing could be added to the finished work of the cross. Salvation is by God's grace through our faith in what His Son did – nothing more. True service comes from a heart overflowing with gratitude and love.

Cheryll and Meredith had taught him how to pray in authority when dealing with sickness, disease or demonic manifestations. He was beginning to get an inkling of the power there is in Jesus name. He had listened to the young woman sharing her faith with others and had learnt much from how she handled what seemed to him to be perennial questions, and he'd reasoned, much like Ray had out in

China, that all men were basically the same. This he took to be yet another firm indicator that we all stem from the same source. The more he read from the bible about Jesus, the more he began to realise the degree to which He transcended the norm. Water into wine, lame sick and blind healed, dead raised back to life and a raging storm commanded to cease! Josh's love and admiration for his saviour grew, day by day. Meredith had also introduced his charge to the concept of prayer and fasting and Josh quickly came to understand that as you deny your body, so your spirit quickens and draws closer to God, which in turn releases more heavenly power into situations. It wasn't long before he was able to utilise his new found strengths.

One weekend Cheryll's brother Mark was visiting from Bristol. He and Josh had hit it off instantly. Mark wasn't saved but was a student at the university. He was highly intelligent, very tall and thin, a great lover of music and, like his sister, into things alternative. He sported a great mop of curly hair and wore John Lennon type glasses. His general attire was an old combat jacket and jeans and he drove a battered old Renault van.

He was rather awkward, and appeared somewhat unsynchronised, walking with a great loping gait. Josh felt that he was probably the least physically co-ordinated guy he had ever met! However, what he lacked in 'cool' was compensated by a warm and caring personality.

A few days before, Tarquin from 'Maen Du' had phoned to say they were having a party at the farm with a couple of bands playing in the barn that weekend, and would Josh and any friends like to come along.

Despite the presence of all the various spirits and foreign gods, Josh always enjoyed visits to 'Maen Du' and its hippie residents. In fact he'd confided in Cheryll that had he not got saved, then he probably would have joined their ranks! She'd smiled and said, "Yes, I know what you mean, most of them are such lovely loving people."

Though some of the residents were strongly opposed to the beliefs of the Christians, - [or rather they were opposed to what they supposed the Christians believed] – all in all they accepted them as they were and often engaged in lively discussions regarding 'churchianity'. As yet none of them had come to Jesus, but many seeds had been sown. Josh and Cheryll prayed for them all regularly, and knew that going there was building bridges. So on Saturday evening they all piled into Mark's van and went to the party. There were a couple of hundred people in attendance and a field was being used as a car park where some were also camping. The bands started at around 10.30 in the barn. Outside there was a large bonfire and folk were sitting around on blankets, smoking and drinking, party fashion. Around 11.15 just after Josh and Cheryll had gone into the barn to listen to the music, the threatening roar of a dozen motorbikes bouncing down the track, heralded the arrival of the local biker gang. They drove into the farmyard at speed, pulling wheelies and scattering some of those relaxing as they watched the flickering flames. Many had to dive out of the way. Round and round the fire they rode, trashing people's blankets and possessions, before heading off into the field where the vehicles were parked, all the while revving their noisy machines.

When Josh and Cheryll had gone in to listen to the band, Mark had gone back to his van to get his tobacco. He was sitting there with the sliding side door open, rolling a joint, when the bikers came past. He had been clearly silhouetted in their headlights. They had continued on into the field, parked their machines and were walking back towards the barn. This route took them past Mark's van. At this point he was sitting there happily smoking his completed joint. One of the bikers ambled over to him, "Smells good man, give me a toke." Ever affable, Mark handed the guy the spliff saying, "Sure, help yourself mate."

The rest of the biker gang was lurking in the shadows as Susie, one of the 'Maen Du' residents, passed by. She knew Josh and Cheryll and had been introduced to Mark earlier. "Hi Mark" she said, just as the biker said, "Give me all your grass man!" An astute young lady, she sensed what was about to go down, especially when she heard Mark reply innocently "Why ever would I do that?"

She disappeared into the darkness and began to run as fast as she could up to the barn. She found Josh and Cheryll quickly, explaining "I think your friend's in trouble, some bikers have got him down in the car park!" Josh turned to Cheryll, "Stay here, pray!" He ran out the door of the barn and was instantly by the back doors of Marks van! He was bemused for a moment, a little disorientated, then he heard a guy threatening Mark "You better give me your grass if you know what's good for you." Josh came from behind the van and stood next to where Mark was now standing by the open sliding door. The biker had hold of Mark's jacket; the situation didn't look good. Josh was aware of about a dozen other bikers, just visible in the shadows, from the interior light of the van. His mind was racing and he could see what was coming.

Josh the man, the ex soldier, veteran of Gulf war action, knew he could take this guy out in half a second. And that then he could probably take out three or four more very quickly. But then the odds would be very much against him, and he knew that Mark couldn't punch his way out of a wet paper bag! Nonetheless, believing there was no other course of action to save Cheryll's brother from physical harm; he was about to unleash a forceful punch against the protagonist's jaw.

Suddenly he felt a power rush down through the top of his head. This power seemed to inflate him and it filled him with righteous indignation. At the same time he lifted his hand, palm outwards and prayed in tongues out loud and forcibly " Shandala bar kiem artoo........" and he continued with great authority. The effect was astonishing. The guy assaulting Mark let go and backed away, and as he continued praying in tongues Josh heard one of the group say "F....... hell! – we've got a f....... born again Christian here and they all backed off mumbling as they disappeared and dispersed into the darkness. Chakine, unseen behind Josh, sheathed his sword and smiled. The young warrior had responded well and used his spiritual weaponry.

Mark, for the most part seemed oblivious to the danger he had been in, except to say, "Hmm, he didn't seem to like your chanting!"

Much later that night the two young Christians gave thanks to the Lord and Josh knew he'd learned a valuable lesson. The reality of the words of the book of Ephesians chapter six had hit home. *Our enemy is not one of flesh and blood!*

The following day, in conversation with Meredith, he mentioned how he'd exited the barn and a second later found himself next to Mark's van which was 200 yards away! "Praise the Lord!" exclaimed the older man, "You were translated. Perfectly biblical, if not the commonest of miracles though!" Josh was quickly shown the passage in Acts chapter eight where Phillip had just baptised the Ethiopian eunuch, and was then 'caught away' and found himself in Azotus, a town some fifteen miles away. "Well," said Meredith with a smile, "I suppose two hundred yards is a start!"

------ O ------

Donna and Vernon, (Ray and Zara's kids), were overjoyed to see their parents again, especially their dad. Their grandparents had taken them to the airport and there was a joyous and tearful family reunion when the tired couple reached arrivals. After a hug, the first thing young Vernon had said was "Show us where the bullets got you dad!" Followed by "What's it like to be shot, did it hurt much?" and then "Did you shoot any of the baddies dad?" during the car journey home the questions were incessant, but Ray answered them all best he could, delighted to be back with his family.

He had purposed to have three weeks at home just chilling out, before he would start work again, and the final week he was particularly looking forward to. It would be the start of the football season, and he could once again watch his beloved team – Manchester United. The Reds. There was only one work related thing he absolutely must do in a fortnight's time. Go to the customs shed at the airport and sign for and pay the duty on, his hard won consignment of jade.

------ O ------

Joshua continued to grow in grace, and in knowledge of the truth, under the steadfast guidance of Meredith and the loving encouragement of Cheryll. He learnt something of church history, of things in the past and of things to come. He learnt about the end times and many of the myths surrounding what is often preached as doctrine. He learnt that some Christians believe the gifts of the Spirit ended with the apostles. This at first bemused, then subsequently amused him as he realised that it just made a complete nonsense of not only all that he was experiencing, but much of what a huge slice of the body of Christ had experienced these last two thousand years. He came to understand that many fellowships operated on 'The traditions of men', though by no means all of them. But he understood that the ones that did had many things in common. Often members would pray in the language of 1642 – "Yea Lord that Thou wouldst pour out Thine unction blessing upon Thy humble servants." or some other such type of prayer language that bore no resemblance to current parlance in the 21st century! Meredith had said "If, when you were greeted at the door of a church, the person greeting you said 'Verily brother, how goest thou, art thou hale and hearty?' and then later on in the meeting prayed in the same vernacular, I could handle that. It would give me no problem at all, except of course I might think it was a bit strange, but if that was how he talked – fine! However the problem is often this: that you'll be greeted on the door in normal 21st century English, only to have people revert to talking like The Pilgrim Fathers during prayer time! Of course, you can't dictate to folk how they should pray, but my concern is that it puts a lot of young people right off, plus it serves no spiritual purpose whatsoever. It is merely a tradition!"

Meredith was imparting the benefit of his experience to equip and enable the young man to cope with what he knew he would ultimately encounter in Christian circles. He continued. "You know, it seems that some of our brothers believe that God wears a suit and tie!" Josh smiled; enjoying what he was learning. "They seem to have completely lost sight of the fact that Jesus, Yeshua, their messiah, was born lived, died and was resurrected in the Middle East! He wore the only garment He possessed. A one-piece seamless robe made of Egyptian cotton. The whole 'suit and tie' thing is once again merely the tradition of man!" Josh rather liked it when his mentor got all fired up. "Now I'm not at all saying that it's wrong to wear a suit and tie, of course not. And if that is the mode of dress in which a minister or believer feels comfortable, then fine, no problem. What gets me however, is when people intimate that God is somehow more pleased or impressed if you dress in that fashion. Or worse still that it somehow indicates your spirituality or position. That sort of thinking is exactly what the Pharisees did, and boy, did Jesus berate them for it!"

Josh had recently read in Mathew chapter fifteen Jesus' tirade against the traditions of men and he had resolved if possible, to never let himself fall into this type of trap.

On another occasion, when Josh and Meredith had taken the dogs for a walk up to Meredith's special place, they had got on to a similar subject. Polly and Boots were running to and fro in the bracken, investigating all and sundry in their usual frenetic canine fashion. Chakine and Salzar, ever alert at the shoulders of their human charges, were talking Angel things. The two men were seated on the fallen tree overlooking the bay and the shining sea, way below. Josh had been talking to the minister of one of the local chapels in town and had felt that the poor man seemed really resistant to anything to do with the movement or power of the Holy Spirit. Meredith attempted to explain.

"Satan got Eve to sin basically by utilising the power of three little words, and he still uses the same tactic today. He questions what The Lord has clearly proclaimed – 'Has God said?' – that's virtually what he presented her with when she replied to his initial temptation to eat from the tree. God's instructions were clear but the Devil sowed seeds of doubt. In the same way God's word is very clear concerning the ministry of the Holy Spirit to believers, and prophecy after prophecy indicates a great movement of the Spirit in the last days. But Satan has sadly been able to blind the minds of many believers and bring them into unbelief through the traditions of man. Same old same old!"

"When I look up at the heavens" said Josh, I'm just amazed at the beauty and enormity of it all, and recently I watched a DVD of photos taken from the Hubble Space Telescope. Oh man, Meredith, they're astonishing! It seems that the universe just goes on and on!" Meredith struck a match and sucked on the stem of his ever-present pipe. Great clouds of aromatic blue smoke swirled around as they sat in momentary silence. Then he said, "We have these little peanut brains yet we often like to think we can suss out the sheer majestic glory, the plans and the extent of the creation of our incredible Heavenly Father. So many people try to limit God when the bible clearly states 'Nothing is impossible to God'! Nothing!" Later, as they walked back down the path to their cottages Josh had the distinct impression that God had done something in him regarding faith.

    During their frequent interactions the two men discussed many things, all pertaining to The Lord, and Josh took on board and assimilated every ounce of wisdom he grasped from Meredith's lucid explanations. The time he and Cheryl spent together also bore fruit and their bond was deepening all the while. In a relatively short time the young warrior had grown in wisdom, discernment and love, and was spending an hour in the morning in prayer and bible study before setting off for work.

------ O ------

Back in the flatlands of Essex Ray was enjoying being pampered, and Zara was pleased to be the perpetrator. He had made contact with Josh and the two friends had talked for a couple of hours on the phone. Josh had again withheld the information regarding his new relationship with Jesus, preferring to tell his old friend face to face, and anyway Ray had done most of the talking, recounting the events of his Chinese adventure. Josh had invited them all down to stay in his cottage and arrangements had been made for them to come in two weeks time.

For the previous two weeks Ray had lounged around the house relaxing, smoking joints and watching DVDs. However, now he needed to go back to the airport customs shed and sort out the payment and paperwork for his consignment of jade carvings. His appointment was for 2pm. He arrived in his van at five minutes to and was ushered into a huge shed piled high with crates and boxes of all shapes and sizes. Once his two crates from China were identified, the customs official explained that they would have to open them for security reasons and Ray happily complied. Simon had made an excellent job of packaging the items, which were all safe, sound, and well padded. In the second crate on top of the rows of small figures all carefully packed in straw and shredded paper, there lay a larger packet, individually wrapped. The customs officer asked Ray to remove the packaging, and was satisfied when it revealed a larger jade carving, a triangle of three intertwined dragons. Signing the various forms, Ray paid the duty, and had his van loaded with the two crates. Pretty soon he was on his way home, the present from Yan-Ti bouncing on the passenger seat next to him.

------ O ------

All of that which Meredith had taught him stayed with Josh, but some things stood out more than others. The latest gem of wisdom had been, in reference to people building doctrines from just one verse, "A text without a context is a pretext!" Josh thought this was brilliant, and would say it to himself over and over. Meredith was at pains to teach him of the truth, reliability and validity of the bible, and that God is not at all limited by man's inability to comprehend His greatness! He was introduced to the works of Charles Spurgeon, Charles S. Price, Derek Prince and Rick Joyner, to name but a few. He quickly came to understand that there is unlimited power in the blood of Jesus and the cross of Calvary.

One afternoon he started to read from the book of Ezekiel for the first time and was completely blown away! The descriptions of the incredible beings and creatures the prophet saw were not remotely like anything Josh had ever seen, even on his wildest acid trip. He had also recently read 'The Final Quest' by Rick Joyner, which is an account of an amazing vision given to Rick by God. He was fascinated by the mystical and otherworldly experiences relayed in the narrative and he resolved to discover more of the spiritual dimension. Very early on after his salvation he had come across this verse: 'Eye has not seen, nor ear heard, nor has entered into the heart of man the things that God has prepared for those that love Him'. [1 Corinthians Ch2 v 9].

This verse alone had 'fired him up' and he understood it to be a promise of an utterly fantastic existence in an incredible place of peace, love, colour and harmony that was way beyond the imagination of man. He had then stumbled upon 'Hunter Ministries' run by Charles and Frances Hunter of Kingswood, Texas, and he was completely blown away by all the verified accounts of fantastic healings and supernatural miracles this lovely old couple had been privileged to be used in. Especially as Frances was now 93 and still ministering!

He was beginning to discover that it *is* possible, within the will of God, to interact with some of these spiritual dimensions. He found that there had been Christian mystics in the past, to whom access to these places had been given.

Meredith however, had very wisely counselled caution, reminding Josh that Satan was skilled in appearing as an angel of light and would like nothing better than to get the young warrior on the wrong track. Heeding this advice yet still feeling led in a mystical direction, Josh prayed for protection, and that God would reveal by His Holy Spirit everything he wanted him to know about, and close the door firmly on anything that was from the enemy.

The following afternoon he decided he would go and sit by the stream at the bottom of the field. This time, for some reason, he felt he should leave Boots at home. Her sad little eyes had made him feel quite guilty as he closed the back door leaving her in her basket, but the feeling to be on his own had persisted. It was a lovely sunny day and Cheryll was in college, Meredith in town. He made his way down the gentle slope the sound of the bubbling water growing louder as he approached. There was a small dry laid old stone wall that bounded the bank of the little stream on one side, and Josh sat himself down in the sunlight, his back against the wall, the stream in front of him. He began to pray. He prayed for his mother, he prayed for Cheryll, Meredith, the fellowship and finally, for Ray and Zara to come to know Jesus.

Suddenly the Spirit said, "Open your eyes Josh." It was a clear and precise voice in his head. He immediately obeyed. Across the field about 250 yards away, he could see some sort of animal approaching but it was in a heat haze and he couldn't make out quite what it was. The Spirit spoke again clearly "Trust me, sit perfectly still."

Josh was sitting cross-legged his hands raised a little, palms upwards. His eyes were glued to the slowly approaching form. At first he thought it was a large dog, as he could clearly see huge paws flicking up as the beast moved in his direction. A long tail that ended in a dark 'pom pom' flicked from side to side and he realised that he was looking at some sort of lion! He estimated its body to be about eight feet long, and it was coming directly towards him! Again the Spirit spoke. "Don't be afraid, trust me. Shut your eyes." The presence of the Spirit was so strong that Josh felt calm and closed his eyes, remaining perfectly still.

He could now hear the creature as it padded ever nearer to him, but his feeling of peace remained. Then he could actually hear its breathing and he felt the vibration of its footfalls through the ground. He realised it was now only feet away, yet the sense of calm persisted and he remained immobile with his eyes shut. Then he could feel its breath on his face! It was right in front of him; in fact it towered over him, its nostrils about level with his forehead.

Josh half opened his eyes, keeping them 'scrunched up' and realised that he was praying in tongues out loud. Abruptly he stopped, shutting his eyes again when he saw how enormous the creature was. It didn't frighten him; it just took his breath away. For several more seconds he sat motionless, still feeling its warm breath on his face. And then it was gone. He opened his eyes and nothing was there. He jumped up and looked 360 degrees all around. Nothing. He scanned the fields from right to left and back. Nothing. Then this Chosen One remembered the prayer he had recently prayed, and the words 'Lion of Judah' came flooding into his mind.

------ O ------

Back over in Essex, Ray Coughlin sat in front of his television in excited anticipation. Zara and the kids were out for the afternoon and Ray was well stocked and ready for his team's first game of the new football season. On the coffee table next to him were several beers and a couple of ready rolled joints, so he wouldn't miss any of the action being distracted by sticking papers together and the like. The screen was a large plasma slim line, mounted on the wall above the fireplace, and Ray was relaxed in his leather recliner with foot support, indulging in a pre-match spliff. There were five minutes to go to kick off and the pundits were giving their usual assessments and opinions. On the mantelpiece below the screen sat Yan-Ti's gift, and in the unseen blackness above Ray's head, a thousand writhing demons schemed and muttered.

------ O ------

Josh was halfway across the field leading back to his cottage when his mobile rang. It was Cheryll and she wanted him to come down into Aberdigan.

A young lad she had been witnessing to was very interested to meet Josh after Cheryll had told him that her Christian boyfriend had once been a professional soldier. Collecting Boots from the cottage, he drove into town meeting Cheryll and the young man in the Castle Café. They'd talked over coffee and then wandered down by the river, and 30 minutes later there was a new member of The Kingdom. Josh was overjoyed, this was the first person he'd led to the Lord. Cheryll was overjoyed for the young man and for Josh. An Angel was immediately dispatched from the courts of Heaven to take his place at the young man's shoulder, and Chakine and Yolan greeted their spirit brother as they swooped and dived victoriously. Up in heaven a great shout went up from the whole angelic host.

". . . There is joy in the presence of the Angels of God over one sinner who repents". [Luke Ch.15 v10]

------ O ------

Around the same time in London, a whistle blew and a great roar resounded around the stadium as Manchester United commenced their battle with Chelsea. The pace was fast and furious and it promised to be a memorable game. Ray, seated in front of his television, exhaled a long plume of marijuana smoke, which enveloped the jade carving on his mantelpiece, curling in, out and around the three sinister dragons.

Manchester United were pushing hard and after five minutes, a brilliant save by the Chelsea keeper from a bullet shot by Wayne Rooney, resulted in a corner kick. The fans began to chant "Come on you Re-eds, Come on you Re-eds!"

Almost imperceptibly at first, the jade statue began to glow and pulsate. Ray was oblivious, his eyes glued to the action. The corner kick was taken, and as it curled towards the far post, Ronaldo rose high in the air, his powerful header sending the ball firmly into the back of the net. The watching army of fans erupted and almost instantly Ray was on his feet doing a little dance in front of the screen and chanting, "C'mon you Reds! C'mon you Reds!" The pulsating glow from the statue was increasing in intensity, but with his senses tuned in to the all-important match, Ray failed to notice it. He was now very stoned and totally into the game. He flopped back into the leather recliner as he popped the ring pull on another can of beer.

------ O ------

Over in Wales, Josh and Cheryll had gone to visit Dave and Lucy from the fellowship. They were brimming over with the news of the young man who had given his life to Jesus, and were pleased to discover Meredith there, already enjoying a mug of tea.

They had noted the young man's details and invited him to attend their meeting in Aberdigan the following day. They met in the old Town Hall each Sunday morning, to give opportunity for members of the public to attend, whereas their mid-week meetings were generally in one another's homes. The others were very happy to hear the news of a young soul saved, and together they all gave thanks to the Lord. They sat for a while chatting and Josh raised the subject of Angels. "Do you think we have Angels with us all the time?" Yolan, Chakine, Salzar and the two Guardians of Dave and Lucy all exchanged smiling glances. "Well," began Meredith "I'd like to think so. I certainly know that I have been helped on many occasions by an unseen force." Dave added, "The bible tells us that 'the angel of the Lord encamps roundabout those that fear Him, and delivers them' [Psalm 34 v 7]

And the Hebrew word 'encamps' literally means 'to dwell', so I would deduce from this, that the Angels <u>are</u> with us all the time." – "Yes good point," continued Meredith, "and we're told in Hebrews chapter one that Angels are all ministering spirits – in other words, they're here to help us." "Not only that," added Cheryll "right across the world there are thousands and thousands of reports of people experiencing angelic intervention, especially where children are concerned."

The five Angels in the room were quite amused by the speculation of their respective charges as to whether they were actually there or not. For a moment, Salzar was tempted to do something that would demonstrate their presence, but quickly dismissed the idea from his mind as being without his master's mandate.

The five humans continued their debate; each contributing something that reflected their individual level of understanding. Finally Josh said "You know the Word says that 'God is a Spirit' and that right in the beginning He spoke everything into being. That is, you, me, the wood of this table," he rapped on the coffee table with his knuckles, "that means that everything that exists, all of it, is born <u>out of spirit!</u>" he threw his hands in the air and looked all around him, "It all has a spiritual source. In other words, reality itself is spiritual <u>not</u> physical." They all looked at him, digesting the enormity of what he had just said. He elaborated. "Let's say you were to trip over and bang your head on this coffee table," he rapped it again, "it would feel pretty real of course, and the lump you would have on your head would no doubt feel extremely real!" They all laughed. "We are here in this third dimension, which is a physical dimension where it seems certain laws of physics are in operation. You step out in front of a truck – you know what will happen. But what I'm saying is that this place we find ourselves existing in, is not the real 'reality'. The real place is God's domain and it's all spirit and it's eternity, because only flesh and blood can grow old and die." Each of the ever-present watching guardians looked very happy, as if they were hearing truth from the lips of a little child. "Look at when Jesus appeared to the apostles in a locked room, it seems He just came right through the wall, or that He just manifested. Whichever way it was, He certainly transcended what we would call the laws of physics. Then He says "Feel me for I am flesh and bone!"

Josh had inadvertently clicked into preach mode, but the little assembly was relishing it, so he continued. "Right after Jesus says 'You must be born again' in John 3, He goes on to say 'That which is born of flesh is flesh and that which is born of spirit is spirit' - God's Kingdom is spirit and the whole of His creation has come out of that realm. The book of Hebrews tells us that we have been made 'a little lower than the Angels', lesser in rank so to speak, and that Jesus himself instead of taking on the nature of the Angels – which is spirit, He took on Himself the seed of Abraham – which is flesh, so He could pay for our sin. My point is, that as the whole of heaven is incorruptible spirit, and full of some pretty strange and amazing stuff, I think we should try and access the spiritual realms a little more, although I have to say that I'm not quite sure how to go about that! – However, I'd just love to have the sort of experiences Ezekiel had!" - "But could you also endure the hardships and persecutions it all involved?" asked Lucy. Josh was about to relate his experience with the lion, then thought better of it. Some things of the spirit are best kept in the heart.

The little band of believers continued their discussions for another hour and a half, at the end of which Meredith said, "You know, I love to watch a bit of football and I could chat about it for ten minutes or so, or talk about art for a little while. But I find I can talk about Jesus and the things of the Kingdom all day every day and it's always fresh and it's always exciting!" Everyone present, including the Angels, agreed.

------ O ------

Back in Essex Ray was completely immersed in the football. It had been a battle royal and with 5 min to go both sides were level at 3 goals each. The room was thick with green glowing marijuana smoke and the smell of alcohol. Several empty cans littered the floor and Ray sucked feverishly on the joint between his lips. The volume of the television masked the low guttural sounds emanating from the jade statue and the inebriated man was oblivious to the demons that were appearing behind him in the room.

Manchester United launched a powerful attack and were breaking through. The cacophonous chants of their fans reached fever pitch, and Ray joined in almost screeching, "C'mon you re-eds! - C'mon you re-eds!"

At that moment a dark and malevolent yellow eyed spirit manifested from the carving and swirled round and round the room and then round and round Ray in ever decreasing circles as though it would constrict him. Ray heard the roar from the crowd as his team scored the winning goal but it seemed to come from far, far away. And as a host of elementals joined those already in residence in his body, the spirit from the carving entered his mouth and the powerful spell of the Dragonmaster began to weave its evil purpose.

Fortunately the kids had decided to stay with their grandparents for the night, so when Zara returned several hours later she was on her own. As she opened the front door she could smell the dope, and the sound of the television was deafening.

Entering the front room she gasped. Ray was lying face down on the carpet, the coffee table was on its side and there were empty beer cans and the contents of an ashtray strewn all over the floor. She ran to him and knelt down by his side, her hand gently shaking his shoulder. "Ray, Ray, what's the matter, wake up Ray!" she shook him again. He made an incoherent burble and began to regain consciousness. He slowly lifted himself up on to his elbows and Zara kissed the top of his head. "Are you ok honey?" she was terrified that it might be something to do with his gunshot wounds, but as he gradually regained clarity she soon realised it was merely the result of several spliffs and six cans of strong beer. "Silly boy," she playfully scolded, getting him back on to the recliner, "I can't leave you for five minutes can I?" Ray shook his head and rubbed his eyes. "I guess it must be because I hadn't had a drink for a couple of months, it just caught me out, and maybe one spliff too many as well!"

Zara quickly cleared up the mess and everything seemed to return to normal, except she noticed that Ray seemed very distant over the next few days. Perhaps the visit to Wales to see his old friend would settle him down again.

------ O ------

Four or five times a year, believers from a wider area would all meet together for a session of praise and worship, with a guest speaker in attendance. Josh was rather looking forward to this gathering, as up to this point he had only met and fellowshipped with the small band of God's people at Aberdigan. The venue was a new and modern village hall some 20 miles away. On the designated evening around 70 believers were gathered. Josh was pleasantly surprised to encounter the Frogett-Smythe sisters and noted that their formal attire was as equally eccentric as their working clothes.

"Hello Mr Fish–man" boomed Wilhemina when she espied him, "Knew the Lord's hand was on you, obvious, obvious, hello Meredith, good to see you, hello Cheryll, I say good lot here this evening what," she gestured around the room, "How's Boots then Mr Fish–man, healthy? happy? "She's wonderful thanks" replied Josh, noting that the dear woman had said all that preceded without once stopping for breath.

The musicians began worship, and as the people took their seats Joshua caught hold of Wilhemina's hand and looking into her eyes he said, "Dominus Vobiscum." A broad smile further creased her wrinkled face, and again Josh felt that wonderful warmth from her eyes and persona.
The worship was rousing and the musicianship good and the host of Angels, who had accompanied their various believing charges, joined their voices to the throng.

The speaker was a well-known man of God with a recognised prophetic ministry, and during his time of sharing he gave several words for people. Anyone he was getting a word for, he would point to and ask him or her to stand up. Eventually he indicated Josh, who duly stood up. "Young man, The Lord says "You are 'apostolos', you are one who is sent. Upon your shoulders God has placed a mantle of Wisdom and Justice, and in your right hand He has placed a sceptre with a golden orb. In your left hand you carry a flaming sword. You must listen carefully and learn to hear from the Still Small Voice. God will use you greatly." Chakine and all the other Angels present drew their swords and shouted, "Hail to the Lord God Almighty - Holy! Holy! Holy!" Here indeed was a warrior.

Sometimes, the Spirit tests those who belong to God and who have been commissioned for specific purposes. One such time occurred as Josh was driving with Cheryll to view a greenhouse that was for sale. His head was full of thoughts of tomatoes, peppers and all the good things it would possibly allow him to grow, and he didn't pay too much attention to a man being pushed along the pavement in a wheelchair. The poor man had encephalitis, and his head was swollen to three times its normal size. As their vehicle passed them the Spirit said to Josh "I want you to pray for that man in the wheelchair." Josh thought it was 'just him' and continued on his journey. Half a mile further on the Spirit spoke again with an inner voice. "I want you to go and pray for that man in the wheelchair." Once more Josh thought it was merely his own imagining. "I'm going over the top on this Christianity." he thought, his flesh battling with the Spirit.

The third time the Spirit spoke they had gone about a mile on from where the poor man was, and Josh just said, "Sorry Lord." and swung the vehicle around in a 'u' turn as he explained to Cheryll. They soon caught up with the wheelchair and Josh pulled up about thirty yards ahead of them. He got out, and walking towards the pair was excited to see what the Lord was going to do. He imagined the poor guy's swollen head miraculously shrinking to normal size and the man leaping from his chair praising God, or some other such supernatural happening. However, when he stopped just in front of them and said to the guy pushing the wheelchair, "Hi, I'm a Christian and God wants me to pray for this gentleman's healing." the only reply was a curt "No, thank you." as the man walked briskly away pushing the chair as fast as he could. Josh was left standing on the pavement, totally bemused and thinking, "What was that all about?" It wasn't until later that he realised it was merely a test of his obedience. When it came to it, would he obey the still small voice of his Master?

------ O ------

Zara had been rather surprised when Ray had suggested that she and the kids should make the journey to Wales on the train, but she agreed that her car was too small for such a long journey and Ray needed to take his van to deliver some furniture and other items for Josh, from his mother's house. The tickets were bought and details finalised. Josh would pick up Zara, Donna and Vernon from Carmarthen station. Ray would arrive the next day in his van.

Zara knew her husband well, and though she wasn't exactly worried, she felt a little uneasy about his behaviour of late. Since the incident with the coffee table and booze, he was definitely not his usual ebullient self. She also thought it a little strange that he had been taking the jade carving everywhere with him. It was getting a little irritating as well, the way he was constantly chanting "C'mon you re-eds, C'mon you re-eds." But she had promised to 'love, honour and obey' and so just put it down to the general after effects and stress of Ray's recent trauma.

That morning at the station as he saw off his family, he seemed to be more like his old self. He kissed the kids and gave Zara a long passionate hug. "No talking to any strange men now." he jokingly cautioned. "No picking up any female hitchhikers!" she countered. They climbed aboard and as the train pulled out of the station, Ray walked briskly alongside waving to his family, until the gathering speed drew them out of his line of sight. Making his way back to the car park, Ray sat in his van and once again read Simon Cheng's translated letter from Yan-Ti.

'Most Eminent Mr. Coughlin - Fellow Dragonmaster,
It was highly pleasing to spend some time with you and to learn something of your distant land and its customs. I was very honoured to receive your gift of a Mirror of Meditation, yet I was saddened to hear of the terrible deeds of the one known as San Jorge. So to show my deep appreciation and to help facilitate the release of all your dragons from their long imprisonment, I give you this special carving, the ancient family symbol of my authority as Dragonmaster here. It is imbued with all the power that is needed to wake your sleeping Dragons and will respond to the chant that you so kindly shared with me when we took the smoke. I have consulted the oracle, and studied the ancient texts and I conclude that you must cast the jade statue into the Black Pool in the Cych valley, which as you know, is an entrance to the underworld in your land. This will raise and once again unleash, the power of the Great Dragon and the land will return to your control'.
Yan-Ti '

Ray sat mesmerised and read the letter again and again, all the while repeating the chant as he swayed gently backward and forward. Safe inside the glove compartment, the jade carving glowed and pulsated.

------ O ------

After its four and a half-hour journey, the train pulled into Carmarthen station right on time and Josh and Cheryll were waiting. A tinge of jealousy flickered through Cheryll's being as Josh greeted Zara, holding on to her for what seemed like ages, and kissing her cheek several times. Cheryll quickly rebuked jealousy, and was duly introduced to the woman who was half of the couple she had heard so much about. She instantly clicked with the kids, and found that she rather liked Zara too!

The 45-min journey to the cottage was peppered with questions from both sides, and young Vernon treated Josh and Cheryll to a graphic description of his father's wounds and adventures. The late summer weather was still warm, and the skies cloudless. As they drove over the mountains toward Aberdigan, Zara gazed wide eyed at the beauty of it all.

------ O ------

Partly emerging from his trance after half an hour or so, Ray had driven to Josh's mother's house and loaded the stuff for Wales. Within the hour he was heading towards the M4 Motorway which would eventually take him to his destination. And all the while he continued quietly chanting, "C'mon you Re-eds! C'mon you Re-eds!"

------ O ------

Back at the cottage Donna and Vernon were having a whale of a time with Boots down at the stream, whilst the adults sat outside in the late afternoon sun, keeping an eye on the kids and chatting. A potentially awkward moment was skilfully averted when Zara pulled out her cigarette papers and began rolling a joint.

Josh and Cheryll had already discussed the whole marijuana issue, realising that Ray and Zara would as a matter of course expect to smoke a few 'spliffs' on their holiday. They had wisely concluded that as it was a free will issue, and they were eminently more concerned about the couple's eternal salvation, they would merely initially inform them that they had given up smoking, and that as such, would they please not smoke indoors. They had also sought Meredith's views.

The older man had counselled, "These are very close old friends of yours Josh, who know you intimately, and who will no doubt assume you still do all the things that for them are a normal part of life. You are a new creature, a new creation that has moved from death to life, and as their old and trusted friend you are in a unique position to introduce them to the love and life changing freedom of Jesus. The bible tells us that as Christians, we must be 'wise as serpents and harmless as doves'. Jesus himself was berated by religious bigots, because he ate and drank with prostitutes and tax collectors. Yet all the while his purpose was to introduce them to the love of the Father. That I am sure is your ultimate goal with your friends. Therefore, wisdom would dictate that just as the Holy Spirit dealt with your bad habits, <u>after</u> you were saved, so He will do the selfsame thing with your friends." They had all agreed.

It was Cheryll who said to Zara as she was building the joint, "Only make enough for yourself Zara, Josh and I have both given up smoking." - "Oh," Zara was genuinely surprised and looked quizzically at Josh, "When was that?" - "Several months ago now wasn't it?" he looked at Cheryll who then said, "Since I stopped I find riding my bike so much easier!" She wasn't lying, she had merely just omitted to add that she had stopped several years earlier. "And I find I can wake up ok now for my early starts in the mornings!" said Josh. They all laughed, marijuana being well known for giving you a great sleep coupled with a desire to remain in bed in the morning! Zara then generously said, "Would you like some to eat instead?" but they declined saying they'd gotten used to being 'straight'.

As they talked with Zara, Cheryll was feeling more and more drawn to this lovely friend of Josh's. For Josh, happy as he was to see her, the more they conversed the more it served to underline how different they now were. How much he had changed.

Cheryll went off to the bathroom and Zara said "What a lovely, lovely girl Josh. I bet the sex is good!" she giggled. They were close enough friends for her to be able to broach the subject. Josh's reply stunned her, knowing him as she did. "Actually, we're not sleeping together, and won't be, unless we ultimately get married." Zara looked at him with an expression that said "This isn't the Joshua Fishmen that I know and love, what on earth has happened to you?" Then she said in an over exaggerated fashion, "Are you ill?" He laughed out loud. "No Zar, I'm well, in fact I'm better than I've ever been my whole life!"

------ O ------

The Severn Bridge was nearly an hour behind him and Ray was on the approach to Carmarthen. He was halfway through the third of the four joints he'd prepared for the journey and the van was purring along. Inside the glove compartment the jade statue continued to glow and pulsate, and in almost robotic fashion, he continued the endless chant.
The automated voice of his Sat-Nav snapped him back to a semblance of reality. "At the roundabout take the third exit." He had punched in the rural postcode of Abercych, the village at the head of the Cych valley where the entrance to the underworld was to be found. He would head there and ask directions.

He passed through the town of Carmarthen and was soon driving on a winding road through wooded valleys, following the path of a fast flowing river. Half an hour later he had reached his destination, the village of Abercych.

The proprietor of the quiet little village shop was at first rather taken aback by the wild-eyed appearance of this unfamiliar stranger. But any a customer is a welcome customer, and he was not dressed like the usual hippies who sometimes came in looking similarly wild-eyed. The fact was, Ray had the raging 'munchies' and he selected three pies, a packet of bacon crisps and a large chocolate milkshake. Informing the shopkeeper he had just driven down from London, he enquired of the whereabouts of the Black Pool and the entrance to the underworld. He was met with a blank stare and shake of the head, "Sorry bach, never 'erd of that then." Ray paid for his goods and left.

Walking back across the road he noticed a fairly new 4x4 parked behind his van, and as he got closer its occupant climbed out. He was a tall man and was dressed completely in black. Black shoes, black slacks and a black roll neck sweater. His hair was jet black, swept backward, and he sported a black moustache and goatee. He spoke in the deepest voice Ray had ever heard. "Good afternoon, I gather you are looking for the Black Pool?"

For the briefest moment Ray wondered "How on earth did this guy know that?" Then, for reasons he wasn't really sure of, chose not to question it. A host of demons shrieked and cackled as Ray proffered his hand. "Ray Coughlin." he said as the icy fingers of the other man closed about his, "Jarvis De'Ath, follow me."

The 4x4 pulled out and around the van, and soon the two were moving in tandem along a narrow tree lined lane. The wooded slopes rose sharply on either side. The sun was beginning to dip behind them and occasionally, as the road wove snake like through the valley floor, they would be in deep shade. They made a left turn onto an even narrower lane that rose sharply up the side of the valley. After a few hundred yards, the 4x4 signalled right and they pulled of the road onto a gravelled parking area surrounded by trees. As Jarvis De'Ath got out of his vehicle he handed Ray a spliff saying, "I assume you do?" Ray smiled and nodded and, taking a huge pull on the joint, said "Indeed I do!"

They were quite high up and totally secluded, surrounded in the folds of the wooded valley. "Do you have boots?" De'Ath asked, "It can be a little muddy where we are going." Ray affirmed his boots were in the back of the van and soon the two men were ready to depart."

"The statue, Mr Coughlin?" De'Ath enquired in a slightly irritated voice. Ray felt amazing but also very, very stoned. He had not realised that what he had just smoked was a mixture of crack cocaine and marijuana. "Oh, yeah, of course!" he said, more to himself than to the other man. Opening the glove compartment he was surprised to see how strongly the jade statue was glowing and pulsating. He felt like he wasn't there, although he knew he was. Everything seemed to be happening around him as if he were watching some bizarre time distorted movie. He removed the statue, and shutting the van door, turned to see his companion who was now dressed in a long hooded robe. He handed one to Ray who put it on without question, whilst all the while wondering "Why am I doing this?"

The two hooded figures followed a little path that led up to a rocky outcrop in the distance.

------ O ------

Zara knew she liked Cheryll immensely, and not only that. In the short time she'd been with her she absolutely knew she was the right girl for Josh. The two young Christians had purposely stayed off the subject of things spiritual, preferring to wait until Ray arrived to 'break the news'. However, in the course of conversation it had been Zara who had broached the subject. "You know, when I was in Beijing at the hospital and Ray was in a coma with all sorts of pipes and leads in him, I really thought at one point that he was going to die. Now I know you'll think this is stupid, but, er.... I really prayed to God to make him better!" She looked very sheepish, as if expecting a tirade of critical negative abuse. Instead she realised that both Josh and Cheryll were smiling broadly, so she continued. "And do you know what, I'm sure that God made Ray better, that He healed him! She said the last three words in an almost defiant tone, daring anyone to say otherwise. "At one point they had to revive him with the electric pad thingy's. His signal on the screen had totally disappeared. Flat lined, I think they call it."

Josh looked at Cheryll and Cheryll looked at Josh and they began to tell Zara about their Lord and Saviour, and about how they had all been fervently praying for Ray, and about all sorts of other wonderful things. Not the least of which being why Zara needed salvation. An hour later, in floods of tears she had given her life to Jesus. Josh had prayed a powerful prayer of deliverance over her and Chakine and Yolan had despatched the various demons as they had tried to flee.

In the heavenly courts an Angel was immediately dispatched to 'encamp round about her' and a new guardian quickly arrived. Taking up his position behind her, he greeted his fellow Angels and joined in the general rejoicing. Then Josh began to pray for Ray, for his salvation and general protection. Meanwhile, Meredith and Dave and Lucy had arrived for a pre-arranged visit, and the small band of believers, led by the Holy Spirit, all entered into fervent warfare prayer for Ray. Cheryll also had a strong leading to pray for protection for all the children at 'Maen Du', Tarquin's place, and the courts of heaven were petitioned accordingly.

------ O ------

The two hooded figures continued to wend their way up the heavily wooded darkened path to the rocky outcrop. They scrambled over fallen trees and boulders and as they went higher eventually they broke out into the sunshine, leaving them looking down on the treetops. Just ahead, at the base of a small rock cliff, a large pool of still dark water lay shimmering in the sunlight. Ray knew it was the Black Pool. The fabled 'Entrance to the Underworld' spoken of in the Mabinogion.

Jarvis De'Ath lit another joint, took several long puffs and passed it to Ray. He actually didn't really want it; he was so 'off his face' already, yet he felt compelled to inhale the sickly smoke. They walked slowly towards the water and Ray began almost involuntarily chanting the battle cry of Manchester United football club. De'Ath began babbling some satanic eulogy as Ray pulled the statue from beneath his robe and held it with both hands at arms length in front of him. Demons were manifesting all around, chanting and urging the two men on. Their combined voices rose to a crescendo and the same guttural growl Ray had heard in Yan-Ti's smoke room suddenly filled the air.

"Now," screamed the other man, "Now, throw it in!" Ray raised the carving above his head and hurled it forward. He watched it spin end over end in agonising slow motion as the arc of its flight brought it ever closer to the shimmering water. Finally, with a great 'PA – LOOMP!' which sent a column of water high in the air, it disappeared into the murky depths. All was completely silent.

The two men stood there for a few minutes motionless. Then, almost imperceptibly at first, the water began to spit and fizzle and Ray felt a very slight vibration in the rock beneath his feet. Then the water began to move more forcefully, as if it were coming to the boil, like a kettle.

They backed away as they began to feel the heat, conscious of the danger of being scalded. And when suddenly a great plume of boiling water erupted and shot twenty feet into the air, they decided it was time to go.

When they got back down to the vehicles and disrobed, all seemed quiet enough and Ray, still in a very weird and dazed state, accepted the offer of a bed for the night, as he wasn't due to arrive at Josh's until the next day. Just as he was about to get into his van, he thought he felt the ground shake. He stood still for a moment and then dismissed it as just his imagination.

Following the 4x4 on the drive to 'Y Draig Goch', Ray's fuzzy head began to clear just a little. All that had just transpired seemed like some strange dream he'd had, especially as he wasn't even really sure why he had done it. Come to that, he wasn't really sure why he was going to the home of this stranger instead of to Josh's where his wife and kids were. Yet at the same time he felt utterly powerless to do anything but go along with it.

He lost track of time following the 4x4, and they made several turns and went up and down many hills and round many bends until they were bouncing down a narrow gravelled track. It was at precisely this time that back at Josh's cottage, the little group of believers were fervently praying for Ray, although as far as they knew he was still in Essex and would arrive tomorrow.

The track continued through a gloomy looking conifer plantation, bounded on the left by a small mountain. Ray could see the sunlight catching the craggy ridge and it reminded him of the back of one of the little prehistoric monster models Vernon had. He felt his head was clearing a little, even though the earlier events of that afternoon were still somewhat hazy.

Ahead he could see a house nestled up against a sheer cliff face that rose to join the mountain to his left. There were two cars parked outside, and as the 4x4 came to rest Ray pulled up behind it.

Somewhere in the back of his mind Ray had begun to wonder how Jarvis De'Ath had known he would be in Abercych that afternoon, yet each time he would think about it, it seemed to be snatched from his mind. From outside the house he could still just see the very top of the ridge to the left, bathed in sunlight. But down here it was almost dark and he shivered with the chill.

The two men exited their vehicles, and with a theatrical bow and accentuated flourish Jarvis De'Ath said "Welcome Ray, to the headquarters of The Temple of The Golden Dawn!"

The front door opened, and there framed in the doorway stood a scantily clad ample bosomed female in her mid twenties. She spoke in what Ray considered a 'posh' accent. "Jaaarvis – you've brought us another playmate!" she said excitedly, in a highly suggestive manner.

As the two men entered the house she moved just slightly to one side, so that they had to brush past her in the narrow hallway. Ray's fallen nature, [urged on by his demonic inhabitants] caused him to speculate on what further delights the evening may hold in store, when he was introduced to four more equally uninhibited young women in the lounge. There were two other men present, both of whom Ray assessed as being in early middle age. Several of the girls were looking at him in what could only be called a 'lascivious' fashion, licking their lips and caressing themselves, and he thought, "Wow! I'm in for some night here!" The air was already thick with marijuana smoke and several joints were on the go.

Jarvis De'Ath stepped into the centre of the room and clapped his hands. He was accorded immediate attention. "Ladies and gentlemen, this is Mr Ray Coughlin, he shall be spending this special night with us." There was a chorus of approval and one young woman cooed, "Will he be in the ceremony?" De'Ath shot her a withering glance, clapped his hands again and said, "Come along, let's eat."

Ray was ushered into another large room with a huge beamed inglenook fireplace and large dining table. A fire roared in the grate and candles flickered and danced in holders on the table and all around the walls, animating the scenario. It was warm and comfortable, yet a part of Ray was vaguely disturbed by the young woman's unanswered question. What sort of ceremony could possibly be happening in this old house? On the wall opposite the fireplace hung a large plaque. It read 'DO WHAT THOU WILT BE THE WHOLE OF THE LAW'.

Something in the back of Ray's mind stirred. Where <u>had</u> he seen that statement expressed before? A joint was passed to him, and as he took a long pull, exhaling a plume of smoke towards the ceiling his memory kicked in. Many years ago, when he and Josh were young lads, they had briefly obtained and read some books on black magic. With mounting apprehension Ray realised that the sentiment expressed on the plaque above the mantelpiece was the 'Mission Statement' of none other than Aleister Crowley, the infamous black magician of the 1920's, also known as 'The Beast'. That's when, with spine tingling clarity, Ray also remembered that Crowley's society had been known as 'The Temple of the Golden Dawn'.

- - - - - - O - - - - - -

High in the craggy mountains of Sheng-Too-Lai, in a windowless smoke filled room in his pagoda, the Dragonmaster rocked back and forth on a black silk cushion, chanting "Khum Oyu Rez, Khum Oyu Rez". On the floor in front of him his large 'Book of Magik' lay open, and in his hand he held Ray's 'mirror of meditation'. All around the room, pentagrams and other occult symbols painted on rice paper, lay on silk cushions. On the wall opposite, a freshly painted mural depicting three intertwined dragons pulsated and glowed eerily, and the same low guttural growl that Ray had heard gradually rose, spiralling to a thundering crescendo!

------ O ------

Although he was totally unaware of it, Ray was now sanctified by his believing wife's trust in Jesus. 'For the unbelieving husband is set apart as holy to God on account of (his relationship with) the (believing) wife...'
[1Corinthians Ch.7 v14] - *Amplified*

So above him in the unseen spiritual plane, and cloaked for security, three warrior Angels kept vigil. Although Ray's name was not in the Book of Life, he was nonetheless temporarily sanctified and as such the law of 'Mortal Danger' was applicable. The little band of believers had continued fervently praying for Ray, believing him to be in Essex preparing for his journey. But now, Josh was starting to feel somehow that his old friend was in danger. He kept this fact to himself as they continued to pray, for fear of frightening Zara, who was blissed out, totally enveloped in prayer and the unfamiliar yet wonderful presence of The Holy Spirit.

------ O ------

Despite the apparent congeniality of his hosts and the excellence of the meal, as the evening wore on Ray found himself struggling to quell a rising paranoia. Paradoxically, he was also wrestling with controlling a mounting lust in response to the highly suggestive and lascivious behaviour of the barely dressed young women around him at the table.

His mind was racing with imaginings. One moment he would relish the thought of the obvious orgy that seemed inevitable. The next he would imagine himself being murdered in some twisted black magician's ritual.
'A double minded man is unstable in all his ways'
[James Ch.1 v 8]

------ O ------

In a small office in a dilapidated building at the rear of Cardiff University, Professor Rees Griffiths was sat in front of a seismograph scratching his head. These readings just didn't make sense. Even as he studied the inked graph, the needle began to scurry wildly from side to side again, and so, he telephoned his colleague in Bangor 150 miles to the North. Similar information was being collated there. It appeared there was sudden and unaccountable seismic activity happening all over Wales. Three more urgent phone conversations confirmed his suspicions and reluctantly he made the call to the media.

On Welsh Television News that evening, for the first time ever, an impending earthquake warning was issued. The estimate was for a possible 4 to a 6.5 on the Richter scale. And it was expected at anytime after 10pm.

The worst fears of the authorities were realised as thousands of people began to panic and converge on the motorways in an effort to escape. The emergency services were stretched to the limit attending multiple pileups in the ensuing chaos. Hordes of terrified motorists headed out of the country at less than sensible speeds, and great bottlenecks of traffic developed. The Severn Bridge was jammed tight and accidents or congestion blocked all the roads to the North of the Principality.

Many people on isolated farms or in secluded cottages, who were involved in pastimes other than that of staring at a screen in the corner of the room, were blissfully unaware of the predicted impending danger This included Josh, Cheryll, Zara, Meredith, and the others, as well as Ray and his hosts at 'Y Ddraig Goch'. Tarquin and the rest of the hippie residents of 'Maen Du' were happily circle dancing in the big barn, whilst at the animal sanctuary, Dulcie and Wilhemina Frogett-Smythe sipped their usual evening cocktails and played cribbage.

------ O ------

The last few joints that had come his way Ray had puffed on but not inhaled. Clinton style. Likewise with the wine he had managed to surreptitiously tip several large glasses into an ornate ceramic plant holder behind him. Consequently his head was clearing somewhat.

When he asked his host for the bathroom, one of the young lovelies jumped up smiling broadly. "I'll show you." She took him by the hand and led him out of a door that accessed a corridor. They walked down to the end past several other doors and, opening the last one, revealing a bathroom, she said. "I'll come in and help you if you like!" Ray declined saying "No, that's ok, I'll be out in a minute." He bolted the door after him.

His ablutions complete, he was washing his hands when he dropped the soap. As he bent to retrieve it, the Pentagram, his good luck gift from Zara, swung out from beneath his T-shirt and he caught sight of it reflected in the bathroom mirror. He had a vague recollection that he had seen this symbol as a child, but he couldn't quite place it. Perhaps it had been during the brief period he and Josh had toyed with black magic, but he wasn't sure.

He dried his hands and slid back the bolt on the door, stepping out into the corridor. His gorgeous young 'minder' was waiting and instantly took him by the hand. Opening the door to her right she pulled him into a room, quickly shutting the door behind her with her foot. Grabbing him with both hands she spun him around and pushed him up against the wall. He was surprised by her strength as she began passionately kissing him, her tongue forcing its way into his mouth. He was aware of a flickering glow in the room, although he could see nothing through her frenzied assault. Her body was pushed up hard against his and his masculinity was beginning to respond.

As she dropped to her knees, intent on undoing his clothing, the room came into view. Ray gasped as he realised he was looking at a huge Pentagram marked out on the floor, with large black candles flickering at each of its five points. He remembered the other girl's earlier question regarding 'The ceremony', and all at once realised he was in way over his head.

------ O ------

In the depths of the Plane of Darkness, Kaisis was addressing hordes of assembled demons. His voice rose in twisted glee. "This will be a glorious night, a night when the magnificent cause of our master will be greatly accelerated, a night when many of those disgusting beings made in His image will perish. A most memorable night, on which we shall exact revenge on many filthy 'white liter's'. Go, wreak havoc and bring chaos, mayhem, death and destruction!"

------ O ------

In his spirit Ray did not want to cheat on Zara, though his body was fast losing the battle with his willpower at the hands of this young courtesan. The decision was abruptly made for him, as suddenly the whole house began to gently shake. Then, the floor of the room buckled, throwing the girl backward. Ray reached up and grabbed the Pentagram round his neck. Tearing it off he flung it into the centre of the room. The lights went out and at the same time the shaking increased in intensity. The girl was screaming and Ray was thrown from side to side as the building continued to buckle and heave. The snapping of timbers sounded like rifle shots and Ray was totally disorientated. A toppled candle set fire to some black silk drapes and the ensuing light illuminated the doorway barely visible through the choking dust.

Ray reached out to the still prostrate girl "Give me your hand!" She grabbed it and was halfway up when a dislodged beam hit her right between the eyes and she dropped lifeless to the floor like a stone. Shocked, confused and feeling like a rat in a trap he just managed to dodge a pile of falling masonry as he turned to make his exit.

At that moment a guy Ray hadn't seen before appeared in the doorway, "Follow me, quickly!" Although it was pitch black in the corridor, somehow Ray could see where he was going and was able to step over every obstacle and move in a reasonably co-ordinated fashion; despite the severe continued quaking of the earth. He followed the stranger into the dining room where part of the inglenook fireplace had collapsed spilling the roaring log fire out into the room. He noticed one of the middle-aged guys and two of the girls sprawled on the floor and was about to try and help them when a section of the upstairs wall cascaded through the ceiling to his left, crushing them like ants. The remaining females were screaming as Jarvis De'Ath and the other man were frantically pulling at the lounge door, which had twisted and was firmly jammed, trapping them in the burning room. The stranger brushed them aside and the door seemed to literally disintegrate as he pushed it with both palms and strode right through, Ray followed and was now in the corridor leading to the front door. More quickly than seemed humanly possible, the stranger had opened the front door, pulled Ray through and shut it firmly behind him.

Fifteen feet away Ray's van was running with the lights on. "Now, go!" the stranger commanded as the ground continued to buck and heave. Ray ran to the van, jumped in and looked to see where the stranger was. Seeing no one, he was about to get out again to see if he could help the others, when a thunderous roar from above caused him to look up. High on the Dragon's Back a great explosion sent thousands of tons of rock plummeting down the mountainside towards the sheer face of the old quarry directly above 'Y Ddraig Goch'. With his foot to the floor Ray gunned the vehicle down the track, swaying erratically from side to side on the shifting terra firma.

He was about 150 yards away when the headquarters of 'The Temple of the Golden Dawn' was buried beneath an avalanche of tons and tons of ancient Preseli Bluestone.

Then, just as suddenly as it had started, the quaking ceased and an eerie silence descended. Ray turned the van around on the old track, and drove the short distance back to where the house used to be. Even in the glare of the headlights it was impossible to tell there had ever been a house there. All that remained was a huge pile of rock at the bottom of the quarry face. No building, no cars, no humans.

Ray called out to see if perhaps the stranger who had saved his life was around, but his "Hello!" just rattled around the mountains, returning as an empty mocking echo. The 'stranger' and the two other Angels sat on the roof of Ray's van, alert and watchful. There had indeed been 'mortal danger'.

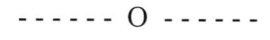

------ O ------

<<<< - - - END OF CHAPTER SIX - - - >>>>

The Dragonmaster

CHAPTER 7 ## As Above So Below

After their marathon prayer session the little band of believers had been chatting over mugs of hot chocolate when the earthquake hit. Generally the level of earthquake in Wales is barely noticeable, but this time the cottage shook gently for nearly a full minute. It had the effect of reinstating the prayer meeting pretty quickly, and the Angels leapt into action in speedy response to the petitions for protection. A few things fell off the sideboard, and some plates committed suicide on the hard stone floor of the kitchen, but otherwise there was no damage aside from some cracked tiles in the bathroom.

A quick look at several television stations revealed bulletins reporting the damage toll in various locations. It seemed that the epicentre had been somewhere in the Preseli Mountains 15 miles across the estuary from Aberdigan, and as yet there was no cohesive account. However other areas were reporting damage and it almost seemed as though there had been several localised tremors throughout the whole country. As is often the case with news stories, conflicting accounts emerged depending on the channel you happened to be viewing.

- - - - - - O - - - - - -

High in the heavenly realms at the Arc of Prayer, the petitions of the small band of believers were transforming into a rich hue of colour and harmony. It was sound and light, dancing and intertwining into beautiful heartfelt melodies of sanctified request. Prayer Angels tenderly gathered and sorted the pleas of believer's worldwide. And the all knowing, all seeing, all loving God of wisdom and justice responded with grace, mercy and infinite love, dispatching ministering spirits in response to the requests of

His people performing His holy will. Captain Cherno was briefed by Micha-el himself, and with a legion of warrior Angels he prepared to enter the earth plane at the appointed time, to do battle with the hordes of Satan.

------ O ------

At the Animal Sanctuary, Dulcie and Wilhemina Frogett-Smythe had been engrossed in their card game when all the dogs had suddenly begun howling. The two ladies were discussing how unusual this was when the earthquake had hit.

The house began to shake violently, showering the pair with dusty debris. Outside, the terrified captive canines were all barking furiously in blind panic, as the ground beneath them buckled and shook. "The dogs!" they shouted almost in unison, making for the doorway. The ancient house, already in a bad state of repair, did not respond well to being shaken like a rat, and as they reached the exit a large old timber lintel dislodged and was falling towards Dulcie's head. In a flash her guardian Angel had caught it, making it seem to hang suspended in the air, as the pair passed safely beneath and out through the door. It fell with a crash behind them.

Sharp edged slate tiles were cascading down from the roof and the guardians of the two sisters deflected them all, covering the women with their wings. As they tried to run towards the labyrinth of cages and runs the bucking ground threw them this way and that and Wilhemina was pitched headlong towards the broken remains of their aluminium greenhouse. Her Angel dived underneath her, breaking her fall and bringing her body to rest, her face an inch away from a jagged pane of broken glass. "I'm ok!" she shouted to her sister who was trying to maintain her balance on the pathway. The next instant, the two sisters were at the doorway of the first set of pens, courtesy of the strong arms of their Angels. As Dulcie fumbled for the keys, the ground still shaking beneath her feet, the padlock just swung open and dropped to the floor.

Inside, several of the dogs were loose, their pens having collapsed, and as the sisters opened the door they were almost bowled over by the terrified little creatures dashing out into the darkness, desperate to make their escape. Clinging to the wire of the pens, the two ladies were making their way in pitch darkness down the inside of the shed, when suddenly there was a great crashing noise, audible even above the cacophony of the dogs and general mayhem. Then, just as if someone had thrown a switch somewhere, all was still. All the lighting was out, and the two eccentric women stood hand in hand in the darkness with the dogs still barking wildly. "Need a torch Will, and some other stuff, best go back to the house what?"

They began to grope their way back along the wire fencing of the pens and soon were outside again. It was totally dark and they couldn't see each other, let alone anything else. They walked very gingerly, feeling in front of them with their hands and feet, in the general direction of the house. They could taste the air was very dusty and both began to cough. Just then the clouds parted and the moon illuminated a scene of total devastation. The house was gone, totally collapsed. All that remained was a heap of rubble and the swirling choking dust visible in the beams of moonlight. The two women sank to their knees, surveying all that remained of their home. "Thank you Jesus, thank you for getting us out of the house in time."

------ O ------

Empowered by the evil blood sacrifice of the young Chinese girl, the jade statue, which Ray had thrown into the Black Pool in the Cych valley, had fired off a chain of events in the spiritual realm. This was now releasing untold evil upon the land that had chosen to bear the symbol of 'That old serpent, the Dragon, Satan', as it's national emblem.
[Revelation Ch 12 v 9 and Revelation Ch 20 v 2]

Ancient dragon spirits, long bound by early Celtic Christian missionaries, had been released. An all-pervading demon infested darkness was rapidly spreading throughout the land in the spiritual realms. This in turn further fuelled the lawlessness and rebellion already rampant in towns and cities across the principality. [2 Timothy Ch 3 v 1- 4]

As the emergency services struggled to cope with the scale of the problem, looters, muggers and rapists took to the streets. In town after town shops were raided, individuals robbed, and scores of women of all ages forcibly ravished.

Kaisis sent wave after wave of spirits of depravity, lust, theft and violence. Fire crews and paramedics were routinely attacked by howling stone throwing mobs, and large department stores were stripped of all their goods by locust like hordes of looters.

Years of government cutbacks and under funding had rendered the police force virtually powerless to deal with civil disobedience on this scale, and no one, despite some noble motives, had a clue how to bring it all under control. No one that is, except for a small number of believers dotted all over the country, who were about to be warned, informed and equipped by the Holy Spirit. One such group was still gathered in Josh's cottage.

Boots and Polly had been outside before the much gentler effects of the violent Preseli quake were felt, North of Aberdigan, at Josh's cottage the other side of the estuary. Shortly before the event they too had begun howling in unison and those inside had been quite amused by the sound until the ground had shaken, revealing the true nature of the dog's pre-emptive concern. Now both of them were curled up on their respective master's laps, their small frames shaking nervously from time to time. The little group of humans sat in the flicker of candlelight, discussing what they had just been through. Josh had the strangest feeling that this wasn't just an earthquake. Not that he was an expert, in fact in common with everybody else in the room this had been his first, and he hoped his last, experience.

They decided to pray again, seeking The Lord as to what they ought to do, and it was whilst they were praying that Josh had a clear and precise word from Him. "Go to Maen Du." - Tarquin's place!

Meredith felt the same leading and they agreed this was confirmation of what they should do. It was also agreed that Josh, Cheryll and Meredith would make the journey.

Dave had a Land Rover and insisted they should take that in case they needed to go off road at any point. Gathering what seemed practical, their mobile phones, several torches, some candles and a first aid kit; they set off in the direction of the Preseli Mountains.

The road towards Aberdigan was clear and showing no sign of any serious damage, and they took the bypass skirting the town centre. In the distance to the right, they could see flashing blue lights in town, and at one point an ambulance, its siren wailing, passed them at speed. Josh stopped at the bridge, carefully scanning the structure for any signs of damage. None were apparent, so they continued over the river and up to the South junction. Leaving the bypass they took the old road and began the long slow climb up into the Preseli's. The further on they went, the more they began to encounter the residual effects of the quake. They were glad to have the Land Rover when they had to skirt some trees that had fallen across the road, and even more so when they were able to pull a car out of a ditch helping its distraught owner.

Josh was enjoying driving the vehicle; it brought back memories of 'Desert Storm' in his army days. Little did he realise he was truly once more going into battle.

------ O ------

Tarquin and the others at 'Maen Du' had been enjoying their evening immensely. He'd left the circle dancing in the barn, which was still in full swing, and was now lying naked on his back in the sweat lodge, enjoying the attentions of an equally naked Susie and Jenny. As was customary at these events the booze and grass had been consumed with abandon and everybody was, in the ways of fallen man, thoroughly indulging themselves.

At the same time, at 'Y Ddraig Goch' on the other side of the mountain, Ray was battling with the urge to ravish the young woman who was pushing her body against him, and her tongue inside his mouth.

Nobody had taken any notice of the howling of the dogs; most of them were too stoned to even care. Without warning the ground began to 'ripple'. Several of those circle dancing in the barn fell over on to the straw covered floor, convulsing with laughter, whilst others stood in complete bewilderment swaying from side to side in those first gentle tremors.

Tarquin barely noticed anything until a stronger shock threw the three of them in a heap, and the red-hot stones from the fire pit through the side of the polythene dome. All hell was letting loose, literally. Atop the Dragon's Back a great juddering explosion had sent hundreds of tons of bluestone granite boulders cascading down both sides of the mountain. The roaring avalanche of stone cut through the zinc sheeted barn like an axe through an apple pie. Those at the top end stood no chance whatsoever, and mercifully were dead in half a second, as a river of solid rock engulfed them.

Those further down had the terrifying ordeal of dodging pumpkin sized rocks periodically crashing through the walls. Avoidance was made suddenly more difficult when all the lights died. Not all were dextrous enough and several had received badly crushed and broken limbs.

Tarquin and the two girls were still being thrown around inside the polythene covered hazel dome. Each time they managed to get their footing another ripple of the swaying ground would cast them down again. Then, quite suddenly it was over, and all that could be heard was the moaning of the injured in the barn.

Tarquin and the girls grabbed their robes and sandals and picking up the sweat lodge flashlight ran towards the teetering remains of the barn. The body of the landslide had missed the main house, but the vehicles, tepees and outbuildings were trashed, buried beneath ton after ton of rock. Several of the poles that carried the phone lines were conspicuous by their absence, and a fire had started in the straw at the remaining end of the barn. Not a great situation for three fit, compos mentis people to have to handle. But for three highly inebriated and very stoned folk, it was the stuff of worst nightmares.

------ O ------

The closer they got to the Preseli Mountains the harder the going became for the three occupants of the Land Rover. More trees littered the road, and in places the tarmac was cracked and buckled. This slowed them to almost walking pace. Josh squinted, and peered warily into the darkness ahead as the 4x4 climbed gradually towards their destination.

At one point they were flagged down by a stranded young couple with a small child, who were most grateful to be ferried the four miles further on to their roadside cottage. On arrival, the little family was overjoyed to discover that their home seemed to be ok. Josh and Cheryll had assisted them in checking things out, discovering that the only apparent damage was a sticking entrance door. A problem readily solved by two male shoulders.

Finally, after an hour and a quarter on a journey that usually took twenty-five minutes, they were approaching the village known in Welsh as 'The Place of the Shivering Ox'. The highest human habitation in the mountains.

There were lights ahead, and as the Land Rover approached they saw that men from the village were busily clearing away debris. Telephone lines were down and bricks and slate roof tiles littered the street. The corner of the village hall had totally collapsed, and a vehicle was through the window of some offices on the right. Meredith spied a couple he knew and asked Josh to pull over. He wound down the window and called to them. They came over. It was Graham and Mary, two Christians Meredith had known for years, who faithfully attended the local fellowship. Graham was a big powerful man and Meredith was not at all surprised to see them out on the street doing whatever they could to help. Introductions were made and the couple described how they had experienced the recent events. They said that they were fine and that mercifully their home had escaped with just a couple of broken windows, unlike some of their less fortunate neighbours. Graham was an electrician, and it had been him who, through use of generators, had facilitated the lighting the volunteers were now using.

Josh liked the big man immediately and felt the presence of the Spirit with both him and his wife. He looked in Graham's eyes and said, "There's more happening here than is apparent on the surface, please get your fellowship praying against the forces of darkness." The big man promised to do just that and the two men shook hands. As the Land Rover pulled away Graham called out "Greater is He who is in you than he who is in the world!"

They continued wending their way through the rubble-strewn street, up the hill towards the garage on the edge of the village. A fire was burning on the side of the road and a couple of guys in reflective coats were monitoring traffic. The great metal awning that used to stand over the petrol pumps was now embedded in the front of the little supermarket next door, and a chasm three feet wide ran right across the road towards the secondary school opposite.

Josh brought the vehicle to a halt, being stopped by the raised hand of one of the guys controlling traffic. It turned out they were firemen, volunteers from the local fire station that was now merely a heap of rubble. Some stout timbers and half inch steel plates formed a temporary bridge over the crack in the road which apparently ran through the playground and right through the school. The sad news was that the both the headmaster and the head of year eleven who had been working together 'out of hours', had been killed in the quake, and much of the school was badly damaged. Two other residents of the village had also perished, victims of falling masonry. A little dismayed by the news, the trio of believers continued their journey, turning right just out of the village on to a narrow lane that would take them to 'Maen Du'.

Back at Josh's cottage Polly and Boots were curled up on the sofa next to Lucy, who together with Dave and Zara were, between cups of strong coffee, sending up periodic prayers for the protection of all those close to them, and everyone in distress. Cheryll had particularly asked them to keep praying for the safety of all the children she knew would be at 'Maen Du'.

------ O ------

Ray sat in his van for a long time with the engine running. Just staring at the great pile of rock illuminated by his headlights. He knew that there were at least eight dead people entombed beneath the rubble, and wondered what the heck he was doing here. Why had he gone to that place yesterday? And how had Jarvis De'Ath known he would be there? What was the great compulsion he had felt to place the jade statue in the Black Pool?

His thoughts drifted back to the time in Yantook when he 'took the smoke' with Yan-Ti. He remembered the peculiar sensation of being 'sucked' into something, and the terrifying yellow green eyes he had seen in the cave. It all swirled round and round in his mind like a nightmare. A little voice whispered to him "You need a joint!" and he began to build one from the stash he kept in his glove compartment. When he was finished, he fumbled around in his pockets looking for his lighter. That's when he remembered – he had left it on the table in the house when he'd gone to the bathroom! With a mounting sense of panic he realised that it was also where he'd left his mobile phone. With the joint between his lips he pushed in the button on his car lighter and waited for it to pop out. And he waited. And waited. Nothing.

On the roof of his van the three warrior Angels assigned to keep him from mortal danger were receiving fresh instructions. The fervent prayers of those upholding Ray had upped the ante, inasmuch as they had been directed not only towards his salvation, but the heartfelt pleas had been to keep him from harm. The warriors knew that a strong enemy attack was imminent, and that Ray getting more stoned was unlikely to assist him in the coming events. In frustration he threw the unlit spliff on to the passenger seat, puzzled as to why to why the lighter which had worked perfectly well this morning, was now malfunctioning.

He could feel his heart was still pounding, and the gravity of the situation he was in suddenly hit home hard. Everyone here was dead, he had no phone, nor did he have the faintest idea where he was or how to get to anywhere he would recognise. It occurred to him that he could use his Sat-Nav and briefly, he felt better, until he remembered that Josh's new postcode was stored in his buried phone. "I need a miracle." he thought, not really ascribing the possibility to God.

For several minutes he sat there thinking of his wife and family who supposed he was still back in Essex. He suddenly longed to see the mother of his children, and tell her how much he loved her. He thought of all the ways in which she cared for him, all the little things she did that he took for granted, and how she never ever complained.

He was so, so glad he had not betrayed her with the unfortunate young woman who now lie buried in the ruins of this house. He thought of how she had flown halfway round the world to be at his bedside and how she had supported him throughout his recovery. He remembered Zara telling him about how she had prayed for him whilst he was in a coma, and how he had derided the idea. Not to her face, he was touched by the childish simplicity, but inside he had thought it was a load of rubbish and that he had recovered due to the expert attention he had received at the hands of the Chinese physicians. Then he haziliy remembered leaving his body and the subsequent terrifying events culminating in being rescued by two Angels. He briefly wondered if her prayers had been anything to do with that, but then decided the whole incident had been down to his delirium from the drugs they had given him. His mind was racing and he kept thinking about the guy that had just rescued him. Finally he concluded that he must have gone back into the house and been killed with the others.

Deciding that doing something would be infinitely better than doing nothing, Ray swung the van around in a wide arc and headed back up the gravel track between the gloomy conifer plantations. He felt he wasn't far from the narrow little tarmac road when he encountered two large trees down, denying any further progress. "Oh great!" he said to himself with a heavy sigh. There was nothing for it but to walk ahead and see if he could find assistance. He collected his flashlight and put on his old fleecy working jacket from the back of the van. It wasn't until he turned off the van's headlights that he fully appreciated just how dark it was. The sky had turned really cloudy and without any streetlights or buildings in the vicinity it was literally like being blind. Flicking on the torch he was thankful that he'd put in a new set of batteries, or rather that Zara had put in a new set of batteries, before he had left from Essex.

Climbing over the now recumbent conifers he walked briskly along the track, his boots crunching on the gravel as he shone the flashlight this way and that.

------ O ------

Back at the cottage Zara had repeatedly tried to phone Ray. In the end, assuming he had gone to bed early in preparation for the long drive, she had finally left a message on his mobile telling him that her and the kids were ok, and warning him of the possible problems with all the disruption.

------ O ------

At the decimated Animal Sanctuary Dulcie and Wilhemina had succeeded in rounding up the escaped dogs and had temporarily housed them in different pens. All their other outside animals had been quite frightened, but thankfully were otherwise all right.

They kept old kerosene lamps in each of the compounds and these were now providing a flickering but useable light. Fortunately their little office shed was untouched by the quake and once they had attended to the needs of the animals, they were able to find comfort and shelter there. Inside the shed, barely visible under piles of paper and old dog food sacks, two battered armchairs provided comfort and rest to the tired and perplexed sisters. The strains of "Who let the Dogs out?" burst upon their senses as Wilhemina's mobile fired off from under a pile of papers on the old bench they used as a desk. She jumped up and rifling through receipts and bills, found the phone. "Rhyd Y Meirch Animal Sanctuary, Wilhemina Frogett-Smythe here!" - "Wilhemina, its Meredith Evans, how is everything, any damage?" she paused for a moment, "Hang on, I'll put you on speaker phone" she switched it over, "Animals are all ok, Dulcie and I are both unscathed, but the house is gorn, finished, no more, a mere heap of rubble!" There was a brief silence on the other end, "Oh Wilhemina, I'm so sorry to hear that, but Praise the Lord that you and Dulcie are okay." - "Praise the Lord indeed!" she retorted, "The Angels have most certainly been encamping round here tonight!"

Meredith sensed the sincerity in the statement and knew she would subsequently have a tale to tell. "Anyway how's things your end Meredith?" chirped Dulcie. He then explained the situation across the country and also the current mission they were on. "Listen girls, Joshua believes The Lord has told him this is more than just an earthquake and that the enemy has unleashed something tonight on a grand scale, so please watch and pray, and contact as many other brothers and sisters as you can and get them to do likewise. We feel the problem has a lot to do with satanic covens, and rituals in the high places."- "We most certainly shall." Wilhemina replied, "Oh and Meredith, tell Mr Fish Man – Dominus Vobiscum!"

The line went dead and she slowly put the phone into the pocket of her knitted cardigan, a puzzled look on her face. She was absolutely certain that she'd taken the phone up to the house to charge it, earlier that evening. She was regimental about such things, a woman of precision and routine and the last thing she always did at closing time was to take the mobile up to the house! The two Angels on the roof of the little shed smiled, and with swords drawn continued their vigil.

Wilhemina spent the next couple of hours phoning with military precision, to all her Christian contacts, passing on the warning and mobilising little groups of prayer warriors.

------ O ------

Just as Meredith concluded his conversation with the sisters, the Land Rover swung off the road and began bouncing down the track to 'Maen Du'. The gate that was usually closed hung half open and Cheryll quickly jumped out and secured it, allowing them through. As they descended, rounding the last bend of the long track, their eyes were greeted with a scene of desolation illuminated by the vehicle headlights.

Where the car park, tepees and outbuildings had been, there was now a huge pile of rock, and to their left, what remained of the barn was a blazing inferno.

Josh swung the Land Rover over to the right as far away as possible from the barn, and the three of them piled out. "Tarquin! Andy! Susie!" Josh was shouting at the top of his voice. Grabbing a handful of candles Cheryll, flashlight in hand, raced off to check the house, scrambling over boulders and flattened vehicles, whilst Josh and Meredith ran around to the end of the barn that was still intact. As they did, they encountered a rather charred looking Tarquin directing a thoroughly inadequate jet of water from a domestic hosepipe into the roaring inferno. Further behind him Susie and Jenny were kneeling on the ground doing their best to tend several injured people. Meredith hurried back to the vehicle for the first aid kit while Josh attempted to calm Tarquin and get him away from the danger. "It's too far gone, Tarquin." Josh shouted over the roar of the flames. "It's my barn, man, my barn!" Tarquin slurred, still drunk from the excesses of the party. Just then a huge burning timber crashed down and Josh barely managed to snatch him clear.

"Tarquin, c'mon man, leave it. It's had it." Another large flaming timber toppled to the ground as part of the remaining roof collapsed. The heat was intense, and in the bright orange glow Josh could see that his hippie friend was burnt on the arms and face.

Just then Meredith returned with the medical kit and began ministering to the injured. He was qualified in First Aid yet had little to use given the degree of injuries. Josh got on the phone to try to summon help, but all the lines were engaged. Succeeding in dissuading Tarquin from further risking his life, he set to, helping Meredith tend the wounded.

As she climbed over the large rocks making her way toward the house Cheryll was glad that she was wearing Doc Martens and not some flimsy fashion footwear. She was almost across when she realised that the poles she was now stepping over were the top of someone's tepee. She stopped for a moment trying to listen for any sound from beneath. She called out, "Is anybody down there?" but all she could hear was the roar of the wind. Then, lying face down, her mouth close by the rocks, she prayed out loud. "Father in heaven, I ask in the name of your son Jesus that if there is anybody under here alive, you send your mighty angels to rescue them."

Wiping the driving rain from her eyes and fighting against the buffeting wind, she staggered to her feet, just hoping no one had been in there when the rocks had hit.

The house was in darkness and by the light of her torch she went up to the familiar side entrance which she knew led to the kitchen. Usually dogs would be barking, fulfilling their role as sentinels. Right now, all was silent. Yolan was right behind her ever alert, and various scuzzy little elementals scurried off as she and the Angel approached.

As a frequent houseguest she knew where everything was, and soon she had lit several candles in the kitchen. Conserving her batteries, she switched off the torch and proceeded by candlelight. The stairs creaked as she approached the first floor, and the flicker of the candle cast deep ominous shadows through the hallway.

She could not see the two demons at the top of the stairs but she certainly felt their dark presence. Her heart rate increased a little and she stopped and took a breath saying quietly, "I have not been given a spirit of fear, but of power, love and a sound mind." [2 Timothy Ch.1v7]

At this point the demons spotted Yolan and took off fast. Cheryll stood on the upstairs landing, listening, aware of things in the shadows.

If only she truly knew. The things she was sensing were far more frightened of her and the great shining warrior Angel at her shoulder. How the Angels wished that their human charges would truly understand the incredible power their master had placed at their command. Awesome power. The power to accomplish every single thing that Jesus had done and more beside. [John Ch.14 v12]

However, amongst the angelic ranks it was common knowledge that very few of the millions of believers ever came anywhere near their full potential in the power of their Master.

The house was eerily silent save for the creaking of the floorboards beneath Cheryll's gentle footfall, and as she cautiously made her way towards the large end bedroom she was praying in tongues. Reaching towards the stripped pine door her fingers closed about the round brass handle and she very slowly turned it. The door creaked as it opened inward and the light from the candle diffused the room revealing dark shapes on several beds. She stood perfectly still, not making a sound as she counted. "Thank you Jesus!" she said quietly, not wishing to wake any of the eight children asleep in the room.

There was one other occupant that she did not see. He was sitting on top of a wardrobe. Yolan smiled and nodded, acknowledging his brother Angel, there because the heartfelt petitioning prayers of the believers had summoned him.

Cheryll quietly made her way back down the stairs and outside, confident that the children were all safe. Across what used to be the yard, the inferno in the barn was still raging. Clambering back over the pile of rocks again she stopped by the tepee poles to listen, just in case. Hearing nothing she made her way over to the fast disappearing end of the blazing barn, feeling the intense heat on her face. Turning the corner she spotted Josh, Meredith, Susie and Jenny all kneeling beside injured people who were laid out on the ground. Tarquin was sitting with his head in his hands, drunkenly lamenting the loss of his barn. She announced loudly the fact that the children were all fine, hoping to bring at least some modicum of comfort to any injured parent, then, she also set to in tending the wounded.

Across the country similar scenes were being played out in towns and villages and on secluded farms. Many people were left to fend for themselves as the emergency services simply could not cope with the sheer volume of calls and requests for assistance.

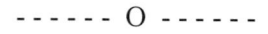

------ O ------

Since Ray had 'taken the smoke' with Yan-Ti, high in the mountains in China, in Wales, coven after coven of dark witches and Satanists had been meeting in the high places and performing rituals of sacrifice. Most of the sacrifices had been animal, though in some cases they were human. And when they were, it was mostly babies.

They would accomplish this by obtaining what they would call 'breeders'. These were usually young homeless girls or runaways who were picked up in desperate circumstances, mainly in the bigger cities. They would be lulled into a false sense of security, given food and often showed 'kindness' and offered free accommodation. Others would be blatantly kidnapped. Whichever way they entered the scene the outcome would be the same. They would be repeatedly raped and sexually abused in disgusting satanic rituals, until they became pregnant. They would often be forcibly injected with highly addictive drugs rendering them pliable and dependant upon their captors to fuel their addiction. Some of the unfortunate young women had borne four or five children in this fashion. Their whole term of pregnancy taking place behind locked doors. The babies born to these girls were never registered, and so never officially missed.

This mode of operation is standard throughout Satanism on a worldwide basis – yet authorities across the world dismiss it as the paranoid ramblings of those crazy fundamentalist Christians. They do this despite a mountain of documented evidence from many girls rescued from dark cults in a variety of countries. However, on reflection, it is hardly surprising when you consider that the authorities, which dismiss such claims, are more often than not the same authorities that will rubber stamp the murdering of unborn children in abortion clinics across the globe.

Spirits do not die. And the demon spirit of the false god Molech to whom the ancients used to sacrifice children, is still around today. It sits over every abortion clinic, over every teenage suicide and over every filthy satanic ritual of the sacrifice of human life.

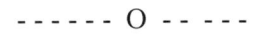

------ O -- ---

Ray had continued walking along the gravel track through the forest of conifers until he had come to a fork. He didn't remember any fork or making any sort of turn on the way in, but then he had merely been following Jarvis's tail lights in his extremely stoned condition. He decided to take the right hand track and strode onward his flashlight flicking this way and that. The only sound he could hear was the 'crunch, crunch, crunch' of his footfall on the gravel, and all he could see was the small patch of track illuminated by the narrow beam from his torch. After a few minutes he was aware that the pathway was steepening and he was steadily climbing. He realised then that this was definitely not the route he had arrived on, but figured that as he didn't know where he was anyway, it didn't really matter as long as he found some sort of habitation. He felt sure this track would lead him to a farm or a cottage.

Up ahead he caught sight of something in the beam. It was a gate! A great feeling of relief flooded his being and he felt certain he would soon be knocking on someone's door. The gate in question was a five bar gate situate at the end of the conifer plantation for the specific purpose of preventing sheep from leaving the grazing grounds at the foot of the Dragon's Back. Beyond this barrier lay open rocky moor land and treacherous bogs.

His spirits somewhat buoyed, and oblivious to the true lie of the land ahead, he slid back the bolt on the gate and passed through, carefully closing it after him. Behind Ray, the three guardians were very much on the alert .This area was an ancient enemy stronghold. It led to a 'high place' where ritual murder had occurred on many occasions past, and from where, one of several Dragon Spirits had just been released from thousands of years of bondage. A few hundred yards away in the darkness, was the exact spot from where the blood of the murdered Princess Angharad still cried out from the ground.

At first it seemed to Ray as if a little breeze had sprung up, and he turned up his collar and hunched his shoulders. But the breeze rapidly intensified into a strong wind that began to buffet him. The gravel path ceased to exist and there were rocks and clumps of spiky grass everywhere. He shone his torch desperately into the inky blackness, this way and that, but there was no sign of any human habitation.

Then in the beam of his torch he spotted tyre marks and what looked like some sort of a track going gently downwards just ahead of him. "That must be it." he said to himself, assuming that just a little way down the track he would find buildings and people. The wind grew even stronger and it began to rain, driving into his face so that he had to shield his eyes with his hand. The ground beneath his feet rapidly turned to mud and as he tried to negotiate the slope he slipped. His legs came out from underneath him and as he instinctively threw out his arms to break his fall, the torch smashed into a rock and died instantly.

A stream of expletives cascaded from Ray's lips as he struggled to his feet .The rain lashed at his face and the wind seemed to be increasing to a furious roar. He literally could not see his hand in front of his face, it was a complete and total inky blackness. He tried to take a few steps and lost his footing again slipping some way down the slope. He staggered to his feet, but he was now sodden, covered in mud and completely disorientated in pitch darkness. Realising that he was actually in some considerable danger, he decided the smart move would now be to get off this muddy track and try and find some shelter. What he had assumed were tyre marks indicating the proximity of human habitation, were in fact tyre marks indicating that this area was favoured by the local motorcycle-scrambling club. Mainly, because of its extreme terrain.

In the blackness above, Kaisis was having one of his best evenings for thousands of years. Everything was following his master's plans and, on the earth plane below him, mayhem, destruction and death were rampant. The dragon spirits were gathering strength and law and order was fast degenerating into a memory. On every high place hordes of demon spirits were descending. None more so than on The Dragon's Back. Ray was stumbling powerless in the darkness a few hundred feet below them. This mountain was the epicentre of the quakes and the spiritual centre of this present dark assault on humanity. In this place there had been many human sacrifices performed by countless generations of Druids, the innocent blood fuelling and empowering strong demonic activity. This place, and its gruesome rituals being the source of, and the power behind, the giant circle of stones at Stonehenge.

The rain was driving heavier, stinging Ray's face and penetrating his inadequate clothing. He began to shiver as he huddled next to a large rock trying to gain respite from the now ferocious wind. He pressed the button that illuminated the face of his wristwatch. The little gleam of light was a brief comforting beacon in the inky howling blackness. It was now 2.45a.m. Ray figured that he'd have to endure at least another three hours of this darkness until he'd be able to see well enough to move around safely. His recently healed wounds were aching and he admitted to himself that he was a little frightened. Not frightened in the same way he had been when the bullets were flying and men were dying right in front of him, but nonetheless he felt fear. This fear was somehow different though, It made the hairs on the back of his neck stand up. It was the fear he had felt when he 'took the smoke' with Yan-Ti, and the same fear he had felt when he 'imagined' he was going to hell. The same fear he had felt when he saw the Pentagram marked out on the floor in Jarvis De'Ath's house and had realised that he'd been wearing this same symbol around his neck for months.

The wind rose to a shrieking howl and at first Ray didn't hear the mechanical sound above the cacophony of the elements. Then he tilted his head, "What was that?" he said to himself as his senses picked up the high pitched whine of a scramble bike. Then he saw the light coming from out of the blackness above him, and in seconds a helmeted rider pulled up on the track just below the rock Ray was sheltering by. "Get on the back Ray," said a cultured voice from a helmeted head. "Put your arms around my waist" Ray immediately complied, too cold and altogether too totally relieved to ask any questions. As he mounted the pillion he felt instantly warm and peaceful. He realised that whoever this guy was he was huge, and he felt like a small child sitting there behind him.

The bike took off down the track; Ray could see nothing as his head only came up to just below the shoulders of his rescuer. He knew they were going fast as the bike slewed this way and that and several times left the ground, expertly manoeuvred by the consummate skill of the rider. The whole time, on what should have been an extremely hair raising journey, Ray felt utterly at peace. After several minutes of travel the bike came to a halt.

Ray dismounted, and the rider, remaining on the bike, pointed towards a fire that was burning in the distance. He angled the handlebars round and the bike's headlight illuminated an ancient track descending in front of them. "Follow the track – it's straight and safe." This said, the rider revved his engine and took off into the darkness. Ray looked towards the flames, then looked back behind him to watch where the biker was going. There was nothing, only the inky blackness and the roar of the wind.

He stood for a while, utterly dumbfounded. It was totally impossible! The rider could not have got out of sight or earshot so quickly. Even in this darkness and on this terrain, you would definitely expect to see his gradually diminishing lights for some distance. And how did he know someone was on the mountain? Not only that but he knew their name?

The driving rain quickly returned Ray's senses to the needs of the moment, and he set out steadily down the track, walking straight towards the distant fire, his mind a whirl of confused thoughts.

------ O ------

Down at 'Maen Du' Josh, Cheryll and Meredith had done their best to make the injured as comfortable as possible. Despite repeated attempts to raise the emergency services, no outside help was forthcoming and Meredith had suggested they try and ferry the injured to a medical station themselves. Josh, with the aid of a sobering bucket of water to the head, had managed to motivate Tarquin, and together the pair had rescued thirty plus bales of hay from the edge of the fiercely burning barn. Parked behind the barn, the old hay trailer was undamaged. They hitched this up to the Land Rover and made a bed of hay with a protective wall of bales all around. Then, as carefully as possible, all the injured folk were put on this trailer. They were then covered with a tarpaulin over poles, making a makeshift, padded, mobile tent.

------ O ------

Wilhemina and Dulcie Frogett-Smythe had performed their allotted task well. Phone call after phone call had informed those who had in turn informed others, and now a Gideon's Army of prayer warriors were storming the courts of heaven across the land and beyond. Little groups of believers from the chapels, churches, house groups and all manner of Christian organisations had been contacted, despite the lateness of the hour. Wilhemina was amazed at the response and the fact that not one of those she'd telephoned had mentioned it being past, or later on, well past, midnight! The Spirit of God was moving!

Meredith had managed to get hold of Graham and Mary in the village known as 'The place of the shivering ox', and Graham had informed him that an emergency medical centre had been set up in the secondary school, and that a doctor and his team would be arriving by 4.a.m. He had also told Meredith that in response to Josh's request, he had organised a 24hour prayer and praise session in the local chapel which was underway already. "God inhabits the praises of His people." he had said to Graham as he signed off.

------ 0 ------

Each time any of those ministering to the wounded got wet and cold, they would just stand a little closer to the remains of the burning barn for a while, and get dried out and warm again. It was during one such drying session that Cheryll learned from Susie how Tarquin had got burnt. Apparently when the three of them, Tarquin, Susie and Jenny, had raced up from the sweat lodge after the earthquake, Tarquin had repeatedly run into the blazing barn and rescued the injured, dragging them out without thought for his own safety. It had been Jenny who had thought to run and bring the hose from the small dairy some twenty feet away. At one point as he dragged out an injured female, Tarquin's sleeves and hair were on fire and Jenny's quick thinking and accuracy with the hose had saved him from serious injury. When Cheryll relayed the incident to Josh, even in the midst of all that was occurring, Josh realised that he had been somewhat guilty of judging Tarquin. He had not seen what had happened before he arrived on the scene, and had erroneously concluded that Tarquin was more interested in his barn than the injured people. Josh asked the Lord to forgive him for being judgmental, and thanked God for a lesson learned in adverse circumstances.

Together they decided that Josh and Meredith would take Tarquin and all the wounded down to the emergency medical centre, whilst Cheryll stayed behind with Susie and Jenny to look after the children.

The survivors were certain that four people were dead, now buried beneath the boulders at the top end of the barn, but another couple who lived in one of the crushed tepees were unaccounted for. They were known to have been in the barn ten minutes before the earthquake but had left, and now were nowhere to be found. Their two children were asleep in the house and it was feared that maybe they were now orphans.

------ O ------

In all situations and in all societies there are always those who will attempt to capitalise on the misfortune of others, or to manipulate and play to their own advantage scenarios which have rendered people vulnerable. Such were Gareth Buttle and his two cronies Rees Phillips and Hywel James. All in their late thirties, and all with totally socially inept and dysfunctional personalities. Buttle was a leering myopic, the product of over friendly cousins. He had lived all his narrow life in these hills and was a bigot and a racist. He drove the delivery van for a local grocer and as such was familiar with every farm, smallholding and isolated cottage in the area. He had never had a girlfriend, and was known for often staring at females almost drooling, which made many of them feel extremely uncomfortable. He was always polite with the local ladies, but whenever he would deliver to a place where alternative types lived, his demeanour would be highly suggestive and his conversation downright lewd. He had been taken to task many times, especially by some of the more liberated females he had tried it on with. However, so poor were his skills in relating to members of the opposite sex, that even on one occasion when an irate target had responded to his indecent suggestion with a hefty kick to his nether regions, he had gone home believing he'd had a 'come on'!

His two associates were of similar ilk and social skills, and the three of them spent most of their time and money in the local public house, topping up on Dutch courage. Over the past few months they had pursued a new hobby. It had started with them driving out on sunny weekends to places where they knew 'hippie' women lived. They would take binoculars and secrete themselves in the hills overlooking a property, in the hope of catching a glimpse of the wild orgies they'd heard took place all the time.

So far, on different occasions, the three voyeurs had been rewarded with seeing several young women sunbathing topless, two totally naked, and one couple making love on a blanket, all of them in what they thought was the privacy of their secluded location.

This had spurred the perverted little trio on to greater things, and of late they had taken to sneaking up on secluded dwellings at night, and peering in through windows. They disguised themselves with ski masks.

That night after leaving the pub, they had driven to an old quarry on a hillside just above a cottage where several hippies lived. The unsavoury trio were making their way down through the woods to the rear of the property, when the earthquake had hit. Literally quite shaken, they had abandoned their immediate voyeuristic plans and made their way back up to where their car was parked. Only to find that the quake had brought down two trees and some rock, which now blocked their exit. They were all quite drunk, and after puzzling for a while as to what they should do, Buttle spied from their elevated vantage point, a large 'bonfire' in the direction of 'Maen Du'. This of course meant that the hippies there were having a wild orgy and dancing naked around the fire. So the inebriates decided they would take the old quarry path that led down to 'Maen Du' via the base of The Dragon's Back. Torches in hand, they set off down the wooded path in their camouflaged waterproofs, with lust in their eyes and evil in their hearts.

------ O ------

With the assurance that he'd return when it was light, Josh kissed Cheryll passionately and climbed into the Land Rover, joining Meredith and Tarquin. Although they'd roped down the tarpaulin covering the injured on the hay trailer behind, it was flapping furiously in the strong wind but nonetheless doing its job in keeping the driving rain off the injured. Cheryll blew a kiss and waved as the Land Rover slowly and gently moved off on its journey of mercy.

The fire in the barn was still blazing, even though the majority of the fabric of the building was now gone. Great showers of sparks spiralled up into the night sky sweeping away in the direction of the howling wind. Cheryll scrambled back up over the rocks towards the house, where Susie and Jenny were making a welcome cup of tea. The wind was so powerful it almost blew her over and she had to lean forward and cling to rocks to make any progress through the driving rain.

Eventually she reached the kitchen door and sanctuary. The familiar smell of marijuana hit her nostrils as she sat dripping at the kitchen table. Susie plonked a large mug of steaming tea in front of her, and Jenny, smoking a fat joint, sat across from her. The table was festooned with flickering candles making the recent events seem like a million miles away. Cheryll studied the pair as the three of them sat in stunned silence. They were all somewhat numbed by what had transpired and the lives that had been so cruelly snatched away. Watching them pass the joint to and fro she felt rather sad at how they always automatically retreated into that which gave the enemy an even greater hold on their lives. Everything was about escaping, moving out of reality and into an insular space where only what you were doing at the time mattered. A foolish philosophy, but one employed by countless thousands to deal with a life devoid of the love of Jesus. A philosophy she herself had once subscribed to.

------ O ------

Buttle and his co-conspirators were halfway down the wooded track to 'Maen Du' when the dark force hit them. They were completely, utterly, totally, overwhelmed and bowled to the ground as demon after demon entered their defenceless bodies, joining those already in residence. Kaisis had launched his major attack and throughout the country similar occurrences were taking place everywhere.

In the heavenlies the 'appointed time' was declared and troops of warrior Angels were dispatched to reinforce, and serve the prayers and needs of the believers.

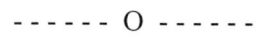

------ O ------

Cheryll was aware that the two girls carried various elementals. They were one track single natured spirits that in themselves could not hurt her. Both Susie and Jenny were friendly people, and she genuinely liked them. She prayed for them often, that they would find salvation and through that, protection from all that assailed them. Cheryll stood up. "I'm gonna go up and sit with the kids a while." she said taking her tea and a couple of candles. None of the children actually belonged to Susie or Jenny and they knew that

Cheryll would be praying for the little ones and watching out for them, so they were quite happy.

On the other track that led to 'Maen Du' Ray had been making steady progress towards the fire in the distance. He was soaking wet and cold in the relentless driving wind and rain, but having a tangible, visible goal kept spurring him on. His three accompanying guardians were extra alert, their swords drawn as they had sensed the evil that was amassing above them on the Dragon's Back. The three warriors had been assigned to him due to the pleas of believers, especially those of his newly saved wife Zara. The Angels knew they would have to be extra specially vigilant in protecting Ray as he was unsaved and already harbouring demons himself. Though these had for the most part been temporarily bound by the sanctification he now had through Zara's belief, they were by no means rendered void.

As the wave of darkness hit, Ray's three guardians met the onslaught with mighty resolve. The force of the impact knocked Ray to his knees, and the guardians were about to be beaten back by sheer weight of numbers when a vast array of shining warriors swooped down with swords flashing. Ray stumbled again, thinking he had just lost his footing, unaware of the battle raging all around him. Yet acutely aware of how the hairs on the back of his neck were reacting. Rising to his feet, he shivered in the biting wind, resolving to carry on towards the comforting glow of the distant fire.

On the other path up in the woods the three miscreants staggered to their feet, drunkenly lurching forward in the direction of their intended target. Their eyes were completely glazed and their twisted motivation absolutely demonic. Like entranced automatons they increased their pace and soon were emerging at the side of the track just down from the burning barn. No naked revelry greeted their lascivious gaze, just a rapidly diminishing fire and a huge pile of rock. Undeterred, they continued towards the house, scrambling up and over the residue of the avalanche, spurred on by a burning all consuming desire to ravage and hurt women.

With the brunt of the attack stopped in its tracks, Ray was able to continue his descent towards the fire as the battle in the unseen realm raged behind him.

In the kitchen, Susie and Jenny were relieved to see the flicker of torches outside, though they quickly tossed the remains of the joint into the stove. Jenny got up and went to the door with a candle. She opened it immediately upon seeing what she assumed to be three military rescue workers. The candle flickered wildly in the ensuing gust and as Jenny put her hand up to shield it, she was pushed roughly backward and the three men surged into the room, grabbing her and Susie almost at once. The girls, very stoned and already in shock from the earlier incidents of the evening, offered little resistance, believing at first that they'd been busted for dope or something, but when Buttle grabbed a kitchen knife and told Susie, "Take your clothes off." the reality of their situation bit deep.

As Ray neared the end of the track, he saw torches flashing to the right of the fire. He shouted as loud as he could, but the fury of the wind stole his voice away. He stumbled into something in the darkness and soon realised it was a gate. Climbing over he made his way toward the waning fire. Shards of burning timber and great volumes of sparks were still being lifted by the howling wind, and in the flickering light he could see a large pile of rock. He reasoned that as he had seen the torches to the right of the fire, the people wielding them must have gone over the rocks. As he scrambled over the mound he stood on something which gave way with a loud 'snap' and clattered down to the ground ahead of him.

Following suit he was soon approaching the side of the house, his guardians' right behind him.

Up in the bedroom Cheryll sat on an empty bed, her knees tucked up to her chest, praying and keeping watch over the children. The roaring of the wind was such that she had not heard a sound from the commotion downstairs and she was calm and unworried, sitting in the flicker of candlelight rocking gently back and forth. Yolan and the other warrior in the room were on high alert, totally aware of what was occurring, but their mandate was to protect Cheryll and the children and this is what they would do. They would not leave their post.

As Ray came level with the kitchen window, he froze in his tracks. Inside, clearly illuminated by the light of several candles, he saw a frightening scene. Buttle held Susie naked on the table with a knife at her throat, whilst Phillips attempted to ravish her. She was struggling hard and obviously distressed. James had Jenny by the hair, she was sat in a chair and he was holding a knife to her throat. The kitchen door was open and banging wildly in the wind.

Ray backed away, momentarily gathering his thoughts. How he wished his old mate Joshua was here. He'd know what to do. Then suddenly he thought of Simon Cheng and events in China. When it had come to it Simon had charged right at the enemy. The element of surprise.

He quickly ran the few yards back to the pile of rock and felt around on the ground in the dark, the rain again stinging his face. After a few seconds his fingers closed around a stout piece of timber, a broken end of one of the tepee poles! Ray stood up holding the wood like a baseball bat and, taking a deep breath strode towards the kitchen door. He had not the faintest idea what he actually looked like, he was soaked to the skin, and covered from head to foot in mud, but he knew what he needed to do.

Buttle shrieked and dropped the knife as this wild-eyed apparition burst into the kitchen screaming "Yaaarrrgh!" Phillips had a nano second of remaining cognisance before a tepee pole struck him hard across the head knocking him senseless. James screamed in agony dropping his knife as Jenny bit hard on that which she had been trying to evade. Susie leapt up from the table, and grabbing a heavy earthenware storage jar, in one fluid movement swung it up and under Buttle's fat chin sending him sprawling backward. With two quick steps and a blow to the back of the head Ray sent the now fleeing James headfirst into a very solid and substantial old dresser.

At the same time Ray's guardians had swiftly dispatched a terrified host of demons that had attempted to escape. The whole event had been over in six seconds, and now Ray stood there in the kitchen opposite a naked Susie and a stunned Jenny. After a couple of seconds of silence he said, "We'd better tie them up." which seemed to galvanise the girls into action. They rummaged around in the utility room while Ray stood guard. Soon they returned with some rope and the unconscious intruders were securely tied together back to back and seated on the cold slate floor at the opposite end of the large kitchen.

Meanwhile Susie had re-robed.

------ O ------

The journey to the emergency medical centre though relatively short, had taken some time as Joshua tried to read every undulation and ride it accordingly, to save bouncing around the injured on the trailer behind. With so much to attend to in the here and now Josh was puzzled as to why the Spirit kept prompting him to pray for Ray, but in obedience he did, each time the leading came. He had discussed it with Meredith as they slowly and carefully made their way to the school. The older man had agreed that Ray was probably in some sort of difficult situation over in Essex, and the pair continued to lift him in prayer. A case of the right diagnosis but the wrong location!

Shortly before the huge enemy offensive an entire platoon of warriors had arrived to reinforce Salzar and Chakine. And when the forces of darkness had hit the Land Rover and trailer like a battering ram, it was the shoulders of the Angels that had prevented them from turning over the vehicle and spilling the precious cargo of injured people. A battle royal had ensued. The clashing of light and darkness was happening over and around the believers and the helpless wounded, as they continued slowly towards their destination. The high winds and lashing rain hadn't helped but eventually they had got there around 4.am. Shortly afterwards the emergency team had arrived. They were met in the car park by Graham, who, after they had offloaded the injured and seen them handed into the care of the medics, led them to a steaming urn of tea. Graham too had been in contact with Wilhemina and Dulcie and confirmed that not only was there a whole battery of prayer cover happening here, but that now, brothers and sisters in the USA and other countries were petitioning heaven too!

------ O ------

The two Angels sitting on top of the shed at the animal sanctuary had been happy to note the arrival of many more of their peers. For several hours now, they had been holding off enemy attacks as well as holding down the roof of the tottering old shed. Wilhemina had been amazed at the amount she had been using her mobile, yet the little bars said it was still fully charged. "Most surprising!" She was also amazed that she and Dulcie were still awake!

Just then another prolonged gust of wind hammered the little shed and it seemed it would disintegrate. The two sisters cried out to the Lord in unison. "Father, please help us!" In the unseen realm warrior Angels fought a desperate battle against demonic powers intent on taking the lives of the two dear ladies. Swords flashed, and shields deflected blow after blow, as attack after attack was successfully repelled.

In other locations in the country, in large towns and cities, murderous demonised mobs rampaged, bringing death and destruction, as wave after wave of Kaisis's forces invaded Godless areas, and penetrated the hearts and minds of unregenerate selfish people.

At Josh's cottage, Dave, Lucy and Zara's guardians were likewise reinforced shortly before a concerted enemy attempt to take them out, and a fierce battle had ensued there. Zara had fallen asleep leaving Dave and Lucy still praying. The frantic barking of Boots and Polly, sensing the raging battle above, had awakened her.

It was all so strange and very new to Zara, yet she nonetheless had grasped what was going on and earlier had fervently prayed for her man, and the protection of Josh, Cheryll and Meredith. Now however, she absolutely had no idea that Ray was only fifteen miles away, standing in a house in a room below Cheryll, brandishing a broken tepee pole, covered in mud and soaked to the skin, with a naked woman opposite him and three unconscious would be rapists sprawled on the floor.

------ O ------

After they had securely tied up the loathsome trio and placed a blanket over their heads, the two girls and Ray settled down over mugs of tea to introductions and a general re-cap of the night so far. They knew that the phone lines were out and that repeated attempts to raise the emergency services had been fruitless.

Ray started his story at the point at which his vehicle had encountered a blocked road ahead, saying he'd been visiting friends. Ever the opportunist, he had modified events somewhat making it seem that he had spotted the fire from up in the hills and had come to offer assistance, thus further enhancing his knight in shining armour role with the two young females. He completely omitted any reference to the rescuing biker.

Susie recounted the recent events at 'Maen Du' merely alluding to Josh and the others as 'good friends' who had come to help. Jenny also related her 'take' on the way it was, adding that one friend 'Cher' was upstairs with the children.

In the peaceful atmosphere generated by the Angels for the children, Cheryll had eventually fallen asleep. She knew nothing of the assault by Buttle and his cronies, nor was she aware of Ray's arrival. She rather disliked being referred to as 'Cher' by Jenny, but it was a small irritation and one she bore well. Had Jenny spoken of Cheryll, then Ray may well have enquired with regard to Josh, as his old friend had talked a great deal about the beautiful young woman he was in love with in their recent phone conversations. But as it was, Ray had made no mental connection.

The two girls had shown him to the downstairs bathroom where he was able to clean up a bit, and also provided him with a nice dry robe whilst his clothes hung over the stove. Wind and heavy rain continued as the first faint rays of dawn began to drive away the darkness.

The three of them sat at the kitchen table, drinking yet more tea and eating a little bread and cheese. Susie was speaking about how worried they were about Andy and Jane, who had disappeared, when Jenny let out a shriek of delight and jumped up from the table. There coming in the back door was the missing couple! The two girls ran to them and in floods of tears embraced them. Ray was moved by the very obvious display of genuine warmth and affection.

Cheryll had woken and was coming out of the bathroom on the first floor when she heard Jenny's excited shriek. She raced down the stairs and into the kitchen, nearly tripping over the still firmly bound and blanketed trio. When she saw Andy and Jane she lifted her hands and eyes and said "Thank you Jesus!" Her entrance hadn't gone unnoticed by Ray who now found himself lamenting the fact that this gorgeous creature seemed to be a 'Jesus freak'. She joined the hugs and then the questions. "What happened to you?" said Susie. "Where have you been?" questioned Jenny. "Tell us all about it." Cheryll added, the three of them talking at once. "Are the children ok?" Enquired Jane, and Cheryll assured her they were fine and all still sound asleep upstairs.

Jenny did the introductions. "Andy, Jane, Cher, this is Ray, our knight in shining armour." She then went on to tell the story to the others and explain why there were now three men tied up beneath a blanket sitting on the kitchen floor. Andy was all for going over and giving them a good kicking, but Cheryll praying in tongues under her breath, was eventually able to dissuade him from that course of action.

They all agreed that as soon as communication was established the police would be informed.

"So tell us what happened then guys?" said Susie to the recent arrivals, placing a steaming mug of tea in front of each of them. Andy exhaled a long sigh. "Whew, well, we were having a real good time and sort of . . . wanted to be alone," The others smiled knowingly. "so we went back to our tepee and well, you know, and then suddenly the ground started shaking." - "Yes the earth really was moving this time!" interjected Jane. All, including Cheryll, laughed. Andy continued, "Next thing we know there's this rumbling sound that's getting louder, the ground underneath us is heaving up and down and then something massive hit us and everything went black." He looked to Jane, she continued, "We weren't hurt or anything at all, at least I wasn't and Andy was on top of me, but the whole tepee had been pushed over." Andy resumed. "One of the tepee poles was right over us almost running from my feet to my head, it wasn't crushing me but I could only move my left arm. I could feel the pole all the way up my leg, back and across the back of my head. There was a space to our left and in the pitch black I felt about and amazingly was able to locate part of one of our candles and a lighter. With the candle lit we could see that we were in a space just big enough for the two of us with a small space to my left." - "It was quite surreal," said Jane "our little 'cave' was lined with the canvass of our tepee wall." Andy again took up the narrative. "I felt upwards and soon realised we were buried beneath solid rock. There was no earth or gravel, even through the canvas I could feel it was solid rock. I couldn't move from on top of Jane and was worried I may be stopping her from breathing. For a minute there, I felt like we were in our grave and neither of us knew how deeply we had been buried."

Andy had grown up in a 'Christian' household, his father had died in an accident when he was young, and his mother had always tried to instill the 'right way' in her only son. However, she had gone about it the wrong way and like so many other parents she had merely finished up presenting her son with a set of highly repressive rules, rituals and observances that had been meaningless to the young man. Sadly he had never been introduced to the love of Jesus, nor had he been adequately shown why he so desperately needed Him. Consequently, the lure of the things of the world had cleverly ensnared him, albeit in a counterfeit culture of free love. Nonetheless, his mother was a believer and belonged to the family of God. She had never ceased praying for the son she loved. In fact earlier that very night she had attended a service specifically to pray for unsaved family members, and she had prayed with fervour.

Andy continued, "I don't know how long we had lain there, 'cos after a while the piece of candle burnt out and I couldn't find any more. We shouted a good few times but all we could hear was the roar of the wind, but it sounded a long way off, like, in the distance." He sipped from his mug of tea. "Then we heard someone praying that God would send angels to rescue us." - "Must have been you Cher!" Jenny interjected. Cheryll just smiled. Andy took another sip from his tea, gathering his thoughts.

He looked at Jane who nodded to him in encouragement. "Well, all of a sudden there was an incredible bright light in our little cave, and a voice said 'Don't be afraid', really, honestly, didn't it babe?" he said looking to Jane for confirmation. She responded, "Yes, I heard it too. You know what, I have never felt so peaceful in my life. I know it sounds weird, what with being buried alive and all, but it's the truth. Absolute, total, utter peace!"

Cheryll was quietly saying "Thank you Jesus, thank you Jesus." as the others sat in stunned silence. "Then suddenly the whole thing lifted off my back, we heard the canvas ripping and we could see daylight above us! I was able to stand up and help Jane up. Our clothes were in the space that had been to our left, so we got dressed and climbed out! It was then that I saw that a huge flat piece of rock had been over us, resting on the tepee poles. It was that which saved our lives." He paused for a moment before adding "It may have been that which physically prevented us from being crushed, but I know it was God who placed it there, and it was Him who sent the Angel to rescue us." He made this statement with great conviction, and Cheryll was glowing inside, knowing Andy was not far from the Kingdom of God.

Ray sat there for a while as the others chatted, weighing up things in his mind. He thought again about his miraculous escape from death in China, his 'dream' when the angels had rescued him from hell, the stranger who had led him to safety out of Jarvis DeAth's house, and then finally his amazing rescue by the phantom biker just last night. He took a deep breath and cleared his throat. "Um, I'd like to say something about angels." All went silent, the floor was his. He related all the previous evening's happenings, but 'tweaked' one or two of the facts regarding how he had come to be at Mr DeAth's residence, saying he'd called there on business. But he did relate pretty much the truth regarding his amazing rescue seconds before the quake. Then he went on to describe being lost on the mountain and his subsequent encounter with the biker who then disappeared. He excused his previous lies to Susie and Jenny on the grounds that he felt they wouldn't have believed him, and they readily accepted his explanation and apology.

The little group excitedly discussed all the amazing events. Cheryll purposely kept a low profile sensing that now was not the time to launch into preaching the gospel. Then Ray said, "Actually, I had another meeting, encounter, call it what you like, with angels just a few months ago. I was on business in China and we got ambushed and I was shot up quite badly." Cheryll's mouth was falling open. Ray continued to relate the incident and how he had flat lined and left his body, then experienced being rescued from hell by two Angels. When he had finished Cheryll was smiling broadly. "You're Ray Coughlin, Josh's friend!" He looked at her, surprised, "How do you know that, do you know Josh?" With her face shining and forming a beautiful smile she looked him straight in the eyes and said, "Know him? - I love him! I'm Cheryll, Josh's girlfriend!" Ray sat there looking stunned, happy, guilty and worried all at the same time. Cheryll leant forward and kissed Ray on the cheek. "Hello Ray, nice to meet my man's best friend, you have a beautiful wife and children, Zara will be so pleased to see you."

It was decided that it would be better if the children didn't come down to find three strangers tied up the kitchen, so Ray and Andy escorted the prisoners to an outhouse and securely locked them inside. They had just returned from this chore when in a cacophony of squealing, shouting and laughter, eight young children cascaded joyously down the stairs, demanding breakfast. Outside there was little respite from the weather, if anything the skies were darkening and the rain increasing.

Just then the honking of a horn outside heralded the arrival of Josh and Meredith, Cheryll felt her heart rate increase in anticipation of seeing her man, and Ray felt his paranoia increase in anticipation of how he was going to explain this all to Zara!

------ O ------

Kaisis was so pleased, he had not kicked anyone so far this morning. A handful of young Chosen Ones had relinquished their Guardians, surrendering the Position of Influence to the Grey Ones as they had succumbed to lust and pornography, drugs and violence in the concerted enemy attack. Many thousands of ordinary people had been invaded by similar demons and he knew his master would be happy with the progress he was making.

Some young people had been drawn into Satanism and witchcraft through cleverly contrived sex parties and freely distributed drugs. And now his master was about to unleash even more misery as a direct result of what had been unwittingly released at the Black Pool.

------ O ------

At the animal sanctuary, despite the atrocious weather, nine of the local young female volunteers had turned up extra specially early to see if any help was needed. They were stunned to discover the house was now a heap of rubble, but relieved to see the two eccentric old sisters were ok and organising things.

It was ten minutes to seven when the first tornado made landfall. The sky had grown progressively more dark and the unrelenting rain had briefly stopped when just north of 'Rhyd-Y-Meirch' a dark snaking tunnel had dropped from the sky, tearing up everything in its path. This phenomena was also simultaneously occurring in several other locations across the country.

Wilhemina and Dulcie were in one of the damaged pens attempting to effect repairs when they first caught sight of the dark raging monster. They stood momentarily transfixed, as the corrugated sheet metal roof of a line of pens 100 yards away exploded, as if some giant hand were ripping it off, casting the sheets high into the air one after another. Sheets, timber, masonry, animals and young girls were torn from their place and flung spiralling into the whirling melee, the iron sheets acting like the blades in a blender.

They were inside a pen and had nowhere to go. Not that they could have moved fast enough anyway. Wilhemina grabbed Dulcie and said "Lord Jesus, receive our spirits." a second before they were swept off their feet and cast upwards in a swirl of deadly spinning debris. On and on it bore tearing the heart out of the sanctuary, extinguishing life and birthing destruction. Despite the swirling, whirling metal and brick, not one piece forcefully struck either of the sisters as they clung to each other spinning madly round and around suspended hundreds of feet in the air. In the madness of it all Wilhemina was suddenly aware of a young girl spinning beside her, then another, and another, then some dogs too.

In the unseen realm, completely encircling the sisters, the little girls and the dogs, a tight circle of warrior Angels, their wings interlocked, had protected these lives from harm as they spun crazily in a roaring cacophony of death and destruction. Then as quickly as it had started it was over. In a trice they were down on the ground, gently lowered into a meadow. Very dizzy, but otherwise unhurt. They sat there for a while orientating themselves in the relative calm, then the two women turned their attention to the welfare of the girls. They were the three youngest volunteers, two aged ten and one eleven. All of them below the age of accountability. Five dogs survived too, and were running around the little group barking and playing. In the meantime the rapidly dissipating twister had sped off into the distance.

The two sisters gave thanks to the Lord for their deliverance, and holding the hands of the young ones begun the mile and a half walk back to what used to be an animal sanctuary.

In similar scenarios across the land hundreds of people were swept into the sky, none of them surviving. Thousands of houses, farms, schools and factories were destroyed and the estimated cost was in billions.

At 'Maen Du' a dark funnel had narrowly missed them, veering away at the last moment as Josh, Cheryll and Meredith had stood, arms raised, in the path of the approaching twister commanding it away in Jesus name. They had stood their ground in faith and in the knowledge that Jesus once calmed a raging storm and has promised his followers "If you believe in me, all these things I do – you will do . . . ." [John Ch.14 v 12]

With seconds to spare it had turned, cutting a swathe through the valley below them. From their elevated position they had counted at least eleven funnels between them and the far distance of mid Wales. Subsequent reports put the overall count at twenty-seven in total.

------ O ------

Way up in The Arc of Prayer, the petitions of the believers were fast accumulating. Many were those whose prayers were effective and fervent and they were fast correlating into a solid frequency of light, sound and colour that would become a breaker anointing.

The prayer Angels were collecting at full speed and the weight and strength of the colour grew deeper and brighter as the golden bowls filled and refilled. The Father's heart was moved as he listened to the beautiful harmonies of the prayers of His children, rising like one righteous voice in condemnation of the dark acts of the evil one, and pleading for release, love and freedom from this yoke.

------ O ------

Josh had been completely surprised and overjoyed on his return to 'Maen Du', to discover his oldest and best friend was there. Cheryll was very moved when she saw the depth of obvious affection between the two men, especially when halfway through his edited version of events, Ray confessed everything, right from the time of his arrival at Yantook and all that had subsequently transpired. In truth he hadn't had a clue what he was getting himself involved in, but now he was beginning to see the awful consequences of what he had innocently done.

Josh outlined all that was happening across the land, and the gravity of the present situation. Realising that he was now largely responsible for the deaths of many people, Ray broke down and cried, feeling desperate, helpless and very guilty. Josh gave him first the reasons why he was already condemned before God, and why he had found himself literally on the brink of hell when he had 'flat lined'. He then used the Ten Commandments to illustrate to Ray why it was that he deserved to go there, and the punishment God says is due to <u>all</u> that sin.

The spirit of conviction fell heavily upon Ray, and Andy, and Susie and when Josh then gave them the Good News about redemption through Jesus, they all grabbed it with both hands, and in a joyous, tearful prayer session they accepted The Lord Jesus Christ as their saviour. Each at that moment obtained a total forgiveness for all their sin, and each inherited eternal life.

Meredith had led Ray through a specific prayer of repentance regarding the statue and all it entailed, and knowing Ray's remorse was genuine, they had, through the power of Jesus blood, completely cut him off from all negative spiritual ties to the event.

Throughout, Jane and Jenny had sat listening, but their body language said it all. Their arms were folded and they both sat 'hunched up'. They were either not ready or didn't want to give up sinning. Whichever way, they had heard the gospel and a seed had been sown.

Straight away three more Angels had manifested and placed themselves at the shoulders of their new charges. Cheryll told Ray about Zara's decision of the previous evening and his heart soared even higher. He decided however that he would wait a while before phoning her, as she wouldn't be expecting a call until he was at the Bridge, which would have been around 1.00pm, and he wanted to surprise her with the news in person.

Meredith suggested they should spend a little time in prayer, seeking the lord's will on what to do, so Jenny and Jane went off to tend to the needs of the children. The new converts were totally amazed when the Spirit of The Living God filled the room with power as Josh, Meredith and Cheryll proceeded to pray. Meredith prayed for each one of the new believers, laying on his hands, and they all went out in the spirit. Their individual deepest spiritual needs being ministered to by God himself. As the three converts lay on the floor resting in the spirit, the others continued praying.

God spoke clearly to Meredith. He was to anoint Josh with oil and pray for the 'breaker' anointing to come upon him. This he did, and the power of God rose up in Josh from his innermost being. He began to shake as the rivers of living water bubbled up inside him and a great and supernatural anointing invigorated and empowered him.

------ O ------

In the heavenlies the order had gone out from the very throne room of God. The petitions of the believers who were praying world-wide had now filled the golden bowls to overflowing, and the glorious melding of sound, light and colour was now cascading down into the innermost being of Joshua Fishmen. The one whom the Almighty had chosen to bear, in the physical realm, the anointing that would break the yoke through the precious blood of Jesus.

------ O ------

The instructions continued. They were then to go up on to the Dragon's Back anointing the land with oil, to reclaim and cleanse the ground from ritual murder, and banish the spirits that had gained rights to the land because of the transgression of God's law. This place was 'the strong man' and once the power here was broken those praying for similar release on other high places would surely get a breakthrough and the darkness would crumble.

When they knew they had the victory, they must then go with Ray to the Black Pool, break the power of Yan-Ti's curse, and close the dark portal that had been opened. Their instructions were clear and precise. They knew that they had the mandate, the anointing, and the authority over all the powers of the enemy, and that as long as they remained in the spirit, nothing could harm them.

They could see The Dragon's Back from the kitchen window. It was now 9.30 a.m. and still howling outside. The consensus of opinion was that they would leave after a good strong cup of coffee.

Back at Josh's cottage, Dave and Lucy had received a call from one of the other believers down in Aberdigan. All night, drunken mobs had rampaged through the town looting shops and terrorising people. The town centre had narrowly missed further destruction that morning, when a twister moved up the estuary sucking boats out of the water until it moved off, dying out in the hills.

A time of concerted prayer had been organised for 10.45a.m. by a networking of believers nation-wide. In the town's immediate area people were going to meet to pray at the old castle.

Zara was still 'buzzing' on her new found faith and although totally out of her depth, aided by Lucy she was doing her best to answer questions about God and Jesus from Donna and Vernon. She was unaware of the tremendous battle that had taken place while she had slept, or how her guardian had valiantly defended her and the children, bravely fighting alongside Dave and Lucy's Angels against vastly superior numbers until reinforcements had arrived. Right now outside the cottage, there were Angels on the roof and in the garden, and Polly and Boots happily wandered to and fro through their ranks, in complete confidence.

At 'Maen Du' the three new believers had got to their feet, and now all six sat at the kitchen table, mug of coffee in hand. Meredith was addressing them. "The Bible tells us to 'Watch out!' because our enemy Satan prowls around like a roaring lion, seeking whom he may devour. It tells us to be sober and watchful, as even though he is a defeated enemy, he is still 'Prince of this world' and acknowledged as such by Jesus. In spiritual terms, the word of God, the Bible, can be likened to an umbrella. If you stay under its covering, if you keep it over your head, the rain can't touch you! And likewise with God's instructions to man. If we stay 'on the path' operate 'within the rules', Satan can't do much more than occasionally hassle us a bit. But if we wander off the protected path, into 'enemy territory' then his snipers will get us every time and his snares and lures will entice us further and further in the wrong direction. Sin is attractive to man's fallen nature, and that's a fact!" The three redeemed sinners had had their first sermon!

Finishing his coffee, Josh looked at the clock. It was now 10.a.m. Time for it!
They said a final prayer for protection and covering, and Josh, knowing his old friend well, suggested it might be

better if Ray abstained from joints for a bit. They arranged to meet him back here as soon as they could.

Putting on their waterproofs they moved out into the greyness of the morning. The wind driven rain stung their faces, it was coming out of the West, straight at them. Like a mocking Goliath beckoning the boy David, the Dragon's Back rose dark and foreboding in front of them. In the unseen realm thousands upon thousands of dark spirits swarmed like ants on its upper reaches and crest. The ancient sacrificial altar of the Druids, long buried beneath mounds of stone by early believers, was now uncovered. And upon it, in defiant confidence, sat the Dark Lord of the West, Kaisis. All around him demon warriors leered and swaggered, intoxicated with pride in their previous night's success. They jeered at and taunted the distant ranks of approaching warrior Angels that ran six deep for a hundred yards either side of the three little humans.

The gently sloping path they were ascending, was the same one Ray had followed down, the previous evening. They walked three abreast, Josh in the middle, and started to sing "Our God is an awesome God, He reigns in heaven above, with wisdom power and love, our God is an awesome God." As they sang, their steps fell in time with the melody, and soon they were in effect marching in dogged resolve. The Angels joined in, and a spiralling wave of praise began to roll up the incline towards the enemy on the summit. Some of the demons started vomiting whilst others paced up and down trying not to hear the awful sound. Kaisis launched an immediate attack, sending a horde of spirits of fear directly at the three humans, backed up by hundreds of warrior demons.

Out of nowhere fear hit them, and it hit them hard. It was tangible, like a barrier Cheryll instantly stopped singing, her voice frozen in her throat as inexplicable fear took an icy grip on her senses.

Meredith couldn't quite catch his breath as the hairs on the back of his neck stood up, and the two of them stopped in their tracks. Quick as a flash, Joshua grabbed their hands and striding forward dragged them with him still singing "Our God is an awesome God!" He literally pulled them along until they too once again took up the refrain and picked up the marching step. Josh bellowed out at the top of his voice "I have not been given a spirit of fear, but of power, love and a sound mind!" [2 Timothy Ch. 1 v. 7]

When the spirits of fear had hit, Chakine, Yolan and Salzar had thrown themselves into the ranks of the demons attacking their charges, their swords exacting heavy toll. But there were so many that they couldn't push them back right away, especially when hundreds of warrior demons came crashing into the Angelic line. The fight was furious, but as the three redeemed humans picked up again on their praises, the Angels started to push forward causing the hordes of darkness to retreat. The determined trio were now striding on, praising God again at the top of their voices!

Wave after wave of spirits flung themselves at the humans, but not one made any further contact. More fear came, but to no avail. Then 'division', 'argument', 'anger' and 'confusion' tried their hands. Each time the Angels beat them off as Josh, Cheryll and Meredith continued to stride forward towards their goal with the praises of God pouring out from their hearts.

Chakine knew what Josh's mission entailed, and as the three children of God climbed steadily higher he could clearly see to his left where they needed to go. Though all trace in the physical realm was long gone, in the spirit realm the Angel could plainly see and hear the blood of Angharad crying out from the ground. [Genesis Ch.4 v 10].

Various demons including 'murder' had been resident on the spot for over two thousand years, feeding on death and everything contrary to God's laws that had been perpetrated here. Chakine 'directed' Josh, who, still holding the hands of his companions, wheeled left off the track and across the boulder strewn moor land. Josh, supernaturally guided by Chakine, 'knew' the exact spot and they stopped. Immediately the warrior Angels encircled them several deep, and continued to repel the unrelenting attacks of the demons.

From his vantage point Kaisis was momentarily puzzled as to why the puny humans had changed course, but he quickly realised. "No-ooo!" he roared, "stop them!" motioning the main body of his forces into the fray.

A great dark screeching wave of demons cascaded down the mountainside intent on breaking the ranks of the Angels. But the warriors of light held firm, meeting the onslaught with fierce resolve and righteous determination.

At the exact spot where Hwyldalach had beheaded his innocent daughter, the three Christians knelt in the driving rain, buffeted by the forces of darkness. Under strong leading they prayed a prayer of release and consecration, as a spiritual battle raged all around them. The words that Joshua spoke were powerful and authoritative and bore the anointing of The Holy One. As he poured the cleansing oil on the ground the demon spirits screamed and relinquished all rights. With no legal tenancy they were instantly dispatched by eagerly waiting sons of light.

Josh stood to his feet, ignoring the rain stinging his face, and the others followed suit. The presence of evil was tangible, hanging heavy in the air. But the power of the Holy Spirit was sustaining and emboldening them and they bravely strode forward, climbing over rock and gorse and patches of heather.

What had been a gentle slope now arched steeply upward, and the sense that they were unwelcome there intensified. Out of nowhere, despite the strong winds, a dense heavy mist was rolling off the mountaintop and cascading down the slopes. It soon enveloped them. They could barely see six feet in front and disorientation was almost immediate. All around them, unseen by human eye, the battle raged. They were still ringed by a deep circle of warrior Angels, and the line of angelic ranks either side of them fought valiantly against the massed forces of evil.

Meredith let out a cry of pain clasping his chest as his shoulders hunched forward and he sank to his knees. A spirit of 'heart attack' had broken through and attached itself to him. He wasn't actually having a heart attack, but this spirit was able to manifest the symptoms, just as all spirits of sickness can. As Salzar furiously fought off other attackers, Cheryll knelt with her old friend and prayed in tongues, rebuking sickness and the powers of darkness. Just above her, Yolan was battling with three heavily armed demons, as here and there the enemy was breaking through.

The advance had come to a standstill, but Josh, unaware of Meredith's plight had continued to climb. Chakine, as ever, was at his shoulder; his sword whirling and his shield battering a path through the ranks of the enemy that had managed to breach the angelic circle. Assuming his earthly companions were just behind him, Josh continued on until it felt as if he were up against an unseen physical barrier. He looked around, but there was no sign of his two fellows in the swirling yellow mist.

Suddenly, a great shaft of intense white light enveloped Joshua from above, like an ultra powerful spotlight. The massed demons in front of him shrieked and backed away, and any that were not fast enough instantly shrivelled to nothing when the holy beam touched them. Like a zip being slowly undone, the ranks of demon spirits parted allowing Josh free movement forward. The battle with the Angels continued unabated, but no demon would even try to resist this light that shone down from the Holy of Holies.

Some thirty feet behind Josh, the power of the false 'heart attack' spirit now broken, Cheryll and Meredith had scrambled to their feet and looked on, transfixed in amazement. Through the mist they could clearly see Joshua up ahead, bathed in a beam of brilliant white light and striding purposefully on towards the summit. They could also now see the Angels. Everywhere! Grabbing the older man's hand, Cheryll encouraged him to move forward. "C'mon Meredith!" and soon they too were moving ever nearer the summit and the ancient altar.

Captain Cherno gave a pre arranged signal, and the two lines of angelic ranks either side of the believers instantly swung around in a three dimensional pincer movement, completely encircling and covering Kaisis and some of his demons, in a 'dome' of warrior Angels. Those demons outside the dome quickly fled into the darkness, as suddenly the heavens above opened. In an explosion of glory a mighty army of the heavenly host manifested, outnumbering the enemy twenty to one!

Joshua could now clearly see the huge wolf headed 'Lord of the West'. He was no longer reclining on the great defiled lump of rock, empowered with the blood of countless victims down through the ages. He was standing, legs apart, and sword in hand, his dripping fangs bared. He glanced above, behind and to both sides and knew there was no escape. As Josh drew near, Kaisis grimaced and snarled, the proximity of the holy light causing him extreme discomfort.

Chakine, at Josh's shoulder and also bathed in the light, was ultra alert and studying the demon for the slightest sign of movement. He knew that if Josh wavered, if he showed any fear or stopped trusting in the Lord God for even the slightest moment, then this powerful entity could kill him in an instant, and as he was already cornered he would have nothing to lose. Meredith and Cheryll had stopped about twenty feet behind Josh and could clearly see the whole eerie scenario through the mist, by the light of the glory of God and the Angels.

Stopping six feet in front of the altar Josh addressed Kaisis in a tone of absolute authority. "Demon! You come here in the name of the son of disobedience and rebellion, the one who was defeated by the blood of my master, shed on the cross at Calvary!"

Kaisis was growling furiously and shaking with rage. Chakine tightened his grip on his sword and readied himself for what he knew was coming. "And by the power of that blood, I command you and every demon here to leave this place, in the name of the Lord Jesus Christ, and never return. Be bound in chains, and go the appointed place to await judgement. Now!"

Chakine saw the lightning fast movement of Kaisis sword as it sliced through the air intent on removing Josh's head from his shoulders, and with speed of light reactions he leapt forward deflecting the blow with his shield. The momentum carried him on and he thrust his sword straight through the howling demon's neck, and at the same time, drop kicked him backwards. He landed standing on his chest with one foot on his neck.

A hundred Angels instantly pounced, binding him with chains. Chakine, pressing his foot harder into Kaisis neck said, with great satisfaction, "How now, demon?" a second before The Dark Lord of the West disappeared to await judgement. The rest of the terrified demons surrendered to their fate and were bound in chains to judgement too.

For the astonished humans, the whole thing suddenly clicked off, as if someone somewhere had thrown a switch. The glorious light of God dissipated, and the Angels were gone. The previously roaring wind dropped to a gentle breeze, the rain stopped and they were alone on the mountaintop. All of them standing there as if nothing had really happened. An all pervading calm descended and the three faith filled warriors lifted their hands heavenward and glorified God. At that same instant, small bands of praying believers on high places right across the country knew that they had the victory! God had answered their prayers. Oppression lifted, people were set free, and many exhibiting crazily uncharacteristic behaviour became calm and returned to normal.

Still surrounded by the now invisible Angels, the three humans were praising God, and making their way back down the track towards 'Maen Du' when suddenly, with a jolt, they found themselves in a wooded area. All three were looking incredulously at one another, and then around at their unfamiliar surroundings, when a voice called out, "Josh!" Looking over his shoulder Josh spied Ray walking up the little woodland path towards them, a look of wonderment on his face. "What ... I ... er, how can this be? One moment I'm in the loo at 'Maen Du', next thing I'm here with you guys!" He was still looking all around, "Wow, this Jesus stuff's amazing!"

It was now starting to sink in to the others what had just happened, and Josh reminded Meredith that he'd told him "Well, 200 yards is a start" when he'd told him about his experience of being supernaturally translated from the barn at 'Maen Du'. Ray was completely blown away. "Wow, this is incredible." he kept saying.

In truth, they were all quite amazed. Suddenly finding yourself 20 miles away from where you were 5 seconds ago is calculated to have that affect. Meredith of course lost no time in reminding them that it was all perfectly biblical. Phillip after baptising the Ethiopian eunuch, was 'caught away' to Azotus a town nearly fiteen miles away. [Acts Ch 8 v 39 – 40]

Recognizing the place, Ray told them where they needed to go. Josh suggested they join hands and pray, before going on up to the Black Pool. This they did, asking for guidance and leading as to what the Holy Spirit wanted them to do here.

Finishing their prayer they followed Ray, as he was the only one who had ever been here before. The track climbed steadily. The rain had long since stopped but the ominous sky was still grey and threatening. Close behind Ray, Josh, Cheryll and Meredith were praying out loud in tongues. The woodland became thinner, giving way to gorse and rough ground, and eventually in front of them was a rocky cliff face. At the bottom of this a dark shimmering pool reflected the grey clouds overhead.

"This is it." Ray said, pointing at the dark water. The four Angels were scanning the immediate area and stood ready behind each of their charges. A sudden distinct change in the atmosphere heralded something dark and dangerous proceeding to manifest. The water began to 'boil' and bubble just as it had when Ray had thrown the jade statue in. A deep guttural growl reverberated from the rock face and a green swirling mist emanated from the dark depths. Very slowly out of this mist a huge snarling dragon spirit materialised. Its head rising over the dark water, its yellow eyes staring menacingly.

Ray was transfixed, and terrified, the other three stood with hands raised praying in tongues and coming against the entity in the name of Jesus.

As they stood praying, out of nowhere a stick the size of a man's arm came flying end over end and struck Josh in the face, glancing off his forehead and causing a trickle of blood to run down. Each of them felt as if something was trying to cave the top of their head in, as dark forces exerted themselves upon the four humans. Meredith, knowing Ray's inexperience and sensing his extreme fear, caught hold of the new believer's hand and shouted "I am washed in the blood of Jesus, you can do nothing to me demon, and you will go from here!" As he repeated it, a fierce swirling wind blew, blowing choking dust, twigs and leaves all around. The others were likewise coming against the entity under the covering of the blood, but its resistance was strong. It continually rose up like a cobra, and dived menacingly at the little group below, the Angels deflecting its strikes with their shields. They all stood their ground as they prayed in authority, but there was no sign of the demon weakening. Josh sent up a silent prayer, "Lord, give me wisdom, I need to know what to do."

The spiralling wind increased in intensity, as did the frenzied 'boiling' of the waters. Josh's answer came almost immediately. The inanimate demon was anchored to the earth plane through the jade statue. The statue had been empowered by human sacrifice and as such the demon had a legal right to remain here as long as the statue existed. Straight away Josh understood what he must do.

He turned to the others and shouted. "Keep praying!" as he waded into the Black Pool. He felt strength and power invigorate his tired body as he pushed forward through the murky water. Chakine was just above him, deflecting blow after blow as the dragon demon centred his attack on the advancing Joshua. On the bank the other two were praying loudly in tongues, whilst Ray, emboldened by Meredith's encouragement, continued to plead the blood of Jesus.

When a crushing blow pushed Chakine backward, sending Joshua sprawling sideways under the water, Salzar and Yolan dove into the fray, leaping upward and attacking the head of the beast. Ray's Angel remained on the bank guarding the others.

Josh struggled to his feet wiping the foul liquid from his eyes and pushed forward, the bubbling water now coming up to his chest. Again the demon beast struck at him, despite the incessant assault of Yolan and Salzar. Hurling his shield upwards and stabbing with his sword, Chakine did his best to diffuse the power of the strike, but again he was pushed backward and again the young warrior was submerged. The voices of those on the bank rose in volume and intensified in authority as they witnessed Josh being pushed beneath the dark water a second time. In the murky, turbulent, inky blackness, Josh's foot struck against something. Rising to the surface he gulped in a breath of air and dove back down. Feeling around from side to side his fingers closed on something hard with uneven surfaces lying on the bottom of the pool. Above him the three Angels were stabbing and slashing at the huge entity, holding it at bay whilst Josh attempted to retrieve the statue.

After what seemed like an eternity, he burst up out of the water, gasping for air, but triumphantly holding aloft the jade carving. The dragon spirit rose up preparing to strike again, and the three Angels launched themselves in unison at its head, as Joshua hurled the statue with all his might against the rocky cliff face.

All four of them watched the scene as if in slow motion. The triangular statue flew spinning corner over corner until it crashed into the hard granite rock, exploding into a thousand pieces.

With a great screeching roar, and like smoke being sucked into a vacuum cleaner, the huge dark spirit disappeared down into the turbulent black water. Instantly the wind dropped, the water stilled, and a shaft of golden sunlight broke through the clouds, illuminating the pool and the rocks behind.

The whole scenario was instantly imbued with perfect peace.

Ray sat down hard on the bank, his mouth hanging open, "Wow! - did that just really happen?" Josh was wading back to the bank and Cheryll ran in up to her knees throwing her arms around him. Meredith stood there quietly praying. "Thank you Jesus, thank you for your anointing and for bringing this young warrior to us."

They all sat for a while giving thanks to the Lord, and then Josh said, "It's all very well this being translated business, but now we've got to walk home!"

The irony of the situation overtook them, and they laughed together in the sunshine all the way back down the track to the road.

---------- O ----------

~ the end ~

The Dragonmaster

Postscript

Buttle and his gang were handed over to the police when a form of normality was restored. This was after they'd spent two days confined in the outhouse. They were subsequently imprisoned for 3 years each. Susie wrote every week, and went to visit them regularly, buying each of them a bible and praying for them often.

------ O ------

Graham and Mary had become frequent visitors to 'Maen Du' after visiting the injured in hospital, and by the spring of the following year most of them were saved and attending the little fellowship in 'The village of the shivering ox'. Jane saw such a tremendous change in Andy, and that subsequently drew her to Jesus too.

------ O ------

The continuing friendship of Cheryll and Josh with Tarquin had borne the fruit of yet another soul saved for all eternity, and those who had not yet seen the light were well on the way. Sadly, all except for Jenny, who resolutely refused to have anything to do with Jesus and moved away.

------ O ------

The Frogett-Smythe sister's animal sanctuary was rescued by a wealthy Christian businessman, whom the Holy Spirit had prompted to finance the rebuilding of 'Rhyd -y- Meirch', and the refurbishment of the animal pens. They now lived in a brand new modern bungalow erected on the site of the old house. Their shiny new sign outside proclaims who they are. And underneath a verse of scripture, in bold letters, are the words 'Dominus Vobiscum'.

------ O ------

Ray and Zara were growing in their faith and attending a church near their home back in Essex. They looked forward to their next holiday in Wales, albeit with a little caution!

Around Christmas time Ray had received a letter from Simon Cheng in China, informing him that on a certain date Yan-Ti had mysteriously died. It seems he had slipped and fallen headlong into a deep and ancient underground well in a cave beneath his pagoda. Ray had checked the calendar. It was the same day that they had battled the dragon spirit at the Black Pool!

------ O ------

Meredith still missed Leah, but he was very happy that Cheryll was now regularly using the little art studio he had built for his wife in the old summerhouse out back. He continued to support and encourage Dave and Lucy, and all those attending the little fellowship in Aberdigan, and his friendship, love and admiration for Joshua grew more with each passing day.

Cheryll adored her man, and the two of them were passionately in love, so much so that it was becoming increasingly difficult to hold on to sexual restraint, though they had so far managed. So it was a joyous, wonderful, exciting day indeed when Josh had finally proposed to her. It had happened like this. . . . .

It was a Friday afternoon in late spring, warm and sunny. Cheryll had finished at Art College and had decided she would go and do some painting in Leah's studio, as she always did on a Friday. Josh would be at home by now and later she would cycle up to see him.

Arriving at Meredith's she parked her bike at the front of the house and walked round to the back and down the short path to the little summerhouse. As she pulled open the door, her senses were immediately assailed by a glorious perfume.

She stared in disbelief. The entire place, walls, bench, easel and floor were covered with red roses! Right in the middle was a stunning heart shaped ceramic mirror, and scrawled across it in lipstick were the words - 'Will you marry me?'- Josh, who had been hiding in Meredith's kitchen, stepped out through the back door, his heart pounding. Cheryll, still unaware of his presence was standing in the midst of the heady scent just staring at the mirror, tears of joy running down her flushed cheeks. He walked up silently behind her. "Well?" She jumped round with a start, and then flung herself into his arms saying, "Yes! Yes! Yes! Yes! Yes!"

Meredith, observing from the kitchen, stood with tears rolling down his cheeks too. Wiping them away with the back of his hand, he popped the cork on the waiting champagne bottle and soon the three of them were toasting the proposed union in the afternoon sunshine.

They were married in the registry office that August and then had a reception in a local village hall, where Meredith conducted a moving and God honouring service of blessing. Many of the guests remarked that they had never seen such a radiantly beautiful bride.

Ray was Josh's best man, and Zara the maid of honour, and the event was a joyous celebration.

A month later, after their return from a wonderful honeymoon in the Greek Islands, they were sitting together outside their little cottage in the late September sun, when Josh said, "You know babe, I keep having these vague feelings that maybe God wants us to go to Africa . . . ."

< - - - - - - - - - - O - - - - - - - - - - >

Still Small Voice Publishing

If you would like to contact the author or have any questions regarding any of the issues raised in this publication, please feel free to send an email to:
questions@ssvpublishing.com

'Spiritchill': - New Christian Music

The Author is also a musician and worship leader and you can find his Christian CD's and other music at:
www.spiritchill.com

COMING SOON!

The Lion - The War and The Witch Doctor

The second novel by Nigel Conway Partis

The next Joshua Fishmen story – Soon to be released!

Still Small Voice Publishing

www.ssvpublishing.com